CLAIRE TURNED HER ATTENTION TO THE WOMAN IN THE BED. . . .

In spite of the dust, the woman did bear a striking resemblance to Sleeping Beauty—or more accurately, given her age, to Sleeping Beauty's mother. It would be easier to work without the shield, but with a bystander to consider, Claire went through the perimeter without disturbing its structural integrity.

The emanations rising from the body were so dark she gagged. Teeth clenched, she forced herself to take a deeper look.

Kneeling beside the cat, Dean watched his new boss stagger back, trip on the edge of the braided rug, and begin to fall. He dove forward, felt an unpleasant, greasy sizzle along one arm, and caught her just before she hit the floor.

Before Dean could ask if she was all right, Austin leaped up onto her lap.

Her lower body still on the other side of the shield, Claire reached out to stop the cat from crossing over.

Too late.

"Evil!" Without actually touching down, Austin twisted in midair, hit the floor running, and raced back into the hall. . . .

D0190909

Tanya Huff
SUMMON THE KEEPER

DAW BOOKS, INC.

DONALD A. WOLLHEIM, FOUNDER

375 Hudson Street, New York, NY 10014

ELIZABETH R. WOLLHEIM
SHEILA E. GILBERT
PUBLISHERS

For the real Austin, and for Sid and Sam and Sasha.
And in loving memory of Emily and Ulysses.

Because there's no such thing as just a cat.

ONE

When the storm broke, rain pounding down in great sheets out of a black and unforgiving sky, Claire Hansen had to admit she wasn't surprised; it had been that kind of evening. Although her ticket took her to Colburg, three stops farther along the line, she'd stepped off the train and into the Kingston station certain that she'd found the source of the summons. It was the last thing she'd been certain of all day.

By the time it started to rain, her feet hurt, her luggage had about pulled her arms from their sockets, her traveling companion was sulking, and she was more than ready to pack it in. She'd search again in the morning, after a good night's sleep.

Unfortunately, it wasn't going to be that easy.

A Great Lakes Hydroecology convention had filled two of the downtown hotels, the third didn't allow pets, and the fourth was hosting the Beer Can Collectors of America, South Eastern Ontario Division. Claire had professed indignant disbelief about the latter until the desk clerk had pointed out the sign in the lobby welcoming the collectors to Kingston.

Some people have too much spare time, she thought as she shifted her suitcase into her left hand, the lighter, wicker cat carrier into her right, and headed back out into the night. *Way too much spare time.*

Pulling her coat collar out from under the weight of her backpack and hunkering down into its dubious shelter, she followed her feet along King Street toward the university, where a vague memory suggested there were guest houses and B&Bs hollowed out of the huge old mansions along the lake. Logically, she should have caught a cab out to the parade of hotels and budget motels lining Highway 2 between Kingston and Cataraqui, but, as logical solutions were rare in her line of work, Claire kept walking.

Thunder cracked, lightning lit up the sky, and it started to rain harder. Down the center of the street, where the reaching leaves of the huge, old trees didn't quite touch, grape-sized drops of water hit the pavement so hard they bounced. On the sidewalk, under the trees, it was . . .

A gust of wind tipped branches almost vertical, dumping a stream of icy water off the canopy and straight down the back of Claire's neck.

. . . not significantly drier.

There were times when profanity offered the only satisfactory response. Denied that outlet, Claire gritted her teeth and continued walking through increasingly deeper puddles toward City Park. Surely there'd be some kind of shelter near such a prominent tourist area even though September had emptied it of fairs and festivals. Tired, wet, and just generally cranky, she'd settle for anything that involved a roof and a bed.

At the corner of Lower Union and King, the lightning flashed again, throwing trees and houses into sharp-edged relief. On the third house up from the corner, a signboard affixed to a wrought iron fence reflected the light with such intensity, it left afterimages on the inside of Claire's lids.

"Shall we check it out?" She had to yell to make herself heard over the storm.

There was no answer from the cat carrier, but then she hadn't actually expected one.

In this, one of the oldest parts of the city, the houses were three- and four-story, red-brick Victorians. Too large to remain single-family dwellings in a time of rising energy prices, most had been hacked up into flats. The first two houses up from the corner were of this type. The third, past a narrow driveway, was larger still.

Squinting in the dark, water pouring off her hair and into her eyes, Claire struggled to make out the words on the sign. She was fairly certain there were words; there didn't seem to be much point in a sign if there weren't.

"Never any lightning around when it's needed. . . ."

On cue, the lightning provided every fleck of peeling paint with its own shadow. At the accompanying double crack of thunder, Claire dropped her suitcase and clutched at the fence. She let go a moment later when it occurred to her that holding an iron rod, even a rusty one, wasn't exactly smart under the circumstances.

White-and-yellow spots dancing across her vision, the faint *fizz* of an electrical discharge bouncing about between her ears, she stumbled toward the front door. During the brief time she'd been able to read the sign, she'd seen the words "uest House" and, right now, that was good enough for her.

The nine stairs were uneven and slippery, threatening to toss her, suitcase, cat carrier, backpack, and all, down into the black depths of the area in front of the house. When she slid into the railing and it bowed dangerously, she refused to consider it an omen. From the unsheltered porch, she could see neither knocker nor bell but, considering the night and the weather, that meant very little. There could have been a plaque warning travelers to *abandon hope all ye who enter here,* and she wouldn't have seen it—or paid any attention to it if it meant getting out of the storm. A light shone dimly through the transom. Holding her suitcase against the bricks with her knee, she tried the door.

It was unlocked.

Another time, she might have appreciated the drama of the moment more and pushed the heavy door open slowly, the sound of shrieking hinges accompanied by ominous music. As it was, she shoved it again, threw herself and her baggage inside, and kicked it closed.

At first, the silence came as a welcome relief from the storm, but after a moment of it settling around her, thick and cloying, Claire found she needed to fill it. She felt as though she were being covered in the cheap syrup left on the tables at family restaurants.

"Hello? Is anybody here?"

Although her voice had never been described as either timid or tentative, it made less than no impact on the silence. Lacking anywhere more constructive to go, the words bounced painfully around inside her head, birthing a sudden, throbbing headache.

Carefully setting the cat carrier down beyond the small lake she'd created on the scuffed hardwood floor, she turned to face the counter that divided the entry into a lobby and what looked like a small office—although the light was so bad, she couldn't be sure. On the counter, a brass bell waited in solitary, tarnished splendor.

Feeling somewhat like Alice in Wonderland, Claire pushed her streaming hair back off her face and smacked the plunger down into the bell.

The old man appeared behind the counter so suddenly that she recoiled a step, half expecting an accompanying puff of smoke—which would have been less disturbing than the more mundane explanation of him watching her from a dark corner of the office.

"What," he demanded, "do you want?"

"What do I want?"

"I asked you first."

Which was true enough. "I'd like a room for the night."

His eyes narrowed suspiciously. "That all?"

"What else is there?"

"Breakfast."

Claire had never been challenged to breakfast before. "If it's included, breakfast is fine." Another time, she might have managed a more spirited response. Then she remembered. "Do you take pets?"

"I do not! That's a filthy lie! You've been talking to Mrs. Abrams next door in number thirty-five, haven't you? Bloody cow. Lets her great, hairy baby crap all over the drive."

Beginning to shiver under the weight of her wet clothing, it took Claire a moment to work out just where the conversation had departed from the expected text. "I meant, do you mind pets staying in the hotel?"

The old man snorted. "Then you should say what you mean."

Something in his face seemed suddenly familiar, but the shadows cast by the single bulb hanging high overhead defeated Claire's attempt to bring his features into better focus. Her left eyelid began to twitch in time with the pounding in her skull. "Do I *know* you?"

"You do not."

He was telling the truth although something around the edges of his voice suggested it wasn't the entire truth. Before she could press the matter, he snarled, "If you don't want the room, I suggest you move on. I don't intend standing around here all night."

The thought of going back out into the storm wiped everything else from her head. "I want the room."

He dragged an old, green, leather-bound book out from under the counter and banged it down in front of her. Slapping it open to a blank page, he shoved a pen in her general direction. "Sign here."

She'd barely finished the final "n," her sleeve dragging a damp line across the yellowing paper, when he plucked the pen from her hand and replaced it with a key on a pink plastic fob.

"Room one. Top of the stairs to your right."

"Do I owe you anything in ad . . ." Claire let the last word trail off. The old man had vanished as suddenly as he'd appeared. "Guess not."

Picking up her luggage, she started up the stairs, trusting to instinct for her footing since the light was so bad she couldn't quite see the floor a little over five feet away.

Room one matched its key; essentially modern—if modern could be said to start around the late fifties—and unremarkable. The carpet and curtains were dark blue, the bedspread and the upholstery light blue. The walls were off-white, the furniture dark and utilitarian. The bathroom held a sink, a toilet, and a tub/shower combination and had the catch-in-the-throat smell of institutional cleansers.

Given the innkeeper, it was much better than Claire had expected. She set the wicker carrier on the dresser, unbuckled the leather straps, and lifted off the top. After a moment, a disgruntled black-and-white cat deigned to emerge and inspect the room.

As the storm howled impotently about outside the window, Claire shrugged out of her coat, wrapped her hair in a towel and collapsed onto the bed trying, unsuccessfully, to ignore the drum solo going on between her ears.

"Well, Austin, do the accommodations meet with your approval?" she asked as she heard him pad disdainfully from the bathroom. "Not that it matters; this is the best we can do for tonight."

The cat jumped up beside her. "That's too bad because—and I realize I risk sounding clichéd in saying it—I've got a bad feeling about this."

Claire managed to crack both eyelids open about a millimeter. No one had ever been able to determine if cats were actually clairvoyant or merely obnoxious little know-it-alls. "A bad feeling about what?"

"You know: this." He paused to rub a damp paw over his whiskers. "Aren't you getting anything at all?"

She let her eyes close again. "I seem to be getting MTV on one of my fillings. It's part of the Stomp tour." Flinching at a particularly robust bit of metaphor, she sighed. "I'm so thrilled."

A furry, ten-pound weight sat down on her chest. "I'm serious, Claire."

"The summons isn't any more urgent than it was this morning, if that's what you're asking." One-handed, she unbuttoned her jeans, pushing the cat back onto the bed with the other. "Nothing else is getting through this headache except a low-grade buzz."

"You should check it out."

"Check what out?" When Austin refused to answer, Claire decided she'd won, tossed off her clothes, and got into a pair of cream-colored silk pajamas—standard operating procedure suggested night clothes suitable for the six o'clock news, just in case.

Tucked under the covers, the cat curled up on the other pillow, she realized why the old man had looked so familiar. He looked like a gnome. And not one of those friendly garden gnomes either.

Rumplestiltskin, she thought, and went to sleep smiling.

"This is weird, my shoes are still wet."

Austin glared at her from the litter box. "If you don't mind!"

"Sorry." Claire poured liquid out of the toe of one canvas sneaker, hung them back over the shower curtain rod by their tied laces, then made a hasty retreat from the bathroom. "It's not that I expected them to be dry," she continued, dropping onto the edge of the bed, "but I was hoping they'd be wearably damp."

It was starting out to be a six of one, half a dozen of the other kind of a day. On the one hand, it was still raining and her shoes were still too wet to wear. On the other hand, her sleep had been undisturbed by signs or portents, her headache was gone, and the low-grade buzz had completely disappeared. Even Austin had woken up in a good mood, or as good a mood as he could manage before noon.

Flopping back against a pile of bedclothes, she listened past the sound of feline excavation to the hotel's ambient noise, and frowned. "It's quiet."

"Too quiet?" Austin asked, coming out of the bathroom.

"The summons has stopped."

Sitting back on his haunches, the cat stared up at her. "What do you mean, stopped?"

"I mean it's absent, not present, missing, not there." Surging to her feet, she began to pace. "Gone."

"But it was there when you went to sleep?"

"Yes."

"So between ten-thirteen last night and eight-oh-one this morning, you stopped being needed?"

"Yes."

Austin shrugged. "The site probably closed on its own."

Claire stopped pacing and folded her arms. "That never happens."

"Got a better explanation?" the cat asked smugly.

"Well, no. But even if it has closed, I'd be summoned somewhere else." For the first time in ten years, she wasn't either dealing with a site or traveling to one where she was needed. "I feel as though I've been cast aside like an old shoe, drifting aimlessly . . ."

"Mixing metaphors," the cat interrupted, jumping up on the bed. "That's better; while there's nothing wrong with your knees, they're not exactly expressive conversational participants. Maybe," he continued, "you're not needed because good has dominated and evil is no longer considered a possibility."

They locked eyes for a moment, then simultaneously snickered.

"But seriously, Austin, what am I supposed to do?"

"We're only a few hours from home. Why don't you visit your parents?"

"My parents?"

"You remember; male, female, conception, birth . . ."

Actually, she did remember, she just tried not to think about it much. "Are you suggesting we need to take a vacation?"

"Right at the moment, I'm suggesting we need to eat breakfast."

The carpet on the stairs had seen better days; the edges still had a faint memory of the pattern but the center had been worn to a uniform, threadbare gray. Claire hadn't been exactly impressed the night before, and in daylight the guest house had a distinctly shabby look.

Not a place to make an extended stay, she thought as she twisted the pommel back onto the end of the banister.

"I think we should spend the day looking around," she said, following the cat downstairs. "Even if the site's closed up, it wouldn't hurt to check out the area."

"Whatever. After we eat."

Searching for a cup of coffee, if not the promised breakfast, Claire followed her nose down the hall to the back of the first floor. *With any luck, that obnoxious little gnome doesn't also do the cooking.*

The dining room stretched across the end of the building and held a number of small tables surrounded by stainless steel and Naugahyde chairs—it had obviously been renovated at about the same time as her room. Outside curtainless windows, devoid of even a memory of moldings, a steady rain slanted down from a slate-gray sky, puddling beneath an ancient and immaculate white truck parked against the back fence.

Fortunately, before she could get really depressed about either the weather or the decor, the unmistakable scent of Colombian double roast drew her around a corner to a small open kitchen. The stainless steel, restaurant-style appliances were separated from the actual eating area by a Formica counter, its surface scrubbed and rescrubbed to a pale gray.

Standing at the refrigerator was a dark-haired young man in his late teens or early twenties, wearing a chef's apron over faded jeans and a T-shirt. Although he wore a pair of wire frame glasses, a certain breadth of shoulder and narrowness of hip suggested to Claire that he wasn't the bookish type. The muscles of his back made interesting ripples in the brilliant white cotton of the T-shirt and when she lowered her gaze, she discovered, after a moment, that he ironed his jeans.

Austin leaped silently up onto the counter, glanced from the cook to Claire, and snorted, "You might want to breathe."

Claire grabbed the cat and dropped him onto the floor as the object of the observation closed the refrigerator door and turned.

"Good morning," he said. It sounded as though he actually meant it.

Distracted by teeth as white as his shirt and a pair of blue eyes surrounded by a thick fringe of dark lashes, not to mention the musical, near Irish lilt of a Newfoundland accent, Claire took a moment to respond. "Good grief. I mean, good morning."

It wasn't only his appearance that had thrown her. In spite of his age, or rather lack of it, this was the most grounded person she'd ever met. First impressions suggested he'd never push a door marked pull, he'd arrive on time for appointments, and, in case of fire, he'd actually remember the locations of the nearest exits. Glancing down at his feet, she half expected to see roots disappearing into the floor but saw only a pair of worn work boots approximately size twelve.

"Mr. Smythe left a note on the fridge explaining things." He wiped his hand against his apron, couldn't seem to make up his mind about what to do next, and finally let it fall back to his side. "I'm Dean McIssac. I've been cook and caretaker since last February. I hope you'll consider keeping me on."

"Keeping you on?"

Her total lack of comprehension appeared to confuse him. "Aren't you the new owner, then?"

"The new what?"

He jerked a sheet of notepaper out from under a refrigerator magnet, and passed it over.

The woman spending the night in room one, Claire read, *is*

Claire Hansen. As of this morning, she's the new proprietor. Except for a small brown stain of indeterminate origins, the rest of the sheet was blank. "And that explains everything to you?" she asked incredulously.

"He's been trying to sell the place since I got here," Dean told her. "I just figured he had."

"He hasn't." So far, everything young Mr. McIssac had said, had been the truth. Which didn't explain a damned thing. Dropping the note onto the counter, she wondered just what game the old man thought he was playing. "I *am* Claire Hansen, but I haven't bought this hotel and I have no intention of buying this hotel."

"But Mr. Smythe . . ."

"Mr. Smythe is obviously senile. If you'll tell me where I can find him, I'll straighten everything out." She tried to make it sound more like a promise than a threat.

Although two long, narrow windows lifted a few of the shadows, the office looked no more inviting in the gray light of a rainy day than it had at night.

"He lives here?" Claire asked sliding sideways through the narrow opening between the counter and the wall, the only access from the lobby.

"No, in here." The door to the old man's rooms had been designed to look like part of the office paneling. Dean reached out to knock and paused, his hand just above the wood. "It's open."

"Then we must be expected." She pushed past him. "Oh, my."

Overdone was an understatement when applied to the room on the other side of the door, just as overstuffed wasn't really sufficient to describe the furniture. Even the old console television wore three overlapping doilies, a pair of resin candlesticks carved with cherubs, and a basket of fake fruit.

Tucked into the gilded, baroque frame of a slightly pitted mirror was a large manila envelope. Even from across the room Claire could see it was addressed to her. Suddenly, inexplicably, convinced that things were about to get dramatically out of hand, she walked slowly forward, picking a path through the clutter. It took a remarkably long time to cover a short distance; then, all at once, she had the envelope in her hand.

Inside the envelope were half a dozen documents and another note, slightly shorter than the first.

"Senile but concise," Claire muttered. *"Congratulations, you're the new owner of the Elysian Fields Guest House."* She glanced up at Dean. "The Elysian Fields Guest House?" When he nodded, she shook her head in disbelief. "Why didn't he just call it the Vestibule of Hell?"

Dean shrugged. "Because that would be bad for business?"

"Do you get much business?"

"Well, no."

"I can't say I'm surprised." She bent her attention back to the note. "*Stay out of room six.* What's in room six?"

"There was a fire, years ago. Mr. Smythe didn't need the room, so he saved money on repairs by keeping it locked up."

"Sounds charming. That's all there is." She turned the paper over but it was blank on the other side. "Maybe these will give us some ans . . ." Her voice trailed off as, mouth open, she fanned the other papers. Her signature had been carefully placed where it needed to be on each of the legal documents. And it *was* her signature, not a forgery. Smythe had lifted it out of the registration book.

Which could only mean one thing.

"Mr. McIssac, could you *please* go and get me a cup of coffee."

Dean found himself out in the office, the door to Mr. Smythe's rooms closed behind him, before he'd made a conscious decision to move. He remembered being asked to go for coffee and then he was in the office. Coffee. Office. Nothing in between.

"Okay, so your memory's going." He ducked under the counter flap. "Look at the bright side, boy, you're still employed."

Jobs were scarce, and he hoped he could hang on to this one. The pay wasn't great, but it included a basement apartment and he'd discovered that he liked taking care of people. He'd begun to think about taking some kind of part-time hotel management course; when there were no guests, and there were seldom guests, he had a lot of free time.

All that could change now that Mr. Smythe had gotten tired of waiting for a buyer and given the place away to a total stranger. Who didn't seem to want it.

Claire Hansen was not what he'd expected. First off, she was a lot younger. Although he'd had minimal experience judging the ages of women and the makeup just muddled it up all the more, he'd be willing to swear she was under thirty. He might even go as low as twenty-five.

And it was weird that she traveled with a cat.

* * *

"I can't feel the summons anymore, because I'm where I'm needed."

Austin blinked. "Say what?"

"Augustus Smythe is a Cousin."

"Augustus?"

"It's on the documents." Claire fanned them out so the cat could see all six pages. "Printed. He knew better than to sign his name. He's been here for a while, so obviously he was monitoring an accident site—a site he's buggered off from and made my responsibility." She dropped down onto a sofa upholstered in pink cabbage roses and continued dropping, sinking through billowing cushions to an alarming depth.

"Are you okay?" Austin asked a few moments later when she emerged, breathing heavily and clutching a handful of loose change.

"Fine." Knees still considerably higher than her hips, Claire hooked an elbow over the reinforced structure of the sofa's arm in case she started to sink again, dropping the change into a bowl of dubious looking mints. It might have made more sense to find another place to sit, but none of the other furniture looked any safer. "The summons wasn't coming from the site, or I'd still be able to feel it. It had to have been coming from Augustus Smythe."

The cat leaped up onto the coffee table. "He needed to leave so badly he drew you here?"

"Since he left last night, which is when the summons stopped, that's the only logical explanation."

"But why?"

"That's the question, isn't it? Why?"

Austin put a paw on her knee. "Why are you looking so happy about this?"

Was she? She supposed she was. "I'm not drifting any more." Starting the day with neither a summons nor a site had been disconcerting. "I have a purpose again."

"How nice for you." He sat back. "We're not going to get our vacation, are we?"

"Doesn't look like it." Her smile faded as she tapped the papers against her thigh. "Why didn't Smythe identify himself when I didn't recognize him?"

"Better question, why didn't you recognize him?"

"I was tired, I was wet, and I had a headache," she pointed out defensively. "All I could think of was getting out of that storm."

"You think he fuzzed you?"

"Where would he get the power? I was distracted, all right? Let's just leave it at that." After another short struggle with the sofa, Claire managed to heave herself back up onto her feet. "Since the site's in the hotel—or Smythe wouldn't have bothered deeding it to me—and since I can't sense it, I'm guessing that it's so small it never became enough of a priority to need a Keeper and Smythe finally got tired of waiting. I'll close it, and we'll move on."

"And the hotel?" Austin reminded her.

"After I seal the site, I'll give it to young Mr. McIssac."

"You think it's going to be that easy?"

"Isn't it always?" She picked up a squat figurine of a wide-eyed child in lederhosen playing a tuba, shuddered, and put it back down. "Come on."

"Come on?" Trotting to the end of the table, he jumped over a plaster bust of Elvis, went under a set of nesting Chinese tables, and beat her to the door. "Where are we going?"

"To get some answers."

"Where?"

"Where else? Where we were told not to go."

Austin snorted. "Typical."

Room six was on the third floor. As well as the standard lock, the door also boasted a large steel padlock on an industrial strength flange. Both locks had been made unopenable by the simple process of snapping the keys off in the mechanism.

"Seems like a lot of fuss over a small site," Austin muttered, dropping down from his inspection.

"Well, he could hardly have guests wandering in on it regardless of size." Releasing the padlock, Claire straightened. There were a number of ways she could gain access to the room, but most of them were labeled "emergency use only" as they involved the kind of pyrotechnics more likely to be deployed during small Middle Eastern wars. "I wonder if young Mr. McIssac has a hacksaw."

"Ms. Hansen?" Dean put the tray down on the desk and pushed his glasses back up the bridge of his nose. She wasn't in Mr. Smythe's suite—her suite now, he supposed—and she wasn't in the office. He hoped she wasn't upstairs packing. *Am I fired if she leaves?*

Footsteps descending the stairs seemed to confirm his worst

fears, but when she came into view, she wasn't carrying her bags. She hadn't even put her coat on.

"Oh, there you are, Dean."

There he was? He hadn't gone anywhere except to get her the coffee she'd asked for. "I brought cream and sugar," he told her as she squeezed under the counter flap. "You didn't say how you took it."

"Definitely cream." She poured some into the mug and frowned at the sugar bowl. "Do you have any packets of artificial sweetener?"

"Sure." As far as he could tell, she didn't need to watch her weight. While not quite a woman a man could see to shoot gulls through, she was on the skinny side and that much cream would pack on more pounds than a bit of sugar. "I'll go get you some."

"Dean?"

He straightened in the lobby and turned to face her over the counter.

"Bring your toolbox, too."

Cradling the coffee mug in both hands, Claire leaned against the wall and watched Dean work. He'd had no trouble cutting the padlock off, but the original lock was proving to be more difficult.

"I think you should call a locksmith, Ms. Hansen. I can't get in there without damaging the door some."

"How much?"

He shrugged. "If I get my crowbar from the van, I could probably force it open. Just stick it in here . . ." He ran a finger down the crack between the door and the jam where the tongue of the lock ran into the wall. ". . . and shove. It'll crack the wood for sure, but I can't say how much."

Claire took another swallow and considered her options. As long as Dean stayed out of the actual room, there should be no problem; only the largest of sites were visible to the untrained eye. "Go get your crowbar."

"Yes, ma'am."

When the sound of Dean's work boots clumping against bare wood suggested he'd reached the lobby, Austin stretched and glared up at Claire. "Couldn't this have waited until after breakfast? I'm starved."

"Could you have actually eaten not knowing what we were in for? Never mind. Stupid question."

"You've got your coffee, the least you could've done was given me the cream."

"The vet said you're not supposed to have cream." She squatted and rubbed him behind the ears. "Don't worry, it'll all be over soon. Waiting out on this side of the door has me so edgy, I'm positive the site's in there."

"In a just world," the cat growled, "it would've been in the kitchen."

His boots wet from the run out to the van, Dean slipped them off at the back door and started upstairs in his socks. Making the turn on the second floor landing, he heard voices. *I guess she's talking to the cat.*

Voices. Plural, prodded his subconscious.

You're losing it, boy. The cat's not talking back.

She had her back to him when he stepped out into the third-floor hall. "Ms. Hansen?"

Claire managed to bite off most of the shriek, but her heart slammed against her ribs as she whirled around. "Don't ever do that!"

Jerking back a step, Dean brought the crowbar up between them. "Do what?"

"Don't ever sneak up on me like that!" She pressed her right hand between her breasts. "You're just lucky I realized who you were!"

Although she was a good six or seven inches shorter than he was and there was nothing to her besides, somehow, that didn't sound as ridiculous as it should have. "I'm sorry!"

Austin banged his head against her shins and she looked down. "You took your boots off."

"They got wet."

"Right. Of course." Bringing her breathing under control, Claire waved him toward the locked door. "Break the lock, then step away. If there was a fire in there, you won't want the mess tracked into the hall."

Dean flashed her a grateful smile as he jammed the crowbar into the crack. Since coming west, he'd found few people who appreciated the kind of problems involved in keeping carpets clean. "Yes, ma'am."

"And stop calling me ma'am. You make me feel like I'm a hundred years old." When she saw him fighting a grin, Claire rolled her eyes. "I'm twenty-seven."

"Okay." A confidence given required one in exchange. "I'm

twenty-one." As he pulled back on the bar, he glanced over at her expression and wondered how she knew he was lying. "That is, I'll be twenty-one in a few months."

"So you're twenty?"

"Yes, ma'am."

The shriek of tortured wood and steel cut off further conversation. Hands over her ears, Claire watched muscles stretch the sleeves of his T-shirt as the lock began to give. When it popped suddenly, it took her a moment to gather her wandering thoughts—although, she assured the world at large, it was purely an aesthetic interest. In that moment, the door swung open, Dean looked into the room, and froze on the threshold.

"Lord thunderin' Jesus! Mr. Smythe's been hiding a body up here!"

"Calm down." Claire put her palm in the center of Dean's back and shoved. She'd have had more luck shifting the building. "And move!" Over the years she'd seen bodies in every condition imaginable—and frequently the imagination had belonged to fairly warped individuals. If this body had merely been left lying around, she'd consider herself lucky.

Dean stayed in the doorway, the breadth of his shoulders blocking her way and her view.

"I don't think," he said, grasping both edges of the doorframe, "that this is something a lady ought to see."

"Well, you got part of it right, you don't think!" Choosing guile over force, she slammed her knees into the back of his at the spot where the crease crossed the hollow. As he collapsed, she pushed past him, one hand reaching out to the old-fashioned, circular light switch.

The room was a little larger than the room Claire had slept in and the decorating hadn't been changed since the early part of the century. An oversized armchair sat covered in hand-crocheted doilies, a Victorian plant stand complete with a very dead fern stood between the two curtained windows, and a woman lay fully clothed on top of the bed, a sausage-shaped bolster under her head and a folded quilt under her feet. Everything, including the woman, wore a fuzzy patina of dust. The air smelled stale and, faintly, of perfume.

Claire could feel the edges of a shield wrapped around the body—which explained why she hadn't been able to get a sense of what room six held. The shield hadn't been put in place by a Cousin. At some point, a Keeper had been by and wrapped the site up so tightly that even another Keeper couldn't get through.

Had Augustus Smythe not needed to leave so badly, Claire could've passed happily through Kingston without ever realizing the site existed. The one thing she *couldn't* figure out was why a Keeper would bother. While people did occasionally manifest an accident site, the usual response was an exorcism, not the old Sleeping Beauty schtick.

A choking noise behind her reminded Claire she had a more immediate problem. The woman on the bed had clearly been there for some years; she could wait a few minutes longer.

When she turned, Dean had regained his position in the door-way. Her movement drew his locked gaze up off the bed, break-ing the connection. For a moment he stared at her, eyes wide, then he whirled around and managed two running steps toward the stairs.

"Dean McIssac!"

There was power in a name.

He stopped, one foot in the air, and almost fell.

"Where are you going?"

Shoving his glasses back into place, he tired to sound as though he found dead women laid out in the guest rooms all the time. "I'm after calling 911." His heart was pounding so loudly he could hardly hear himself.

"After calling?"

He rolled his eyes anxious to be moving, impatient at the delay. "After calling, going to call; it's the same thing."

"Why?"

"I don't know!" Frustration had him almost shouting. Sud-denly self-conscious, he ducked his head. "Sorry."

Claire waved off the apology. "I meant, why are you going to call 911?"

"Because there's a body . . ."

"She isn't dead, Dean, she's asleep. If you look at her chest, you can see she's breathing."

"Breathing?" Without moving his feet, he grabbed the splin-tered doorjamb and leaned in over the threshold. "Oh." Feeling foolish, he shrugged and tried to explain, "I was raised better than to stare at a woman's chest."

"You thought it was a corpse."

"Doesn't matter."

"Who *raised* you?"

"My granddad, Reverend McIssac," Dean told her, a little de-fensively.

Claire had her doubts at how often a twenty-year-old male actually followed that particular dictum but had no plans to discourage admirable intentions. "Well, good for him. And you. Now, could you do something for me?"

"Uh, sure."

"Could you go get me another cup of coffee, *please*."

He looked at her like she was out of her mind. "What? Now? What about the woman on the bed?"

"I don't think she's going to want one."

"No, I meant, what *about* the woman on the bed!"

Claire sighed. She hadn't actually thought it would work, but since it was the simplest temporary solution, it had seemed foolish not to try. Unfortunately, curiosity was one of the strongest motivating forces behind humanity's rise out of the ooze and, unsatisfied, it invariably caused problems. The safest way to deal with questions was to answer them, then, after all the loose ends were neatly tied up, wipe the whole package right out of Dean's mind. "If I promise to explain everything later, will you do me a favor? Will you wait quietly while I deal with this?"

"You know what's going on then?"

"Yes. Mostly," she amended, conscience prickling.

"And you'll explain it to me?"

"When I'm done with her."

"Done what?"

"That's one of the things I'll explain later."

Feeling a pressure against his shins, Dean glanced down to see Austin rubbing against him. It was such a normal, ordinary thing for a cat to do, it made the rest of the morning seem less strange. "Okay," he said, dropping to one knee and running his fingers along the silky fur. "I'll wait."

"Thank you."

With her unwelcome audience temporarily taken care of, Claire turned her attention back to the bed. In spite of the dust, the woman did bear a striking resemblance to Sleeping Beauty— or more accurately, given her age, to Sleeping Beauty's mother. Then it became obvious that the blonde curls had been bleached, the eyebrows had been plucked and redrawn, and the lips were far, far too red. The severe, almost military-style clothing covered a lush figure that could by no means be called matronly. For some reason, Claire found the line of dark residue under all ten fingernails incredibly disturbing. She didn't know why—dirty fingernails had never bothered her before.

It would be easier to work without the shield, but with a by-stander to consider, Claire went through the perimeter without disturbing its structural integrity.

The emanations rising from the body were so dark she gagged. Teeth clenched, wishing she hadn't had that coffee, she forced herself to take a deeper look.

Kneeling beside the cat, Dean watched his new boss stagger back, trip on the edge of the braided rug, and begin to fall. He dove forward, felt an unpleasant, greasy sizzle along one arm, and caught her just before she hit the floor. Under the makeup, her face had gone a pale gray and her throat worked as though she wanted to throw up. Before he could ask if she was all right, Austin leaped up onto her lap.

Her lower body still on the other side of the shield, Claire reached out to stop the cat from crossing over.

Too late.

"Evil!" Without actually touching down, he twisted in midair, hit the floor running, and raced back into the hall.

That was enough for Dean. Hands under Claire's armpits, he half carried, half dragged her out of the room. When her legs cleared the threshold, he reached over her and pulled the door closed. The damage he'd done to the lock plate meant it no longer latched, but he managed to jam it shut.

Pressed tight against Dean's chest, her head tucked into the hollow of his throat, Claire shoved on the arm holding her in place. While she appreciated him catching her before her skull smacked into the floor, his interference in something he had no hope of understanding created the distinct desire to drive her elbow in under his ribs as far as it would go. Only the certain knowledge that any blow would bounce harmlessly off the rip-pled muscle she could feel through the thin barrier of the T-shirt prevented her. That, and the way the position she found herself in radically restricted her movements. Not to mention her ability to breathe. "Let go of me!" she gasped. "Now!"

He jerked and looked down at her like he'd forgotten she was there but eased up enough so she could squirm free. Wedging her shoulder under his, she managed to get him out of the doorway.

His back against the wall, Dean slid down to sit on the hall floor, feeling much as he had at ten when the local bully had smacked him around with a dead cod. "The cat talked."

Having just reached Austin's side, Claire shook her head. "No, he didn't."

"Yes, he did."

Scooping the cat up into her arms, she said in a tone specifically crafted to make the recipient doubt his own senses, "No, he didn't."

"Yes, he did," Austin corrected, his voice a little muffled.

"Excuse me." Holding him tightly against her chest, she turned so that her body was between Dean and the cat. "I'll just be a minute." Tucking her thumb under the furry chin, she lifted his head and whispered, "Are you all right?"

"I'm fine." His tail, still twice its normal size, lashed against her leg. "I was startled. I hit the nasty on the other side of that shield and I overreacted."

"And what are you doing now?"

"He's a part of this."

"Are you out of your walnut-sized mind? He's a bystander!"

"Granted, but you're going to need his help."

"For what? With what? With *her*?"

"Maybe. I don't know yet."

"You *are* out of your mind! Do you know what that is in there?"

"Excuse me?"

"What?" Dean's voice pulled Claire's attention back across the hall.

Caught between a cruel and capricious sea and an unwelcoming hunk of rock, Newfoundlanders had turned adaptation into a genetically encoded survival trait. True to his ancestry, Dean had progressed from stunned disbelief through amazement to amazed acceptance by the time he'd interrupted.

When he saw he had their attention, he said, "I could still hear you. Sorry."

"Well, she wasn't exactly keeping her voice down," Austin pointed out.

Dean met Claire's gaze almost apologetically. "The cat talks."

"The cat never shuts up," Claire replied through gritted teeth.

"He seems to think I can help."

"Yeah, well when I need something cleaned or cooked I'll let you know. OW!" Sucking on the back of her hand, she glared down at Austin. "What did you scratch me for?"

He retracted his claws. "You were being rude."

"Scratch me again and I'll show you rude," she muttered.

"You're frightened, that's understandable. Even I was almost frightened. You think you can't handle this, you think it's too big for you . . ."

"Stop telling me what I think!"

". . . but that's no reason to take it out on him."

"You're frightened?" Dean ducked his head to get a better look at her face. "You are frightened."

Obviously, she hadn't been hiding it as well as she'd thought.

"Of what? Oh . . ." The talking cat had temporarily driven all thoughts of their other discovery out of his head. "Of her?" *Evil,* the cat had said. Rubbing the lingering, greasy feel off the arm that had been closest to the bed, Dean found that easy to believe. "Don't worry." He straightened where he sat. "On the last of it, she'll have to go through me to get to you."

"Foreshadowing," Austin muttered.

Giving the cat a warning squeeze, Claire realized that Dean's offer was in earnest. He was the sort of person who went out of his way to pick worms off the sidewalk and put them back onto the lawn. She drew in a deep breath and let it out slowly. "First of all, I can take care of myself. Second, if you ever face that woman awake, you'd better hope she kills you immediately and doesn't play with you for a while. And third, there's nothing you can do."

"The cat said . . ."

"He says a lot of things."

"*You* said you'd explain."

"After I'd dealt with her. And I haven't."

"I could help you with her."

"You don't know what's going on."

"I would if you explained."

"I've had as much as I can take of this," Austin grumbled. "I'll explain." Wriggling out of Claire's arms, he crossed the hall and locked a pale green stare on Dean's face. "Do you believe in magic?"

"That's an explanation?"

"Just answer the question."

"Sure."

"Sure? What kind of an answer is sure? Do you or don't you?"

Dean shrugged. "I guess I do."

"Good." Stretching out, Austin ripped at the carpet. "Because that's what we're dealing with."

"Magic?"

"That's right. The woman in the room behind you was put to sleep by magic."

Dean shifted a little farther down the hall. Drawing his knees up, he laid his forearms across them and frowned. "Like Sleeping Beauty?"

Austin's ears went back. "The opposite. This time the bad guy—her—got put to sleep by the good guys."

"Why?"

"How should I know?"

"I just thought . . ."

"At this point we don't know much more than you do." He frowned thoughtfully. "Actually, we know a whole lot more than you, but we don't know *that*. The important thing for you to remember is that, if you're lucky, the woman in there is the worst thing you're ever going to come in contact with. She's evil sleeping in size eight pumps."

Dean's eyes widened. "How do you know her shoe size?"

"I don't."

"But you said . . ."

"I was making a point," Austin sighed. "Which obviously didn't make it through your thick head."

Watching the cat stalk back across the hall and rub his head against a denim-clad hip, Dean suddenly remembered the feel of a body clutched tightly against his. Under normal circumstances, it wasn't a feeling he'd have forgotten. His ears turned red as he realized just which bits had gone where and he suspected he should apologize for something. "Uh, Ms. Hansen . . ."

"You might as well call me Claire," she interrupted wearily, picking at a loose thread in the cleanest carpet she'd ever seen. "If Austin's right . . ."

"And I am," Austin put in, not bothering to glance up from an important bit of grooming.

". . . we're going to be working together. That is," she added after a moment's pause, "if you still want to keep your job."

Austin snorted. "Weren't you listening to me?"

"Dean has to decide for himself if he's going to stay."

Dean shifted nervously under the weight of their combined attention. "What is it we'll be doing together?"

Claire put her cupped hand over the cat's muzzle before she answered. "Fighting evil."

"You're a superhero?"

Austin jerked free. "Don't," he suggested sternly, "give her ideas."

"No, I'm not a superhero. I don't even own a pair of tights. Are you blushing again?"

"I don't think so."

"Good."

"*I* am one of the good guys. And *this* is a bad situation. The woman in there . . ." Claire nodded toward the broken door. ". . . is only half the problem. Somewhere in this building is a hole in the fabric of the universe."

About to protest that there were some stories even a *dumb Newfie* wouldn't believe, Dean hesitated. They'd found a dust-covered woman, dressed in 1940s clothing, asleep in room six and he'd just had the situation more or less—mostly less—explained to him by a talking cat. Evidence suggested it wasn't a bam. "A hole in the fabric of the universe," he repeated. "Okay."

"We refer to it as an accident site. At some time, somebody did something they shouldn't have. The energy coming through the hole is keeping the woman asleep." Crossing her legs at the ankle, Claire rocked up onto her feet. "That's how I know there *is* a hole and Augustus Smythe wasn't here merely to monitor her." As Dean opened his mouth, the next question obvious on his face, she held up a silencing hand. "It's nothing personal, but right at the moment, my questions are more important than yours. Since I'm not going back in there to find the answers . . ."

"You don't want her to wake up," Austin muttered at Dean. "You *really* don't want her to wake up."

". . . I've got to find the accident site. Unfortunately, it seems to be at least as well shielded as she is and we're going to have to search every threadbare inch of this place, unless . . . you know where it is?"

"The accident site?" He stood. "The hole in the fabric of the universe?"

"That's right." She'd never had to explain herself to a bystander before. It was hard not to sound patronizing.

"Sorry. I haven't the faintest idea of what you're talking about." Squaring his shoulders, he hiked the tool belt up on his hips. His world had always included a number of things he'd had to take on faith. He added one more. "But I'd like to help."

"So you're staying?"

"Yes, ma'am."

"Claire." When he looked dubious, she sighed. "What?"

"You own the hotel, you're my boss; I can't call you by your first name. It wouldn't be right."

About to tell him that he was being an idiot, Claire suddenly remembered the feel of his arms and the warm scent of fabric softener and decided it might be better to maintain some distance. "What did you call Augustus Smythe?"

"To his face?"

Austin snickered.

"Yes. To his face."

"I called him Boss." Dean considered the possibility of calling an attractive woman the same thing he'd called a cranky old man and wasn't entirely convinced it would work. "I *guess* I could call you Boss."

"Good. Glad we've got that cleared up."

"Should I wire this door shut before we start searching, um, Boss?"

Although Dean don't seem quite comfortable using the title, Claire found she liked it. It made her feel like the lead in an old gangster movie. "You might as well." It would be a useless precaution since it was unlikely any of them would now wander into room six by accident, but it would give Dean something to do that he understood. "Just let me turn out the light first."

The remainder of the third floor, two double rooms and a single, was empty of everything except the lingering smell of disinfectant. Inside the storage cupboard across from room six, Claire emptied the shelves of toilet paper and cleaning supplies, then peered down the laundry chute.

"Don't even think about it!" Austin spat as she turned and studied him measuringly.

"Suppose it's between floors?"

"Then it'll just have to stay there."

"I'll keep you from falling."

"Oh, sure." He squeezed in behind a bucket of sponges and peered balefully at her over the edge, ears flat against his head. "*That's* what you said the last time."

"Those were extraordinary circumstances. Never happen again."

"I said no."

"Okay, okay." She tried and failed to open the narrow door next to the chute. "What's in here?"

"Stairs to the attic." Dean eyeballed the opening of the laundry chute, was relieved to find he wouldn't fit, and found the required key on his master ring.

Filling an area barely five feet square, a narrow set of metal stairs spiraled upward toward an uninviting square hole cut out of the ceiling.

"Are there lights?"

"Don't think so. You stay where you're at, girl, and let me . . ." At the look on her face, his voice trailed off. "Never mind, then."

"Girl?"

"It's just a way we have of talkin' back home," he explained hurriedly, his cheeks crimson and his accent thickening. "I don't mean nothing by it."

"Then don't do it again."

"Yes ma'am, Ms. Hansen." A deep breath and he tried again. "Boss."

"Are you certain he's a part of this?" she demanded, turning toward the cat.

"Yes. Get along."

Claire sighed. Metal rungs ringing under her feet, she ran to the top of the stairs, crossed her fingers and stuck her head up into what looked like one large room filled with decades of discards, barely lit by the two filthy dormer windows cut into the sloping roof on either end of the building.

It was still raining.

"It'll take us months to search that place thoroughly," she announced a moment later backing carefully down the stairs. "Let's leave it for later. With any luck we'll find the hole someplace more accessible."

"Oh, sure, accessible like the laundry chute," Austin muttered as Dean relocked the attic door.

The second floor was as empty as the first—more so since there was nothing to match the occupant of room six. Remembering the mess she'd left spread out on the bed, Claire vouched for her room without opening the door. Room four, a corner single with two outside walls and no window, suggested a more thorough search.

Leaning on the edge of the bureau, Dean watched Claire slip into the bed alcove and try the bolt on the inside of the alcove's steel door. "You know someone actually asked for this room last spring."

"How would I know that? I just got here." The high box bed had one shallow drawer under the mattress and two deeper drawers below that. Hands slid between the mattress and the frame found no sign of evil but did turn up a silver earring.

Mortified, Dean apologized for a sloppy job as Claire dropped the piece of jewelry on his palm. "When we're done searching, I'll clean this room again."

"If it makes you happy," Claire muttered, checking in the bedside table. As far as she could see, the room was spotless.

Dean's expression softened as he bounced the earring on his

palm. "She was a musician. Sasha something. I can't remember her last name, but she was some h . . ." Then, he remembered who he was talking to. His boss. A woman. Some things he couldn't say to a boss. Or a woman. "Cute. She was some cute."

"H . . . cute?" Shaking her head, Claire brushed past him.

Mouth partly open, Austin whipped his tail from side to side. "I don't like the way this smells."

"Then since it'd take a sledgehammer to air it out, let's go." Claire could feel a perfectly logical reason for the design hovering just beyond the edge of conscious thought, but when she reached for it, it danced away and taunted her from a safe distance. *Later,* she promised and added aloud, "What did you say?"

Dean paused at the top of the stairs. "I said, do you think we should search the rest of Mr. Smythe's old rooms, then?"

"He wouldn't have been living with it," she snapped dismissively. Then feeling like she'd just kicked a puppy, a large and well-muscled puppy, she added a strained, "Sorry. Where Augustus Smythe is concerned, I shouldn't take anything for granted."

The sitting room violated a number of rules concerning how many objects could simultaneously occupy the same space, but the only accident it contained involved the head-on collision of good taste with an apparent inability to throw anything away. The bedroom wasn't quite as bad. Dominated by a brass bed, it also held an obviously antique dressing table, a wardrobe, and two windows. One of them framed into an inside wall.

"Probably the window missing from the room upstairs." Jumping up onto the bed, Austin began kneading the mattress. "This isn't bad. I could sleep here."

Before Claire could stop him, Dean tugged the burgundy brocade curtain to one side and closed it again almost instantly, setting six inches of fringe swaying back and forth.

"Are you okay?" she asked warily. If it was the accident site and he'd been exposed, there was no telling what he might have picked up.

Cheeks flushed, he nodded. "Fine. I'm fine."

"What did you see?"

"It was, uh, a bar." He cleared his throat and reluctantly continued. "With, uh, dancers."

"Were they table dancing?" The cat snickered. "Upon admittedly short acquaintance, that seems like the sort of scene old Augustus would go for."

"Not exactly table, no." Shaking his head, Dean lifted the curtain again. "It was dark but . . ." His voice trailed off.

Claire peered around his shoulder and almost went limp with relief. "That doesn't sound like a bar to me. Looks like Times Square. And over there, in front of the hookers, isn't that a drug deal going down?" Leaning forward, she rapped on the glass and nodded in satisfaction. "That put the fear of God into them.'

The curtain fell closed again. Dean's voice threatened to crack as he asked, "What was it?"

"We call it a postcard."

"We?" He waved an overly nonchalant hand toward the cat. That smacked-with-a-cod feeling had returned. "You and Austin?"

"Among others." She glared at the curtain. "Smythe couldn't have managed this on his own; he had to have been pulling from the site."

"Is that bad?"

"Well it isn't good. I'll know more when we find the hole."

"Wherever it is," Austin agreed.

"Since we know it's not in the dining room, what's left?"

The basement held, besides the mechanicals, the laundry room, Dean's sparsely furnished and absolutely spotless apartment, several storage cupboards holding sheets, towels, and still more cleaning supplies, and, across from the laundry room, a large metal door. Painted a brilliant turquoise, it boasted not one but two padlocked chains securing it closed.

"Dean, did you know this was down here?"

He frowned, confused by the question. Since he obviously spent a lot of time in the basement . . . "Sure."

"Why didn't you mention it earlier?"

"It's just the furnace room."

"The furnace room." Claire exchanged a speaking glance with the cat. "Have you ever been in this alleged furnace room?"

"No. Mr. Smythe did all the furnace work himself."

"I'll bet." The keys were hanging beside the door. The security arrangements were clearly not intended to keep people out but to keep something in. "What was he heating this place with," she muttered, dragging the first chain free. "A dragon?"

Dean took the chain, removed the second length, and hung them both neatly on the hooks provided. "Are you kidding?"

"Mostly. Any virgins reported missing from the neighborhood?"

"*Pardon?*"

"Forget it." Claire pulled the door open about six inches and leaned away from the blast of heat. "Do you mind?" she asked as

Austin slipped in ahead of her. "Try to remember what curiosity killed." Moving forward, she felt remarkably calm. At first she thought she was just numb—it had, after all, been a busy morning—but when she stepped over the threshold, she realized that the entire furnace room had been wrapped in a dampening field.

Much more powerful than a mere shield, it not only deflected the curious but was quite probably the only thing allowing people to remain in the building.

Down nine steps, inscribed into the rough surface of a bedrock floor, was a complicated, multicolored, multilayered pentagram. The center of the pentagram was an open hole. A dull red light, shining up from the depths, painted lurid highlights on the copper hood hanging from the ceiling. Ductwork directed the rising heat up into the hotel.

Must have a helluva filter system, Claire thought, wrinkling her nose at the stink of fire and brimstone.

And then it sank in. Unfortunately, the dampening field had no effect inside the furnace room.

Heart pounding, hot sweat rolling down her sides, she bent and scooped up Austin, who'd flattened himself to the floor. With the cat held tightly against her chest, she forced herself down the first three steps.

"Where are you going?" he hissed, claws digging into her shoulder.

"To check the seal."

"Why?"

"Because Augustus Smythe couldn't have held this."

"Then obviously someone else is. And there's only one someone else in this building."

"She's holding it, it's holding her." Claire went down another three steps and nodded toward the pentagram. "There's her name. Sara."

"Don't . . ."

"It's all right. If her name could get through the field, they'd have woken her years ago." There was a vibration in the air, just on the edge of sound, an almost hum as though they were walking toward the world's largest wasp's nest. "On the other hand, you know that low-level buzz I mentioned last night? There seems to be some seepage."

"But you couldn't feel it this morning."

"Not outside this room, no. Augustus Smythe probably used it up making his getaway."

"That's bad."

"Well, it's not good." Placing her feet with care, she backed up the stairs, squeezed over the threshold, shoved Dean away from the door, and very, very gently, pushed it closed.

"*Was* it a dragon?" Dean asked, not entirely certain why he hadn't followed her inside but untroubled by the uncertainty.

"No." As the dampening field began to take effect, it became possible to think again. "It wasn't a dragon."

"Then was it a furnace?"

"Sort of." She unhooked Austin's claws from her shoulder and settled him more comfortably in her arms, her free hand rhythmically stroking his fur and sending clouds of loose hair flying. He tucked his head up under her chin, and left it there.

"Was it the hole?"

Claire giggled. She couldn't help it, but she managed to cut it short; she hadn't expected such a literal example of the explanation she'd created to fit a bystander's limited world. "Oh, yes, it was the hole." Still cradling the cat, she started toward the basement stairs, head up, back straight. "Could you please replace the chains and the locks?"

Dean had the strangest feeling that if he tapped her shoulder as she passed, she'd ring out like a weather buoy. "Are you all right, then?"

"I'm fine."

"Where are you going?"

"Upstairs."

He shook his head, thought about opening the door and taking a look for himself and for reasons he wasn't quite clear on, decided not to. "Hey, Boss?"

It took Claire a moment to realize who he was talking to. Three steps up, she paused and leaned out from the stairs so she could see him. "Yes?"

"What are you after doing?"

"I'm going to do what anyone in this situation would do; I'm going to get a second opinion."

"From who?"

Her smile looked as if it had been borrowed and didn't quite fit. "I'm going to call my mother."

Behind the chains, behind the turquoise door, down the stairs, and deep in the pit, intelligence stirred.

HELLO?

When it realized there'd be no answer, it sighed.

DAMN.

TWO

"Hansen residence."

The voice on the other end of the line was not one Claire had expected to hear. "Diana?" Unable to remain still, she picked up the old rotary phone and paced the length of the office and back. "What are you doing home? I thought you were doing fieldwork this weekend."

"Hong and I had a small argument."

"Like the argument you had with Matt?"

"No."

There was a lengthening, a scornful pronunciation of that second letter that only a teenager could manage. At twenty, the ability was lost. *Three years,* Claire told herself, *just three more years.* She'd been ten when Diana was born and the sudden appearance of a younger sister had come as a complete surprise. Over the years, although she loved Diana dearly, the surprise had turned to apprehension—being around her was somewhat similar to being around sweating dynamite. "These people are supposed to be training you. You could assume they know what they're doing."

"Yeah, well, they're old and they never let *me* do anything."

"I haven't time to get into this with you right now. Put Mom on, please."

"Duh, Claire, it's Sunday morning."

She took a minute to whack herself on the forehead with the receiver. She'd completely forgotten. "Could you ask her to call me the moment she gets home from church?"

"You didn't say the magic word."

"Diana!"

"Chill, I'm kidding. What's the matter anyway? You sound like you just looked into the depths of Hell."

Reflecting, not for the first time, that her little sister had an appalling amount of power from someone with an equally appalling amount of self-confidence, Claire smoothed the lingering tremors

out of her voice. "Just ask her to call me—please." She read the
number off the dial. "It's important."

Dean could hear Claire talking on the phone as he came up the
basement stairs. Ignoring the temptation to eavesdrop—as much
as he wanted to know what she was saying, it would've been
rude—he continued on into the kitchen, where he found Austin
attempting to open the fridge.

"They build garage door openers, push of a button and you can
park your car, but does anyone ever think of building something
like that for a fridge. No." He pulled his claws out of the rubber
seal and glared up at Dean. "What does a cat have to do to get
breakfast around here?"

"Are you okay?"

"Why wouldn't I be?"

"A few minutes ago . . ."

Austin interrupted with an explosive snort. "That was then,
this is now." Rising onto his hind legs, he rested his front paws
just above Dean's denim-covered knee, claws extended only
enough for emphasis. "You look like a nice guy, why don't you
feed me?"

"Austin!"

"That's my name," he sighed, dropping back to all four feet.
"Don't wear it out."

As Claire came around the corner, she was amazed at how familiar it seemed, as though this were the twenty-second not
merely the second time she'd walked into the kitchen. Layered
between the sleeping Sara and Hell, there was a comforting do-
mesticity about the whole thing. She shuddered.

"Are you okay?" Dean asked.

"I'm fine. I just had a vision of an unpleasant future." Shaking
her head, hoping to clear it, she added, "My mother wasn't home,
but I left a message with my sister. She'll call later."

Austin jumped up onto the counter. "Why was your sister
home!"

"The usual."

"Anyone get hurt?"

"I didn't ask."

Leaning back against the sink, Dean looked down at his sock-
covered feet. Had she not been his boss, he would've asked her if
she wasn't a little old to be calling her mum when she ran into a
problem.

"Dean?"

He glanced up to see Claire staring at him.

"Penny for your thoughts?"

Instinct caught the coin she tossed, and to his surprise he found himself repeating his musing aloud.

"No, I am *not* too old to call my mother," she said when he finished, ignoring the cat's muttered, "Serves you right for asking."

"My mother has been in the business a lot longer than I have, and I could use her professional advice since not one thing that happened this morning was what I expected. Not room six, not the furnace room, not you."

"Not me?"

"If Austin wasn't so convinced that you're a part of this whole mess, we'd be sitting down to rearrange your memories right about now."

Dean squelched his initial response—why ask if she could do it when there was absolutely nothing in that statement to suggest she couldn't. "If it's all the same to you, I'd like to keep my memories the way they are."

"Good for you." Austin sat down and stared pointedly at the fridge. "So if we're not going to adjust the status quo until your mother's had a look, what are we waiting for? When do we eat?"

Claire sighed. "I think Dean's waiting for an explanation."

"I already explained," Austin protested, twisting out from under Claire's hand. "He told me he believed in magic. I told him that's what was going on."

"That's not much of an explanation."

"It's enough to tide him over until after breakfast."

They surrendered to the inevitable. While Dean cooked for Claire, she ran up to her room to get a can of cat food.

As she put the saucer of beige puree on the floor, Austin glanced down in disgust and then glared up at her. "I can smell perfectly good sausages," he complained.

"Which you're not allowed to have. Remember what the vet said, at your age the geriatric cat food will help keep you alive."

"One sausage couldn't hurt," Dean offered, his expression as he looked into the saucer much the same as the cat's.

Claire caught his wrist and moved the hand holding the fork holding the sausage back over the plate. "Austin's seventeen years old," she told him. "Would you feed one of these to someone who was a hundred and two?"

"I guess not."

"You won't live forever; it'll only seem that way," Austin muttered around a mouthful of food.

As Dean carried the loaded plate over to one of the small tables in the dining room, Claire attempted to organize her thoughts. Of the morning's three surprises, four if she counted Augustus Smythe disappearing and leaving her the hotel, Dean was actually the one she felt least qualified to deal with. When it came right down to it, Sara and Hell and Augustus Smythe were variations on a theme—extreme variations, *really* extreme variations, granted, but nothing entirely unique. On the other hand, in almost ten years of sealing sites, she'd never had to explain herself to a bystander. Manipulate perceptions so she could do her job, yes. Actually—to tell the truth, the whole truth—no.

When Dean set down the plate, she stared aghast at the scrambled eggs, sausage patties, grilled tomatoes, and three pieces of toast. "This is more food than I'd usually eat all day."

"I guess that's why you're so . . ."

"So what?"

"Nothing."

"What?"

"Skinny." Hie ears slowly turning red, Dean set the cutlery neatly on each side of the plate and hurried back into the kitchen. "I'll, uh, get you another coffee, then."

While his back was turned, Claire rolled her eyes. She was not skinny; she was petite. And *he* was so—in rapid succession she considered and discarded intense, earnest, and stalwart. Before she worked her way down to yeomanly, she decided she'd best settle on young and leave it at that. "Aren't you having any?" she asked as he returned with her mug.

A little surprised, he shook his head. "I ate before you got up."

"That was hours ago. Bring another plate, you can have half of this."

"If *I* bring another plate . . ." Austin began.

"No." When Dean hesitated, Claire prodded at his conscience. "Trust me, I'm not going to eat all of it; it'll just get thrown out."

A few moments later, a less intimidating breakfast in front of her and Dean eating hungrily on the other side of the table the way only a young man who'd gone three hours without eating could, Claire turned suddenly toward the cat and said, "You're *sure* he's a part of this?"

"I'm positive."

"You were positive that time in Gdansk, too."

Austin snorted. "So my Polish was a little rusty, sue me." He stared pointedly up at her, his tail flicking off the seconds like a furry metronome.

"All right. You win." Chewing and swallowing a forkful of tomato delayed the inevitable only a few moments more. Feeling the weight of Dean's gaze join the cat's, she lifted her head and cleared her throat. "First of all, I want you to realize that what I'm about to tell you is privileged information and is not to be repeated. To anyone. Ever."

Wrapped in the comforting and lingering odors of sausage and egg, Dean ran through a fast replay of the morning's events. "Nothing personal, but who'd believe me?"

"You'd be surprised. When I got up today, I didn't expect I'd be telling it to you." Eyes narrowed, she leaned forward. "If this information falls into the wrong hands . . ."

Unable to help himself, Dean mirrored her movement and lowered his voice dramatically. "The fate of the world is at stake?"

"Yes."

When he realized she meant it, he could've sworn he felt each individual hair rise off the back of his neck. It was an unpleasant sensation. He pushed his chair away from the table, all of a sudden not really hungry. "Okay. Maybe you'd better not tell me."

Claire shot an annoyed look at the cat. "Too late."

"But you don't even know me. You don't know you can trust me."

The possibility of not trusting him hadn't crossed her mind. Total strangers probably handed him their packages while they bent to tie their shoelaces. If a game needed a scorekeeper, he'd always be the one drafted. Mothers could safely leave small children with him and return hours later knowing that their darlings had been fed, watered, and harmlessly amused. *And he does windows.*

"I know we can trust you," Austin muttered, leaping up onto an empty chair and glaring over the edge of the table at a piece of uneaten sausage. "Get on with it. I'm old. I haven't got all day. Are you going to finish that?"

"Yes." While she cleared her plate, Claire created and scrapped several possible beginnings. Finally, she sighed. "I suppose Austin's right . . ."

"Well thank you *very* much."

". . . it begins with believing in magic."

"And ends with?" Dean asked cautiously.

"Armageddon. But if it's all the same to you, I'd rather leave that for another day." When he indicated that Armageddon could be left for as long as she liked, Claire continued. "Magic, simply put, is a system for tapping into and controlling the possibilities of a complex energy source."

"Energy from where?"

"From somewhere else." It was clear that she'd lost him. She sighed. "It doesn't have a physical presence, it just is." In fact, a part of it had reputedly once explained itself by saying, "I AM." but that wasn't a detail Claire thought she ought to add.

"It just is," Dean repeated. Since she seemed to be waiting to see if he was willing to accept that, he shrugged and said, "Okay." At this point, it seemed safest.

"Let's compare magic to baseball. Everyone is more-or-less capable of playing the game but not everyone has the ability to make it to the major leagues." Pleased with the analogy, Claire made a mental note to remember it. She could use it should she ever be in this situation again—owning a hotel complete with sleeping evil, a hole to Hell in the basement, and a handsome, young caretaker to whom her cat spilled his guts. *Yeah, right.* Her nostrils flared.

Taken aback by the nostril flaring, Dean shuffled his feet under the table, glanced around the familiar dining room, and finally said, "Could I do it?"

"With training and discipline, lots of discipline," she added in case he started thinking it was easy, "anyone can do minor magics—so minor that most people don't think they're worth the effort."

Feeling like he'd just been chastised by his fifth grade teacher, an intense young woman right out of teacher's college whom every boy in the class had had a crush on, Dean slid down in his chair until his shoulders were nearly level with the table and his legs, crossed at the ankle, stretched halfway across the room. "Go ahead."

"Thank you." An irritated *so kind* came implied with the tone. Who did he think he was? "Most of the energy magic deals with comes from the center part of the possibilities. The upper end is for emergency use only and the lower end is posted off-limits. For the sake of argument, let's call the upper end 'good,' and the lower end 'evil.' " She paused, waiting for an objection that never came. "You're okay with that? I mean, good and evil aren't exactly late twentieth century concepts."

"There were at my granddad's house," Dean told her. Tersely invited to elaborate, he shrugged self-consciously. "My granddad was an Anglican minister."

"This is the Reverend McIssac, the grandfather who raised you?"

He nodded.

"What happened to your parents?" Claire didn't entirely understand his expression, but as the silence went on just a little too long, she suspected he wasn't going to answer. "I'm sorry, that was tactless of me. I'm not actually very good with people."

"*Quel surprise,*" Austin muttered, head on his front paws.

"No, it's okay." Dean spun one of the breakfast knives around on the table, eyes locked on the whirling blade. "They died when I was a baby," he said at last. "House fire. It happens a lot when the woodstove gets loaded up on the first cold night of winter and you find out what condition your chimney is really in. My dad threw me out the upstairs window into a snowbank just before the building collapsed."

"I'm sorry."

"I never knew them. It was always just me and my granddad. My father was his only son, see, and he wouldn't let any of my aunts raise me. He's the one who taught me to cook." All at once, Dean had to see Claire's expression. Too many girls fell into a "poor sweet baby" mood at this point in the story and things never really recovered after that. Catching the knife between two fingers, he looked up and saw sympathy but not pity, so he told her the rest. "They could've saved themselves if they hadn't gone upstairs for me. I've always known, without a doubt, how much they loved me. There's not a lot of people who can say that."

Swallowing a lump in her throat, Claire reached over and lightly touched the back of his hand. "No wonder you're so stable."

He shrugged self-consciously. "Me?"

"Do you see anyone else around here who isn't a cat?" Austin reached up and batted the knife off the table. "Thank you for sharing. Now, can we get on with it?"

Partly to irritate the cat, and partly to allow emotions to settle, Claire waited while Dean dealt with the smear of butter and toast crumbs on the floor before picking up the scattered threads of the explanation. "You ready?"

He nodded.

"All right, back to good energy and evil energy. Between this energy and what most of the world considers reality, is a barrier. For lack of a better term, let's keep calling it the fabric of the universe. Those who use magic learn to pierce this barrier and draw off the energy they need. Unfortunately, it also gets pierced by accident." She took a long swallow of coffee. "In order to continue, I'm going to have to grossly oversimplify, so please don't think that I'm insulting your intelligence."

"Okay." It still seemed to be the safest response.

"Every time someone does something good, it pokes a hole through the fabric, releases some of the good energy, and everybody benefits. Every time someone does something evil, it releases some of the evil energy and everybody suffers."

"How good?" Dean wondered. "And how evil?"

"The holes are proportional. If say, you sacrificed yourself to save another or conversely sacrificed another to save yourself, the holes would be large." She paused to watch raindrops hit the window behind his head, the drops merging until their weight pulled them in tiny rivers toward the ground. "The problem is that small holes can get bigger. Evil oozing out a pinprick inspires more evil which enlarges the hole which inspires greater evil . . . Well, you get the idea."

"Unless he's dumber than kibble," Austin growled. "I can't believe that was the best you could come up with."

Claire stared down at him through narrowed eyes. "All right. You come up with a better explanation."

Twisting around on the chair seat, the cat pointedly turned his back on her. "I don't want to."

"You can't."

"I said, I didn't want to."

"Ha!"

"Excuse me?" Dean waved a hand to get Claire's attention. "Is that what happened in the furnace room? Someone did something evil and accidentally made a hole?"

"Not exactly," she said slowly, trying to decide how much he should know. "Some holes are made on purpose. There are always people around who want what they're not supposed to have and are arrogant enough to believe they can control it." Recalling an accident site she'd come upon her first year working solo, she shook her head. "But they can't."

Dean read context if not particulars in the movement. "Messy?"

"It can be. I once found a body, an entire body, in the glove compartment of a 1984 Plymouth Reliant station wagon."

"The 1.2 liter GM, or the Mitsubishi engine?"

"Does it matter?"

"It does if you need to buy parts."

Claire drummed her fingernails against the tabletop. "I'm talking about a body in a glove compartment, not a shopping trip to Canadian Tire."

"Sorry."

"May I continue?"

"Sure."

"Thank you. Most holes can be taken care of with the magical equivalent of a caulking gun. Some are more complicated, and a few are large enough for a significant amount of evil to break through and wreak havoc before anything can be done about them."

His eyes widened, appearing even larger magnified by the lenses of his glasses. "Has this ever happened?"

She hesitated, then shrugged; this much she might as well tell him. "Yes. But not often; the sinking of Atlantis, the destruction of the Minoan Empire . . ."

"The inexplicable popularity of Barney," Austin added dryly.

Claire's eyes narrowed again, and Dean decided it might be safer not to laugh.

"Holes," she announced, her tone promising consequences should the cat interrupt again, "that give access to evil draw one of two types of monitors."

"Electronic monitors?"

"No." She paused to rub a smear of lipstick off her mug with her thumb. This was turning out to be easier than she'd imagined it could be. At the moment, before the tenuous connection they'd acquired over the course of the morning dissolved back into the relationship of almost strangers, she suspected Dean would accept almost anything she said.

GO AHEAD, TAKE ADVANTAGE. HAVE SOME FUN. WHO'LL KNOW?

The mug hit the table, rocking back and forth.

Dean grabbed it before the last dregs of Claire's coffee spilled out onto the table. "Are you okay?"

"Yes." She blinked four or five times to bring him back into focus. "Of course. Did you hear anything just now?"

"No."

He was clearly telling the truth.

"Are you sure you're okay?"

"I'm fine." The voice had sounded slightly off frequency, as though the speaker hadn't quite managed to sync up with her head. Considering the nature of the site in the furnace room, there could be only one possible source for that personal a temptation. And only one possible response.

"Right, then, the monitors. Now what?" she demanded when the pressure of Austin's regard dragged her to a second stop.

"Nothing."

"You're staring."

"I'm hanging on your every word," he told her.

He was looking so irritatingly inscrutable, Claire knew he suspected something. Tough. "The monitors," she began again, fixing her gaze on Dean and blocking the cat out of her peripheral vision, "are magic-users known as Cousins and Keepers. The Cousins are less powerful than the Keepers, but there're more of them. They can mitigate the results of an accident, but they can't actually seal the hole. They watch, and wait for the need to summon a Keeper.

"For the sites that *can't* be sealed because the holes have already grown too large, Keepers, who're always referred to as Aunt or Uncle for reasons no one has ever been able to make clear to me, essentially *become* the caulking and seal the hole with themselves. A lot of eccentric, reclusive old men and women are actually saving the world."

Dean took off his glasses and rubbed the bridge of his nose. "So the Keepers are the good guys?"

"That's right."

"And the woman asleep upstairs is one of the bad guys?"

"She's a Keeper gone bad." The words emerged without emotion because the only emotion applicable to the situation seemed a bit much to indulge in over the breakfast dishes. "An evil Keeper."

"An evil auntie?" he asked, unable to keep one corner of his mouth from curving up.

"It's a title, not a relationship," Claire snapped. He looked so abashed she couldn't help adding, "But, essentially, yes. We found her name written in the furnace room. For safety's sake, we can't tell you what it is."

Replacing his glasses, Dean straightened in his chair, shoulders squared, both feet flat on the spotless linoleum. "Written in the furnace room? On the wall?"

"The floor actually." It was very nearly the strongest reaction he'd had all morning. Claire wasn't entirely certain how she felt about that.

"Okay. As soon as you're done, I'll get right on it."

"On it? And do what?"

"Get rid of it. I've got an industrial cleanser designed for graffiti," he told her with the kind of reverence in his voice most males his age reserved for less cleansing pleasures. "Last spring, some kids decorated the side wall, the one facing the driveway, and this stuff took it right off the brick. Took off a bit of the mortar, too, but I fixed that."

"You'll just stay out of the furnace room, thank you very much." Although it would be a unique solution, it wasn't likely to be a successful one. Fortunately, the dampening field would keep him from attempting it on his own.

Brow creased, he shook his head. "I hate to leave a mess. . . ."

"I don't care." Claire smiled tightly across the table at him. "This time, you're going to."

"Okay. You're the boss," he sighed, slumping back into his chair. "But why can't you tell me her name?"

"Because Austin was right. . . ."

"I usually am," the cat muttered.

". . . and we really don't want to wake her."

Dean nodded. "Because she's evil. What did she do? Try to use the power coming out of the hole for her own ends?"

Claire felt her jaw drop. "That's exactly what she tried to do? How did *you* know?"

"I just thought it was obvious. I mean, she was corrupted by the dark side of the force, but another Keeper showed up to stop her just in time, and although she was beaten in a fair fight, she couldn't be killed because that would bring the good guys down to her level, so they put her to sleep instead as kind of a temporary solution."

Mouth open, Claire stared across the table at him.

Dean felt his cheeks grow warm. "But I'm just guessing." When she didn't respond, he squirmed uneasily in his chair. "It's what they'd do in the movie."

"What movie?" The question slipped out an octave higher than usual.

"Not an actual movie," Dean protested hurriedly, not entirely certain what he'd done wrong. "It's just what they'd do in a movie. If they did a movie. But they wouldn't." He'd never actually heard a cat laugh before. "I still don't know why her name would wake her."

Ignoring Austin, who seemed in danger of falling off the chair, Claire wrapped the tattered remains of her dignity around her, well aware that this bystander seven years her junior had offered his last statement out of kindness, deliberately handing back control of the conversation. "Names," she said, coolly, "are more than mere labels; they're one of the things that connect us to each other and to the world." Which was one of the reasons she wasn't planning on identifying the hole in the furnace room. If Dean thought of Hell by name, it could give the darkness a connection and easier access.

One of the reasons.

What they'd do in the movie, indeed.

"If she does get woken up," Dean wondered, frowning slightly, "is she able for you?"

"Say what?"

He hurriedly translated his question into something a mainlander could understand. "Is she stronger than you?"

"No!"

Austin snorted.

"All right. I don't know." Claire glared at the cat. "She's a powerful Keeper, or she wouldn't have been able to seal the hole, not to mention attempting to use it. But . . ." Her eyes narrowed. "I am also a powerful Keeper, or I wouldn't have been summoned here. Waking her would be the only way to find out which of us is stronger, and I'm not willing to risk the destruction of this immediate area on a point of ego."

"So she's still sealing the hole? Like a cork in a bottle?"

"Essentially."

"You're here to pop her out and close the hole?"

"It's more complicated than that."

"And that's why you called your mother?"

"Yes."

"Okay." He took a deep breath, and laid both hands flat on the table. "The woman in room six is an evil Keeper."

"That's right."

"And you're a good Keeper?"

Claire leaned back and pulled a vinyl business card case out of her blazer pocket. "My sister made these for me. She meant them as a joke, but they're accurate enough."

> Aunt Claire, Keeper
> your Accident is my Opportunity
>
> (abilities dependent on situation)

The card stock felt handmade and the words had the smudgy edges of rubber stamp printing. "Should *I* call you Aunt Claire?"

"No."

He'd never heard such a definitive *no* before. There were no shades of *maybe,* no possibility of compromise. When she indicated he could keep the card, he slipped it into the pocket of his T-shirt. "I've always wanted to see real magic."

Claire leaned forward, eyes half lidded, palms flat on the table. "You should hope you don't get the chance."

It would've been more dramatic as a warning had she not placed one palm squarely on a bit of spilled jam.

Dean handed her a napkin and managed not to laugh although he couldn't quite control a slight twitch in the outer corners of his mouth. "So was Mr. Smythe a Keeper, too?"

Claire showed her teeth in what wasn't quite a smile. "Augustus Smythe was, and is, a despicable little worm who walked out and left me holding the bag. He's also a Cousin."

"Did he put her to sleep?"

"No, a Cousin can't manipulate that kind of power." As much as it irritated her to admit it, Dean's little synopsis had to have been essentially correct. "At some point, there was another Keeper involved."

"But Mr. Smythe is a Cousin, and you said Cousins monitor unsealed sites."

"Your point?"

"You said this site is sealed, that she was sealing it like a cork in a bottle . . ."

"No, you said like a cork in a bottle."

"Okay. But if the hole is sealed, what was Mr. Smythe doing here?"

"Probably monitoring the seal since she can't and monitoring *her* since the power that's keeping her asleep is coming from the site."

"Evil power is keeping her asleep?"

"Trust me . . ." She tossed the napkin down onto her plate. "It's not likely to corrupt her."

"But if it was a temporary solution, why has Mr. Smythe been here since 1945?"

"Has he?"

"Sure. He complained about it all the time." With a flick of two fingers, Dean began spinning the knife again. "Why did Mr. Smythe sneak out like he did?"

"I have no idea." The handle of her mug creaked slightly in her grip. "But I'd certainly like to ask him."

"What are you after doing now?"

"Nothing hasty. Nothing at all until I get that second opinion. When I have more information, I'll get to work closing things up but as long as the hole remains sealed, it's perfectly safe. We're in no immediate danger."

"No immediate danger?" Dean repeated. When she nodded, he leaned back in his chair, continuing to spin the knife. "That's, um, interesting phrasing. What about long-term danger?"

"That depends."

"On what, then?"

"I can't tell you."

"There's a whole lot you're not telling me, isn't there?"

"There's a whole lot I don't know."

"Mr. Smythe was supposed to leave you more information?"

Claire snorted, sounding remarkable like Austin at his most sardonic. "At the very least."

"Which is why we need you," the cat told him, looking up from a damp patch of fur. "Smythe's not here, and you are."

"But I don't know anything," Dean protested.

"You should make a good pair, then. She thinks she knows everythi . . . Hey!" he protested as Claire picked him up and dropped him onto the floor. "It was a *joke!* Keepers," he muttered, leaping back up onto the chair, "no sense of humor."

The wisest course, Dean decided, would be to ignore that observation altogether. Stilling the knife, he looked up from her elongated reflection in the blade. "If you don't mind me asking, where do Keepers and Cousins come from?"

"Just outside Wappakenetta." When both Dean and Austin stared at her blankly, she sighed. "We have a sense of humor, it's just no one appreciates it. If you're asking historically, Keepers and Cousins are descendants of Lilith, Adam's first wife."

Dean started to grin.

"I'm not joking."

"You're not serious! Adam's first wife?"

Enjoying his reaction, she waved off his question with a dismissive gesture borrowed from Marlon Brando in *The Godfather*. "I only know what I'm told, but some of our people are very into genealogy."

"But you're talking about *Adam and Eve!*"

"No, I'm talking about Adam and Lilith."

"The Bible, the Christian Bible, as literal truth?" Dean suspected that his granddad, who held some fairly radical views for an Anglican minister, would be appalled.

"No. Not truth as such. The lineage—that is, Cousins and

Keepers—consider all religions are attempts to explain their energy. Think of them as containing capital T Truths as opposed to merely being true."

"But you said Adam and Lilith," Dean reminded her. "Twice."

Were all bystanders so literal, she wondered, or was it just this one? "Forget them. Forget them twice. If you prefer, there had to have been, at some point, a breeding pair of what was essentially the first humans. Postulate, a second female, with genetic coding to handle magic that the other didn't have. It's the same story in a different language."

"Okay." He took a deep breath, followed that theory out to its logical conclusion, and half prepared to duck. "So essentially, you're not—that is, not entirely—human?"

She took it better than he'd thought she would and seemed more intrigued than insulted, as though the idea had never occurred to her before. "I suppose that depends on where you set your parameters. If you're speaking biologically . . ."

"I wasn't," Dean interrupted before she could add details. Unfortunately, it didn't stop her.

". . . we're certainly able to interbreed, but that doesn't really mean anything because so could the old Greek gods."

"They were real?"

"How should I know?" One painted fingernail tapped against the side of her mug as she thought it over. "Under those parameters, I suppose you could say, we're . . ." She smiled suddenly and taken totally by surprise, he found himself lost in it. ". . . semi-mythical."

Austin snorted. "Spare me. Semi-mythical indeed."

"It does cover all the bases," Claire protested.

"You want to cover the bases? Play shortstop for the Yankees." Swiveling his head around, Austin stared up at Dean. "She's human. The Keepers are human. The Cousins are human. I barely know you, but I'm assuming you're human. I'm not saying this is a good thing, it's just the way it is."

"Okay." Dean held up both hands in surrender. "So, if Mr. Smythe is a Cousin, and she's a Keeper, what are you?"

Austin drew himself up to his full height, his entire bearing from ears to tail suggesting he'd been mortally insulted. "I am a *cat*."

"A cat. Okay."

While Dean did the breakfast dishes and slotted the morning's experiences into previously empty places in his worldview,

Claire went through the papers Augustus Smythe had left in the hotel office in the hope of discovering some answers. If the registration books were complete, the hotel had never been a popular destination and bookings had fallen off considerably after Smythe had changed the name from Brewster's Hotel to The Elysian Fields Guest House in 1952.

"Might as well call it The Vestibule of Hell," she muttered mockingly, turning yellowed pages and not at all impressed by her earlier flash of prescience. It appeared that windowless room four had been popular throughout the existence of the hotel, and the guests who stayed in it seemed to have had uniformly bad handwriting.

She had to call Dean out of the kitchen to open the safe.

"The very least Augustus Smythe could've done," she grumbled, arms folded and brows drawn into a deep vee over her nose, "was leave me the combination."

"He left you Dean," Austin observed from the desk. "Something he probably figured you'd get more use out of."

Ears red, Dean cranked the handle around and got up off his knees as the safe door swung open. "Anything else, Boss?"

Having chased Austin halfway up the first flight of stairs before being forced to acknowledge that four old legs sufficiently motivated were still faster than two, Claire ducked back under the counter. "Not right now."

As she straightened, their eyes locked. "What?"

Dean felt a sudden and inexplicable urge to stammer. He managed to control it by keeping conversation to a minimum. "The combination?"

"Good point. Write it down. Use the back of that old bill on the desk," she added, walking over to the safe. Squatting, she heard pencil move against paper then the combination appeared over her shoulder. "Six left, six right, seven left?"

"That's right. I should, uh, finish the dishes now."

"Good idea." As he returned to the kitchen, Claire grinned. He really did turn a very charming color at the slightest opportunity. Then she looked back down at the piece of paper and shook her head. Six sixty-seven. Cute. Hell was in the basement; the safe was on the first floor, one up from the Number of the Beast. *First the Elysian Fields, now this.* Augustus Smythe seemed to delight in throwing about obscure hints. *A cry for help or sheer bloody-mindedness?*

In the safe, she found a heavy linen envelope marked with the sigil for expenses. On the back, *Taxes, Victuals, Maintenance,* and *Staff* had been written in an elegant copperplate. Another, later hand had added, *Electricity* and *Telephone*. The envelope was empty.

No outstanding bills. Claire put the envelope back in the safe and closed the door. *Great. When the seal goes and something calling itself Beelzebub leads a demonic army out of the furnace room, the lights'll stay on and a well-fed staff can call 911 as they're disemboweled.*

As she sat back on her heels, a flash of brilliant blue racing along the inside edge of a lower shelf caught her eye. Thumb and first two fingers of her right hand raised, just in case, she leaned over and with her left hand yanked a dusty pile of ledgers onto the floor. The hole in the corner was unmistakably mouse.

Which didn't mean that only mice were using it.

Mice weren't usually a brilliant blue.

She moved closer and sent down a cautious probe.

"Problem?"

"OW!" Rubbing her head, she crawled back from the shelf and glared up at Dean. "Try and make a little more noise when you sneak up on people!"

"Sorry. I've finished the dishes and I was wondering if you want me to put a new padlock on room six."

"Definitely." It was an emotional not a rational response. Sara wouldn't be leaving the room any time soon and—should she decide to—a padlock wouldn't stop her, but for peace of mind there had to be a perception of security. "I'll have a locksmith repair the door plate."

"But he'll see her."

"No, he won't."

It was another one of those statements, like *"rearrange your memories,"* that Dean had no intention of arguing with. "Okay." He squatted beside her and peered at the hole. "Looks like a new one. I'll set out some more traps."

"Mousetraps?"

The sideways look he shot her seemed mildly concerned. "Yeah. Why?"

"Have you caught anything?"

"Not yet." Rising, he held out his hand. "They're smart. They take the bait and avoid springing the trap."

Claire debated with herself for a moment, then put her hand in his. "They might not be mice," she said as he lifted her effortlessly to her feet. "All I'm reading is the residual signature of the seepage, but this place could easily be infested with imps."

Which would explain why her running shoes had still been wet this morning.

"Imps?"

"I saw something and it was bright blue." A little surprised that he hadn't released her, Claire pulled her fingers free of his grip.

"Imps." Dean sighed. "Okay. Is there anything I can do about it now?"

"Not now, no."

"In that case, I'll be upstairs if you need me."

"Don't go into the room."

He looked uncomfortable. "I was thinking about dusting her."

"Don't."

"But she's covered in . . ."

"No."

According to the site journal, found tucked under a stack of early seventies skin magazines in the middle left-hand drawer of the desk, three Keepers had sealed the hole before Sara; Uncle Gregory, Uncle Arthur, and Aunt Fiona. Aunt Fiona had died rather suddenly which explained why Sara had been summoned off active service at such a relatively young age—she'd been the closest Keeper strong enough to hold the seal when the need had gone out.

"Relatively young age," Claire snorted, rubbing her eyes. The yellowing papers she studied seemed to soak up the puddle of illumination spilled by the old-fashioned desk lamp without the faded handwriting becoming any more legible. "She was forty-two."

Sara had made it very clear in her first entry in the site journal that she hated the hotel and everything to do with it. It was also her one and only entry.

"Oh, this is a lot of help. A considerate villain would've had the courtesy to keep complete notes."

Confident of her abilities, Claire had no doubt that she'd been summoned to the hotel to finally close the site. It was the only logical explanation. Unfortunately, sealing the hole would cut the power that kept Aunt Sara asleep, and Claire had meant it when she'd told Dean she didn't want to find out which of them was more powerful.

Keepers capable of abusing the power granted by the lineage were rare. Claire had only heard of it happening twice before in their entire history. The battles, Keeper vs Keeper, good vs evil, had been won but both times at a terrible cost. The first had resulted in the eruption of Vesuvius and the loss of Pompeii. The second, in disco. Claire had only a child's memories of the seventies, but she wouldn't be responsible for putting the world through that again.

Augustus Smythe's entry, which should have, and possibly did describe how he'd come to monitor the site, was unreadable. Ink had been spilled on the last third of the ledger, had soaked through the pages, and dried to create what could most accurately be described as an indigo blue brick. The skin magazines would've been as helpful.

"Coincidence?" Claire asked the silence. "I don't think so." The sound of something scuttling merrily away inside the wall only confirmed her suspicions.

She was searching through yet another pile of paid bills in the top drawer of the desk when, for the first time that day, the phone rang. Used to the polite interruptive chirp of modern electronics, Claire had forgotten how loud and demanding the old black rotary models could be.

Coughing and choking, she picked up the receiver. "Hello?"

"Claire?"

"Mom . . ."

"What's the matter?"

Startled by the intensity of the question, Claire jerked around but could neither see nor hear anything moving up on her. "What do you mean? What do you know?"

"You were choking."

"Oh, that." Wiping her chin with her free hand, Claire relaxed. "The phone startled me, and I tried to breathe spit. It's nothing." Breath back, she explained the problem.

"Oh, my."

"Exactly. Do you think you could come and have a look at it? At them. Tell me what you think."

"I'd like to help you, Claire, but I don't know. If I were needed, I'd have been summoned."

"I need you. Who says a summons can't use the phone?" She could feel her mother weakening. "This is huge. I'd hate to screw it up."

"Under the circumstances, that wouldn't make anyone very happy." She paused. Claire waited, poking her finger through the black coils of the cord. "It would be nice to spend some time with you. Would you like me to bring your sister?"

"I don't think so, Mom."

"You haven't seen her for almost a year."

"We talk on the phone."

"It's not the same."

"Yes, I know. But, please, leave her home anyway." The thought of Diana within a hundred miles of an open access to Hell brought up an image of the Four Horsemen trampling the world under their hooves as they fled in terror.

After supplying detailed directions, Claire hung up, glanced out into the shadowed lobby, and sighed. "Are your work boots dry, Dean?"

"He looked down at his feet. "They should be. Why?"

"You walk too quietly without them. *Please,* put them on."

With no memory of turning, he'd taken three silent, sweat sock muffled steps toward the back door before he recalled what he'd come out to the lobby to say. "I made a fresh pot of coffee, if you're interested. And pecan cookies."

Dean stared at Claire over his seventh cookie. "So your mother is your cousin?"

"No. She's *a* Cousin."

"And your father's . . . ?"

"A Cousin, too."

"And you and your younger sister, Diana, are both Keepers?"

"Yes."

Behind his glasses, his eyes twinkled. "So, you're your mother's Aunt?"

"No."

"But . . ."

"Look, I didn't make up the stupid nomenclature!" Strongly suspecting that Dean was being difficult on purpose, Claire tossed back her last mouthful of coffee, choked, and ended up spraying the tabletop and both her companions.

"Oh, thank you very much." Austin jumped down onto the floor and vigorously shook one back leg. "I just got that clean!"

After handing the still sputtering Keeper a napkin, Dean quickly used another to mop up the mess. When things got back to normal, and when the cat had been placated, he asked, "Why won't your mother be here until tomorrow afternoon?"

"That's when the train from London gets in. Tomorrow morning she'll get a lift from Lucan into London, then catch the train from London to Toronto to connect with the 1:14 out of Union Station, which means she'll be here about four."

"Oh." He'd been half hoping to hear that the delay involved

vacuuming the flying carpet or waiting until the flight path cleared for low altitude brooms. After the excitement of the morning, he was ready for his next installment of weird. Things hadn't been this interesting since he'd left home. Actually, things hadn't been this interesting *at* home—although his granddad's reaction to his cousin Todd getting an eyebrow pierced had come close. "Why doesn't she drive?"

"Because she can't. None of us can."

Dean blinked. Okay, *that* was the weirdest thing he'd heard so far. "None of your family?"

"None of the lineage."

"Why not?"

"Too many distractions. We see things other people don't."

There'd been a couple of members of Dean's family who'd seen things other people hadn't, but they were usually laid out roughly horizontal and left to sleep it off. "Things like blue mice?" he asked innocently, biting into another cookie.

"No. They're nothing at all like blue mice," she told him curtly. If she responded to his teasing, he'd keep doing it, and she already had one younger sibling; she didn't need another. "They're bits of the energy, small possibilities that . . . Austin! Get out of there!" Leaping to her feet, she snatched the butter dish out from under the cat's tongue. "Do you know what this stuff does to your arteries?" she demanded. "Are you trying to kill yourself?"

"I'm hungry."

"There's a bowl of fresh, geriatric kibble on the floor by the fridge."

"I don't want that," he muttered looking sulky. "You wouldn't make your grandmother eat it."

"My grandmother doesn't lick the butter."

"Wanna bet?"

Claire turned her back and pointedly ignored him. "Small possibilities," she repeated, "that sometimes seep through and run loose in the world."

Dean glanced around the dining room. "What do they look like?"

"That depends on your background. You're a McIssac so, if you had the Sight, at the very least you'd see traditional Celtic manifestations. Given that Newfoundland has a wealth of legend all its own you'd also probably pick up a few indigenous manifestations."

"You're not serious?" he asked her, grinning broadly. "Ghoulies and ghosties and things that go bump in the night?"

"If you want."

His grin faded. "I don't want."

"Then don't mention it."

Down in the furnace room, having spent the last few hours testing the binding, the intelligence in the pit rested. It would have been panting had it been breathing.

NOTHING HAS CHANGED, it observed sulkily.

Although physically contained, the pentagram could not entirely close it off from the world. There was just no way it was that easy.

It seeped through between the possibilities.

It tempted. It taunted. And once, because of the concentration trapped in that one spot, it had managed to squeeze through a sizable piece of pure irritation.

THE OLD MALE IS GONE.

THE YOUNG MALE IS STILL HERE.

The heat rose momentarily as though Hell itself had snorted. THAT GOODY TWO SHOES. WHAT A WASTE OF TIME.

THERE'S A NEW KEEPER.

WE'VE DEALT WITH KEEPERS BEFORE.

WE DIDN'T EXACTLY DEAL WITH THE OTHER. WASN'T SHE INTENDING TO CONTROL . . .

SHUT UP!

It also talked to itself.

THREE

"If you don't hurry," Austin complained from the bedroom, "I'm going down to breakfast without you."

Claire rummaged through her makeup case, inspecting and discarding a number of pencils that needed sharpening. "I'm moving as fast as I can."

They'd spent the night back in room one even though Dean had reiterated that the owner's rooms were now rightfully Claire's. Although willing to spend the evening watching television and eating pizza in Augustus Smythe's sitting room, Claire wasn't quite ready to sleep in his bed.

"I don't see why you bother with all that stuff."

"This from the cat who spent half an hour washing his tail." One eye closed, she leaned toward the mirror. Her reflection remained where it had been. "Oh, no." Straightening, she put down the pencil and looked herself in the eyes—not at all surprised to notice that they were no longer dark brown but deep red. "Now what?"

A skull, recently disinterred, appeared in the reflection's left hand. "Alas, poor Yorik. I knew him, Horatio, a fellow of infinite jest."

"And oft times had you kissed those lips." Claire folded her arms and frowned. "I'm familiar with the play. Get to the point."

The reflection lifted the skull until it could gaze levelly into the eye sockets. "Now get you to my lady's chamber, and tell her, let her paint her face an inch thick, to this favor she must come . . ." A fluid motion turned the skull so that it stared out from the mirror. ". . . make her laugh at that."

"Not bad, but I imagine you have access to a number of actors. Your point?"

"Open the pentagram. Release us. And we shall see to it that you remain young and beautiful forever."

"You're kidding, right? You're offering a Keeper eternal youth and beauty?"

The reflection looked a little sheepish. "It is considered a classic temptation. We thought it worth a try."

"Oh, please."

"That means no?"

Claire sighed and, both hands holding the edge of the sink, leaned forward. "Go to Hell," she told it levelly. "Go directly to Hell, do not pass go, do not collect two hundred dollars."

The skull vanished. Her reflection began answering to her movements again.

"Was that wise?" Austin asked from the doorway.

"What? Refusing to be tempted?"

"Making flippant comments."

"It wasn't a flippant comment." She finished lining her right eye and began on her left. "It was a stage direction."

"Hel-lo!"

"Mom?" In the kitchen, using a number of household products in ways they'd never been intended by the manufacturers—not even the advertising department which, as a rule, had more liberal views about those sorts of things—Claire was attempting to remove the ink from the latter third of the site journal. While not technically an impossible task, it did seem to be, as time went on, highly improbable. Laying aside the garlic press, she dried her hands on a borrowed apron—borrowing it hadn't been her idea— called out that she'd be right there, and tripped over the cat.

By the time she reached the lobby, Austin was up on the counter, having his head scratched and looking as though *he* hadn't been waiting as impatiently as anyone.

"You're certainly right about those shields," Martha Hansen said, as Claire came into the lobby. "I can't feel a thing."

Catching Austin's eye, Claire mimed wiping her brow in relief. Austin looked superior; *he'd* had a bad feeling about it from the start. So there. "Thanks for coming, Mom."

"Well, I could hardly refuse my daughter's call for help, now could I? Besides, your sister's in the workshop today and it's your father's turn to deal with the fire department." The three of them winced in unison. "And it did seem a shame not to work in a quick visit with you so close. You're looking well." She wrapped Claire in a quick hug. "Maine must've agreed with you."

"I was in and out too fast for it to disagree with me. Easiest site I ever sealed."

"Good. At least you're not facing this site exhausted and cranky."

"Cranky?" Claire repeated, shooting a warning look at the cat. "Mom, I'm twenty-seven. I'm a little old for cranky."

Her mother smiled. "I'm glad to hear that. How did you sleep last night?"

"Like a log. I expect it's another effect of the dampening field."

"I expect it is." Unzipping her windbreaker, Martha turned back toward the counter. "What about you, Austin?"

"*I* slept like a cat." One ear flicked back. "I always sleep like a cat."

"That's very reassuring. Any developments since you called, Claire?"

"Nothing much. We might have an imp infestation—I'm fairly certain it, or they, damped down my shoes the first night I was here." She saw no point in mentioning the voice. Not only had it been a highly subjective experience, but she'd stopped telling her mother everything that went on in her head the day Colin Rorke had kissed her behind the football bleachers. "This morning, my reflection offered me eternal youth and beauty."

Martha sighed as she shrugged out of her jacket. "I've said it before and I'll say it again, evil has no imagination. Probably why so much of it ends up in municipal politics. They'll be back, you know, and the temptations will escalate as they come to know you better."

"I expect I'll seal the site before that becomes a problem."

"But surely it's already sealed."

"No, Mom, I mean seal it closed."

"Closed?"

"That must be why I'm here," Claire asserted. "I couldn't possibly have been summoned to an epistemological babysitting job as though I were too old to do anything but slap my power over a site and make sure nothing creeps out around the edges."

"This hole . . ."

"Is huge, but it doesn't change the job description."

"And have you determined how you're going to close the hole and simultaneously take care of . . ." She jerked her head toward the third floor.

"Not yet, but I'm working on it. I was hoping that you, with your greater experience and years of work in the field, could throw a little light on the problem."

"Suck up," Austin muttered.

Lips twitching, Martha bent and picked up her overnight case. "Let me drop this off in my room, and then I'll go take a look at your problems. The sooner I see them, the sooner I can tell you what you need to hear."

Claire grabbed the key to room two and hurried to catch up on the stairs, frowning as she got a good look at the feet she followed. "I wish you wouldn't wear socks and sandals, Mom."

"It's the end of September, Claire, I can hardly wear either alone."

"But they make you look like an aging hippie."

"Truth in advertising; nothing wrong with that. Now, *I* wish you'd wear a little less makeup. It makes you look like . . ."

"Don't start, Mom."

My. This *is* medieval." Walking slowly, examining each line, Martha circled the pit. "In my experienced opinion," she said after a moment, "you do, indeed, have a hole to Hell in your furnace room. Or more specifically a manifestation of evil conforming to the classic parameters of Hell—the popularity of which, I've never entirely understood." Glancing up at the ductwork, she added, "Mind you, I expect it keeps the heating costs down." Her hand shot out and jerked Claire back a step. "Don't pace on the pentagram."

Folding her arms, Claire mirrored her mother's élan. Mostly, it was an act although as the second exposure came without the shock of discovery, she found it a little easier to cope. "I *know* it's a hole to Hell," she said, trying to sound as if her teeth weren't clenched together. "But since it's linked rather irrevocably to room six, I was hoping you might have some ideas on how to separate them. Some advice on what I should do first."

YOU COULD RELEASE US.

"Nobody asked you."

WE'D BE GOOD.

"Liar."

WELL, YES.

"I don't think you should argue with it, Claire." Slipping on her glasses, Martha pointed toward the lettering etched into the bedrock, being very careful not to trace anything in the air that could be interpreted as a pattern. A Cousin shouldn't be able to affect an accident site but, given the site in question, that wasn't a tenet she intended to test. "That," she said, "is the name of the person responsible for this situation. I expect he died right after he finished the invocation. Notice the similar pattern around Sara's name."

Eyes beginning to water from the sulfur, Claire studied the design. It wasn't an exact match, but close enough for Keeper work. "Just as we thought, she tried to gain control. If Hell offered her power in exchange for freedom, that must've come as an unpleasant surprise."

"I can't say that I find myself feeling too terribly sorry for it," her mother murmured.

NO ONE EVER DOES, Hell sighed.

"Do shut up. Now then, I think we've been in here long enough." Martha took hold of her daughter's arm and guided her up the stairs. "Hopefully, we'll find out more from a thorough examination of Aunt Sara."

GIVE HER OUR REGARDS.

"Don't count on it."

"Well?" Austin asked from the top of the washing machine as they tightened the chains across the closed door. He had point-blank refused to go back into the furnace room.

"She wants to go see *her*," Claire told him, pointing upward.

"You should take Dean with you."

"Are you out of your mind? Has he been feeding you on the sly?"

The cat's eyes narrowed. "Read my lips, he's a part of this."

"You don't have lips."

"A moot point. Your mother will have to meet him sooner or later."

"She can meet him later."

Martha started toward the other end of the basement. "Are his rooms down here?"

"Yes, but . . ."

"Austin thinks we should take Dean, and I'm inclined to agree."

Claire threw up her hands. "Mom, Austin thinks baby birds are a snack food."

"What does *that* have to do with this?"

"Listen to your mother, Claire," Austin murmured as he padded by.

She managed to resist kicking him and hurried to catch up, wishing she'd remembered that her mother's professional opinion carried personal baggage along with it. "I don't want Dean told about what's in the furnace room."

"You don't think he deserves to know the truth?"

"He knows there's an accident site; telling him that he's bedding down next to a hole leading to a classical manifestation of a Christian Hell will only compromise his safety."

"In what way?"

"He's a kid. Minimal defenses. The knowledge could give Hell access to his mind."

"I think you're afraid he'll leave if you tell him," Austin said, rubbing against the edge of a low shelf. "And you don't want him to leave."

"Of course I don't want him to leave—he cooks, he cleans, I don't. But neither do I want him blundering into situations he has no hope of understanding." She turned to her mother. "He's already in deeper than any bystander I've ever been in contact with. Isn't that enough? How am I supposed to protect him?"

"If he's been here since last February, I'd say he has pretty powerful protections of his own," Martha said thoughtfully. "But you're the Keeper, it's your decision whether you tell him or not."

"Then why isn't *this* my decision?" Claire asked as her mother knocked at the basement apartment. She didn't expect an answer, which was good, because she didn't get one.

Dean came to his door holding a mop.

"Merciful heavens." Unable to stop herself, Martha glanced down at his feet.

Claire hid a smile. It seemed clear that any member of the lineage meeting Dean for the first time couldn't help but check for tangible evidence of how very grounded he was.

Completely confused, Dean set the mop to one side, scrubbed his palm off on his jeans, and held out an apprehensive hand. "Hello. You must be Claire's mother."

"That's right, I'm Martha Hansen." Recovering her aplomb, she took his offered hand in a firm grip. "Pleased to meet you, Dean. Claire's told me so little about you."

Half expecting a female version of Augustus Smythe, Dean was pleasantly surprised to find there were no similarities whatsoever. Mrs. Hansen looked remarkably like many of the artists who spent their summers in the outports. She wore her long, graying hair pulled loosely back off her face, no makeup, baggy pants, a homespun vest over a turtleneck and the ubiquitous sandals. Dean wasn't sure why sandals were considered artistic, but they certainly seemed to be. While a resemblance to the summer people wasn't entirely a recommendation, working for Mr.

Smythe had taught him it could've been a lot worse. "You've been in the furnace room already, then?"

"We have. How could you tell?"

He felt his ears redden. "You're sweating. Mr. Smythe was always sweating when he came out of the furnace room."

Martha smiled and dabbed at her forehead with a tissue pulled from her vest pocket. "How observant of you. We have, indeed, been in the furnace room, but we're on our way up to room six now and we'd like you to come along."

He glanced over at Claire and noticed her slight hesitation before she nodded. "I don't want to be in the way."

"Nonsense. As Austin says, you're a part of this."

"Then just let me hang up my mop."

When he disappeared into his apartment, Martha turned toward her daughter. "He's a kid?"

"He's barely older than Diana."

"Sweetie, I hate to tell you this, but your sister isn't exactly a kid any more either." When Claire's brows drew in, she patted her on the arm. "Never mind. I don't think you'll have any problems with Dean. He's a remarkably stable young man, not to mention very easy on the eyes. I like him."

Forced to agree with the first two sentiments, Claire snorted. "You'd like an Orchi if it did housework."

"This is incredible." Remaining within the shielded area, attention locked on the sleeping Keeper, Martha moved around to the far side of the bed. "Just think of all the factors involved in achieving such an intricate balance of power."

"I am thinking about it, Mom. Or more specifically, I'm thinking about what'll happen if I unbalance it, ever so slightly."

"Don't."

Safely outside the shield, Claire sighed. Had she forgotten her mother was prone to those sorts of facetious comments? "I don't suppose you can see a way to break the loop without percipitating disaster?"

"No, I can't. I've never seen anything so perfectly in balance. I'm very impressed. Such a pity I'll never have a chance to tell the Keepers who designed it."

"Keepers."

"Oh, yes, this definitely took two people. You can see a double signature in the loop."

"Where?"

"Here. And here."

Claire pressed the back of her hand against her mouth. She shouldn't have missed the signs her mother had just pointed out. After all, she was a Keeper and her mother only a Cousin. "How can you stand to get so close to her?"

"I concentrate on the binding, not on her. Still . . ." Dusting off her hands, she stepped out through the shield. ". . . that was nasty."

Crouched in the doorway, rubbing Austin behind the ears to keep him distracted, Dean shook his head. They were like TV cops standing over a body matter-of-factly discussing multiple stab wounds. "You don't get disturbed about much, do you, Mrs. Hansen?"

Martha turned to face him. "Actually, I'm very disturbed."

"It doesn't show."

"After a few decades spent dealing with various sundry and assorted metaphysical accidents, I've gotten good at hiding my reactions. Also, the lineage is trained to remain calm about these sorts of things. It wouldn't do to have us yelling 'Fire!' in a crowded theater, now would it?"

Not entirely certain that he understood the analogy, he let it go.

"Don't worry about it," Austin murmured. "Just try sharpening your claws on the sofa and you'll see how disturbed she gets."

Arms folded, Claire frowned down at the woman on the bed. In a strange way, Hell was the lesser of two evils. Unlike Aunt Sara, hell had done nothing it wasn't supposed to. "All right, Mom, you've seen the situation. Where should I begin?"

"I suggest we begin by leaving the room." Shooing Dean, Claire, and Austin out in front of her, she pulled the door closed then frowned at the splintered wood. "Then I suggest you get this fixed. Thank you, Dean." She stepped aside as he snapped the padlock back on. "Finally, I suggest you get used to the idea of being here a while."

"I never thought I'd work out how to close this down in a day or two, Mom."

"You may not be intended to close it down, Claire. You may have been summoned here as a monitor."

Claire blinked. "I find that highly unlikely. The last monitor was a Cousin."

"And the site was clearly too strong for him to manage. It needs a Keeper."

"If it needs me," she said, her eyes narrowing, "then it *doesn't* need a monitor."

"I can't see a way for you to safely interfere with the current arrangement. I think Dean's idea is correct; given there was a war on, the Keeper, or Keepers, who dealt with this situation probably intended their solution to be a temporary measure. They plugged in the first available Cousin, then were killed during the fighting. Augustus must have been quite young and would have agreed to watch the site until the Keepers returned. They never did, and he was held by his word until another came along.

"Just at the point where the site was about to destroy him utterly, there was Claire, drawn by his need to leave. I realize I'm speculating here, but I find myself feeling quite sorry for him."

"I don't." Claire flinched under her mother's gaze. "All right, yes I do. He got a raw deal, but I don't see why I should be happy to have the same one."

"Not exactly the same deal, if the site was intended to have a Keeper as a monitor."

"Or," Claire insisted, "if that Keeper was intended to close the site down. I'll tell you what I'm going to do, I'm going to find the Historian, find out exactly what those two Keepers did, then undo it. I have no intention of either allowing this to continue or of spending the rest of my life here."

"The Historian is seldom easy to find."

"That's only because I've never gone looking for her."

"True enough. Meanwhile," Martha glanced up and down the hall. "You have a guest house to run."

"Run?" Claire stared at her mother in astonishment. "Have you forgotten what's in the basement?"

"This was probably set up as a guest house because of what's in the basement. This is a unique situation. The more you think about the site, the more attention you pay it, the stronger it becomes. You need a distraction, something to occupy your time."

"But the guests . . ."

"They're here two or three nights at most. Hardly long enough for a sealed site inside a dampening field to have much effect."

"But I already have a job; I'm a Keeper. I don't know the first thing about running a guest house."

"Dean does." Martha looked remarkably like Austin as she added, "And you said you didn't want him to leave."

"Because I need a cook and a caretaker," Claire explained hurriedly, picking at a wallpaper seam.

"You still do."

"If I'm really a part of what's going on," Dean broke in, "I couldn't just walk out."

"You couldn't walk out on old Augustus," Austin sniggered, "and he didn't have Claire's . . ."

Claire's head jerked up. "Austin!"

". . . sunny personality."

"Good, that's settled." Martha smiled on them both in such a way it became obvious the problem had been solved to her satisfaction.

Since there seemed to be no point in continuing the argument, and since she wasn't entirely certain which argument to continue, Claire started down the stairs, her heels thumping against the worn carpet. Dean fell into step beside her. "I want you to know that things are not going to continue the way they were under Augustus Smythe. I am not going to watch passively. I'm going to take action."

"Okay." When she glared at him from the corner of one eye, he smiled and added, "Sure."

"Are you laughing at me?"

"I was trying to cheer you up."

"Oh. Well, that's all right, then."

As they disappeared down the stairwell, Austin wrapped his tail around his toes and looked up at Claire's mother. "Nice to have things settled."

Smoothing down the wallpaper Claire'd been picking at, Martha frowned. "It's hard to believe that all this has been sitting here for so many years with no one aware of it."

"It was a bit of a surprise," the cat admitted. "You can't blame Claire for wanting to wrap it up and leave."

"Staying does ask a lot of her."

"Not the way she sees it. She thinks she's been declawed."

"That's only because she was looking forward to doing things, not merely waiting for all hell to break loose."

"Oh, that's clever," Austin snorted as he stretched and stood. "Come on, just in case the world's about to end, you can feed me."

"Mr. Smythe has prog enough to last through freeze up," Dean explained, setting the supper plates on the table.

"Very reassuring, or it would be if I had the slightest idea of what you meant."

"I mean he has food enough to last the entire winter."

"Then why didn't you say so." Claire moved her chicken aside and tentatively tried a forkful of the wild rice stuffing. Her eyes widened as she chewed. "This is good."

"Try not to sound so surprised, dear, it's rude." Her mother waved a laden fork in Dean's direction. "You cook, you clean, and you're gorgeous; do you have a girlfriend?"

"Mom."

"It's okay." His father'd had six older sisters and after twenty years of holiday dinners with his aunts, Dean pretty much expected both the comments and the question from any woman over forty. They didn't mean anything by it, so it no longer embarrassed him. "No, ma'am, not right now," he said, sliding into his seat.

"Are you gay?"

"Mom!"

"It's a perfectly valid inquiry, Claire."

"It's a little personal, don't you think? *And* it's none of your business."

"It will be if you're here for any length of time. I could introduce him to your uncle."

"He's *not* gay."

"He most certainly is."

"I wasn't talking about Uncle Stan! I was talking about Dean."

"And why are you so certain he's not?"

"I'm a *Keeper!*"

Ears red, Dean stared intently into his broccoli. *That* was not a question he'd expected, at least not from Claire's mother, although Uncle Stan did make a change from being set up with *my best friend Margaret's youngest daughter, Denise.* "Um, excuse me, I was wondering, who's the Historian?"

"Heavens, I'd have thought you'd had enough exposition for one day."

Claire sighed. "He's attempting to change the subject, Mom, you've embarrassed him." She ignored her mother's indignant denials. "The Historian is a woman . . ."

"We don't know that for certain, Claire," Martha interrupted. "You may see her as a woman, but that doesn't mean everyone does."

"Do *you* want to tell him?"

"No need, you're doing fine."

"The Historian," Claire repeated through clenched teeth, "who *I see* as a woman, keeps the histories of all the Keepers."

"Is she a Keeper?" Dean asked, bending to pick up his napkin and slipping a bit of chicken under the table to the cat.

"We don't know."

"Then what is she?"

"We don't know."

"Okay. Where is she?"

"We don't know that either; not for certain at any given time. The Historian hates to be bothered. She says she can't finish collecting the past with the present interrupting, so to protect her privacy she moves around a lot."

"Then how do you find her?"

"I go looking."

Dean paused, wondering if he was ready for the next answer. *Oh, well, the boat's past the breakwater, I might as well drop a line.* "Where?"

"She usually sets up shop just left of reality."

"What?"

"If reality exists, then it stands to reason that there must be something on either side of it." Claire tapped the table on both sides of her plate with her fork as if that explained everything.

He ate some chicken, delaying the inevitable. "Okay. Why *left* of reality?"

"Because the Apothecary uses the space on the right."

"Dean? If I could have a few words?"

"Sure, Mrs. Hansen."

"Martha." She took the tea towel from his hand. "Here, let me help."

He watched as she dried a plate, decided her standards were high enough, and plunged his hands back into the soapy water. "Where's Claire?"

"Watching the news. I was wondering, did she explain her family situation?"

"Both you and Mr. Hansen being Cousins?"

"That's right. It's a very rare situation, two Cousins together, and it's why both our girls are Keepers. Now, usually Keepers become aware of what they are around puberty . . . are you blushing?"

"No, ma'am."

"Must be the light." She took a dry tea towel off the rack. "Because of their double lineage, my girls not only knew what they were from the start but were unusually powerful. Although they're better socialized than many Keepers—my husband and I tried to give them as normal an upbringing as possible—they've been told most of their lives that with great power comes great responsibility—clichéd but true, I'm afraid. Now, Claire's willing to give her life for that responsibility, but, like all Keepers, it's made her more than a little arrogant."

Dean set the plate he was washing carefully back into the water and slowly turned. "What do you mean, give her life?"

"Evil doesn't take prisoners." Martha shook her head, wiping a spoon that was long dry. "That sounds like it should be in a fortune cookie, doesn't it?"

Pulling the spoon from her hand, Dean locked eyes with the older woman and said softly, "Mrs. Hansen, why are we having this conversation?"

"Because all power corrupts and the potential for absolute power has the potential to corrupt absolutely. This site has already corrupted a Keeper and made a Cousin, at best, bitter and, at worst, mean. I don't want that happening to my daughter. She's going to need your help." When he opened his mouth, she raised her hand. "I realize your natural inclination is to immediately assure me you'll do everything you can, but I want you to take a moment and think about it. Their abilities tend to deemphasize interpersonal relationships; she can be downright autocratic at times."

He dropped the spoon in the drawer. "What happens when she finds this Historian?"

"I don't know."

"She thinks she's too powerful to be here just as a monitor, doesn't she?"

"Yes."

Dean watched the iridescent light dance across the soap bubbles in the sink. "I'll tell you, Mrs. Hansen . . ."

"Martha."

". . . I don't know Claire and I don't really understand what's going on, but if you say she's after needing me, well, I've never turned away from someone who's needed me before and I'm not after starting now."

Long years of practice kept her from smiling at the confidence of the young. At twenty-five that speech would've sounded pompous. At twenty, it sounded sincere. "She won't make it easy for you."

"You ever gone through a winter in Portuguese Cove, Mrs. Hansen?"

"Martha. And no, I haven't."

"Once you can do that, you can do anything. Don't worry, I'll help her run things and I'll try not to let her push me around because of what she is."

"Thank you."

"*Everyone* likes to be needed."

She studied him thoughtfully for a moment, then said, "You're taking this whole thing remarkably well, you know. Most people wouldn't be able to cope with having their entire worldview flipped on its side."

"But it wasn't my entire worldview, now was it?" He plunged his hands back into the soapy water. "The sun still comes up in the east sets in the west, rain falls down, grass grows up, and American beer still tastes like the water they washed the kegs out with. Nothing's changed, there's just more around than I knew about two days ago." With a worried lift of his brows, he nodded toward the rest of the silverware on the tray. "If you could, please finish that cutlery before the water dries and makes spots . . ."

They worked in silence for a while, the only sound the wire brush against the bottom of the roasting pan.

"Mrs. Hansen?"

"Martha."

"What is it you do?"

"Claire's father and I watch over the people who live in an area where the barrier between this world and evil is somewhat porous."

"But I thought Cousins couldn't use the caulking gun."

Martha stopped drying one of the pots and stared at him. "The what?"

"The magical equivalent of the caulking gun that seals the holes in the fabric of the universe." Dean repeated everything he could remember of Claire's explanation.

When he finished, Claire's mother shook her head. "It's a bit more complicated than that, I'm afraid." Then she frowned as she thought it over. "All right, perhaps it isn't—but it's certainly less rational. We're not dealing with a passive enemy but a malevolent intelligence."

"Does Claire know this?"

"Of course she does, she's a Keeper. But she's young enough to believe—in spite of what you might think of her advanced age," she interjected at his startled expression, "that it's not the energy that's the problem, it's what people do with it. While that may be true in a great many cases, there's also energy that you simply can't do good with, no matter what your intentions are."

"Evil done in God's name is not God's work. Good done in the Devil's name is not the Devil's work." He set the last pan in the rack to drain. "It's what my granddad used to say before he clipped me on the ear."

"Your granddad was very wise."

"Sometimes," Dean allowed, grinning.

Without really knowing how it happened, Martha found herself grinning back. "To finish answering your actual question, the site we monitor is too porous to be sealed—think T-shirt fabric where it should be rubberized canvas—so there's constant mopping up to do. I do the fieldwork, and my husband teaches high school English."

"Teaching high school doesn't seem very . . ." He paused, searching for a suitable word.

"Metaphysical?" Martha snorted, sounding like both her daughter and the cat. "Is it possible you've already forgotten what it's like to be a teenager?"

"Are you going to be all right?"

"I'll be fine, Mom." Claire reached out and fixed the collar on her mother's windbreaker as the early morning sun fought a losing battle with a chill wind blowing in off Lake Ontario. "And don't worry. I'll monitor the situation while I gather the information I need to shut it down."

"I would never worry about you not fulfilling your responsibilities, Claire, but it took two Keepers to create the loop. What if it needs two Keepers to close it?"

"Then I'll monitor the situation until the other Keeper shows up. This is not going to be my final resting place."

Because even Keepers needed the comfort of hope, Martha changed the subject. "Be nice to Dean. He's exactly what he seems to be, and that's rare in this world."

"Don't worry about Dean. Austin's on his side."

"Austin's on the side of enlightened self-interest." A pair of vertical lines appeared above the bridge of Martha's nose. "I think you'll manage best with Dean if you treat him like a Cousin."

"A Cousin?" She stared at her mother in astonishment. "He's a nice kid, Mom, but . . ."

"He's not a kid."

"Well, not technically and certainly not physically, but you've got to admit he's awfully young."

"And how old were you when you sealed your first site?"

"That's beside the point. He's not of the lineage."

"No, he's not, but he is remarkably grounded in the here and now, and he's going to be your main support. The less you hide from him, the more he'll be able to help."

"Mother, I'm a Keeper. I don't need help from a bystander. All right," she went on before her mother could speak, "I need his help running the guest house but not for the rest."

"Just try to be nice to him, that's all I ask." She gripped Claire's hands in both of hers. "If you must check the contact points of the loop, be very, very careful. You don't want to wake her up, and you don't want to believe anything *they* tell you. Don't lose track of time when you're searching for the Historian; you know what'll happen if you come back before you've left. Try and make Austin stick to his diet, and you should eat more, you're too thin."

Claire opened her mouth to argue but said instead, "Here's your ride," as a battered cab pulled up in front of the guest house and honked.

"If you need me, call." She frowned as the cabbie continued to hit his horn, the irregular rhythm echoing around the neighborhood. "Would you do something about that, Claire?"

The echo gave one last, feeble honk, then fell silent.

"Thank you. Come to think of it, even if you don't need me, call. Your father's likely to be worried about you being in such proximity to the hole in the furnace room."

"There's really no need to tell him about Hell, Mom."

"He's teaching in the public school system, Claire. He knows about Hell."

Standing in the open doorway, Claire released her hold on the horn as the cab pulled away. Through the broad back window of the vehicle, she could see her mother giving emphatic instructions. If the driver thought he knew the best way to the train station, he was about to discover he was wrong.

At the last possible moment, Martha turned and waved.

Claire waved back.

"So. It seems I own a hotel." A distraction, something to keep her mind off what was in the furnace room. "Who knows," she said with more resignation than enthusiasm. "It might be fun."

Raising her body temperature enough to fight the chill, she went down to have a look at the sign. To her surprise, her first impression had been correct. The sign actually said "Elysian Fields 'uest House," the "g" having disappeared. "Dean's going to have to repaint this." She frowned. "I wonder what I'm paying him?"

A low growl drew her attention around to the building on the other side of the driveway. An apple-cheeked, old woman with brilliant orange hair, wearing a pale green polyester pant suit and a string of imitation pearls, stood on the porch, waving at her enthusiastically. Also on the porch was the biggest black-and-tan Doberman Claire had ever seen.

"Hello, dear!" the woman caroled when she saw she had Claire's attention. "I'm Mrs. Abrams—that's one b and an ess—who are you?"

"I'm Claire Hansen, the new owner of the guest . . ."

"New owner? No, dear, you can't be." Her smile was the equivalent of a fond pat on the head. "You're much too young."

"I beg your pardon?" The tone could stop a political canvasser in full spate. It had no effect on Mrs. Abrams.

"I said you're too young to be the owner, dear. Where's Augustus Smythe?" She leaned forward, peering around like she suspected he were hiding just out of sight. The Doberman mirrored her move—twitching as though anxious to get down and check it out personally.

Claire fought an instinctive urge to back up and held her ground. "Mr. Smythe's whereabouts are none of your con . . ."

"None of my concern?" A flick of her hand and a broad smile took care of that possibility. "Of course I'm concerned, you silly thing; I live next door. He's avoiding me, isn't he?"

"No, he's gone, but . . ."

"Gone? Gone where, dear?"

"I don't know." When Mrs. Abrams' expression indicated profound disbelief, Claire found herself adding, "Really, I don't."

"Well." The single word bespoke satisfaction that years of suspicions had finally been justified. "They took him away, did they? Or did he run before they arrived? If truth be told, I can't say as I'm surprised." She fondled one of the dog's ears. The twitching grew more pronounced. "You would never, not ever, hear me say anything against anyone—live and let live is my motto, I'm very active in my church's Women's Auxiliary you know, they couldn't get along without me—but Augustus Smythe was a nasty little man with an unnatural dislike of my poor Baby."

Showing more teeth than should've been possible in such a narrow head, Baby's growl deepened.

"Would you believe that he actually had the nerve to accuse my Baby of doing his business in your driveway?" Her voice dropped into caressing tones. "As if he didn't have his own little toilet area in his own little yard. He didn't repeat those vile and completely unfounded accusations to you, did he, dear?"

It took Claire a moment to straighten out the pronouns. "He did mention . . ."

"And you didn't believe him, did you, dear? I'm afraid to say that he told a lot of, well, lies—there's no use sugar coating it. I don't know what else he told you, Caroline . . ."

Claire opened her mouth to protest that her name was not actually Caroline but couldn't manage to break into the flow of accusation.

". . . but you mustn't believe any of it." A plump hand pressed against a polyester-covered, matronly bosom. "Now, me, I'm not like some people in this neighborhood, I mind my own business, but that Augustus Smythe . . ." Her voice lowered to a conspiratorial tone Claire had to strain to hear. "He not only lied, but he kept secrets. I wouldn't be surprised if he had unnatural habits."

Neither would Claire, but she was beginning to feel more sympathetic. No wonder Baby twitched.

"I'd love to stay and chat longer, dear, but it's time for Baby's vitamin. He's not a puppy any more, are you, sweetums? He's a lot older than he looks, you know."

"How old is he, Mrs. Abrams?"

"To be perfectly honest, Christina—and I assure you I am always perfectly honest—I don't actually know. The little sugar cube showed up on my doorstep one day—he knew I'd take him in, you see, dogs always know—and we've been together ever since. Mummy couldn't do without her Baby. Ta, ta for now!" She yanked the dog around and, with a cheery wave and a bark that promised further confrontation, they disappeared inside the house.

Stepping to the edge of the driveway, Claire peered toward the back of the property. Too far away to make a positive identification, a large brown pile had been deposited, nicely centered in the lane.

"Unfounded accusations," Claire muttered, carefully climbing the stairs and going back inside.

Stretched out in a patch of sunshine on the counter, Austin yawned. "Where have you been?"

"Out meeting the obligatory irritating neighbor. How do you tell if a pile of dog shit came out of a Doberman?"

The cat looked disgusted. "How do *I* tell? *I* don't."

"All right, how would I tell?"

"Check it for fingers. Why are we talking about this?"

"I'm beginning to think Hell wasn't the only thing Augustus Smythe wanted to get away from."

"Are you staying in the official residence, then?" Dean asked as Claire came down the stairs with her belongings. Sliding his hammer into the loop on his carpenter's apron, he leaped down off the ladder and held out his hands. "Can I help?"

"Yes." Pride not only went before a fall, it also went before dropping everything she owned. She shoved her suitcase at him, caught her backpack as it slid off her shoulder, and barely managed to hang onto the armload of clothes that she hadn't bothered to repack. "What were you doing?"

"Attaching that bit of molding over the door. It'd gone some squish. Out of plumb," he added as her brows dipped down.

"I see." Glancing at the repair, Claire wondered what, as his employer, she was supposed to say. Her mother wanted her to be nice to him . . . "Good work. You matched the ends up evenly."

"Thank you." He beamed as he held up the folding section of the counter and waited for her to go through.

She didn't think he was being sarcastic. Stopping by the desk, she lowered her backpack to the center of the ancient blotter. "Since this appears to be the only available desk, I guess I'm leaving my computer out here. I can use it for hotel business."

"Laptop?" Dean wondered, studying the dimensions of the pack curiously.

"No." Once everything else had been dumped in the sitting room, she returned to the desk. Opening the backpack, she pulled out a fourteen-inch monitor and stand, a vertically stacked CPU with two disk drives and a CD-Rom, and a pair of speakers.

"You've got to love the classics," Austin snickered, watching Dean's jaw drop. "Now pull out the hat stand and the rubber plant."

"Hat stand and rubber plant?" Dean repeated.

"Ignore him," Claire instructed, untangling the cables. "I'm hardly going to put a rubber plant in here with all these electronics."

Dean removed his glasses, cleaned them on the hem of his T-shirt, and put them back on just as Claire unpacked a laser printer. "This is incredible. Absolutely incredible."

She shrugged, rummaging around for the surge suppressor. "Not really, it only prints in black and white."

*   *   *

"Boss?"

Squinting a little in the glare from the monitor, Claire leaned left and peered out into the lobby. Although all available lights were on, her computer screen was still the brightest source of illumination in the entire entryway. "What is it, Dean?"

"I thought I'd head downstairs and I just wondered if there was anything I could get you before I went."

"Nothing, thank you. I'm fine."

"You could get *me* a rack of lamb, but we all know who'd object to that," Austin muttered without lifting his head from the countertop.

When Dean showed no sign of actually heading anywhere, Claire sighed and saved her file. "Was there something else?"

Fingers tucked second-knuckle-deep into the front pockets of his jeans, he shrugged, the gesture more hopeful than dismissive. "I was just wondering what you were doing."

"I'm treating this site like any other I've been summoned to seal." She was not going to surrender her life to a run-down hotel; no way, no how, no vacancy. "I'm writing down everything I know, and I'm prioritizing everything I have to do."

Head cocked speculatively to one side, Dean grinned. "I wouldn't have thought you were the 'lists' type."

"Oh?" Both eyebrows rose. "What type did you think I was."

"Oh, I guess the 'dive right in and get started' type."

Either he hadn't heard her tone, or he'd ignored it. Claire took another look at his open, candid, square-jawed and bright-eyed expression. Or he hadn't understood it. "Well, you're wrong." His smile dimmed, his shoulders sagged slightly, and his head dipped a fraction—nothing overt, nothing designed to inflict guilt, just an honest disappointment. She felt like such a bitch, her reaction completely out of proportion to his. "But how would you know differently?" Impossible not to try and make amends. "I do have something for you to do tomorrow, though."

"Sure." His head lifted, erasing the fractional droop. "What?"

"The *G* needs replacing on that sign out front."

"No problem." Smile reilluminated, he glanced down at his watch. "I'd better get going, then; it's almost time for the game on TSN."

"If he had a tail, he'd be wagging it," Austin observed dryly as Dean's work boots could be heard descending the basement stairs. "I think he likes you."

Claire found herself typing to the rhythm of heels on wood and forced herself to stop. "I'm his new boss. He just wants to make a good impression."

"And has he?"

"How can you make such an innocent question into innuendo?"

The cat looked interested. "I don't know. How?"

The room was completely dark. The air smelled faintly of stale cigar smoke. The silence was so complete, the noises her body made were too loud to let her sleep. The cat was taking up most of the room on the bed.

That, at least, she was used to. The rest, she decided to do something about. Slipping out from under the covers, she felt her way over to the window in the outside wall.

There's nothing out there but the driveway. No harm in opening the curtain a bit and letting in some air.

It wasn't that easy. After forcing her will on a heavy brocade curtain that didn't want to open and struggling with the paint that sealed the sash, Claire managed to shove the window up about half an inch. Breathing heavily, she knelt on the floor and sucked an appreciative lungful of fresh air through the crack. As her eyes grew accustomed to the dark, she made out a window across the drive, the silhouette of pointed ears and, beside them, a pair of binoculars resting on their wider end.

No wonder Augustus Smythe had kept the curtains so emphatically drawn.

A thump behind her warned her to brace herself for the furry weight that leaped onto her lap and then onto the windowsill.

"Could I have a little light here?" Austin murmured.

"What for?" Claire asked as she cast a glow behind him. "You can see perfectly well without it."

"I can," the cat agreed placidly. "But he can't."

Across the drive, the pointed ears flicked up and Baby threw himself at the window.

Claire doused the light, but the damage had already been done. Baby continued to bark hysterically. She grabbed the cat and let the curtains fall closed as a lamp came on and a terrifying vision in pink plastic curlers snatched up the binoculars.

Austin squirmed out of her arms and jumped back onto the bed. "I think I'm going to like it here."

CAN WE USE THE CAT?
DON'T BE RIDICULOUS.

FOUR

Augustus Smythe had wanted his breakfast every morning at seven o'clock. He'd had a bowl of oatmeal, stewed prunes, and a pot of tea, except on Sunday when he'd had a mushroom omelet, braised kidneys, and indigestion. Guests, and in his experience there'd never been more than one room occupied at a time, ate between eight and eight-thirty or they didn't eat at all.

Dean found himself in the kitchen, water boiling and bag of oatmeal in his hand before he remembered that things had changed. He'd been feeding Claire like she was a guest, but she wasn't. Nor, he'd be willing to bet, was she the stewed prunes type.

She wasn't only his new boss, she was a Keeper; a semimythical being monitoring the potential eruption of evil energy out of a possibly corrupting metaphysical accident site in the furnace room. Cool. He could handle that.

The question was: What did she want for breakfast?

"How should I know?" Foiled in his attempt to gain access to the refrigerator, Austin glared down at the fresh saucer of wet cat food. "But if she doesn't want the kidneys, I'll take them."

The hot water pipes banged at a quarter to eight. Dean had no idea how long women usually took to get ready in the morning, but his minimal experience seemed to indicate they were fairly high maintenance. He waited until eight-thirty, then brewed a fresh pot of coffee.

At nine, he began to worry. Austin had eaten and disappeared, and he'd heard nothing more from Claire's suite. By nine-thirty, he couldn't wait any longer.

Had she fallen getting out of the shower? Did that sort of thing happen to the semimythical?

Tossing his apron over the back of a chair, he walked quickly up the hall, ducked under the edge of the counter, and hesitated outside her door. If she'd gone back to sleep, she wouldn't thank him for waking her. Maybe he should go away and wait a little longer.

If, however, she were lying unconscious by the tub . . .

Better she's irritated than dead, he decided, took a deep breath, and knocked.

"Come in."

It took a moment, but he finally spotted Austin on a pie-crust table beside a purple china basket of yellow china roses. "Is Claire . . ."

"Here? No."

"She went out?" He hadn't heard the front door.

"No. She went in."

"In?"

"That's right. But I'm expecting her back any . . ." The cat's ears pricked up and he turned to face the bedroom. "Here she comes. I hope she picked up those shrimp snacks I asked for."

Brow furrowed, Dean stepped forward. He could've sworn he heard music—horns mostly, with an up-tempo bass beat leading the way. Through the open door, he could see an overstuffed armchair and the wardrobe Mr. Smythe had used instead of a closet. Obviously Claire hadn't quite caught on as her clothes were draped all over the chair.

The music grew louder.

The wardrobe door opened and Claire stepped out. Several strings of cheap plastic beads hung around her neck, and a shower of confetti accompanied every movement. She didn't look happy.

"What do you bet they were out of shrimp snacks," Austin muttered.

Glancing into the sitting room, the Keeper's eyes widened. "What are you doing here?"

"I live here."

"Not you." She dragged off the thick noose of beads and pointed an imperious finger at Dean. "Him."

"You were in the wardrobe."

It wasn't a question, so Claire didn't answer it. "Don't you ever knock?"

"I *did* knock." Flustered almost as much by the implication that he'd just walk in to her apartment as by her emergence from the wardrobe, Dean jerked his head toward the cat. "He told me to come in."

Austin stretched out a paw and pushed a pottery cherub onto the floor. It bounced on the overlap of three separate area rugs and rolled unharmed under the table.

Claire closed her eyes and counted to ten. When she opened them again, she'd decided not to bother arguing with the cat—experience having taught her that she couldn't win. Bending over, she flicked confetti out of her hair. "If that's coffee I smell, I could use a cup. It isn't safe to eat or drink on the other side."

"The other side of what?" Dean asked, relieved to see that the bits of paper disappeared before they reached the floor. Well, maybe relieved wasn't exactly the right word. "Where were you?"

"Looking for the Historian. The odds of actually finding her are better early in the morning before the day's distractions begin to build." Straightening, Claire scowled at the pile of beads. "I lost her trail at a Mardi Gras."

"In September?"

"It's always Mardi Gras somewhere." She reached into her shirt to scoop confetti out of her bra, noticed Dean's gaze follow the motion and turned pointedly around. So much for his grandfather's training.

Dean felt his ears burn. "It's *somewhere* in the wardrobe?"

"The wardrobe is only the gate." When she turned back to face him and caught sight of his expression, she added impatiently, "It's traditional."

"Okay." First he'd ever heard that Mardi Gras in a wardrobe was traditional, but at least the music had stopped. If his life was after picking up a soundtrack, he'd prefer something that didn't sound like a marching band after a meal of bad clams.

"I could really use that coffee," Claire prodded, taking his arm and propelling him toward the door.

"Right." Coffee, he understood, although, since he'd thought he understood wardrobes, coffee would probably also be subject to change without notice. "We, uh, we need to work out your meals."

"What's there to work out? You do your job, I'll do mine. You cook, I'll eat."

"Cook what?" Dean insisted. "And when?"

Suddenly aware she still had fingers wrapped around the warm, resilient curve of a bicep, Claire snatched her hand back. "I'll eat anything, I'm not fussy, but I can't cope with brussels sprouts, raw zucchini, dried soup mixes, and anything orange. Except oranges."

"Anything orange except oranges," he repeated. "So carrots . . ."

"Are out. For as long as I'm here, lunch at noon, supper at five-thirty, so I can watch the news at six. I'll have cold cereal or toast for breakfast and that I *can* make myself."

"You're after saving the world on a bowl of cold cereal?"

"I'd really rather you didn't start sounding like my mother," she told him sharply, stepping out into the office just as the outside door opened.

"Yoo hoo!" Clinging to the latch, Mrs. Abrams peered around the edge of the door. "Oh, there you are, dear!" She straightened and rushed forward. "You remember me . . ." It was a statement of fact. ". . . Mrs. Abrams, one bee and an ess. You should keep this door locked, you know, dear. The neighborhood isn't what it was when I was a girl. These days with all the immigrants you never know who might wander in off the street. Not that I have anything against immigrants—they make such interesting food, don't you think?" Penciled eyebrows lifted dramatically toward a stiff fringe of bangs when she spotted Dean standing on the threshold behind Claire. "How nice that you two young people are getting along."

"What did you want, Mrs. Abrams?" Claire didn't see much point in asking *her* if she ever knocked.

"Well, Kirstin . . ."

"Claire."

"I beg your pardon, dear?"

"My name is Claire, not Kirstin."

"Then why did you tell me it was Kirstin, dear?" Before Claire could protest that she hadn't told her any such thing, Mrs. Abrams waved a dismissive hand and went on. "Never mind, dear, I'm sure anyone might get confused, first day at a new job and all. I stopped by because Baby heard something in the drive last night—it might have been burglars, you know, we could have all been murdered in our beds—and I had to come over and see that you were all right."

"We're fine. I . . ."

"I see you have a computer." She shook her head disapprovingly, various bits of her face swaying to a different drummer. "You have to be careful about computers. The rays that come off them make you sterile. Has that nasty little Mr. Smythe returned yet?"

Finding it extremely disconcerting to speak to someone whose eyes never settled in one place for more than a second or two,

Claire came out from behind the counter. "No, Mrs. Abrams, he's gone for . . ."

"I remember how this place used to look, so quaint and charming. It needs a woman's touch. I hope you realize that you can call on my services at any time, Karen dear. I could have been a decorator, everyone says I have the knack. I offered to give the place the benefit of my own unique skills once before, but do you know what that Augustus Smythe said to me. He said I could redecorate the furnace room."

Claire managed to stop herself from announcing that the offer was still open—although whether she was sparing Mrs. Abrams or Hell, she wasn't entirely certain.

"Have you done anything with the dining room, dear?"

Short of a full tackle, Claire couldn't see how she could stop Mrs. Abrams from heading down the hall.

"I haven't seen the dining room for years. I hardly ever set foot in here with that horrible man in . . ."

Although dimmed by distance and masonry, Baby's bark was far too distinctive to either miss or mistake.

"Oh, dear, I must get back. Baby does so love to greet the mailman, but the silly fool persists in misunderstanding his playful little ways. Mummy's coming, Baby!"

Claire rubbed her temples, throwing an irritated glance at Dean as he finally stepped off the threshold and closed the door to the sitting room. "You were a lot of help."

"Mrs. Abrams," Dean told her with weary certainty, "doesn't listen to men."

"I doubt Mrs. Abrams listens to anyone."

The barking grew distinctly triumphant.

"I'm not criticizing," Claire said stiffly, ducking back under the counter and going to the front window, "but why *wasn't* the front door locked?"

Dean followed her. "I unlock it every morning when I get up. For guests."

They winced in unison as Mrs. Abrams could be heard shrilling, telling Baby to let it go—where *it* did not refer to the mailbag.

"Were you actually expecting guests?"

"Not really," he admitted.

The mailman made a run for it.

"I can't say as I'm surprised." As she left the office, a wave of her hand indicated the cracked layers of paint on the woodwork and the well-scrubbed but dingy condition of the floor. "This place doesn't exactly make a great first impression."

"So what should we do?"

"Do?" Claire turned to face him and was amazed to find him looking at her as though she had the answers. Behind him, Austin looked amused. "*We* aren't going to do anything. *I'm* going to work at sealing this site. You . . ." About to say *"You can do whatever it is you usually do on a Tuesday,"* she found she couldn't disappoint the anticipation in his eyes. "Since it's not raining, you can get started on repainting that G on the sign."

With the site journal soaking in a clarifying solution, Claire spent the morning going through the rest of the paperwork in the office. By noon, the recycling box was full, her hands were dirty, and she had two paper cuts as well as a splitting headache from all the dust.

She'd found no new information on either Sara, the hole, or the balance of power maintained between them. Someone, probably Smythe, had scrawled, *the Hell with this, then* in the margin of an old black-and-white men's magazine and that was as close as she'd come to an explanation.

"What a waste of time."

"Some of those old magazines are probably collectible."

Claire's lip curled. "They're not exactly mint."

"Good point." Gaze locked on her fingers, Austin backed away. "You're not planning on touching me with those filthy things, are you?"

"No." She dropped her hands back to her sides. "You know what the worst of it is? I have to go through Smythe's *suite,* too. There's no telling what he's crammed in there over the last fifty-odd years."

"No point in picking the lock if there's a chance of finding the key," the cat agreed.

"Spare me the fortune cookie platitudes." Searching for at least the illusion of fresh air, Claire walked over to the windows. Outside, the wind hurried up the center of the street, dragging a tail of fallen leaves, and directly across the road two fat squirrels argued over a patch of scruffy lawn. It was strange to feel neither summons nor site. Because of the shields, she had to keep reminding herself that this was real, that she shouldn't be somewhere else, doing something else.

The sound of Dean's work boots approaching turned her around to face the lobby.

"Hey, Boss, find anything?"

"No more than on the last two times you asked."

"Would lunch help?"

"Helps me," Austin declared, leaping down off the counter.

Claire's stomach growled an agreement. Outvoted, she started toward the door to Smythe's old suite. "Just let me wash up fir . . ." The sound of her shin cracking against the bottom drawer of the desk drowned out the last two letters. Grabbing her leg, she bit back her first choice of exclamation, and then her second, and then there really didn't seem to be much point in a third.

"Are you okay, Boss?"

"No, I'm not okay." Air whistled through clenched teeth. "I'm probably crippled for life."

A LIE!
AN EXAGGERATION.
CAN'T WE USE IT ANYWAY? Hell asked itself hopefully.
OH, DON'T BE SUCH A GIT.

"And you know what the worst of it is?" The question emerged like ground glass. Claire tugged her jeans up above the impact point. "I closed the drawer. I *know* I closed the drawer."

Obviously, she hadn't, but Dean knew better than to argue with a person in pain. "Here, let me look at that, then." Ducking under the counter, he dropped to one knee and wrapped his hand around the warm curve of Claire's calf.

Her first inclination was to pull free. Her second . . .

NOW *THAT* WE CAN USE.

Reminding herself of the age difference, she banished the thought.

DAMN.

"You didn't break the skin, but you'll have some bruise." Stroking one thumb along the end of the discoloration, he looked up at her and forgot what he was about to say.

"Dean?"

The world shifted most of the way back into focus. "Liniment!"

"No, thank you. You can let go of me now."

Feeling his ears begin to burn, he snatched both hands away, then, suddenly unable to cope with six inches of bare skin, lightly stubbled, reached out again and yanked her jeans back down into place.

"Watch it!" One hand clutching her waistband, she grabbed his shoulder with the other to stop herself from falling.

Stammering apologies, Dean stood.

Things got a little tangled for a moment.

When a minimum safe distance had been achieved, Dean opened his mouth to apologize yet again and found himself saying instead, "What's that noise?"

"It's a cat," Claire told him. "Laughing."

Claire refused to be constrained over lunch. So what if Dean kept his gaze locked on the cream of mushroom soup, that was no reason for her to act like a twenty-year-old. Biting into a sandwich quarter, she swept a critical gaze around the dining room.

"This is ugly furniture," she announced after chewing and swallowing. "In fact, it's an ugly room."

Grateful for a change of subject, even though the original subject hadn't actually been broached, or even defined, Dean acknowledged the pitted chrome and worn Naugahyde with a shrug. "Mr. Smythe wouldn't buy anything new."

"It's not new we need." Claire tapped a fingernail thoughtfully against the table. "I'll deny this if you repeat it, but Mrs. Abrams gave me an idea that could bring in more guests."

"Is that a good idea?" Austin asked, jumping up onto an empty chair. "You're a Keeper, remember? You *have* a job."

"And I'll do my job, thank you very much," she snapped, turning to glare at him. "But a short break before I face the chaos in that sitting room won't bring about the end of the world." She paused and considered it a moment. "No. It won't. Besides, I have no intention of allowing this hotel to slide any farther into oblivion during my watch. There's a hundred things that need to be done, that should've been done years ago. If Augustus Smythe had kept busy, he'd have been happier."

The cat snorted. "Have you seen the rest of those postcards? He kept plenty busy."

"He kept one hand busy at best." Claire put down her spoon and folded her arms. "He was a disgusting little voyeur. Is that how you suggest I fill my time?"

"Actually, I was about to suggest you share your soup with the cat."

"I still don't understand what we're doing." Dean twisted the key around in the attic lock and dragged the door open. "There's nothing up here but junk."

"The furniture in the dining room is junk," Claire amended. "The furniture in the attic is antique." Switching on the larger of the two flashlights, she ran carefully up the spiral stairs.

Dean watched her climb, telling himself it wasn't safe to have both of them on the stairs at once and almost believing it. When she stepped off the top tread into the attic, he followed her up.

"Look at all this!" Although sunlight streamed in through the grime on the windows, the volume of stored furniture kept most of the attic in shadow. The flashlight beam picked out iron bedsteads, washstands, stacks of wooden chairs, lamp shades dripping with fringe, and rolls of patterned carpet. "Nothing's been thrown away since the hotel opened."

"And nothing's been cleaned since it was put up here."

Thankful that they'd found the accident site before they'd had to spend days shifting clutter, Claire turned the flashlight on her companion. "What is it with you and this obsessive cleaning thing?"

"It's not obsessive."

"It's not normal." She pointed the flashlight beam toward room six, one floor below. "You even wanted to dust *her*."

"So?" Reaching down, Dean effortlessly shifted one end of a carpet roll out of his way. "My granddad always said that cleanliness was next to godliness."

Cleanliness was living next to a hole to Hell, but Claire hadn't changed her mind about letting him know it. Not even if he flexed that particular combination of muscles again. "See if you can find the old furniture from the dining room."

"From the look of this place, we'd be as likely to find the Ark of the Covenant and the Holy Grail."

She shuddered. "Don't even joke about that."

Squeezing past a steamer trunk plastered with stickers from a number of cruise ships, including both the *Titanic* and the *Lusitania,* Claire worked her way toward the back of the building. It was farther than it should have been; one of the earlier Keepers had obviously borrowed a little extra Space.

Well, I hope they kept the receipt. . . . Out of the corner of one eye, she saw a bit of red race along the top of a wardrobe and disappear behind a pink-and-gray-striped hatbox. "Oh, no."

"Trouble, Boss?" She could hear furniture shoved aside as Dean struggled toward her.

"Not exactly, but I saw something; something small moving very fast. Unfortunately, it would take at least two hours of excavation or an Olympic gymnast to get to the spot."

The sound of distant movement ceased. "It was just a mouse. There's prints and turds all over up here."

He sounded so positive, Claire didn't bother pointing out that mice seldom came in a bright fire-engine red.

"Don't worry about it, okay? I'll bring some traps up later."

So would she, and she rather thought hers would be more successful.

Ignoring the way her reflection moved slightly out of sync, Claire ducked around an elaborate, full-length mirror and finally ended up under the sloping edge of the roof. "This," she said, turning off the flashlight, "is certainly strange."

Displayed in relative isolation by one of the windows was a bed and mattress, a set of drawers, an old radio, a washstand with a full china set, and a pair of ladder-back chairs.

As Claire stepped forward, she caught sight of something that drove all thoughts of V.C. Andrews-style decorating out of her mind. Just at the edge of the "room" was the very table she'd been looking for. It could easily seat twelve, and all it needed was a bit of polish.

"Dean! I've found it!" She swept a pile of papers onto the floor and had barely emerged, sneezing and coughing from the cloud of dust, when Dean stepped out from between a stack of washstands and yet another steamer trunk, having discovered a slightly wider route to the spot.

"It looks solid enough," he admitted, circling the table. Frowning thoughtfully, he heaved one end into the air. "It's some heavy. How are you after carrying it downstairs?" Releasing the table edge, he bent under it for a closer inspection, highlighting the joints with his flashlight beam. "Those stairs are narrow, and it doesn't come apart."

"I'll get it down the same way they got it up." Dismissing the little voice in the back of her mind that suggested she was showing off, Claire carefully reached through the possibilities and pulled power. "First, I stack the chairs and tables currently in the dining room, out in the hall."

Listening hard, Dean thought he heard the faint sound of stainless steel chiming against stainless steel and the slightly louder sound of an irritated cat.

"Then . . ." She traced a design in the dust on the table. ". . . I send this beauty down to replace them."

The table disappeared.

"*Rapporter cette table!*"

Waving one hand vigorously in front of her face, Claire peered through the reestablished dust cloud at Dean. "What did you say?"

He sneezed. "Wasn't me."

In the silence that followed his denial, they could hear the dust settling.

"It's quiet."

"Too quiet," Claire corrected.

With a sinister rustle, scattered papers rose into the air, riding an invisible whirlwind. They spun for a moment in place, faster, faster, then whipped forward.

Claire dove for Dean just as he reached out to rescue her. Foreheads connected. They hit the floor together as the papers flew overhead.

Ears ringing, Claire scrambled to her knees. "What do you think you're doing?"

"Trying to save you!"

"Oh? How?"

"Like this!" He flung himself at her and returned her to the floor as the papers made their second pass. The edge of an envelope opened a small cut on his cheek.

"Get off me!"

"You're welcome!" Too buzzed with adrenaline to be embarrassed, he rolled onto his back and watched her climb to her feet. "What are *you* doing?"

"Putting a stop to this!" She pointed a rigid finger at the papers. "Right now!"

Everything except a postcard plummeted to the floor. The postcard made one final dive.

"You, too!" Claire snapped.

It burst into flames and fell as a fine patina of ash over the rest.

Hands on her hips, she glared around the open space where the table had been. "We can do this easy or we can do this hard. Your choice."

The silence picked up a certain mocking quality.

"Just remember, I warned you."

"Now what?" Dean asked, standing slowly, keeping a wary eye on those larger items, like chairs, that might also be considered movable.

Claire bent down and smudged a bit of ash on her left forefinger. "Now, I'm going to make whatever it is show itself."

"You can do that?"

"Of course," she snapped. "Check the card."

"The card?"

"The business card I gave you."

He pulled it out of his wallet as she walked over to the window ledge and smudged a bit of dust on her right forefinger.

> Aunt Claire, Keeper
> Your Accident is my Opportunity
>
> (spiritual invocations a specialty)

"It didn't say that before."

"It didn't need to. Now, be quiet." With both hands out at shoulder height, she pulled power. The symbol drawn by her left hand glowed green, the symbol drawn by her right glowed red. "Ashes to ashes, dust to dust. Appear because I say you must."

Dean glanced back down at the card. It now read: (poetry optional). Claire's sister apparently had a good idea of Claire's limitations.

Between the symbols, fighting the invocation every inch of the way, the figure of a man began to materialize. Still translucent, he jerked back and forth trying to break the power that held him. When he finally realized he couldn't win, he snapped into focus so quickly the air around him twanged. Medium height and medium build, he wore a bulky black turtleneck, faded jeans, and a sneer.

The symbols lost their color, glowing white.

"Your name," Claire commanded.

"Jacques Labaet." Squinting, he tossed shoulder length, dark-blond hair back off his face. "And I am *not* at your service." When he tried to stride forward, lines of power snapped him back between the symbols. Brows drew in over the bridge of a prominent nose. "All right. Perhaps I am."

"Give me your word you won't attack again, and I'll release you."

"And if I do not?"

The symbols brightened. "Exorcism."

One hand raised to shield his eyes, Jacques shook a chiding finger at her. "You are a Keeper. You cannot do that. You have rules."

"You drew blood." Claire nodded toward the cut on Dean's cheek. "Yes, I can."

"Ah." He pursed his lips and thought about it. "*D'accord.* You win. I give you my word."

The symbols disappeared.

"You are a woman of *action rapide,* I allow you that." Blinking away afterimages, he stepped toward her. "For all you are so . . . beautiful." His mouth slowly curled up into a lopsided smile that softened the long lines of his face, creating an expression that somehow managed to combine lechery and innocence. Claire found it a strangely attractive combination. *"Tes yeux sons comme du chocolat riche de fonce.* . . . Your eyes they are like pools of the finest chocolate; melting and promising so very much sweetness. Does anyone ever tell you this?"

"No."

"Are you certain?"

He sounded so surprised she had to smile. "I'd have remembered."

"So foolish are mortal men." After a dramatic sigh, his voice deepened to a caress. "Your lips, they are like the petal of a crimson rose, your throat like an alabaster column in the temple of my heart, your breasts . . ."

"That's quite far enough, thank you." There was such a mix of sincere flattery and blatant opportunism in the inventory that Claire found it impossible to be insulted.

Jacques spread expressive hands. "I mean only to say . . ."

Standing at the edge of the cleared space, Dean cleared his throat. "She said that was enough."

"Really? *Et maintenant,* what did I say of mortal men?" One brow flicked up to punctuate a disdainful glance. "Ah, *oui,* that they are fools. Are you mortal, man? No, wait, it is not a man at all; it is a boy."

Moving up behind Claire's left shoulder, Dean dropped his voice. "What is this?"

"This is Jacques Labaet." She couldn't decide if she were amused or irritated by Dean's interruption, mostly because she couldn't decide if he were being supportive or protective. "He's a ghost."

"A ghost?" Dean repeated. He turned his head and found himself nose-to-nose with the phantom.

"Boo," said Jacques.

"We have just left Kingston, steaming for Quebec City; the weather, she is bad, but she is always bad on the lakes in the fall and we think anything is better than being stuck in with the English over freeze up. We barely reach Point Fredrick when things, they go all to Hell."

Claire winced, but there was no response from the furnace room.

"*Pardon*. Such language I should not use around a lady." Blowing her a kiss, Jacques continued his story. "The wind she came up, roaring like a live thing. I remember something hard, I don't know what, catching me here." He tapped the sweater just below his sternum. "I remember cold water and then, *rien*. Nothing." His shoulders rose and fell in a Gallic shrug. "They said I wash up on shore, more dead than alive. Me, I don't know why they bring me here. Two days later, I died."

"And you're a ghost." Dean wanted to be absolutely clear on that. Every community back home had at least one story of a local haunting—ghost husbands, ghost stags, ghost ships—and if this annoying little man was the real thing, then the old stories could be real as well and there were a significant number of apologies owed. He'd have to make some phone calls when the rates went down.

"*Oui*. A ghost." Jacques favored the younger, living man with a long, hard stare, then deliberately turned away from him. "First, I haunt the room I die in. That was not so bad although, I tell you, this place is not so popular with the living. When that Augustus Smythe, that *espece de mangeur de merde*, he moves everything up to the attic, I must go as well and I am haunting this place ever since."

"As a ghost."

"Does he have to keep repeating?" Jacques demanded of Claire. Before she could answer, he spun around to face Dean. "Would you feel better if I disappear? All of me?" He faded out. "Bits of me?" His head reappeared.

"You've been dead seventy-two years," Dean reminded him disdainfully. If the ghost had thought to frighten him with all the appearing and disappearing, he hadn't succeeded. The whole performance too closely resembled the Cheshire cat in the Disney version of *Alice in Wonderland*. "Seventy-two years, that's some time to be dead. You're used to it, I'm not."

Jacques' body came back into focus as he stood, hands curled into fists and chin in the air. "Nobody asks you to be used to it, *Newfie*. You don't like it, then you can get out!"

Rising slowly and deliberately to his feet, Dean was significantly larger. "I live here."

"And I died here, *enfant*, long before you were born on that hunk of rock in water!"

"You know, you've got a real bad attitude for a dead guy!"

"Say you?"

"Yeah."

"This is why we have cats castrated," Claire said to no one in particular. "Sit down. Both of you. You're acting like idiots." While she understood how males were hardwired to defend their territory, this was ridiculous.

"Only for your sake, *ma petite sorcière*," Jacques muttered sulkily, throwing himself back down onto the bed, "would I tolerate this lump of flesh."

Dean moved toward the chair, then shook his head and remained standing. "No. He called me a Newfie like it's an insult. I don't take that from anyone, living or dead."

"You think I am to apologize?" Leaning back on one elbow, Jacques raised his free hand scornfully. "I think not."

"Okay." Full lips pressed into a thin line, Dean turned on one heel and started toward the stairs. "I'm sorry, Boss, but if you want me, I'll be in the kitchen."

"Ha! Go on, run away! I scare off better men than you!" When Dean disappeared behind the stacked furniture, Jacques quieted and turned a speculative glance on Claire. "You will not stop him?"

"How?"

"*Ah, oui,* you cannot wave the dreaded exorcism over him." Then his expression softened, and he laced his fingers behind his head, the lopsided grin not so much suggestive as explicit. "Or perhaps you want to be alone with me as I want to be alone with you. Yes?"

"No. Did you intend to drive him away?"

"*Non.* But I intend to take advantage of it."

Claire rolled her eyes. "I think not. Perhaps I should leave, too."

"You would leave me alone?" Letting his head fall back against the mattress, Jacques sighed deeply. "For still more long and weary years. Alone." He paused for a moment then repeated, "Alone."

All the playacting, all the cheerful seduction, had disappeared. Although she knew she should maintain both a professional and personal distance, Claire couldn't help responding emotionally. Rising out of the armchair, she walked over and sat down on the edge of the bed. It sagged under her weight. "You don't have to stay here alone, Jacques; not any more. I can send you on."

"On to where? That is the question." His eyes serious, he laid his hand over hers. "I tell you, Keeper, I was not the best of men.

A bad man, no, but I cannot say and be certain that I was a good man. I would like to be certain before I go on."

Claire could understand that. Especially considering what waited in the furnace room.

"So." He rolled over on his side and his fingers tightened around hers. "Since I seem to be remaining for a time and we seem to be alone together, so conveniently on a bed, perhaps we could get to know each other better?"

Snatching her hand through his, his grip no more confining than cool smoke, Claire leaped to her feet. "Don't you ever let up? While I appreciate your need for companionship, I do not appreciate being continually propositioned!"

His eyes widened, his expression injured innocence. "But when first I see you, you are so beautiful, how can I not want you?"

"That has more to do with how long you've been alone than it does with me."

"I do not want that Dean and I see him, too," he pointed out reasonably. "And I am not to blame that it has for me been such a very long time."

"What do you expect? You're dead."

Back up on one elbow, he rested his chin on his palm and waggled both brows suggestively. "The spirit is willing . . ."

"But the flesh is nonexistent."

"You are a Keeper. For a time, I can be incubus for you."

Claire groped behind her for a chair and sat down rather abruptly. "How do you know that?"

"There was a Keeper when I was dead no more than ten or fifteen years. She came to my room, *de temps en temps*—that is, from time to time. She is not so young as you, but when no one else makes offers . . ."

The hair lifted off the back of Claire's neck and she fought the urge to turn and check the space behind her. "Bleached blonde, full-figured, pouty mouth, very red lipstick?"

"*Oui.*" His eyes narrowed. "You know Sa . . ."

"Don't say her name. She's still here."

"Then I . . ." He disappeared. ". . . am not."

A little surprised, Claire scanned the area, trying to find him. She didn't want to have to compel him to return. "I thought you two . . . you know?"

"*Non.* You do not know." His voice came from near the window. "There are legends about women like her, try to suck a man's soul out his . . ."

"I get the picture," Claire interrupted hurriedly, not really in the mood for a graphic description in either language.

"Why is that one *still* here?"

How much to tell him? "Do you know what Keepers do?"

"*She* told me. They guard the places where evil can enter the world." He rematerialized, cross-legged on the bed, expressive features folded into worry. "But me, I think *she* want the evil for herself. I do not know what happened, but all at once, *she* did not come and Augustus Smythe was here. He is not a Keeper."

"No, he's a Cousin. Less powerful. *She* . . ." It was impossible not to pick up Jacques' inflection. ". . . was put to sleep for trying to take over the, um, evil." Claire could see no reason to be more specific, especially considering Jacques' transitional state and his lack of certainty over his final destination.

"*She* was put to sleep?" His voice rose, making it more a shriek than a question. "And if *she* wake up?"

"It won't happen."

"So you say. Me, I learn a lullaby or two. And now, what happens? To me?"

Claire frowned, uncertain of what he meant. "Nothing happens to you. *She* can't do anything while she's asleep or she'd have done something by now."

"*Je ne demande pas ce* qu'elle *peut faire a moi!*" Agitation threw him back into French. "I know what *she* can do to me." He raised both hands and made a visible effort to calm down. "I am asking what do you do now with me."

"What do I do?" He was persistent, she'd give him that. "Nothing."

"Nothing happens to me for years." Jacques lay down again and flung an arm up over his eyes.

"Could you please reattach that? It looks disgusting."

Jacques sighed but complied. "At least will you visit?"

"When I can."

"Ah, you have no time because you must guard the place where evil can enter the world?"

"I'm working at sealing the hole."

"And when the hole is sealed?"

"Then I'll move on."

Opening one eye, he peered up at her. "Will you bring back my table?"

"No. You don't need it." When he began a sorrowful protest, Claire cut him off. "You began haunting the attic when Augustus

Smythe moved the furniture up from the room you died in, right?"

"*Oui.*"

She chewed on a corner of her lower lip. "Did he know you were there?"

"He knew. He did not care." Jacques rolled back up onto his side. Misery made his eyes surprisingly dark. "For so many years with no one who cared; do you know, *cherie,* I think that is worse than Hell."

Which explained why there was no response from the basement. Hell appreciated pain. "I have an idea."

Something heavy hit the floor in the room above the dining room. Dean and Austin stared at the ceiling.

"What do think she's doing up there?"

"She's still in the attic," Austin told him. "And so the question becomes, what's she doing up *there?*"

Dean leaned into his polishing cloth with a certain amount of violent activity. "Finding antiques."

"I'm amazed you left them up there together." The cat flopped down on the polished end of the table and stretched to his full length. "A woman. A man. Didn't you say he was a sailor? You know what they say about sailors."

"They don't say it about dead sailors." He peered sideways at the cat. "Austin, can I ask you a personal question? Were you castrated?"

Austin rolled over and blinked up at him. "My, that *is* personal. Why do you ask?"

"Something Claire said."

"She sees all, she tells all." The cat snorted. "If you must know, yes, I was. I was with a less enlightened—and, as it turned out, allergic—family before I moved in with Claire."

"How do you feel about it?"

"It broadened my horizons. I was no longer forced by biology to endlessly pursue females in heat and could turn my attention to philosophy and art."

Dean nodded, understanding. "It pissed you off."

"Of course it pissed me off!" Ears back, Austin glared up at him. "Wouldn't it piss you off? But . . ." he spent a moment grooming the dime-sized spot of black fur on the side of a white paw. ". . . I got over it. Eventually it was a relief to be able to go outside and not come home with my ear shredded by some feline Goliath out to overpopulate the neighborhood."

"Did you talk to the other family?"

"Not after *that*."

A crack of displaced air heralded the sudden appearance of a ladder-back chair in the far corner of the dining room. Closely followed by Jacques, who displaced no air but made up for it in personal volume.

"*Liberté!* I am free! She was right! I go where the furniture is!" He advanced on Dean, his arms flung wide. "Freed, I gladly apologize to you."

Dean backed up a step as Jacques walked through the table.

"You are not a Newfie like an insult even though you are from the colony of the despicable British."

"Newfoundland joined Canada in 1949," Dean told him stiffening.

"*Bon*. Just what this country need, more *Anglais*. It has no matter, we start again, you and I. So tell me, Dean, why do you stay here in such a place?" He paused and looked him up and down. "Should you not be fishing or whacking on the seals or something?"

Dean folded his arms. "I stay," he said through clenched teeth, "because Claire needs me."

"For what?" As Dean's expression darkened, Jacques raised both hands, palms out. "No, no, it is not another insult. I want to know because I think of you. Since I must stay, you can go if I can do for Claire what you can do." His volume dropped dramatically. "You know of *her?* Sleeping upstairs? I tell you, it is not safe for a young man in a building where *she* is."

"You must think I'm really stupid," Dean snarled. "It's sure as scrod not my safety you're thinking of." If he'd ever even considered packing it in and shipping away from this weirdness, he certainly had no intention of going anywhere now.

"Then think of the Keeper's safety. When you are here she must protect you all the time. Her attention it is divided."

"I can protect myself!"

"How?"

"His strength is the strength of ten," Austin muttered, dropping his chin onto his paws, "because his heart is pure."

Nose-to-nose, both men ignored him.

"If Claire allows me a body . . ."

"If Claire *what*?" Dean interrupted.

The cat looked up. "It's an incubus kind of a thing. Not generally approved of by the lineage, but there have been exceptions."

"And I have been already excepted," Jacques announced smugly, and disappeared.

"I hate it when they do that," Austin said, dropping his head again. "You never know when they're really gone." As Dean turned toward him, eyes wide behind the lenses of his glasses, he added, "I know, of course, but you don't."

"*Is* he gone?"

"Yes." Claire answered as she came into the dining room brushing cobwebs off her shoulders. "He's upstairs investigating the rest of the hotel. I spread the stuff from the room he died in as widely as possible."

"In *my* apartment?"

"Of course not. I didn't put anything in the basement at all."

Dean folded his arms. "Is it true what he said?"

"That depends. What did he say?"

"That you . . ." She lifted an eyebrow and Dean suddenly found it difficult to continue. "That you gave him a body."

"He said I gave him a body?"

Her tone lowered the temperature in the room about ten degrees. His crossed arms now a barricade, Dean couldn't stop himself from stepping back. "Not exactly."

"What *exactly* did he say?"

It wasn't a request. Moistening dry lips, Dean repeated the conversation.

Claire sighed and lifted her right hand into the air, fingers flicking off the points. "First, according to my mother and my cat, you don't need my protection and, as things stand right now, there's nothing to protect you from. Second, I need you to run this place. Jacques certainly isn't going to be cooking, cleaning, or unclogging toilets. Third, I didn't make the exception for him, *she* did."

Feeling both foolish and reassured, Dean watched his finger rub along the edge of the tabletop. "Will you?" The silence drew his gaze back to Claire's face. "Uh, never mind."

"Wise choice," Austin muttered.

Claire sighed again. Her life used to be so simple. "Look, Dean, I realize Jacques made it sound like he and I, that we . . ." She paused, wondering why she was so embarrassed about something that hadn't happened. Maybe because somewhere deep in the back of her mind she'd considered it? Clearing her throat, she started again. "Put yourself in his place, trapped between life and death, trapped alone in that attic for decades."

"Okay. I guess I feel sort of sorry for him," Dean allowed reluctantly. "But every ghost story I've ever heard says he'll be a nuisance at best."

The can of furniture polish crashed suddenly to the floor.

"See?"

"That was Austin."

A cupboard door opened and one of the plastic salt shakers put out for guests flung itself halfway across the room.

"*That* was Jacques."

"Just meeting expectations." He materialized by Claire's side, grinning wickedly.

"Ground rules," Claire told him, folding her arms and trying not to smile. "First, no throwing things."

"He started it." Jacques nodded at the cat.

"If he took poison, would you?"

"What would be the point?"

She had to admit that under the circumstances it was a stupid question. Actually, under most circumstances it was a stupid question. "Second, when you're in a room with either Dean, or me, or both of us, you must be visible."

"And thirdly? There is always a thirdly, yes?"

"Thirdly, if we're all going to live together for a while, let's make an effort to get along."

"I cannot go down there with you." Jacques squatted at the top of the stairs to better watch Claire descend. "Why not?"

"Because there's nothing of yours in the basement."

"Is it because he lives in the basement and you keep us from fighting over who is most important in your life?"

"Something like that." Claire smiled as she moved out of his line of sight. For the moment, it was surprisingly entertaining being the center of someone's universe.

"Cleaning is woman's work." Sprawled on the bed, the ghost peered around the room.

Dean very carefully coiled the vacuum cleaner cord around the back of the machine. "Is it?"

"*Oui.* Any man would know."

"Like you know it?" He picked up his divided bucket of cleaning supplies.

"*Oui.*"

"Why don't you tell Claire?"

"That cleaning is woman's work?"

"Yeah."

"I cannot. She is in the basement."

Dean mourned the missed opportunity. Even after only three days he had a fairly good idea of Claire's response to a declaration of that type.

"I think you need to rub harder."

"Don't you have something to do?" Dean growled, scowling up at the ghost. While searching for paint for the sign, he'd come across a can of paint remover and, although the dining room was still a catastrophe, Claire had decided he should spend the rest of the afternoon stripping the front counter.

Sitting on the countertop, Jacques thought about it, soundlessly drumming his heels. "No," he said cheerfully after a moment. "I will remain here and watch you."

"Don't."

"Dean."

He leaned around the flailing legs. "Yeah, Boss?"

Carrying a second box of triple-X videos from the sitting room, Claire pushed her hair up off her face with the back of her hand. "Jacques isn't hurting anything. He'd help if he could."

"I would," Jacques agreed cheerfully. "Truly I would help if I could."

"Yeah. Sure." Until this point, Dean had always been able to give any new acquaintance the benefit of the doubt. Until this point they'd all been alive, but if he disliked Jacques solely because he was dead, didn't that make him as much of a bigot as if he disliked him because he was French Canadian? Now, if he disliked him because of the way he acted around Claire, that opened a whole . . .

He threw his weight behind the scraper.

. . . new . . .

Muscles bulged in his jaw as he gritted his teeth.

. . . barrel of fish.

"I think you reached the wood right there," Jacques pointed out conversationally.

"Claire?"

She paused, one hand on the doorknob. "What is it, Jacques?"

"You have put nothing of me in your bedroom." Standing on the threshold, he pushed against an invisible barrier. "I cannot come in."

"I know."

He stared soulfully at her. "I want only to be where you are."

"Why don't you try being back in the attic where your bed is and I'll see you in the morning." She pushed the door closed.

"Even though you close the door on my face, I still desire you!"

She had to smile. "Good night, Jacques." Switching off the light and dropping her robe, she climbed into bed.

"Claire?" His voice came faintly through the door. "I would just sit in the chair. My word as a Labaet."

"Good *night,* Jacques." After a moment, she sighed. "Jacques, go away. I can still feel you standing there."

"I am on guard so that your sleep is not disturbed."

"The only thing disturbing my sleep is you. Why won't you go away?"

"Because . . ." He paused and she felt him sigh. Or she felt the emotion behind the sigh; as he wasn't breathing, he didn't actually exhale. "Because I have been so many years alone."

Alone. Once again, the word throbbed between them, and once again it evoked an emotional response. Claire couldn't deny the urge to bring the small tapestry cushion—the cushion that gave him access to her sitting room—into the bedroom. She couldn't deny it, but she managed to resist it. "You can stand at the door if you want to." After a moment, she pushed her face into Austin's side and murmured, "This could become a problem."

"I told you so."

"No, you didn't."

"Well, I would've if I'd been there." He touched her shoulder with a front paw. "You're attracted to him, aren't you?"

"Don't be ridiculous, I'm a Keeper."

"So?"

"I feel sorry for him."

"And?"

"He's *dead.*"

Down in the furnace room, the flames reflected on the copper hood were a sullen red. It could have told the Keeper that the spirit was trapped in the same binding that held it—accidentally caught and held.

BUT SHE DIDN'T ASK US.

It would have been even more annoyed had it not recognized all sorts of lovely new tensions now available for exploitation.

FIVE

At seven-forty the next morning, at the far end of the third-floor hall, the vacuum cleaner coughed, sputtered, and roared into life. Three-and-a-half seconds later, Dean smacked the switch and it coughed, sputtered, and wheezed its way back to silence. Heart pounding, he stared down at the machine, wondering if it had always sounded like the first lap of an Indy race—noisy enough to wake the dead.

Or worse.

Which is ridiculous. He'd vacuumed this same hall once a week for as long as he'd worked here with this same machine and the woman in room six had slept peacefully—or compulsively—through it. Contractors had renovated the rooms to either side of her and obviously she hadn't stirred. Mrs. Hansen had all but stuck pins in her, and still she slept on.

The odds were good that he wasn't after waking her up this morning.

His foot stopped three inches above the off/on switch and Dean couldn't force it any closer.

Apparently, his foot didn't like the odds.

So he changed feet.

His other foot was, in its own way, as adamant.

You're being nuts, boy. He carefully cleaned his glasses, placed them back on his nose, and, before the thought had time to reach his extremities, stomped on the switch, missed, and nearly fell over as his leg continued through an extra four inches of space.

Clearly, parts of his body were more paranoid than the whole.

Okay, uncle. He unplugged the machine and rewound the cord. There had to be an old carpet sweeper up in the attic, and he could always use that.

On his way back to the storage cupboard, he bent to pick up a small picture of a ship someone had left on the floor. He had no idea where it had come from; guests had found Mr. Smythe's taste in art somewhat disturbing, so the walls had been essentially art free ever since the embarrassing incident with the eighteenth-century prints and the chicken.

Upon closer inspection, the picture turned out to be a discolored page clipped from a magazine slid into a cheap frame. A cheap, filthy frame.

Holding it between thumb and forefinger, Dean frowned. What was it doing leaning against the wall outside room six? And could he get it clean without using an abrasive?

"Put that down!"

Behind his glasses, Dean's eyes narrowed as he raised his gaze from the felted cobwebbing to the ghost. "Is it yours, then?"

"It is mine as much as it is anyone's."

If the picture belonged to Jacques, that explained why he'd never seen it before. "Why should I put it down?" he asked suspiciously.

Jacques' expression matched Dean's. "Why do you hold it?"

"I found it on the floor."

"Then put it back on the floor."

"There?" A nod indicated the picture's previous position against the wall—far, far too handy to the sleeping Keeper.

"*Oui,* there! What are you, *stupide*?"

"*Why* do you want me to put it there?"

"Because that is where it was!"

"So?"

"Do you try to block my way, *Anglais*?"

"If I can," Dean growled, taking a step toward the dead man. The way he understood it, Jacques had been dead as dick and haunting the hotel at the same time as the evil Keeper's attempt to control the accident site. It wouldn't surprise him to discover the ghost had been her accomplice and now, with Claire unwilling to give him a body, he had only one other place to turn. Dean couldn't let that happen, not after everything Claire and her mother and the cat had said. "What are you planning, Jacques?"

Jacques folded his arms and rolled his eyes. "I should think," he said scornfully, "that what I, as you so crudely say, plan, would be obvious even to a muscle-bound *imbecile* like yourself."

"You're after waking her?"

"Waking her?" The ghost shot a speculative look in Dean's direction. "*Oui,* if you like. I wake her to new sensations. And when I tell Claire that you gather what allows me to walk within the hotel, that you try to keep me from her, she will not like that, I think."

. . . what allows me to walk within the hotel. Dean's scowl faded as he realized, for the first time in his life, he'd leaped to the worst possible conclusion, his response based solely on his irrational reaction to a dead man. The picture had nothing to do with the sleeping Keeper. Working from the attic, Claire must've sent it to the third floor hall without considering where it might end up.

He'd completely forgotten about Jacques' anchors. He opened his mouth to explain and was amazed to hear himself say, "Sure, run and hide behind Claire."

"Run and hide?" Anger blurred Jacques' edges.

"Too dead to stand up for yourself?"

"Claire . . ."

"This has nothing to do with Claire." Dean set the picture back on the floor—as far from room six as he could put it without appearing to give ground—then straightened, shoulders squared. "This is between you and me."

"Me, I think this has everything to do with Claire," Jacques murmured, studying the younger man through narrowed lids. "But you are right, *mon petit Anglais,* this is between you and me."

Claire had been vaguely disappointed not to find Jacques waiting for her when she passed through the sitting room on her way to the bathroom. Thoughts of him spending the night pressed up against her bedroom door had inserted themselves into her dreams and jerked her awake almost hourly. She'd wanted to share her mood with him while she still felt like giving him a body in order to wring his neck.

It didn't help that the morning's measurements had shown a perceptible buildup of seepage. With no access to the power sealing the hole, she couldn't cut it off, and she certainly couldn't let it build up indefinitely.

Teeth clenched, she gave the shower taps a savage twist, snarled wordlessly when the pipes began banging out their delivery of hot water, and bit back an extremely dangerous oath when the temperature spent a good two minutes fluctuating between too hot and too cold.

She finally began to calm as she lathered the Apothecary's shampoo—guaranteed not tested on mythical creatures—into her hair, and by the time she'd sudsed, rinsed, and dried, she'd relaxed considerably. When Hell actually let her blow-dry and style in peace, she left the bathroom feeling remarkably cheerful.

Her good mood lasted through dressing and right into the day's search for the Historian.

Curled up on a pillow, Austin lifted his head as the wardrobe door opened and Claire emerged soaking wet. "You're cutting it close," he said. "You've just barely left. What happened?"

"Tropical storm," Claire told him tightly, pushing streaming hair back off her face. "Came up on shore after me and followed me about ten kilometers inland. Good thing I was driving an import, or I'd never have stayed on the road."

"One of the Historian's early warning systems?"

Claire shrugged, her sweater sagging off her shoulders. "Who knows?" Trailing a small river behind her, she picked up some dry clothes, held carefully at arm's length, and headed for the bathroom.

Dumping her wet clothes in a pile on the floor, she dressed quickly and, stomach growling, picked up her blow-dryer. "This one's going to be quick and sleazy," she muttered, bending over and applying the hot air. "I'm too hungry for style."

When she straightened, Jacques stared at her from out of the mirror.

"Oh, hell," she sighed.

"Got it in one, *cherie*." His lips curled up into the lopsided smile that raised his looks from passable to strangely attractive— strangely attractive were it not for Hell's signature substitution of glowing red eyes. "I'm sorry I missed you earlier."

"Just get on with it."

The image shook its head. "You would think," it said teasingly, "that you were in a hurry to get somewhere. You can't leave, *cherie*." The smile disappeared. "Neither of us can leave. We have been thrown together here, why not make the most of it?"

She had every intention of leaving, but her mother's suggestion that she not argue with Hell had been a good one. "What did you have in mind?"

"With the power of the pentagram, you could give me a body nightly as easily as you could snap your fingers."

Claire frowned. "Don't you mean opening the pentagram would give me that power?"

"Things are not sealed so tightly as all that." Red eyes actually managed a twinkle. "Augustus Smythe knew the benefits of using the seepage. How do you think he kept himself amused?"

"I think *that's* fairly obvious." She folded her arms. "If I can use the seepage without releasing the hordes of Hell, what's in it for you?"

He looked hurt. "Must there be something in it for us?"

"Yes."

"Perhaps we find that a happy Keeper is a Keeper easier to live with."

"I'm sure that Augustus Smythe was a joy."

"He was Cousin, *cherie*. You are a Keeper. Surely you are stronger?"

"That has nothing to do with it."

"Perhaps." The image saddened. "You get so few chances to have another's life touch yours. A frenzied fumbling in the dark—and we have nothing against that, *cherie*—and then you move on. Only when Keepers are old do they stay in one place long enough to find a mate for the soul and, by then, they are too old to recognize such a one. You have a chance, *cherie,* a chance few Keepers get."

Claire's nostrils flared. "He's dead."

"Ah, I see. You will not take the risk, even though there is no danger to you, because it is what a Keeper does not do. A Keeper does not take risks for such a minor thing as happiness." The image saddened. "For once in your life, *cherie,* can you not give in to desire without questioning if it is what a Keeper should do?" It raised its left hand and pressed it against the inside of the glass "Can you not reach out and meet me halfway?"

She felt her right hand lift and forced it back down by her side. "You're good," she snarled.

The image in the mirror let its hand fall back as well, fully aware that the mood had been broken "Technically, no. But we accept the compliment."

"Give me back my reflection. Now!"

"As you asked so nicely, *cherie* . . ." Jacques' image faded slowly, calling her name as though he were being pulled into torment.

"You're not Jacques," Claire told it, and found herself talking to herself.

"Claire!"

When she opened the bathroom door, Austin tumbled in and rolled once on the mat. He took a moment to compose himself, then said, with studied nonchalance, as though he hadn't just been trying to dig his way through the door, "Dean and Jacques are fighting."

"You mean they're arguing."

"No. I mean they're fighting."

"That's impossible."

"So one would assume, but they seem to have found a way."

She tossed her blow-dryer down by the sink and ran her fingers through her hair, forcing most of it into place. "All right," she sighed, "where are they?"

"The third-floor hall." Austin paused, licked his shoulder, and stepped out of the way. "Directly in front of room six."

His foresight kept him from being trampled as Claire raced for the stairs.

The effect depended on who delivered the blow. If Dean punched his fist through Jacques' immaterial body, then Jacques felt it. If Jacques drove his immaterial fist through Dean's body, then Dean felt it. It wasn't much of an effect either way, being closer to mild discomfort than actual pain, but neither the living nor the dead cared. The point was to score the point.

"Stop it! Stop it this instant!" Breathing heavily from her run up the two flights of stairs, Claire flung herself between the combatants, then sucked in a startled gasp as Jacques' hand sliced through her body from hip to hip dragging a sensation of burning cold behind it. When she staggered back, she found herself pressed up against the warm length of Dean's torso and that was almost as disconcerting.

Jerking forward, she turned sideways and presented a raised hand to each man. "That will be quite enough! Would one of you like to explain what the h . . . heck is going on?"

Silence settled like three feet of snow.

"I'm waiting."

"It is not your business . . ." Jacques began. His protest died as Claire turned the full force of her disapproval in his direction.

"*Everything* that happens in this building is my business," she told him. "I want an explanation and I want it now."

Jacques smoothed back translucent hair. "Ask your houseboy."

"I'm asking you."

"Why? *Le cochon maudit,* he started it."

As Claire turned to face him, Dean bit back an answering insult.

"Well?" she prodded.

"He accused me of picking up his anchors. Of keeping him from walking around the hotel."

"Were you?"

"No!" When he saw Jacques' mouth open, he shifted his weight forward and said, "Okay, I picked up that picture there, but I didn't know it was one of his anchors."

"You accuse me of hiding behind Claire."

"And look where you are."

"*Fini! Je suis a bout!* I have had it up to here!"

"FREEZE!"

Jacques stopped his forward advance, and Dean rocked back on his heels.

Arms folded, Claire turned slowly to face Dean. "Did you really say that?"

Dean nodded sheepishly, gaze locked on the carpet.

"Why?"

Ears red, he shrugged without looking up. "I don't know."

Since he was telling the truth, Claire ignored the rude noises coming from behind her. "All right, then, I suggest—no, this needs something stronger than a mere suggestion—I *insist* that we continue this, whatever this is, downstairs. We're uncomfortably close to her."

"*Her?*" Jacques repeated, coming between Claire and the stairs. "By her, I am wondering, do you mean, *her?*"

"*She's* in room six," Claire told him, pointing with broad emphasis at the splintered door. She opened her mouth to demand he get out of her way when she realized all his attention was on Dean. The air crackled as he moved past her.

"You thought that I, Jacques Labaet, did want to wake *her?*"

Several hundred childhood stories of vengeful spirits passed through Dean's head, but he held his ground, wondering why adults thought it necessary to scare the snot out of kids. "I only thought it at first."

"You dare to give me this insult!"

"The picture was right by her door."

"And so were you!"

"I was vacuuming!"

"The carpet," Jacques spat, drifting up so they were nose-to-nose, "is clean! Perhaps you mean to wake *her,* and I come in time to stop you!"

It was only twenty after eight, but Dean had already had a bad morning. The carpet was not clean, it hadn't been vacuumed in a week and it didn't look as though it was going to get vacuumed any time soon. Sure, he'd discovered a suspicious side of himself he didn't much like, but he didn't think he deserved to be accused of treachery by someone intent on necrophilia. Of a sort. "You go to Hell," he said with feeling.

Jacques disappeared.

"Oh, shit!" Claire clamped a hand over her mouth, but it was too late.

Dean's eyes widened and, fumbling for his keys, he raced for room five.

With no time to explain, Claire flung herself down the stairs. *How could he have done that?* She missed a step, fell five, caught her balance, and picked up speed. *There's no way he should've been able to do that.* By the time she turned onto the basement stairs, her sock-covered feet barely touched the wood. One more floor and she'd have been the first Keeper to fly without an appliance.

She turned the chains and padlocks to rice and then kicked piles of it out of the way as she dragged open the furnace room door.

"Claire!" Suspended over the pit, Jacques flickered like a bulb about to go out. "Help me!"

Skidding to a halt at the edge of the pentagram, Claire hadn't the faintest idea of what to do. Because of the seal, Jacques hadn't gone directly to Hell, but there was sufficient power in the area directly over the pit to shred his ties to the physical world. When the last strand ripped free, his soul would be absorbed, seal or no seal.

"Claaaaaaaaire!"

She could barely hear her name in the panicked wail. Making it up as she went along, she reached out with her will.

HE WAS GIVEN TO US!

"It doesn't work that way." Slowly, she wrapped possibilities around the thrashing, flickering ghost. "You know the rules."

RULES DO NOT APPLY TO US.

"You wish. Souls come to you by their own actions. They can't be given to you."

BUT HE'S DEAD.

"So?" It was like scooping a flopping fish out of a tidal pool with a net made of wet toilet paper.

WE HAVE THE RIGHT TO JUDGE HIS ACTIONS.

"Not on this side you don't."

WE'RE HELPING HIM PASS OVER.

"Not if I have anything to say about it." Holding him as securely as possible, Claire began to pull Jacques toward the edge of the pit. His struggles made it difficult to tell how quickly he was moving, but after a few tense moments he was definitely closer to the side than the middle.

When eldritch power crawled like a bloated fly over the part of her will extending over the edge of the pentagram, she realized Hell was analyzing the rescue attempt. She felt it remove its attention from Jacques and gather its resources. There was barely time to brace herself before an energy spike thrust up out of the depths, dragging both her will and Jacques back toward the center of the pit.

LET HIM GO. HE IS NOTHING TO YOU.

"That's not what your recent temptation implied."

WE'RE BIG ENOUGH TO ADMIT WHEN WE'RE WRONG.

Sock feet slid closer to the edge of the pentagram.

ON SECOND THOUGHT, DON'T LET HIM GO.

If she let him go, the odds were good she wouldn't fasten onto him again before Hell tore through the bonds holding him to the world. If she didn't let him go, she'd be dragged through the pentagram and his fate would be a minor footnote to the cataclysm as the seal broke. Her toes dug through her socks and into the imperfection in the rock floor, but that only slowed her.

Jacques or the world?

It was the sort of dilemma Hell delighted in. Claire could feel its pleasure in the certain knowledge that she'd have to sacrifice Jacques for the lives of millions.

Then strong arms wrapped around her from behind. Her toes stopped millimeters from disaster.

"Bring him in," Dean told her, tightening his grip one arm at a time. "And let's get out of here."

Constrained by the pentagram, Hell stood no chance against the deeply ridged treads on a pair of winter work boots designed to get the wearer up and down the chutes of St. Johns.

Weight on his heels, Dean stepped back, once, twice, dragging Claire back with him, dragging Jacques with her. At the outside edge of the pentagram, the tension snapped and flung all three of them against the far wall of the furnace room; first Dean, then Claire, then Jacques, who slapped through them both like a cold fog to smash in turn against the rock.

Teeth gritted, Claire pried herself up off of Dean, used the wall to pull herself to her feet, and attempted to blink away the afterimages caused by impact with limestone closely followed by

Jacques' left knee passing between her eyes. "Is everyone all right?"

"I guess." Dean braced himself against the floor, separated himself from Jacques' right arm and shoulder, and stood.

"Jacques?"

"*Non.* I am *not* all right. Where are we?"

"The furnace room," Dean answered, before Claire had a chance.

"What? In the hotel?" The last syllable rose to a shriek.

"Yeah. The furnace room in the hotel." Dean shot a look both wounded and disapproving at Claire. "But I don't think we should stay."

Jacques glanced wide-eyed toward the pentagram. "It is real?"

"It is," Claire told him, holding her head in both hands. When they'd broken free, her will had retracted and she had the kind of headache that came with trying to fit approximately twelve feet of power in an eight-inch skull.

"Then we talk in the dining room." Still flickering around the edges, he disappeared.

"The dining room," Claire repeated. "Good plan." Staggering slightly, she started up the stairs.

One hand out to catch her if she fell, Dean followed, still far, far too angry to give in to the faint gibbering he could hear coming from inner bits of his brain. "Why didn't you tell me there was a hole to Hell in the furnace room?"

"I'm a Keeper, it's my duty to protect you."

"From what?"

"Living in terror."

A LIE. A VERITABLE FALSEHOOD!

Claire sighed. She couldn't believe a headache could pack so much mass; it felt as though she had the weight of the world on her shoulders. "From having to bear more than I thought you could."

"Didn't think much of me, did you? Do you?"

Heaving herself up another step, she waved more or less toward the pit. "Dean, it's Hell!"

"We've a saying back home . . ."

"Please, spare me."

". . . some don't be afraid of the sea, they goes down to the sea, and they be drowned. But I be afraid of the sea, and I goes down to the sea, and I only be drowned now and then."

"What the h . . ."

SAY IT.

". . . heck does that mean?" she snarled.

"Fear can keep you alive. You should've told me."

KEEPERS, ALWAYS THINK THEY KNOW WHAT'S . . .

Claire slammed the door shut on the last word, spraying uncooked rice all over the basement.

A single grain of those pushed inside the furnace room flew down the stairs and tumbled end over end across the stone floor. It stopped no more than its own width away from the outermost edge of the glyphs that sealed the pentagram.

DAMN.

"Look, Dean, you knew what you needed to know." Claire kicked at a mound of rice, guilt making her sound petulant even to her own ears. "I told you there was a major accident site down here; I just didn't name it."

His back against the furnace room door, Dean stared at her, unable to believe what he was hearing. "You didn't name it? It's not like you forgot to tell me it was called Fred or George or Harold. It's Hell!"

"Technically, it's energy from the lower end of the possibilities manifesting itself in a format the person who called it up could understand."

"And that *format*?"

"Is Hell; all right?" Sagging back against the washing machine, she threw up her hands. "You win."

Dean jerked a hand back through his hair. "It's not about winning." He paused, trying to figure out what it was he'd won. "Okay. Maybe it is. You're admitting you should have told me, right?"

"Right."

"That you were wrong?"

She found enough energy to lift her head. "Don't push it." One fingernail traced the maker's name stamped into the front of the washer. "So now you know, what are you going to do? Are you going to leave?"

"Leave?" Leave. He hadn't actually thought it through that far.

"What's the point?" his common sense wanted to know. *"There's nothing there that hasn't been there for the last year."*

"Shouldn't you be telling me to pack?"

"Too late."

"Dean?"

He took a step away from the furnace room. He wanted to ask her if she really thought she could close up *Hell,* but the sound of a hundred grains of rice being ground to powder drew his gaze to the floor. "What's with all the rice?"

"Conservation of mass," Claire explained wearily. "It used to be the chains."

"You changed the chains into rice?"

"It had to be something I could get through even though it weighed the same as the chains."

The area immediately in front of the furnace room door looked as though a small blizzard had wandered through on its way to Rochester. Crouching, Dean scooped up a handful of the tiny white grains and frowned as they spilled through his fingers. "Instant rice?"

"What's wrong with instant?"

"Nothing. I mean, it's not like you're cooking with it." He straightened, dusting his hand against his thigh. "Are you after changing it back?"

Claire shook her head and regretted the motion. "I can't. I couldn't change my mind right now."

"Then should I replace the chains? Mr. Smythe kept a box of extras," he added in response to her expression.

Claire glanced at the door. The chains, like the locks on room six, were wishful thinking. If Hell got loose, chains wouldn't stop it. "Why not."

Picking rice off her socks, she watched him walk to a storage cupboard at the far end of the basement, return, and efficiently secure the door. When he turned to face her, she realized there was a reserve in his expression, a new wariness in his gaze, that made her feel as though, somehow, she'd failed him. She didn't like the feeling.

Keepers weren't in the habit of apologizing to bystanders. But then, Keepers didn't usually have to look Dean McIssac in the eye, knowing they were wrong. "All right." She tried to keep her nostrils from flaring and didn't quite manage it. "I'm *sorry* that I didn't tell you."

"I told you so." Enjoying the startled reaction his unexpected declaration had evoked, Austin picked his way across the laundry room. "What's with the rice?"

"It used to be the chains and locks," Claire told him.

"I see. Well, the mice will certainly be pleased."

"How many times do I have to tell you, I don't think they're mice!" The need to vent at something pushed the volume up until she was almost shouting.

Austin snorted. "Oh, that's right; you're the Keeper and I'm just a cat. What do I know about mice?"

She smiled tightly down at him. "You should know they don't come in primary colors. Were you looking for us?"

"No. But I was wondering why Jacques is having hysterics in the dining room while you two are hiding out down here." Fastidiously finding a clean bit of floor, he sat down, wrapping his tail around his toes. "After what I overheard, I'm not wondering any more, but I was.

"This is only a guess," he continued as Claire raced for the stairs, "based on the really pissed-off ravings of a dead man, but did someone use the h-word out of context and almost condemn his soul to everlasting torment?"

Dean blanched as he realized that was exactly what had happened. "If you'd told me," he called, hurrying to catch up, "I wouldn't have done it!"

"Her mother wanted her to tell you."

"Shut up, Austin."

When they reached the dining room, a plastic salt shaker, a box of toothpicks, and six grapes flew out of the kitchen. Claire ducked and Dean took the full impact.

"J'ai presque ete a l'Enfer!"

Wiping crushed grape off his chin, Dean stepped forward. His French wasn't up to an exact translation, but the infuriated shriek suggested a limited number of possibilities. "I'm sorry. I didn't mean it. It was . . ."

"It was an accident!" With a well-placed hip, Claire moved Dean out of her way. "Granted, he said the words, but he didn't mean them as an instruction. He should be able to say what he wants with no effect."

Austin snorted and whacked the salt shaker under the dining room table. "That thing's been down there for over a century and the power seepage has permeated this whole building. I'm only surprised that he never told old Augustus where to go."

"I couldn't say that to my boss," Dean protested.

"Not without a union," the cat agreed.

Jacques surged through the table to stand face-to-face with Claire. "I don't care what he should have been able to do! All I know is that he tried to throw me into Hell!"

"And then he pulled you out again."

"You think that makes up for him putting me there?"

"Would you listen to me, Jacques!" Had she been able to get hold of him, she'd have shaken him until his teeth rattled. "He didn't *know* it would happen. He didn't even know what was in the furnace room."

"He did not know!" Jacques stepped back in disbelief, half in and half out of the table. "You did not tell him?" All at once, he frowned. "Come to think on it, you did not tell me!"

"*You've* been in the same building with it for seventy-two years!" Claire met indignation with equal indignation. "Knowing it's there won't change anything."

His eyes darkened. "You are wrong, Claire. It changes what I know."

She couldn't argue with that, even if she'd wanted to. "Okay. Fine. I should've told you. I should've told you both. But I didn't. I'm sorry." And that, she decided was the last time she was apologizing for it. "You both know now. I'm going to have another shower even though it won't do any good because the touch I can feel is inside my head, and then I'm going to get some breakfast because I'm starving. All right?" Her chin rose. "Is there anything *else* you'd like me to tell you?"

The two men, now side by side, exchanged interrogative glances.

"*Non,*" Jacques said after a moment. "I cannot think of anything."

"No more secrets," Dean added.

"God forbid *I* should have secrets." Her ears were burning and she didn't want to think about a probable cause. "My cat can't keep his mouth shut, and suddenly my life is an open book."

"Hey!" Austin stuck his head out from under the table. "You let the ghost out of the attic all on your own, and *I* said you should tell them about the furnace room."

"You did not."

He thought about that for a moment. "Well, I never told you not to."

Claire swept a scathing glance over the three of them, suggested they watch their language, and stomped out of the dining room. It would've been a more effective exit had she not been in socks and had her heels hitting the floor not set up a painful reverberation in her head, but she made the most of it.

"There will be secrets," Jacques observed, as the door to her suite slammed shut. "Women must have secrets."

"Why?" Dean asked, going into the kitchen.

"Why? Because, *espece d'idiot,* between a man and a woman, there must be mystery. The worst of Hell is that there is no mystery."

* * *

ROSEBUD IS HIS SLED. When silence was the only response, Hell sighed. GET IT? NO MYSTERY. ROSEBUD IS HIS SLED. . . . DOESN'T ANYONE CARE ABOUT THE CLASSICS ANYMORE?

Dean turned to face the ghost, feeling slightly sick when he thought of what he'd nearly done. "I can only keep saying I'm sorry."

"That is right, *Anglais,*" Jacques agreed. "You can keep saying you are sorry."

"The way I see it," Austin said, leaping from chair to countertop, "you're even. You unjustly accused each other of wanting to wake *her.* You, Dean, accidentally almost sent Jacques to Hell, but then you purposefully went in and rescued him."

"*Non.* Not even." Jacques glared over the cat's head at Dean. "He also accuses me of hiding behind Claire."

"Yeah, and you called him something pithy and insulting."

"You speak French?"

"I'm a cat."

"Look, I overreacted," Dean admitted. He paused while the hot water pipes banged out the rhythm of Claire's shower. "It's just you've been pretty obvious about how much you want a body."

"I would take a body from the cat before I took a body from *her.*"

"Don't hold your breath," Austin recommended.

Pulling the toaster from the appliance garage, Dean shook his head. He couldn't help feeling he should be more upset about the reality of a hole to Hell in the furnace room except that *reality* and *hole to Hell* in the same sentence just didn't compute. "Why does *she* bother me more than Hell?"

"I could go into the deep psychological problems men experience when they come face-to-face with powerful women . . ."

"We do not!" both men exclaimed. Standing with their arms crossed, they regarded each other warily.

The cat snickered. ". . . but it's simpler than that. Hell is too nasty for mortal minds to comprehend, so they trivialize it, knock it down to size. It's a built-in defense mechanism."

Brow furrowed, Dean stared down at the cat. "So *she* bothers me more than Hell because I don't have any natural defenses against *her?*"

"And because the original Keepers put a dampening field around the furnace room. Without it, business would be worse than it is, as difficult as that may be to imagine, and any sane person would run screaming once they found out what was in the basement."

"And with it?"

"Unnerving but endurable. Kind of like opera."

"A dampening field to dull the reactions." Rubbing at the perpetual stubble along his jaw, Jacques nodded. "That does explain why I take this so well."

"That," Austin agreed, assaulting the lid on the butter dish, "and because you're dead. The dead don't get worked up about much."

"Except getting their rocks off," Dean muttered.

"You desire I should tell Claire why we were really fighting?" the ghost demanded.

"If you know, why didn't you tell her upstairs?"

"Two reasons. If you do not know, me, I am not the one to tell you. And two . . ." He shrugged. "I remember in the neck of time . . ."

"Nick of time."

"What?"

"Not neck," Dean told him. "Nick."

"*D'accord.* In the nick of time, I remember that women do not always appreciate being fought over the way those who fight might assume."

"Oh." Opening the fridge, Dean stared at the contents, ignored the little voice suggesting that, under the circumstances, it was all right to have a beer before noon, and closed the door again, saying, "That's pretty smart for a dead guy."

"I was, as you say, pretty smart for a live guy."

"You're bonding," Austin observed sardonically. "I'm touched. Well, what would you call it?" he asked when both the living and the dead fixed him with an identical expression of horror.

"We're not bonding," Dean declared.

"Not even a little bit," Jacques added. "We are . . ." He looked to the living for help.

"Not bonding," Dean repeated.

"*Oui.*" Settling himself cross-legged an inch above the table, the ghost leaned back on nothing and studied the other man. "Me, I have no choice, but you, now you know, do you stay?"

"Claire asked me that, too." He folded his arms. "I don't run away from things."

"Perhaps it is wiser to know when to run."

"And leave you alone here?"

Jacques spread his hands, the pictures of wronged innocence, the gesture far more eloquent than words.

"Fat chance." Shoving his glasses up on his nose, Dean headed for the basement stairs.

"Where are you going?"

He made the face of a man who once a month scrubbed the concrete floor with a stiff broom and an industrial cleanser. "I'm after sweeping up the rice."

"You've had a busy twenty-four hours, Claire. Are you sure you're all right?"

"I have a vicious headache." Cradling the old-fashioned receiver in the damp hollow between ear and shoulder, she fought with the childproof cap on a bottle of painkillers. Teeth clenched, she sat the pill bottle on the table and pulled power. The bottle exploded.

"Claire, what are you doing?"

There were two pills caught in the cuff of her bathrobe. "Just taking something for my headache." She swallowed them dry.

On the other end of the phone, Martha Hansen sighed. "You aren't the first Keeper who's had to apologize to a bystander, you know."

"It's the first time *I've* ever had to do it."

"It's the first time a bystander's ever been involved in what you do."

Claire opened her mouth to disagree, then realized that her previous involvements with bystanders were not something she wanted to discuss with her mother. Nor, she acknowledged with a small smile, were they something she had to apologize for.

"Claire?"

Pleasant memories fled as the current situation shoved its way back to the forefront of her thoughts. "At least I needn't worry about it happening again. Dean's too nice a guy to even think of doing it on purpose."

"And Jacques?"

Her lip curled. "Jacques is dead, Mom. He can't affect anything."

"Ah. Yes."

Claire decided she didn't want to know what that meant. Had the phones been Touch-Tone, she'd have suspected Austin had been talking to her mother behind her back. Since there was no way the cat could use a rotary phone . . . All at once, this conversation was not making her feel any better. "I'd better get dressed and get back to work."

"I hope it helped you to talk about it, Claire. You know you can call any time. Speaking of calling, you haven't heard from your sister, have you?"

She could feel her jaw muscles tightening up. "No. Why?"

"We had a bit of a disagreement, and she stormed out of here last night. I'm not worried, I know where she is, I was just wondering if she'd spoken to you."

"No."

"If she does call, would you please explain to her that turning the sofa into a pygmy hippo for the afternoon might be very good transfiguration, but it's rather hard on the carpets and it confuses the hippo."

A dry, tearing sound, the sound of something large and ancient clearing its throat, pulled Dean up from the basement. Fighting against the natural inclination of his legs to get the rest of his body the hell out of there, so to speak, he made his way to the dining room where he found Claire on her hands and knees, surrounded by pieces of broken quarter-round, ripping up the linoleum.

"She's venting frustrations on inanimate objects," Austin explained from the safety of the countertop. "You should consider yourself lucky."

"Boss?"

She shuffled backward and tore free another two feet of floor covering before the section detached from the main. "There's hardwood under here. We're going to refinish it."

"But I thought . . ."

"Congratulations."

". . . that you were after working on closing the site."

"To close the site, I need to study it. To study it, I need to get close. To get close, I need to be calm." Claire ripped up another ragged section. "Do I look calm?"

"I guess not." Amazed by the extent of the mess, Dean wasn't entirely certain he wouldn't rather have faced the demon he'd expected. "But what about the front counter, out in the lobby."

"I know where the front counter is, Dean." She tossed aside a crumbling piece of linoleum. "I'm not asking you if you want to refinish the floor, I'm telling you we're going to."

Dean glanced over at the cat who looked significantly unhelpful. "Where's Jacques?"

"Staying out of my way."

"Ah." He cleaned his glasses on his shirttail and squinted unenthusiastically at the exposed wood. "Should I go rent an industrial sander?"

"Yes, you should." Claire rolled up onto her feet and headed down the hall toward the office.

"Why should we be the ones who suffer?" Dean muttered at the cat as he turned to follow. "She was in the wrong."

"And you're just going to keep that thought to yourself, aren't you," Austin told him.

Dean knew the envelope Claire pulled the money from—Augustus Smythe had paid him out of it every Friday. He could've sworn it had been empty on Saturday when he'd unlocked the safe. "Where did you get the cash?"

"Lineage operating funds." Claire tossed the envelope back in the safe and closed the door. "When people, or institutions, or pop machines lose money, it becomes ours, available to draw on when we need it."

"*This* is where lost money goes?" Fanning the bills he counted four twenties, three tens, and a five with Mr. Spock's haircut penciled onto the head of Sir Wilfred Laurier. It was a remarkable likeness. "What about socks?"

"Socks?"

"Where do lost socks go?"

Claire stared at him as though he'd suddenly sprouted a third head. "How the he . . . heck should I know?"

When Dean returned just before noon, all the furniture in the dining room had been rearranged on the ceiling and the linoleum had been completely removed. It was still lying around in messy heaps, but it was no longer attached to the floor.

Tired and filthy, Claire watched appreciatively as he wrestled the heavy machine in through the back door. Having actually been able to accomplish something had put her in a significantly better mood.

They ate soup and sandwiches sitting on the counter, discussing renovations in perfect harmony. Two hours later, the debris bagged, Claire left to finish sorting through Augustus Smythe's room while Dean used the sander.

As the layers of glue and old varnish began to disappear, he grew more confident. Finished with the edging, he began making long, smooth passes up and down the twenty-three-foot length of the room. After the third pass, he began to pick up speed. All at once, a body appeared too close to the drum to avoid.

Jacques screamed in mock agony as the sander split him in two.

Somehow, Dean managed to maintain enough control so he only gouged a three-foot, shallow, diagonal trench into the floorboards before he got the machine turned off. Ripping off his ear protectors with one hand and the dust mask with the other, he whirled around and yelled, "That's not funny!"

Jacques waved a hand made weak by laughter. "You should see your face. If I am here another seventy years, I will never see anything so funny." As Dean sputtered inarticulately, he started laughing harder.

"Why have you stopped? Have you finished?" Claire halted in the doorway, took in the tableau, and shook her head. "Jacques, pull yourself together!"

"For you, *cherie*, anything." Continuing amusement kept his upper half vibrating and Jacques finally had to reach down, grab his jeans, and yank his legs back onto his torso.

"Was there an accident?"

"No, not an accident," Dean growled. "The jerk suddenly showed up in front of me. Look at what he made me do to the floor! I should've run over his head."

"Be my guest," Jacques told him, still snickering.

"Jacques!"

The ghost set his head back on his shoulders.

"You know," Claire told him pointedly, "just for the record, I don't find that sort of thing attracti . . ." She jumped as an air raid siren began to sound. "Mrs. Abrams. I set up an alarm on the front steps to give us a little warning. Jacques, you'd better disappear."

"Why can't I meet this Mrs. Abrams?"

"Yeah, Boss, why *can't* he?" Dean asked with feeling. "Why should we have all the fun."

The siren shut off as the front door opened. "Yoo hoo!"

Jacques flinched and disappeared.

Suddenly inspired, Dean switched the sander back on.

As clouds of dust billowed up around him, Claire dragged herself reluctantly out to the front hall.

"Oh, there you are, dear." Her voice rose easily over the background noise roaring out of the dining room. "As I was letting Baby out into his little area I heard horrible sounds coming from the back of this building and I rushed right over in case the whole ancient firetrap had begun coming down around your ears."

Claire crushed an impulse to ask her what she would have done had it been. "We're refinishing the floor in the dining room, Mrs. Ab . . ."

"Of course you are. Didn't I say this fine old building needed a woman's touch? So nice you have a strong young man around to do the work for you." She darted purposefully down the hall, caroling, "I'll just go and have a little look-see," as she went.

For a woman of her age and weight, Mrs. Abrams moved remarkably quickly. The defensive line of the Dallas Cowboys might have been able to stop her, but Claire didn't stand a chance without using power. With no time for finesse, she reached out and slammed to her knees.

Five feet out in front, Mrs. Abrams didn't even notice.

Blinking away afterimages, Claire dragged herself up the wall. *It's that damn sander,* she decided, perfectly willing to condemn it to the flames. *How's anyone supposed to concentrate through all that noise?*

Innate good manners forced Dean to turn the sander off when Mrs. Abrams charged into the room.

"Mercy." She coughed vigorously into a handkerchief she pulled from her sleeve. "It is dusty, isn't it? And this room looks so small and dreary with no furniture in . . ." Her voice trailed off as she noticed just where the furniture was. "Oh, my. How did you ever . . . ?"

"Clamps," Claire told her. The older woman looked so relieved she could almost hear the sound of possibilities being discarded. Meeting Dean's incredulous gaze, she shrugged—the gesture saying clearly, *people believe what they want to believe.*

A LIE!
A LIE IN KINDNESS. THEY CANCEL EACH OTHER OUT. NEITHER SIDE IS STRENGTHENED. NEITHER SIDE IS WEAKENED.
BUT . . .
INTENT COUNTS. Had anyone been there to overhear, they might have thought that Hell spoke through clenched teeth. IT'S IN THE RULES.

Suddenly inspired, Claire took hold of one polyester-covered elbow and turned the body attached to it back toward the front door. "You shouldn't be in here without a dust mask, Mrs. Abrams. What would Baby do if you got sick?"

"Oh, I mustn't get sick, the poor darling would be devastated. He's so attached to his mummy." Craning her head around, she took one last look at the dining room ceiling. "Clamps, you say?"

"How else?"

"Of course, clamps. How else would you be holding furniture on the ceiling. How very clever of you, Karen, dear. Have you heard from that horrible Mr. Smythe?"

"No, and my name isn't . . ."

"He's going to be so surprised at all you've done when he comes back. Are you going to open up the elevator?"

"The what?"

"The elevator. There's one in this hall somewhere. I remember it from when I was a girl.

Claire opened the front door, but Mrs. Abrams made no move to go out it.

"You ought to open the elevator up, you know. It would lend the place such a historical . . ." Her eyes widened as the sound of frenzied barking echoed up and down the street. She darted out the door. "What can be wrong with Baby?"

"The mailman?" Claire asked, following from the same compulsion that stopped drivers to look at car accidents on the highway.

"No. No. He's long been and gone."

They were side by side as they crossed the driveway. Claire, on the inside track, looked toward the back in time to see a black-and-white blur leap from the fence to the enclosure around the garbage cans to the ground and streak toward the hotel.

When Claire stopped running, Mrs. Abrams never noticed.

The noise coming from Baby's little area—after a few years of Baby, it could no longer be called a yard in any domestic sense of the word—never lessened.

If the flames reflected on the copper hood were sullen before, they were downright sulky now.

IT ISN'T FAIR.

WHAT ISN'T?

THAT THE KEEPER SHOULD ALWAYS WIN. IF WE HAD ONLY PULLED HARDER. WE WERE SO CLOSE.

CLOSE! The repetition resounded in the heated air like a small explosion. CLOSE ONLY COUNTS IN HORSESHOES AND HAND GRENADES.

AND DANCING.

WHAT?

CLOSE DANCING.

SHUT UP.

SIX

"I would like a room."

Kneeling behind the counter, attempting to send a probe down into the mouse hole and settle the imp question once and for all, Claire felt icy fingers run along her spine. Shivering slightly, she carefully backed out from under the shelf and stood, curious to see if it was the customer or the possibility of actually renting a room that had evoked the clichéd response.

The woman on the other side of the counter was a little shorter than her own five feet five, with a close cap of sable hair, pale skin, and eyes so black it was impossible to tell where the iris ended and the pupil began.

Claire felt the pull of that dark gaze, found herself sinking into the dangerous embrace of shadow, jerked back, and said, "Room four?"

"How perceptive." The woman smiled, teeth gleaming between lips the deep burgundy of a good Spanish port. "Where is the Cousin?"

"Gone. This is my site now." It was almost, but not quite, a warning.

"I see. And should I worry that things have changed enough to need the monitoring of a Keeper?"

"You are in no more danger here than you ever were."

"How fortunate." The woman sagged forward, planted her elbows on the counter, and rubbed her eyes. "'Cause I'm bagged. You have no idea how much I hate traveling. I just want to dump my gear in the room and find something to eat."

Claire blinked.

"Oh, come on." Smudged mascara created raccoonlike circles on the pale skin. "Surely you hadn't planned on continuing that ponderous dialogue?"

"Uh, I guess not."

"Good. 'Cause I'll be staying the rest of the week, checking out Sunday evening if that's cool with you. I've got a gig at the university."

"Gig?"

"Engagement. Job. I'm a musician." She stretched an arm across the counter, thin, ivory hand overwhelmed by half a dozen heavy silver bangles and the studded cuff of her black leather jacket. "Sasha Moore. It's a stage name, of course. I do this kind of heavy metal folk thing that goes over big on most campuses."

Her skin felt cool and dry and her handshake, while restrained, still put uncomfortable pressure on mere mortal knuckles.

There was power in a name and trust in the giving of it. Claire wasn't certain how that applied in this case—while Keepers maintained a live-and-let-live attitude toward the vast bulk of humanity, they tended to avoid both actors and musicians; people who preferred to be in the public eye made them nervous—but she did know that her response would speak volumes to the woman maintaining an unbreakable grip on her hand. If the hotel was no longer a safe haven for her kind, Sasha Moore would want to know before dawn left her helpless.

"Claire Hansen." Hand freed, she flipped open the registration book, and pulled a pen out of the *Souvenir of Avalon* mug on her desk. "Sign here, please."

"Rates the same?"

Rates? Claire hoped she didn't look as confused as she felt. Rates. . . .

Sasha leaned against the counter, dark eyes gleaming. "Room rates?"

"Right. Of course." She had no idea what the rates were, but it was important not to show weakness in front of a predator. "They've gone up a couple of dollars."

"Couple of bucks, eh?" Her signature a familiar scrawl, the musician spun the register back around. Her smile held heat. "You're not charging me for breakfast, are you?"

"Breakfast?" Unable to stop herself from imagining the possibilities, Claire's voice rose a little more than was necessary for the interrogative.

"'Cause if you are, there's nothing I like more than a big, juicy, hunk of . . ."

"Boss, there's a red van parked out back. Do you know whose it is?"

As Dean stepped out into the entry hall, Sasha winked at Claire and turned gracefully to face him. "The van's mine. I'm just checking in."

About to apologize for interrupting, Dean found his gaze caught and held. For a moment, the world became a pair of dark eyes in a pale face. Then the moment passed. "I, I'm sorry," he stammered, feeling his ears burn, "I didn't mean to stare, but you're Sasha . . . uh . . ."

"Moore."

"Yeah, Moore, Sasha Moore, the musician. You were here last spring."

"My, my, my. I must've made an impression."

"You had a black van then. Late eighties, six cylinder, all season radials."

"What a memory."

Claire's eyes narrowed. So this was the h . . . cute guest from room four. She slapped the keys down on the counter and tried not to feel pleased when Dean jumped at the sudden sound.

Sasha's smile broadened as she swept her attention back around to Claire. "I'll just go get my stuff out of the van while you make up the room."

"Make up the room?"

Dark eyes crinkled at the corners. "You are new at this, aren't you? Sheets. Towels. Soap. The usual." Her gaze turned speculative. "Which one of you will be making up the bed?"

Dean stepped forward. "I always did it for Mr. Smythe . . ."

Claire cut him off. "You're in the middle of staining the floor. I'll do it."

"Since it doesn't matter to me . . ."

Glancing over at Dean, Claire wondered if he heard the blithe innuendo.

". . . you two argue it out. I'll be right back." She disappeared into the night before the front door had quite closed behind her.

"Making up the rooms is part of my job," Dean explained, walking over to the counter and reaching for the keys. "Renovations are no reason to slack off my regular work."

"Refinishing the dining room floor is hardly slacking off." Claire snatched the keys out from under his hand. Realizing he remained unconvinced, she added, "The sooner that urethane's done and dry, the sooner you'll be able to deal with the mess."

His eyes lit up at the thought of restoring the kitchen to its usual pristine state. "If you're sure."

"Believe it or not, I'm fully capable of making a bed and hanging up towels. Keepers are trained to be self-sufficient in the field."

"Living off the land?" When she nodded, he frowned at the image that conjured up. "Hunting and fishing?"

"No. But I *can* locate a fast food restaurant within three minutes of arriving in a new area."

He looked appalled.

"It's a joke," she pointed out curtly. "Although, ninety percent of all accident sites do occur in an urban environment. Some Keepers spend their entire lives in the same city, trying desperately to keep it from falling apart."

"What about the other ten percent?"

"Big old houses in the middle of nowhere with at least one dead tree in the immediate area."

"Why a dead tree?"

"Ambience."

His smile was tentative and it disappeared entirely when she didn't join in. "Not a joke?"

"Not a joke." Closing the registration book, Claire came out from behind the counter. Dean was not going to be alone in that room when Sasha Moore returned and that was final—no matter what sorts of demanding tasks she had to perform. She was strong enough to resist the temptation the musician represented but he, however, was a man, and a young one, and expecting him to decline that kind of invitation on his own would be expecting too much. Whether or not he had succumbed during the previous visit was immaterial; this time, she was here to help. "Where do we keep the supplies?"

"In the supply cupboard."

From anyone else, she'd have suspected sarcasm.

"I could wait here and help Ms. Moore carry her bags upstairs. She looked tired."

Ms. Moore could carry you upstairs; one-handed. But that wasn't Claire's secret to reveal. "You know, the longer you leave that floor unattended the greater the odds are that Austin will take a walk and track dark oak stain all over the hotel."

"He'd notice the floor was wet."

"Of course he'd notice. He wouldn't do it by accident."

"But . . ."

"He's a cat." She waited until Dean started back toward the dining room then, jaw set for confrontation, headed upstairs.

"So she's h . . . cute, is she?" Yanking out a set of single sheets, she piled them on top of the towels. "I don't care if he's been providing breakfast, dinner, and midnight snacks, it's dangerous and it's going to stop. I won't have my staff snacked on."

"Who is snacking on your staff?" Jacques floated down from the floor above and settled about an arm's reach away. "And does that mean what it sounds like it means, or is it some prissy *Anglais* way to talk of what is more interesting?"

"It means what it sounds like it means." Two small bars of soap were dropped on the pile. "Did I put one of your anchors in here?"

"Oui."

"I wonder why I did that."

"So we could have more time alone together?" He lifted a lecherous brow but at her protest pressed it back down onto his forehead. "Because you felt sorry for me?" His whole body got involved in looking mournful, shoulders slumped, gaze focused on the loose interlacing of his fingers.

Claire rolled her eyes at the dramatics but couldn't help smiling.

Peering up through his hair, Jacques caught sight of the smile and flashed her an answering grin. "Ah. That is better, no? You should be in a happy mood. I am saved from the pit, and you . . ." He waved a hand at the gathered supplies. ". . . you have someone to stay at your hotel."

"You seem to have recovered from this morning's experience." Claire struggled toward the door, decided she was being ridiculous, wrapped the whole unwieldy pile in power and floated it out into the hall. "I expected the trauma to have lasted a little longer."

Jacques shrugged. "A man does not allow himself to be held captured by his fears. Besides, as Austin reminds me, I am dead. The dead exist in the now; this morning is as years away. Tomorrow may never happen. When I am with you, only then do I think of a future."

Which said something, something unpleasant, about the lingering effect of Aunt Sara. Not to mention country music lyrics.

Inside room four, Claire brought the bedding and towels and sundries to rest on the bureau and picked a small shaving mirror and stand up off the floor.

"What are you doing?"

"You can't have access to rooms that guests are in."

"Why not?"

"Because they might not like it."

"How can they not like me?"

"You're dead." She set the mirror out in the hall and carried the towels into the bathroom.

"Hey, who's the dead guy?"

The sound of the hall door closing brought Claire back out into the dressing room. "He's none of your concern."

"Count on it." She grinned and shrugged out of her jacket. "I don't ask for much from my dates, but they do have to be alive. Now that piece of prime rib in your basement . . ."

"Stay away from him."

"Why?" She polished nails much the same length and color as Claire's against her black sleeveless turtleneck. "You think I'm too hard an act to follow?"

"I have no intention of following you or anyone else. I don't know and I don't care . . ." Claire ignored a raised ebony brow, obviously intended to provoke. ". . . about what happened when Augustus Smythe ran the site, but while I'm responsible, Dean McIssac is under my protection."

"Really? He seemed like a big . . ." A reflective moment later, she resumed. ". . . very big boy. And you're not his guardian, Keeper, so chill. But, as it happens, I never feed in the crib unless things get desperate and, if that's the case, your mother hen act will be the least of my problems. Besides, it'd be easier to throw myself on your mercy. After all, Keepers respond to need." A startlingly pale tongue flicked over burgundy lips. "You're what, O negative?"

"What does that have to do with anything?"

"It doesn't. It's just nice to know you're one of my favorite flavors. Just in case."

Busying herself with the bed, Claire pointedly did not respond.

Behind her, Sasha laughed, neither insulted nor discouraged. "From the way you spoke of him, I assume the little man isn't dead. What did he do? Bugger off and leave you holding the stick?"

"That's not how it works."

Sasha laughed again. "Not generally, no, but Keepers don't take over sites from Cousins who took over from Keepers, so clearly it ain't working the way it should."

"How do you know all that?"

"I've been around a while."

Claire remembered the years of signatures in the registration book—not one of them, unfortunately, occurring in the few short months Sara held the site. "Do you know about . . . ?" A jerk of the head to room six finished the question.

"Well, duh. It's not like it's possible to hide something like that from me. I mean, after four or five visits it got kind of hard to ignore this unchanging life just hanging around upstairs." The musician shrugged into an oversized red sweater. "Gus said it was a woman the Keepers had done a Sleeping Beauty on and that was all I needed to know."

"You called him Gus?"

"Sure. And I'd love to know how he stuck you with this place, but if you don't want to spill, hey, that's cool." She ran her fingers through her hair and quickly changed her lipstick to match the sweater. "He never filled me in on his summoning either—the obnoxious little prick. But man, at your age, it must be driving you nuts hanging around here when you could be out saving the world."

Before Claire could answer, Dean's voice, calling her name, drifted up the stairwell.

Sasha tilted her head toward the sound. "And right on cue we have a reminder of the fringe benefits."

"He's not a benefit," Claire protested.

Cool fingers cupped her chin for a heartbeat. "Foolish girl, why not?" Then, with a jangle of silver bracelets and a careless, "Don't wait up—" she was gone.

Her touch lingered.

Later that night, as Claire climbed into bed, Austin uncurled enough to mutter, "I understand you're renting a room to a bloodsucking, undead, soulless creature."

"Does that bother you," Claire asked.

"Not in the least." He yawned. "Anyone who can operate a can opener is okay by me."

"She came back into her room just before dawn. I think that she saw somebody in town last night." Jacques' hands traced euphemistic signals in the air. "If you know what I mean. She had a cat who has eaten canary look."

Sprawled on top of the computer monitor, Austin snorted. "She looked like she was about to hawk up a mouthful of damp feathers?"

"That is not what I mean."

"You shouldn't spy on the guests," Dean told him, tightening his grip on a handful of steel wool. "It's rude."

"I was not spying," Jacques protested indignantly. "I was concerned."

"Pull the other one."

"You do not have to believe me."

"Good."

"Why do you suppose such a pretty girl stays in a room with no windows?"

Descending from an hour spent studying the power wrapped around Aunt Sara—as long as she could spend so close to such evil without wanting to rent movies just so she could return then un-rewounded—Claire waited on the stairs for Dean's answer.

"Ms. Moore's a musician." His tone suggested only an idiot couldn't have figured it out on his own. "She works nights, she sleeps days, and she doesn't want the sun to wake her."

"Such a good thing there is the room, then," Jacques mused.

Claire frowned. What would happen if Jacques put one and one together and actually made two? If the ghost found out about the vampire, who could he tell? Dean? Only if it would irritate or enrage him.

What if Dean found out? She was fairly certain he would neither start sharpening stakes nor looking up the phone numbers for the tabloids. The vampire's safety would not be compromised.

Dean's safety was another matter entirely. Many humans were drawn to the kind of danger Sasha Moore represented. While not necessarily life-threatening, it was a well known fact that the intimacy of vampiric feeding could become addictive and that wasn't something she was going to allow to happen to Dean. He wasn't going to end up wandering the country, a helpless groupie of the undead.

And I'd feel the same way about anyone made my responsibility, she insisted silently. *Including guests while they're in this hotel.* Which, in a loopy way, made Sasha Moore her responsibility as well.

The sudden realization jerked her forward. Catching her heel on the stair, she stumbled, arms flailing for balance, down into the lobby. She'd have made it had the pommel on the end of the banister not come off in her hand.

Her landing made an impressive amount of noise. It would have made more had she been permitted the emotional release of profanity.

"Claire!" Dean tossed the steel wool aside, peeled off the rubber gloves, and started to rise. "Are you all right?"

"I'm *fine.*"

Moving toward her, he found Jacques suddenly in his way, hands raised in warning.

"I wouldn't," the ghost murmured by the other man's ear. "When a woman says she is fine in that tone, she wishes you to leave her alone."

Since he couldn't push the ghost away, Dean went through him and dropped to his knees by Claire's side. "What happened?"

"I slipped."

"Are you hurt?" Without thinking, he reached for her arm but drew back at her expression.

"I said, I'm *fine.*"

"Told you so," Jacques murmured, drifting up by the ceiling.

Claire pushed herself into a sitting position with one hand and gave Dean the banister pommel with the other. "If you're looking for something to do . . ." A triple boom not only cut off Dean's response but spun her around, hand over her heart as she futilely tried to keep it from beating in time. "What the . . ."

"Door knocker," Dean explained, then clapped his hands over his ears as the sound echoed through the lobby again.

Except that Dean had no reason to lie, she'd never have believed that the brass knocker she'd seen on her first night could have made the noise. *At least we know it's not Mrs. Abrams; she never knocks.* As Dean ran for the door before their caller knocked again and they all went deaf, Claire got to her feet, telling Jacques to disappear.

"Why?" he demanded, floating down to the floor.

"You're translucent in natural light."

"What means translucent?"

"I can see through you."

"That is because to you, *cherie,* I have nothing to hide." He blew her a kiss and vanished as the door opened.

A graying man in his mid-forties peered over a huge bouquet of red chrysanthemums, his slightly protruding eyes flicking back and forth between Dean and Claire. "Flowers for Ms. Moore."

"She's sleeping," Dean told him, adding helpfully, "if you leave them here, I'll see that she gets them when she wakes up."

The deliveryman shook his head and held out a clipboard. "I gotta have her sign for 'em."

"But she's asleep."

"Look, all I know is that I gotta have her signature and room number on this or I can't leave the flowers." He looked suddenly hopeful. "Maybe you could just fake it for me? Then I'd leave 'em with you. It'd *really* help me out."

"I don't know . . ."

Claire did. "I'm sorry," she said, crossing the lobby, "but we don't give out the room numbers of our guests. If you can't leave the flowers with us, you'll have to come back."

"Look, lady, it's my last delivery. What difference would it make?"

"You're missing the point." Moving in front of Dean so she stood eye to eye with the deliveryman, who was no taller than her own five-feet-five, Claire folded her arms and smiled. "We don't give out the room numbers of our guests."

"But . . ."

"No."

He looked up at Dean. "Come on, buddy, give me a break, eh."

Claire snapped her fingers under his nose, drawing his attention back down to her. "What part of no don't you understand?"

"Okay. Fine. You're responsible for Ms. Moore not getting her flowers, then."

"I can live with that." It was nice to have a responsibility so well defined.

"Yeah, well, thanks for the help." Lip curled, he spun around and missed his step on the uneven stairs. Flowers flailing, he began to fall.

"Boss!" Dean's exclamation prodded at her conscience. "He could get hurt!"

Reminding herself of where temptations came from, Claire sighed, took her time reaching for power and, just as he began to pitch forward, set the deliveryman back on his feet.

He never noticed. Stomping down the remaining steps, he flung the flowers into his car and, tires squealing, drove away.

Claire watched until he turned onto King Street. "I wonder who the flowers were from?"

"A fan?"

"I guess." She reached out and gave the small brass knocker an investigative flick. When the resulting boom faded, she followed Dean back inside. "But how did they know she was staying here?"

"Maybe she told them."

"Maybe," Jacques put in, rematerializing, "they were from the one last night. Flowers to say, *Thanks for the memories*."

"I don't think so; she wouldn't have told anyone she was staying here."

"Why not?"

"Because she told me she valued her privacy."

LIAR, a triumphant little voice announced in her head.

A lie to protect another, Claire pointed out. *Circumstances must be weighed. And get out of my head!*

THE LIE INVITED US IN.

Fine. Now I'm telling you to leave.

"Claire?"

Her eyes refocused. "Sorry, what were we talking about?"

"Ms. Moore's privacy."

"Right. We're going to respect it." She looked pointedly at Jacques. "And that means all of us."

Later that afternoon, as the last flat bit of counter emerged from under the twenty-seventh layer of paint, Baby could be heard barking furiously in his area.

Dean glanced up to see Austin still sprawled out on top of Claire's monitor. "Mailman must be late today."

"Only if he's out in the parking lot."

"What?"

The cat leaped down onto the desk, knocking a pile of loose papers and a pen to the floor. "According to Baby, who functions remarkably well on only two brain cells, there's a stranger in the parking lot."

"My truck!" Springing to his feet, he raced toward the back door, peeling off another pair of gloves as he went.

Claire, on her way up from testing the dampening field, stepped in his path. "Hold it! Remember the urethane!"

He spun on the spot, retraced his steps, and flung himself out the front door.

By the time Claire reached the back of the building, having paused in the lobby for a brief explanation, Dean was disappearing over the waist-high board fence to the west. To the south, Baby continued barking. Dean's truck, a huge white gas-guzzling monster named Moby, and Sasha Moore's van both seemed untouched.

"Carole! Carole, dear!" Mrs. Abrams voice didn't so much rise over Baby's barking as cut through it. "What's going on? What's happening?"

Slowly, Claire turned. "We had a prowler, Mrs. Abrams."

"What's that? Speak up, dear, don't mumble."

"A prowler!"

"What, in the middle of the afternoon? What will they think of next? You don't suppose it's that same ruffian who was lurking about the other night?"

"No, I . . ."

"We'll all be murdered in our beds! Or assaulted. Assaulted and robbed. That'll show them!"

Just in time, Claire stopped herself from asking, *Show who?* She didn't really want to know.

"Has that nice young man of yours gone after him?" Mrs. Abrams didn't actually pause for breath let alone an answer. "How I do miss having Mr. Abrams around, although to be honest with you, dear, he was never what I'd call a capable man; had an unfortunate tendency to wilt a bit in stressful situations. He passed away quite suddenly, you know, with such a queer little smile on his face. I'm sure he's as lost without me as I am without him. Never mind, though, I get on. As a matter of fact, I can't stand and chat, I have our local councilman on the phone. The dear man depends on my advice in neighborhood matters." A beringed hand lightly patted lacquered waves of orange hair. "He simply couldn't manage on his own. Baby, be quiet."

Baby ignored her.

"That's Mummy's good boy."

As Mrs. Abrams returned to her telephone, Dean vaulted back over the fence and dropped into the parking lot. "I'm sorry. I lost him. He had a car on Union Street. Got into it and away before I got around the corner." Frowning like a concerned parent, he quickly checked over both vehicles. "Seems like Baby chased him away before he could do any damage. Good dog!"

To Claire's surprise, the Doberman wuffled once and fell silent.

"I wonder if this is his?" Dean pointed to a handprint on the van's driver side window.

Staring at the greasy print, Claire felt her own palms tingle and was suddenly certain she knew who the prowler had been. "It's the deliveryman."

"Pardon?"

"The guy with the flowers this morning."

"I knew who you meant. Are you, uh . . ." He waggled his fingers in the air.

"Manipulating power? No. It's just a hunch."

"A hunch. Okay." Pulling his sweatshirt sleeve down over his palm, he scrubbed the window clean.

Since she couldn't point out that he'd just ruined any chance Sasha Moore might've had of picking up the intruder's scent, Claire shrugged and went back inside to find Austin waiting by his dish.

"Catch him?"

"No. I didn't know you understood dogs."

"What's the point of insulting them if they can't understand what you're saying?"

"You speak dog?"

In answer, Austin lifted his head and made a noise that could possibly be considered a bark had the listener never actually heard a dog larger than a Pekingese.

"And what does that mean?" Claire asked, trying to keep from laughing.

"Roughly translated . . ." Austin stared pointedly down at his dish. ". . . it means, feed me."

That evening, Claire was waiting at the desk when Sasha Moore came downstairs. "Can I speak to you for a moment?"

"Is it going to take long?"

"Not long, no."

"Good, 'cause I really need to eat before I go onstage or the audience is one major distraction; kind of like performing in front of a buffet table."

Since there didn't seem to be anything she could safely reply, Claire stood and silently led the way into her sitting room.

"I see old Gus didn't take much with him."

She didn't want to know the circumstances under which Sasha had been in these rooms before. It was none of her business.

"You still got his dirty pictures up in the bedroom?"

"I'm removing them as soon as I have time."

"Uh-huh." The musician dropped onto the couch and draped one crimson-spandex-covered leg over the broad arm. "So what did you want to talk to me about?"

Claire perched on the edge of the hassock, it being the only piece of furniture in the room that was neither overstuffed nor covered in knickknacks. "I think you're being stalked."

Long lashes, heavy with mascara, blinked twice. "Say what?"

Editing for time, Claire recited the day's events and her interpretation of them.

"Look, I appreciate your concern, but the flowers were probably sent by a fan, and you never actually saw the guy in the lot. It could've been one of the local kids taking a shortcut."

"To his car?"

Sasha snorted. "Trust me, parking sucks in this neighborhood."

"All right, then, if it was a fan who sent the flowers, how did he know you were here? I can't believe you'd tell anyone where you spend the day."

"He must've seen me last night at one of the bars and followed the van."

"Doesn't that worry you?"

She reached out and slapped Claire on the knee. They were close enough that Claire could smell the mint toothpaste on her breath. "Why should I worry? You seem to be worrying enough for both of us." Standing, she bared her teeth. Exposed, they were too long and far, far too white. "I can take care of myself, Keeper. If a fan gets too close, I'll see that he gets just a little closer still." She paused at the door. "Oh, by the way, did you know you have mice?"

Feeling her lips press into a thin line, Claire pried them apart enough to say, "I don't think they're mice."

The musician shrugged. "They sure smell like mice."

"Told you so," Austin muttered as the door closed behind her.

Claire jumped. She hadn't noticed him tucked up like a tea cozy under the television. "If they're mice," she snapped, "why don't you catch one."

He snorted. "Please, and do what with it?"

Friday morning started badly for Claire. First Hell, by way of her mirror, suggested she invite Sasha Moore to dinner and twisted her reaction to such an extent that when she finally regained her reflection, she was edgy and irritable and had no idea of who'd won the round. Then she got completely lost looking for the Historian, was gone almost nine hours' wardrobe time, and returned absolutely famished to discover Dean had just laid down the last coat of urethane and she couldn't get to the kitchen.

"Go . . . l darn it!"

Thanks to the two huge, plate glass windows in the back wall, any solution had to take the possibility of Mrs. Abrams into account. Making a mental note to buy blinds as soon as possible, she grabbed power and shot into the air so quickly she cracked her head on the hall ceiling.

"Scooped up the seepage," Austin said with a snicker.

Both hands holding her head, Claire glared down at him. "I didn't *mean* to."

"You wanted it quick and dirty, didn't you?"

"Well, yes, but . . ."

"That's what you got. Still, I doubt you've permanently warped your character."

"This wasn't the first time. When I tried to stop Mrs. Abrams yesterday, I got knocked to my knees."

"Once, twice; what's the harm?"

"That's probably what Augustus Smythe used to think." The faint buzz of building seepage seemed to have disappeared; it was hard to be certain given the ringing in her ears from the impact. Drawing power carefully from the middle of the possibilities, she sank down until she was about two inches off the floor and then skated slowly forward. Another time, she might've been hesitant about continuing buoyancy initiated by seepage from Hell but right now she was too hungry to care.

Breathing *eau de sealant* shallowly through her mouth, she sat down by the sink, poured a bowl of cereal, and began to eat. She'd started a second bowl when Jacques appeared beside her.

"I think you should know," he said, "that the man who deliver the flowers yesterday, he is just come in the front door."

"What?"

"The man, who deliver the flowers yesterday . . ."

"I heard you." Dropping her cereal in the sink, she flung herself off the counter and raced for the front of the hotel . . .

. . . unfortunately forgetting the section of tacky polyurethane she had to cross.

"Fruitcake!"

The emotional force behind the substitute expletive transfigured the toaster and the smell of candied fruit soaked in rum rose briefly over the prevailing chemicals.

Jacques studied the cake thoughtfully. "What would have happened, I wonder, had you actually used that old Anglo-Saxon expletive with you and I here together?"

"Do you have to!" Claire snapped, loosened her laces, pulled power, and floated to the hall, leaving her shoes where they were stuck.

"Not exactly have to," Jacques murmured.

As Claire ran for the lobby, the deliveryman ducked out from behind the counter, holding what seemed to be the same bouquet of red mums. "I was just lookin' for a piece of paper," he said hurriedly. "The boss said I could leave the flowers, and I was gonna leave you a note."

He was lying. Unfortunately, unless she knew for certain he was a threat to the site, Claire couldn't force him to tell the truth.

OH, WHY NOT?" asked the little voice in her head. *"WHO'S GOING TO KNOW? YOU KNOW YOU WANT TO."*

"Shut. Up." Claire held her hand out for the flowers. "I'll see that Ms. Moore gets these," she said aloud.

"Sure." Watching her warily, he backed along the edge of the counter toward the door, reaching behind him for the handle. He slipped out, still without turning, and paused, peering through the crack just before the door closed. Yellowing teeth showed for an instant in an unpleasant smile. "Give Ms. Moore my regards."

Setting the flowers down, Claire glanced into the office, but nothing seemed to have been disturbed. "Yeah, well, we'll see about that." Ducking under the counter, she lifted her backpack off a hook and rummaged around in the outer pocket. A few moments later, she pulled out the tattered remains of what had once been a large package of grape flavored crystals and poured what was left of the contents onto the palm of one hand.

"Sorry your shoes got stuck to the floor, Boss. I figured you'd notice it was still . . ." Dean's voice faded out in shocked disbelief as he watched Claire fling a fistful of purple powder into the air.

The powder hung for a heartbeat, a swirling purple cloud with added vitamin C, then it settled into a confused jumble of foot and handprints leading from the front door into the office and back to the door again. A fair bit of the powder settled around the flower stems.

"What a mess," Claire sighed. "This tells me nothing except that he was in here and I knew that already."

"Who?"

"The flower deliveryman. I was trying to find out what he was up to."

"With . . ." Dean rubbed a bit of the residue onto the end of a finger and sniffed it. ". . . grape Koolaid?"

"Actually, it's generic. Why waste name brands if you're just going to throw it around?"

"Okay." He pulled a folded tissue from his pocket and carefully wiped his finger. "I'll start cleaning this up."

"Great. I need coffee."

"The floor . . ."

"I know." A careful two inches above the purple, she floated down the hall.

Unfortunately, the flavor crystals had been presweetened. It took Dean the rest of the morning to clean up the mess, and when he finished, he still wasn't certain he'd got it all.

He was right. Although he glanced inside when he cleaned the purple prints off the key cabinet, he didn't notice the small smudge that marked the end of the one empty hook.

"Look, why don't you guys come over to the pub tonight and if this bozo's there, you can point him out to me. I'm always eager to meet my fans."

Dean looked doubtful. "What if he's dangerous?"

"If he is, you'll be there to help." The musician smiled languorously up at him. "Won't you?"

"Sure." Ears red, Dean stepped sideways until he stood behind the masking foliage of a fake rubber plant that filled the southeast corner of Augustus Smythe's sitting room. Until this moment he'd thought he'd gotten past those awkward, mortifying years of spontaneous reaction.

"What do you mean when you say *sure*?" Claire demanded from the other side of the room.

As far as he could tell, she had no idea why he'd moved. He glanced down at Sasha Moore, and his ears grew so hot they itched.

"Dean!"

Twisting one of the plastic leaves right off the plant, he dragged himself out of the warm, dark, inviting depths of the musician's eyes. "I mean, uh, that is . . . uh, Ms. Moore, could you please look somewhere else. Thank you." He took a deep breath and slowly released it. "I mean, that since we'll be there, if anything happens, we'll help."

"You've decided we're going to be there?"

"Sure. I mean, no." He shot a helpless look at Claire. "I mean, you don't *have* to go. I could always go without you."

"He's right, Claire, you don't *have* to go. He could stay late and help load the van." A pink tongue flicked out to moisten crimson lips. "I could give him a ride home."

"I'll go."

"Good, then, it's settled." Twisting lithely in the chair, Sasha stood and made her way through the bric-a-brac to the door. "I'm going out for a bite. I'll see you both at the pub."

As the door closed behind her, Jacques materialized, eyebrows lifted toward Dean. "Showing off?" He laughed at the panicked embarrassment in Dean's eyes, turned to face Claire, and said with patently false dismay, "He is so strong, no? He tore a leaf off your rubber plant."

"Don't worry about it," she snorted dismissively. "It's plastic. I'm more concerned about this pub thing."

"What pub thing?" Austin asked, coming out of the bedroom and stretching. When Claire explained, he jumped up onto her lap. "Go," he told her, butting his head against the bottom of her chin. "Take advantage of the fact you're not actually sealing the site. If anything comes up, I'll contact you."

"What would happen if you were actually sealing the site," Jacques wondered.

"I wouldn't be able to leave the building."

"Just like me."

"Except he's dead," Austin pointed out. "Since you're not, why don't you prove it."

"By going out?"

The cat sighed. "Ladies and gentlemen, we have a winner. Go out. Have fun. Aren't you the one who keeps saying you're not planning to be stuck here?"

"I didn't mean I should be going out to pubs," Claire protested indignantly.

"Why not?"

"I never get to go anywhere," Jacques said mournfully an hour later as he and Austin stood in the front window watching Claire and Dean walk toward King Street.

"Look at the bright side," Austin observed as Mrs. Abrams hurried down her front path too late to corner them. "It can be a dangerous world out there."

"What does she look at?"

One hand shading eyes squinted nearly shut, Mrs. Abrams stared up toward the window.

The cat stretched. "She's probably wondering if I'm the same cat who got Baby to hog-tie himself with his own chain."

"Are you?"

"Of course." He jumped down off the windowsill. "Come on, it's Friday night, let's go watch TV."

With a last curious look at Mrs. Abrams, Jacques turned and followed. "TV? Is it like radio?"

"You know radio?"

"*Oui.* Augustus Smythe, *le petit salaud,* he leaves in the attic a radio. I have energy enough to turn it on and off, but I cannot make different channels. Over many years, I have learned English from the CBC."

Austin snorted. "Well, that explains a lot." ·

"A lot?"

"You don't talk like a French Canadian sailor who died in 1922."

"So I have lost my identity to the English."

"Although you still sound French Canadian . . ."

THE CAT IS ALONE!

YEAH. SO?

A gust of heated air wafted up from the pit. GOOD POINT.

"Why is it so dark in here?" Claire demanded, stopping just inside the door of the Beer Pit.

Feeling the pressure building behind them, Dean cleared his throat. "Uh, Boss, we're blocking the entrance."

"Technically, you're blocking the entrance, they could get around me." But she moved across the painted concrete floor toward one of the few empty tables. "Why is the ceiling so low?" Before Dean could point out that the pub was in a basement, she added, "And look at the size of these things. Why are the tables so small?"

"More tables, more people, more money."

Claire shot him a look as she sat down. "I knew that. The floor's sticky. You'll notice, I'm not asking why. Do you see the deliveryman?"

"It's pretty crowded . . ."

"I'd suggest you wander around and search for him, but you can't move in here. I guess we wait until he tries something. Why is it so smoky?"

Dean nodded toward the other side of the room. "There's a smoking section."

"And it's got one of those invisible barriers to keep the smoke away from the rest of us."

"It does?" After the events of the last week, he wouldn't have been surprised.

"No. I was being sarcastic. I could create a barrier, we do it all the time when we have to contain some of the more noxious site emissions, but it would be fairly . . ." The spatial demands of a beefy young man in a Queen's football jacket caused an involuntary pause. ". . . obvious by the end of the evening when the smokers started suffocating in their own toxic exhalations," she finished, shoving her chair back out from the table.

The arrival of the waitress stopped conversation until the arrival of the drinks.

"Three seventy-five for a glass of ginger ale?" Claire tossed a ten onto the girl's tray. "I could buy a liter for ninety-nine cents!"

"Not here," the waitress said tartly, handing back her change.

"You don't go to pubs much, do you?" Dean asked, putting his own change back in his wallet and his wallet in his front pocket.

"What was your first clue?" She took a mouthful of the tepid liquid just as Sasha Moore stepped up onto the small stage at the other end of the room.

Dean pounded her on the back as she choked and coughed ginger ale out onto the table. "Are you okay?"

"Except for a few crushed vertebrae, I'm fine." Eyes wide, Claire stared at the woman in the spotlight. All masks were off. She was danger. She was desire. She was mystery. And no one else in the room realized why. Claire couldn't believe it. Sasha Moore had done everything but sit under a big neon sign that said, "vampire," and no one made the connection although everyone responded. Brows drawn down she watched Dean shift in his seat. Everyone. "There are none so blind . . ." she muttered.

"What?"

"Nothing." Claire half expected Sasha to rely on the "rabbits caught in the headlight" effect that predators had on prey, but she played it straight. At the end of the first set, after a heavily synthesized version of "Greensleeves," she acknowledged the applause and cut her way easily through an adoring audience to the table.

"A soft drink?" An ebony brow rose as her dark glance slid from Dean's beer to the glass in front of Claire. "If you don't drink beer, the house wine isn't bad."

"I don't drink wine," Claire told her.

Sasha smiled, her teeth a ribbon of white in the darkness. "Me either. So, is he here?"

"We haven't seen him."

"Then I guess you'll have to stay until the end."

Although she'd been about to say that they might as well leave, Claire found herself responding to the challenge. "So it seems."

Dean glanced from one to the other and realized there were undertows here strong enough to suck an unwary swimmer in deep over his head. He didn't understand what was happening, so he let instinct take over and did what generations of men had done before him in similar circumstances; he opened his mouth only far enough to drink his beer.

"So how was she?" Austin asked, his eyes squinted shut against the light.

"Pretty good, I guess." Claire lifted the cat off her pillow and got into bed. "They made her do two encores."

"Ah, yes." He climbed onto her stomach and sat down. "The creatures of the night, what music they make."

"Go to sleep, Austin."

"The boss not back yet?"

"No, not yet." Austin sprang up onto the coffee table and shoved aside a shallow bowl carved from alternating colors of wood and filled with a dusty collection of old birthday cards. "She got a late start this morning."

"You know she doesn't want me in here before she gets back."

"I wanted my head scratched."

"She's likely to be angry."

"It's a worthy cause."

Although he knew he should just turn around and leave, Dean sighed and scratched where indicated, unable to resist the weight of the cat's stare.

"Hey, go easy, big fella. I'm not a dog."

"Sorry."

"Of course you are," Claire said stepping out of the wardrobe. "The question is, why are you here?"

"It's Saturday."

"I knew that." Setting a pair of plastic shopping bags—one stamped with a caduceus and the other with an ankh—down beside the cat, she began pulling out small packages tied up with string.

"On Saturdays, I do the grocery shopping."

Understanding dawned. "And you need money?"

Dean was quite certain he saw one of the packages move. Just to be on the safe side, he stepped back from the table. "Unless you've already done it?"

"Not quite." Leading the way to the office, she unwrapped half a dozen pieces of six-inch-high iron grillwork as she walked. "I'm making imp traps this morning so instead of searching for the Historian, I went to the Apothecary for supplies." The envelope had seventy dollars in it. Handing over the money, she said,

"Get what you usually get, but add a dozen bagels, ten kilograms of plain clay kitty litter, and a bag of miniature marshmallows—the plain white ones. The Apothecary only had four left, and that won't be enough if I have to reset the traps."

"Four bags?"

"Four marshmallows."

"You trap imps with marshmallows?" Dean asked, folding the money into his wallet.

"We've discovered they work as well as newt tongues and get you into a lot less trouble with Greenpeace."

"What are the bagels and the kitty litter for?"

Claire snorted. "The bagels are for breakfast, and the kitty litter is for Austin to . . ."

Dean raised a hand and smiled weakly. "Never mind."

"I thought we were going up to the attic?"

"We are." Claire took several deep, calming breaths and picked up a bread stick from the counter. "But first, I'm going to ward the door."

Austin rubbed against her shins. "Why don't you just lock it?"

"Lock it?"

"Yeah, you know, that thing you turn that keeps the door from opening without a key. Remember what your mother always said."

"Ripped underwear attracts careless drivers?"

"I was thinking more of 'try a simple solution before looking toward more exotic possibilities.' "

"Warding the door is hardly exotic."

"Locking it's simpler."

"True enough." The tumblers fell into place with a satisfying clunk. Picking up a pair of imp traps, she followed the cat upstairs.

"A question, she occurs to me." Floating just below the ceiling, Jacques watched Claire set the second trap beside the pink-and-gray-striped hatbox. "What will you do with an imp if you catch one?"

"I'll neutralize it."

"What does that mean, neutralize?"

"Imps are little pieces of evil; what do you think it means?" Precariously balanced on a pile of old furniture, Claire extended her right leg and probed for the first step down.

"A little more to your left," Jacques told her.

She moved her foot.

"Your other left," he pointed out as she fell. "Are you hurt, *cherie*?" he called when the noise had stopped but a rising cloud of dust still obscured the landing site.

Shoving a zippered canvas bag filled with musty fabric off her face, Claire sucked a shallow, dust-laden breath through her teeth, then took inventory. Her left elbow hurt a lot, and she seemed to have landed on something that squashed. "Where's Austin?"

"Right here." He leaped up into her line of sight, balancing effortlessly on a teetering commode. "Are you okay?"

"I'm fine."

"You're just saying that, aren't you?" Jacques drifted toward her, wearing an expression of poignant concern. "I wish I had hands to help you up, arms to carry you, to comfort, lips to kiss away the hurt.

His eyes were dark, and Claire found herself thinking of Sasha Moore. "I wish you did, too."

"You could make it so."

Austin snorted. "Does she look like Jean Luc Picard?"

"Who?"

The cat sighed. "I have so much to teach you, Grasshopper."

"What?"

Reflecting how nothing could spoil the moment like a cat, Claire got her legs free, rolled onto her side, and noticed, right at eye level, a stack of ten-inch baseboards. As far as she could tell, given her position, they'd been taken from the wall in ten- or twelve-foot lengths. "This is great!"

"Falling?"

"Baseboards." Scrambling to her feet, she retrieved her flashlight from a pile of old *Reader's Digest Condensed Books*—part of the obligatory attic door—and headed for the stairs. "They were probably taken off when they replaced the plaster and lathe with drywall. Come on. I've got to measure the walls in the dining room because I think baseboards go on before the wallpaper."

Happily working out a renovation schedule that would keep Dean busy for the next six or seven lifetimes, Claire raced down the attic stairs, along the third floor hall, and down to the second floor where she stopped cold. There was a man at the other end of the hall; at the door to room four.

Instinct overwhelmed cognitive function and she ran toward him. "Hey!"

When he spun around, she saw it was the deliveryman—no big surprise—and that he was picking the lock.

So much for the simple solutions. "Get away from there!"

"Don't try and stop me." The clichéd warning made his voice sound harsher than it had, the voice of a man barely clinging to sanity.

One hand searching her clothing for a thread, Claire reached for power, touched seepage, and hesitated.

The intruder dove toward her, grabbed her upper arms, and threw her against the wall. He was stronger, much stronger than he looked; madness lending strength.

"Why?" he demanded, smashing her head against the wall on every other word. "Why are you protecting that undead, blood-sucking, soulless creature?"

Limp in his grasp, unable to concentrate enough to use even the seepage, Claire was only vaguely aware of being dragged toward the storage cupboard. Through a gray haze and strangely shifting world view, she saw Jacques swoop down from the ceiling, shrieking and howling and having no effect at all.

Oh, swell, she thought, as the cupboard door swung open. *He believes in vampires but not in ghosts.* A heartbeat later, the implications of that sank in and she began to struggle weakly.

She hit the floor beside the mop bucket, barely managing to keep her head from bouncing, and collapsed entirely when a heart-stopping screech set the bottles of cleanser vibrating.

A deeper howl of pain rose over the noise the cat was making; then, just as Claire attempted to sit up again, the door slammed shut and Austin landed on the one thing guaranteed to break his fall.

For a moment, the need to breathe outweighed other considerations; then, lying in the dark listening to Austin hiss and spit, she grabbed for the first power she could reach and used it to clear her head. Sucking up seepage had just become a minor problem. "I understand how you feel, Austin, but shut up. We haven't time for this."

A whiskered face pressed into her cheek. "Are you all right?"

"No. But I'm fixing it." Anger burned away the damage, power riding in on her rage to replace what she spent. At the moment, it didn't matter where that power came from. With all body parts more-or-less back under her control, she stood and flung herself at the door. The impact hurt—a lot—and bounced her onto her butt. The door didn't budge.

He'd done something to hold it in place.

"Calm down!" the cat snarled. "You nearly landed on top of me!"

"Calm?" Claire struggled back onto her feet. "What do you think a murder in this building will do to the pentagram's seals?" Breathing deeply, once, twice, she placed her hands on the wood and blew the door off its hinges.

Staggering slightly, she raced down the hall, through Jacques, and into room four.

He was standing over the bed, a sharpened stake in an upraised hand.

There was no seepage left, blowing the door had wiped it clean. Sagging against the wall, Claire reached into the possibilities, knowing she wouldn't be in time.

A black-and-white streak landed on his back as the stake came down.

Pulling Austin clear with one hand, Claire tossed her bit of thread with the other. As the deliveryman stiffened, she shoved him behind her to fall, shrieking, wrapped in invisible bonds, onto the floor of the outer room.

The stake protruded from Sasha Moore's chest just below the collarbone. At first, in the forty-watt glow of the bedside lamp, Claire thought it was all over, then she realized that he'd missed the heart by three full inches. Either he had a poor understanding of biology or Austin's leap had misdirected the blow.

"She is Nosferatu! She must die!" The crazed voice echoed in the closed room. "Those who protect her have made a covenant with evil!"

"Hey! Don't tell me about evil," Claire snapped at him over her shoulder. "*I'm* a trained professional." She spread her fingers and one of the bonds expanded to cover his mouth.

His tail still twice its normal size, Austin panted as he looked from the stake to Claire. "Now what?"

"Now we pull it out." There was a pop of displaced air as the first-aid kit from the kitchen appeared on the bedside table. "And we bandage the wound and see what happens when she wakes up."

"I'm guessing she'll be hungry."

Claire glanced toward the man thrashing impotently about and grunting in inarticulate rage. "I think we can find her a bite of something."

AT THIS RATE, THE DAMPENING FIELD WILL NEVER GO DOWN. SHE BARELY CLEARED THE WAY FOR FUR-

THER SEEPAGE. THE COUSIN DID MUCH MORE DAMAGE WITH HIS TOYS AND DIVERSIONS.

PATIENCE.

PATIENCE . . . The word sounded as though it had been ground out through shards of broken glass. . . . IS A VIRTUE!

The ruddy light reflected in the copper hood grew brighter, as though Hell itself blushed. SORRY.

SEVEN

Sunset was at seven-forty-one. Claire called the local radio station for the exact time and, while she had them on the line, asked them to play "Welcome to My Nightmare." The song, discovered on one of her parents' old albums, had meant a lot to her during the earliest years of her sister's training and the events of the afternoon had made her nostalgic for those simpler, albeit equally dangerous, times.

At seven-thirty, she started up the stairs.

At seven-thirty-five, she unlocked the door to room four, passed the man lying in the dressing room, who stirred restlessly in his involuntary sleep, and entered the cubicle holding the bed and the wounded Sasha Moore. In the dim light of the bedside lamp, she stood by the wall and waited for sunset.

At seven-forty-six, either the radio station or her watch off by the longest five minutes in recorded history, she saw the vampire's lips, pale without their customary sheen of artificial color, slowly part and draw in the first breath of the night. Ebony brows dipped in as both wound and bandage pulled with the movement of the narrow chest. Muscles tensed beneath the ivory skin. Eyes snapped open. A dark gaze swept over the red-brown stains along the left side of the bed and then locked on Claire's face.

"Spill, Keeper," Sasha Moore snarled. "What the fuck is going on here?"

At seven-fifty-two, as the newly awakened vampire-slayer began to whimper, Claire stepped out into the hall and locked the door to room four behind her.

"How did you know I wouldn't kill him when he had every intention of killing me?"

"He's crazy, you're not," Claire answered calmly. "You've lived too long to risk exposure by modern forensics." She turned her attention to the glassy-eyed man, who swayed where he stood, oblivious to his surroundings. Centuries of arriving at ac-

cident sites after the inevitable, and invariably messy, cause and
effect had already taken place, had given Keepers a distinctly fa-
talistic, some might even say unsympathetic attitude toward people who played with matches. A Keeper's responsibility involved
keeping the whole metaphorical forest from going up, and they
figured the more people who got their fingers burned, the less
likely that was to happen. Claire shuddered to think of what
might have occurred had she stayed in the attic a few moments
longer. "How much will you allow him to remember?"

A spark of cruel amusement gleamed in the shadowed eyes.
"Let's put it this way: He's going to piss himself whenever he's
outside after the sun goes down and he's not going to know
why."

"Isn't that a bit extreme?"

"What? For trying to kill me?" Sasha tossed her head disdainfully. "I think not. Besides, it's nothing a few dozen years of
therapy won't clear up." Silver bracelets chiming softly, she
stroked the velvet length of Austin's back. "Imagine living two
hundred and twenty-seven years only to die at the hands of yet
another amateur van Helsing. What a frigging waste."

"Yet another amateur van Helsing?" Austin rolled so she could
reach his stomach. "This has happened before?"

"Once or twice; the nutballs come out every time we get
trendy." Crimson nail polish glistened like drops of blood against
the white fur. "But this . . ." Her other hand lightly touched the
bandage under her clothes. "This is as close as anyone's ever
come." When she lifted her gaze from the cat, Claire realized that
for the first time since the other woman had arrived at the hotel,
her eyes neither threatened nor promised. "Thank you for my
life, Keeper."

"You're welcome. But it was no more or less than I would
have done for anyone. Murder creates the very holes the lineage
exists to seal."

The vampire sighed, a fringe of sable hair dancing as she
shook her head. "You really lean toward the sanctimonious, you
know that?"

"I'm a Keeper," Claire began defensively, but cool fingers tapping the curve of her cheek cut her off.

"My point exactly. Try to get over it."

Speechless, Claire watched as Sasha turned her would-be exe-
cutioner unresistingly toward the door and, when she opened it,
finally gave up trying to put together a sufficiently scathing response, settling for: "What are you going to do with him now?"

Pausing on the threshold, the night spreading out behind her like great, dark wings, Sasha locked one hand around her captive's wrist to prevent him from moving on and turned back toward the guest house. "I'm going to take him to his car and release him."

"But the sun's down."

White teeth flashed between carmine lips. "Obviously."

"And people complain about the way *cats* play with their food," Austin snorted as the door swung shut.

"I'm not sanctimonious, am I?"

"You're asking me?"

Claire's eyes narrowed. "Is there anyone else around?"

"Just the dead guy on the stairs."

Jacques gave the cat a scathing look as he materialized. "I only arrive this moment, and if he says I am here all along, he lies."

"Cats never lie," Austin told him, leaping from the counter to the desk to the chair to the floor. "There's not much point is there, not when the truth can be so much more irritating. If you two will excuse me, I have things to do."

"What sorts of things?" Claire asked suspiciously as he started down the hall.

The black tail flicked sideways twice. "Cat things."

Elbows still propped on the counter, Claire let her head drop forward into her hands. Cat things could cover everything from a nap on top of the fridge to the continuing attempt to twist Baby's already precarious psyche into still tighter knots. If it was the former, she didn't need to know. If the latter, she didn't want to.

"I thought," Jacques said softly, "that there were no more secrets between us."

Without lifting her head, Claire sighed. "No more secrets that concern you. This doesn't."

"You think it does not concern us that Sasha Moore is Nosferatu?"

"No." She wondered when Jacques and Dean had become an *us* and whether it would last longer than this conversation. "You're dead. Dean is off limits."

"But you get hurt defending her and, if we knew, we could be there."

"You *were* there."

"Ah. Oui." His face fell. "And I could do nothing to save you. But I am dead." The realization perked him up. "What can a dead man do? And besides, my failure does not change your silence.

You do not tell me. You do not tell Dean—which is, of course, of not so great a consequence."

"It wasn't my secret. If she wanted you to know, she'd have told you herself."

"And yet, now I know."

Claire straightened, both hands gripping the edge of the counter. "Now you know," she agreed. "Now what?"

He grinned. "Well, I am thinking; you do not want Dean to know so, if I do not tell Dean, *tu me does un recompense.*"

"I owe you for not telling Dean?"

"Oui."

"And what do I owe you?"

His grin warmed and his eyes grew heated under half-lowered lids as he leaned so close his breath, had he been breathing, would have stroked her cheek. "Flesh, for one night."

"Just *one* night?"

"One night," he told her, his voice low and promising, "is all I ask for. After that one night, I no longer need to ask."

She turned so she was facing him. He was a comfortable amount taller than she was, unlike Dean who loomed over her, and it would only take a tilt of her head to bring their mouths together. She wanted to push his hair back off his face, run her thumbs down the stubble-rough sides of his jaw, watch everything he felt dance across his expression as she slid her arms up under his sweater. She didn't understand the attraction, but she couldn't deny it. "Think highly of yourself, don't you?"

"Not without reason."

Someone, or something giggled. She frowned, stepped back, and almost saw a flash of purple disappear beneath the shelf.

"Claire?"

"Forget it, Jacques." Squatting down, she peered at the imp trap. It had been moved from across the mouse hole leaving a tiny opening clear on the left side.

"Then not a night." He dropped down beside her, his knees making no impact with the floor. "An hour. An hour only and I can convince you."

"No, not a night, not an hour." The miniature marshmallows were missing. "Not ten minutes."

"Ten minutes would not be worth the effort. I have no interest in a quick and frenzied pawing."

That drew Claire's attention away from the imp trap. She turned to face the ghost, both brows lifted almost to her hairline.

"D'accord. I will take a quick and frenzied pawing if it is all I

can get. But to be truly intimate with a woman requires a little more time. Give me that time, *cherie,* and you will be like plaster in my hands."

"Putty."

"Pardon?"

Even though she knew he'd take it the wrong way, Claire couldn't stop herself from smiling. "Like putty in your hands."

"Oui. Putty." His accent softened the word, made it malleable. He leaned close again. "Are you afraid that if we become lovers, it will hold you here?"

"What will hold me here?"

"Passion. Pleasure. Complete . . ." The pause lingered on the edge of being too long, preparing the way for the presentation of each separate syllable. ". . . satisfaction."

Claire blinked.

"Just give me a chance, *cherie.*"

"A chance to do what?"

Feeling as though she'd been caught by her father in a clinch on the rec-room couch, hoping her ears weren't as red as they felt, Claire straightened and noticed for the first time that Jacques floated high enough off the floor so that he looked Dean—who was a good four inches taller—directly in the eye. "He wants me to give him flesh."

Dean shrugged. "If it'll help, there's a leftover pork chop in the fridge."

"Not that kind of flesh!" The ghost looked appalled.

"Beef? Chicken? Fish?"

The suggestions emerged too close together for Jacques to reply, but with each he grew more and more indignant.

"Sausage?"

His image began to flicker. *"Mon Dieu!* Are you so irritating on purpose?"

"Difficult to be that irritating by accident," Claire murmured. The ridiculous list had banished embarrassment. Suddenly realizing that might have been his intent, she took a closer look at Dean and found his expression of solid helpfulness offset by a distinct twinkle behind the glasses.

"I thought you might want to know that Austin's outside," he said. "I opened the back door for him about five minutes ago."

"Any response from Baby?"

"Not yet."

"So you thought she wanted to know, and now she is told." Folding his arms, Jacques regained control of his definition.

"You may go now, *Anglais.* The Keeper and I, we have a private conversation."

"About giving you flesh?"

A finger, fully opaque in the artificial light of the lobby, jabbed at the air inches from Dean's chest. "Do *not* start that again!"

Dean ignored him. When he turned to Claire, the twinkle was gone. "You wouldn't, would you?"

"And why wouldn't she?" Jacques asked matter-of-factly. "She is young, she is healthy, she has needs."

"Jacques!" Her elbow went right through him.

"I only say that since there is no one else, I am here." He turned on Dean, who was shaking his head. "What?"

"You're dead!"

"And you cannot stand the thought of a dead man achieving that which you . . ."

This time Claire protested with power.

"OW!" Pulling himself together, the ghost turned to face her. "I have to say, *cherie,* I am not at this moment thrilled by your touch. Obviously, the mood has been broken. I will leave you now but, you have my word as a Labaet, I will keep my part of the bargain until we have a chance to speak again."

"What did he mean," Dean asked as Jacques vanished, "about keeping his part of the bargain?"

Claire shrugged, running her thumb along the edge of the counter. "Who knows what he thinks."

A LIE! A LIE!
A PREVARICATION. WE CAN'T USE IT.
SAYS WHO?
THE RULES.
DAMN THE RULES.
Heated air, redolent of sulfur and brimstone, gusted up into the furnace room. DON'T THINK WE HAVEN'T TRIED.

Before Dean could answer, Claire lifted her head and actually noticed what he was wearing. "Are you going out?"

He shoved his hands into the pockets of his faded, leather football jacket. "Yeah. I meet some friends from back home every Saturday night." He hesitated, then continued in a rush. "Do you want to come, then?"

For a moment, she thought it might be nice to spend an uncomplicated evening with Dean and his friends, going to another pub, listening to music, with Dean and his very young friends, in another dark, smoky, crowded, overpriced pub, listening to overloud music not being sung by a vampire. "Thanks for asking, but no thanks."

"My friends wouldn't mind."

A LIE!
IN KINDNESS.
BUT . . .
OH, GIVE IT UP.

Claire hid a smile. "It's okay. I've got things to take care of."

"I, uh, heard Ms. Moore's van leave."

He was far too nice to look as relieved by her refusal as she knew he felt. "It's her last night at the pub."

"The stalker?"

"I think he got scared off."

He thought, as she'd intended him to, that she meant he'd been scared off when he'd been chased away from the vans. "Will you be okay alone?"

"I'll be fine."

"And what on earth do you think you could do if I wasn't?" remained mostly silent.

Should I have insisted? Dean asked himself as he paused halfway down the front stairs to let his eyes grow accustomed to the dark. From what he understood of Claire's life, it had to be a lonely existence, constantly on the move with few opportunities to make real friends.

A sudden vision of Claire sitting at the Portsmouth with the guys and Kathy, listening to them swap stupid mainlander stories, picking up her round of beer in turn, stopped him from going back into the lobby. They wouldn't be rude. In fact, they'd be glad to see another woman in the group, but she wouldn't fit in.

And she wouldn't try to, he admitted. *Maybe you should stay with her, boy. Keep that dead freak away.* Wondering just how Jacques knew what Claire's needs were, he turned toward the office window in time to see her drop to her knees and out of sight. *Oh, man, not the imps again.*

Fists in his pockets, he continued down to the sidewalk, navigating the uneven brick steps with the ease of familiarity, and made his way out to the bus stop on King Street without looking back. What with scraping the front counter and refinishing the dining room floor, not to mention the weirder stuff, it had been some long week and he wasn't up to another argument about the types of vermin infesting the guesthouse. Now that he thought about it, he was really looking forward to a nice, normal evening, finding out how many mainlanders it took to screw in a light-bulb, and watching George drink until he puked.

Claire sat back on her heels and glared at the trap. After replacing the marshmallow pieces, she'd moved the cage back over the hole and was now trying, unsuccessfully, to convince herself that an imp, or imps, had taken the bait without being caught. Unfortunately, the evidence suggested one of two possibilities and she didn't care much for either. The first implied that the power she'd wrapped about the trap wasn't strong enough to hold even a minor piece of evil, and the second involved her being wrong from the start.

"And I just don't think I can handle multicolored mice," she muttered, getting to her feet. Had Austin been privy to her thoughts he'd have reminded her that what she *really* couldn't handle was being wrong but, since he wasn't, the emphasis remained on the mice.

"Still, they've been breeding around a major accident site for generations," she allowed as she locked the lobby door—Sasha and Dean both had keys and if by some strange stroke of misfortune any guests happened to wander by, she'd hear the knocker. "I suppose they should consider themselves lucky if color is the only variation. I mean," she added to no one in particular, entering her own suite, "look at the platypus."

Picking her way through the sitting room in the dark, she tripped only twice, and was feeling pretty pleased with herself when she flicked on the bathroom light.

"Sweet heaven."

At first she thought the letters on the mirror had been written in blood, but then she noticed the crushed remains of her favorite lipstick in the sink. Claw marks on the metal case and a perfect, three-fingered, *Jaded Rose* handprint pressed onto the porcelain identified the graffiti artist beyond a shadow of a doubt. Imps.

Or at least, imp.

This was exactly the sort of petty, destructive mischief they excelled at.

"Mice. Ha!" Claire exchanged a triumphant look with her reflection. "This will prove my point once and for all. I'll just go and get . . ."

Then the actual words sank in.

Someone, it said, in barely legible cursive script, *needs to get laid.*

"You'll go and get who?" her reflection asked, eyes faintly glowing.

"Shut up." Jacques would never give her a moment's peace. Dean would be so horribly embarrassed she'd feel like a slut. And Austin—Claire was only glad that Austin hadn't been around to hear Jacques declare she had needs. Obviously, she couldn't show the message to any of them. And there wasn't anyone else. "Nuts! Nuts! Nuts!" At her last declamation, she slapped both hands down on the counter.

A pair of dusty guest soaps turned into a pair of equally dusty pecans.

"Temper, temper," warned her reflection, shaking an amused finger behind the lines of lipstick.

"You think this is temper?" Claire muttered, reaching past the seepage and pulling power. One hand shading her eyes from the flash of light, she ran a clean cantrip over the mirror. "Wait until I catch that imp." Her lip curled. "Then you'll see temper."

Later that night, Dean let himself into his apartment through the door in the area. The evening had been no different than any other Saturday evening but still, something had been missing. It no longer seemed to be enough that these people were his best friends, his link to home in the midst of those who'd never heard of Joey's Juice and couldn't seem to figure out how to wipe their feet.

Undressing in the dark, he lowered himself carefully onto the bed, locked his hands behind his head, and stared at nothing, wondering why the world outside the guest house suddenly seemed smaller than the world within. Wondering why a hole to Hell and an evil Keeper seemed less important than the Keeper sleeping overhead. Wondering why the world had started to spin. . . .

Because you drank a whole lot of beer, his bladder reminded him.

When his bladder turned out to be the only organ offering solutions, Dean surrendered to sleep.

Still later, after letting herself in and relocking the front door, Sasha Moore paused by the counter and listened, separating out the individual rhythms of four lives. One, upstairs. Too slow and unchanging for mortal sleep. Two, downstairs. Slow and regular, a man sleeping the sleep of the just and the intoxicated. Three, close by. A Keeper, tossing restlessly in an empty bed. The vampire acknowledged temptation, then shook her head. Keepers took themselves far too seriously; regardless of how it turned out, she'd never hear the end of it. Four . . . She smiled and raised an ivory hand, a greeting to another hunter in the night. A greeting between equals.

A rustling, a scrabbling of claws on wood, lifted her gaze to the ceiling. "Mice," she murmured.

"That's what I keep telling them," Austin agreed from the shadows.

The temperature dropped overnight, October arriving with the promise of winter. By morning, the air in Claire's bedroom had chilled to an uncomfortable sixty-two degrees. She put it off for as long as she could, monitoring the seepage levels from under the covers, but she finally ran out of excuses to stay in bed. When her bare feet hit the floor, she sucked her breath in through her teeth. Nothing rose through the brass register except perhaps a sense of anticipation.

"If you think I'm heading in there to open a vent, think again," she muttered. It would be simple enough to temporarily ward off the chill by adjusting her own temperature. Simpler still, since it wasn't likely to warm up any time soon, to put on a second sweater.

Rummaging through the pile of clothes on the floor, she realized she hadn't done laundry since she'd arrived. Fully aware that, in time, she wouldn't think twice about wearing an orange sweater over a purple turtleneck with navy sweats—as they aged, surviving Keepers grew less and less concerned with how the rest of the world perceived them—Claire tried not to think about how she looked as she shoved dirty clothes into a pillowcase.

"Running away to the circus?" Austin asked testily, emerging from under a carelessly thrown fold of blanket.

"Doing laundry," she told him, jumping off the chair with three socks and a bra she'd found on top of the wardrobe.

He stretched out a foreleg and critically examined a spotless, white paw. "Well, you know, I hadn't wanted to say anything . . ."

"Then don't."

* * *

Hearing Claire descend to the basement, Dean gratefully left off his attempt to fit old lengths of baseboard into the new dimensions of the dining room and followed. To his surprise, he found her stuffing clothes into the washing machine. Taking in the layered sweaters, he realized she had no intention of turning up the heat. He couldn't say that he blamed her. "Did you, uh, need help with that, then?" he asked when she turned and flashed him an inquiring glance.

"I can manage, thank you."

About to mention that she should sort her colors, Dean forced himself to hold his tongue. Maybe Keepers never ended up with gray underwear.

She looked different. For the first time since she'd arrived, he was seeing her without makeup. Without the artfully defined shadows, she seemed younger, softer, less ready to take on the world. A sudden image of her riding into battle in the traditional, Saturday-afternoon-Western warpaint made him smile.

"What?" she demanded.

"Nothing."

"If it's the clothes, I don't usually dress like this."

"I hadn't noticed." Except he had. "You mean the sweaters." He pulled at the waistband of his Hyperion Oil Fields sweatshirt. "I could go out and buy some electric heaters."

Claire's eyes narrowed. Obviously Augustus Smythe had never used electric heaters, or there'd be some already in the building. "No. Thank you." She closed the lid of the washing machine, started the cycle, and turned to face the furnace room door. "I'll go in and adjust the vents."

"I wasn't criticizing."

"I never said you were."

"I understand why you don't want to go in."

Her chin lifted. "Who says I don't want to go in?"

"The sweaters . . ."

"I was referring to the color combination."

"The colors?"

"That's right. But since you're cold . . ."

"I never said I was cold."

"Then why offer to buy heaters?"

"I thought you were cold."

"I never said I was cold."

"No, but the sweaters . . ."

"Oh, I see. Well, if I can't put on a sweater without people thinking I can't do my job, maybe we'd just better get a little heat in here. And no, I don't need you to go with me," she added, crossing to the turquoise steel door. The chains were heavier than they looked and made ominous rattling sounds as she dragged them free, indignation lending strength. About to drop them to one side, a large hand reached over her shoulder and effortlessly lifted them from her grip.

"I'll hang these here, on the hooks, where they go."

"Fine." Claire pressed her right palm against the steel, a little surprised at how warm it was until she realized that her exposed skin had chilled to the point where an Eskimo Pie would've seemed toasty. In fact, she could feel the heat radiating off of Dean and he was standing . . .

She turned to face him, and her eyes widened.

. . . rather temptingly close. Her breathing quickened as her hindbrain made a detailed suggestion. *"Hey! Get out of my head!"*

WHAT MAKES YOU THINK YOU DIDN'T COME UP WITH THAT ON YOUR OWN?

"Most people's joints don't bend that way."

THEY DON'T?

"Get out!"

"Instead of lurking around down here, go up to the dining room and let me know when there's heat coming through the register."

Dean hesitated. "You'll be all right, then?"

"Augustus Smythe adjusted these vents for fifty years and he was . . ."

The realization of what Augustus Smythe was, or at least of what he'd become, filled the narrow space between them.

". . . a Cousin," Claire finished. "I am a Keeper." She turned back toward the door and took a deep breath. Then another.

"They say that as long as it's sealed, it's perfectly safe."

Tapping her nails against the heavy latch handle, she snorted. "Who says?"

"You did."

Hard to argue with such an unquestionable source. "Just yell down the register," she said, shoving open the furnace room door. "I'll hear you." She paused, one foot over the threshold. All things considered, it might be best to tie up loose ends before she went any farther. "Dean?"

"Yeah, Boss?"

"Thanks."

Anyone else would've asked her what for, and then she'd have had to face Hell with a caustic comment still warming her lips. Anyone else.

He smiled. "You're welcome."

By mid-morning the hotel had warmed about ten degrees, Dean had discovered how the pieces of baseboard fit together, Austin had eaten breakfast, made his morning visit to Baby, and gone back to bed, and Claire had been forced to spend half an hour leaning over the dryer.

"I don't understand," Dean had said earnestly, checking out the machine after the third time it had shut off. "It's never done this before." After a moment's rummaging behind the switch with a variety of screwdrivers, he'd replaced the cover and added, "There's nothing wrong. Try again."

The dryer had worked perfectly while they were there, but the moment Claire had stepped off the basement stairs and out into the first floor hall, it had stopped. "Never mind," she'd grumbled as Dean moved back toward the stairs, "it's my laundry and you've got things to do. I'll just grab a cup of coffee and go watch it run."

"And that'll keep it going?"

"It should."

And it had.

The imp had, no doubt, been switching off the dryer and, with her standing guard, had now gone off to find other ways to irritate, leaving behind no proof she could use. Weighing the alternatives while her clothes dried, Claire figured that the imp must've come through before Augustus Smythe. Or very soon after he arrived, before he began using up the seepage as it emerged.

She wished she knew how long it had taken, how many accidental uses, before it became habit. It would have been so much easier for him to use the seepage—power just lying around for the taking—than to reach into the narrow area of the possibilities that the Cousins could access.

How many excuses had it taken before he didn't bother making excuses anymore? Before he used what he wanted. And every time he used it, it corrupted him a little more.

Which explained why Dean, who'd lived next to Hell for eight months, hadn't been affected. He couldn't use the power. At least Claire hoped he hadn't been affected. "I shudder to think of what he must've been like if he's this nice *after* Hell's been working on him."

She'd cleared the seepage twice, and she'd only been there a week. They were admittedly low levels of seepage, nothing like the buzz she'd felt on her first night, but she'd still have to start being a lot more careful.

When her laundry was finally dry, she'd lost three socks and gained a child's T-shirt. Claire would've liked to have placed the blame on Hell, but this particular irritant was the result of human error. Given the metaphysical design flaw inherent in clothes dryers, those in the know were fond of pointing out how the loss of an occasional sock was nothing to complain about considering the odds against everything else coming back.

"Jacques, get away from the window!" Running her blade along a piece of molding, Claire scraped off a long curl of medium green paint. The counter had probably never been that actual color—when scraping paint there always had to be a medium green layer. "Anyone walking by and looking up can see right through you."

"Perhaps they would not see me at all. The vampire-hunter, he did not see me."

"He didn't believe in ghosts."

"I do not see why that should matter."

"Neither do I, but it does."

"If you gave me flesh, it would not happen," he pointed out reasonably.

"Just move," she told him without looking up.

Jacques glanced down toward the sidewalk, opened his mouth to say something, and shook his head. Floating closer, he sat down on the floor with his back against the outside wall. "So, if someone who believed walked by . . . ?"

"They'd see the sunlight streaming right through you."

"And that would be a problem because?"

"People who see ghosts seldom keep the information to themselves." Carefully working stripper-soaked steel wool carefully along the grain of the wood, she wrinkled her nose at the smell. "And I don't feel like dealing with tabloid reporters."

"I know reporters, but what are tabloids?"

"Sleazy newspapers that deal in cheap sensationalism. Hundred-year-old woman has lizard baby, that sort of thing."

"Is that not what Keepers deal in?"

"No."

"Hole to Hell in basement?"

"It's not the same."

"Woman sleeps for fifty years?"

Shifting her weight back onto her heels, she turned and glared at him. "You know what your problem is? You never know when to quit!"

He cocked an eyebrow and spread his hands. "*Evidentment.* If I knew when to quit, I would not be haunting this place, and if I were not haunting this place, I would not have met you. *Voila,* all is for the best." Wrapping a weightless grip around Claire's fingers, he leaned forward and murmured, "Have I ever told you how sexy I find big, pink rubber gloves?"

She laughed in spite of herself, pulling her hand back through his. "You're unbelievable." The laughter vanished when he started to fade. "Jacques?"

"If you do not believe," he told her mournfully, "you cannot see me."

"Stop it!"

Rematerializing, he grinned triumphantly. "You do not want to lose me."

Lips pressed tightly together, Claire bent back over the bit of unstripped molding on the counter. Her search for the Historian had ended up at a medieval bazaar selling Japanese electronics, and her hour with Sara had brought her no closer to an answer. She'd have to study both ends of the balance if she wanted to figure it out and that meant spending time next to the pit. Since she'd been in the furnace room once already today and since stripping the counter had been her idea . . .

She'd like to see it finished before she left. She'd like to see the dining room finished, too—wallpaper, trim, blinds, maybe new light fixtures.

This is nuts. The steel wool stopped moving. When she closed this site, need would summon her to another. It might be in Kingston—there were, after all sixty thousand people in the city and townships and population density was directly proportional to how often a Keeper was needed—but it might be across the continent. Or on another continent entirely. *I am not getting attached to this place.*

"Claire? I do not want to lose you either. Please, I am sorry. Come back to me."

"I haven't gone anywhere." The silence clearly stated he didn't believe her. She shifted from knee to knee and finally sighed, "Could I give you flesh to help me finish this?"

"Non." Although she didn't turn to look she could hear the relieved smile in his voice. "I can take flesh only to give you pleasure."

"It'd give me pleasure to have some help with this."

"It does not work that way."

She sighed again, resting her forehead on the edge of a shelf. "Why," she asked dramatically, "am I not surprised?"

Sasha Moore checked out that evening, paying for her room in cash. "Will I see you in the spring?" she asked, effortlessly swinging her heavy duffel bag up onto one shoulder.

Claire stared at her, aghast. "The spring?"

"Comes after winter. The snow melts. The dog crap lies exposed on the lawn."

"I won't be here in the spring."

"I hope you're not expecting old Gus to come back. He's blown this popsicle stand for good." The vampire paused at the door. "Oh, yeah; Dean's memory of me's going to get a bit foggy. I don't like to leave too many specifics behind." Ebony brows rose and fell suggestively. When it became obvious that Claire was not going to respond to this mild provocation, she snapped pale fingers. "Hey, Keeper!"

Wandering thoughts jerked back to the lobby. "What?"

"Domo arigato on that lifesaving thing. I know, I know, you'd do it for anyone, but this time you did it for me. In return, can I offer you these words of wisdom, culled from a long and eventful existence? You needn't bother answering 'cause I'm going to anyway.

"First of all, at the risk of sounding like Kenny Rogers, God forbid, you should make the best of the hand you've been dealt. Second, a genuine, unselfish offer of help is the most precious gift you'll ever be given. And third, remember that you never have to travel alone . . ." Teeth flashed. ". . . hitchhikers make a handy protein supplement when on the road. Thanks for coming, you've been a wonderful audience, maybe we can do this again sometime—less the asshole trying to kill me, of course."

Claire stared at the closed door for a moment, then jerked around to the window as the red van roared down the driveway, honked twice, and disappeared into the night.

"Is Ms. Moore gone?"

Dean's voice seemed to come from very far away. She nodded, without turning.

"Did she say if she'd be back in the spring?"

It was only just October, not even winter yet, spring was impossibly far away. "I won't be here in the spring. I'll have finished up and moved on."

"Okay." That wasn't what he'd asked, but since it was clearly on Claire's mind . . . "That, uh, book you've got soaking? It's starting to stink up the fridge."

"It needs to soak a little longer."

"But . . ."

"I need that information, Dean, and I'm not going to risk losing it because you don't like the way it smells."

"Is Claire coming out for breakfast?"

"In a minute," Austin told him, staring alternately at his empty dish and Dean. "She has to have another shower first. The Historian appears to have led her through an area populated by ruminants."

"Say what?"

"She crawled through some cow shit. Are you going to feed me, or what?"

Weighing the bag of geriatric kibble in one hand, Dean scratched the back of his neck with the other. "There should be a lot more in this."

"Not necessarily. I told the mice they could help themselves. With any luck we'll run out on the weekend when the vet's closed, and you'll have to feed me something decent."

The next morning, Dean handed Claire a cup of coffee and watched in concern as she slumped against the sink and stuffed a whole piece of toast into her mouth. "Manage to avoid the cow shit this morning?" he asked hesitantly.

Claire snorted, blowing crumbs onto the spotless stainless steel. "This morning," she said, and paused to swallow, "I crawled through the cow. Same end result though," she added after a moment.

"You know, lady, I got a cousin who does renovations. Not too expensive," the locksmith assured her as he screwed down the new plate. He nodded toward the charred, smoke-damaged interior of room six. "Why leave a room in that condition when you can fix it up and use it, that's what I say. You gotta spend money to make money, you know?"

"We're not that busy. Which," she added dryly, "is a good thing. I called you four days ago."

"Hey, I couldn't have got here faster if you'd been Old Nick himself."

WANNA BET?

The locksmith pulled bushy brows down toward his nose. "Did you say something?"

"No."

"Thought I heard . . . Never mind. You know, you don't have to stay with me. I can just come down when I finish up."

"Like I said," Claire told him, keeping the glamour centered over the actual contents of the room, "we're not that busy."

"Oh, I get it. Lonely, eh? I know how you feel; some days when I don't leave the shop, I'm ready to climb the walls by four, four-thirty. No one to talk to, you know? What was that?" He leaned around the door, staring at the floor by the curtained window, then settled back on his heels, shaking his head. "It sorta looked like a bright blue mouse."

"Trick of the shadows," Claire said tightly. It figured that the locksmith would see the imp when neither Dean nor Austin ever had.

A few moments later, his weight on the newly installed doorknob, the locksmith heaved himself to his feet and flicked the open flange with his free hand. "Quite the secondary locking system. I guess you can't be too careful about this kind of thing, eh? I mean, one tourist wanders in here, hurts himself on a bit of loose board and the next thing you know, you're being sued."

Peering through the glamour, Claire checked that Aunt Sara remained undisturbed by all the banging. "If a tourist wandered in here, being sued would be the least of my concerns. But you needn't worry, this is only a temporary measure."

"So you are going to fix it?"

"Sooner or later."

"Hopefully sooner, eh?" He pulled the door closed and nodded with satisfaction as the lock clicked into place. "When the time comes, and you need some help, don't forget my cousin."

Claire had a vision of the locksmith and his cousin facing down the hordes of Hell. It was strangely comforting.

The ink soaked out of the site journal had turned the onions blue. The brine had been absorbed and the whole thing smelled like pickled sewage. With a cheese sauce.

When Claire opened the plastic container, Austin left the building.

Breathing shallowly through her mouth, she used a fork to

tease apart the pages. The process had been partially successful. The few pages of Augustus Smythe's notes now legible made it clear he knew an incredible number of dirty limericks but offered no other useful information.

The first four pages after his summoning remained stuck together in a glutinous blue mass.

"One more week should do it," Claire sniffed at Dean, peeling another three onions and dropping them into fresh brine.

"Great," Dean gasped. He snuck a look at the card.

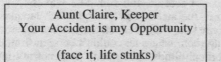

Aunt Claire, Keeper
Your Accident is my Opportunity

(face it, life stinks)

Later, he threw out the fork.

"This is the sixth morning in a row she's come out of that wardrobe looking wiped. Two days ago, she fell asleep in that old armchair up in room six, and yesterday she didn't have enough energy to take the chains off the furnace room door."

Austin lifted his head off his paws and gazed across the dining room at Claire, who'd fallen asleep with her cheek on an egg salad sandwich. "Did you take them off for her?"

"No. I figured if she was too tired to open the door, she was too tired to face Hell."

"I've said all along you're more than just a pretty face. What did Claire say?"

Dean grinned. "That I was an interfering, idiotic bystander."

"That's all?" The cat snorted. "She must've been tired."

"What's happening in that wardrobe, Austin?"

"From the steely-eyed determination on her face when she goes in, I'd say she's trying too hard. The other side has kind of zen thing going, you can't force it."

"So she's doing it to herself, then?"

"Well, I don't think she'd have chosen to fight her way through those pre-Christmas sales this morning but, yeah, essentially."

"If there's anything I can do, will you let me know?"

"Sure."

As Austin laid his head back down, Dean's concern evolved into full-blown worry. Any other morning, that question would've brought a suggestion that he feed the cat.

* * *

"What have you done, that Claire suddenly try so hard to find this Historian?"

"I didn't do anything," Dean told him, getting a can of oven cleaner out from under the sink. "I'm not the one exposing myself to Mrs. Abrams."

"I do not expose myself. She has no business to be in the parking lot to peer through the windows while you attach the blinds. I vanish the moment I see her."

"But did she see you?"

"She did not scream and run. She waves to you, puts two thumbs up in the air, and leaves quietly." Jacques pressed his back up against the wall between the two windows, the one place in the dining room where he couldn't be seen from outside when the new vertical blinds were open. "It is not my fault she is always looking in."

Dean might have believed him had he not sounded so defensive. "You're careless. You don't care how much trouble you cause."

"I am causing trouble?"

"That's what I said."

"So, you say it is my fault that Claire tries so much harder to leave us?"

Shrugging, Dean dropped to his knees in front of the stove. "If the shroud fits."

"And what does that mean, if the shroud fits?"

"It means you're always all over her. Give me flesh, give me flesh." His accent was a passable imitation of the ghost's. "You're too pushy."

Jacques disappeared and reappeared sitting on the floor behind the peninsula. "I am too pushy? You are too . . . too . . . too nice!"

"Too nice?"

"*Oui.* You are like mushy white bread and mayonnaise. *And . . .*" He folded his arms triumphantly. ". . . you are always cleaning things. If I could, I would leave also."

"Then leave. Claire said she could send you on."

"And leave her with you? She would be too bored in a week."

"Lecher."

"Monk."

"Bottom feeder."

"Betty Crocker."

"Stereotype!"

Before Jacques, reeling under a direct hit, could come up with a response, the ka-thud, ka-thud of a galloping animal filled the house, growing overwhelmingly louder the closer it came. The glasses in the cupboard began to chime as the vibrations brought their edges together. "Something is out of the pit," he moaned as Austin threw himself around the corner and into the kitchen.

The noise stopped.

He glared down at the cat. "That was you? But you weigh only what, two kilos?"

"Can we discuss my weight another time," Austin snapped. "Claire's in trouble!"

TROUBLE IS GOOD.
BUT WE DIDN'T CAUSE IT.
SO?
Hell sounded sulky. IT'S THE PRINCIPLE OF THE THING.
WE DON'T HAVE PRINCIPLES!
OH, YEAH.

EIGHT

Jacques slammed into an invisible barrier at the door to Claire's room. The impact flung him backward into the sitting room, past Dean, past Austin, right through the bust of Elvis.

"Thang you, thang you vera much."

"Nobody asked you," he snarled at the plaster head. "*Anglais!* I cannot follow you without an anchor."

Just on the far side of the threshold, Dean rocked to a halt and spun around. "An anchor?"

"*Oui.* Come and get *la coussin,* the cushion." His fingers swept through the horsehair stuffing. "Take it with you to Claire's room."

"You don't have an anchor in here?"

"Did I not just say that? And wipe that *stupide* grin off your face! You think I would not allow Claire her privacy?"

Actually, he did. But he was too nice a guy to say so. And the stupid grin seemed to want to stay where it was. Three long strides and he snatched up the cushion. Three more and he was back in Claire's room, Jacques by his side.

"About time you goons got here," Austin growled, pacing back and forth in front of the wardrobe.

Except for the cat and the furniture, the room was empty.

"Where's the boss?" Dean demanded, throwing the cushion down on the bed.

"Where do you think?"

Three heads, one living, one dead, one feline, turned toward the wardrobe.

"How do you know she is in trouble?" Jacques asked. "She goes every morning to search for the Historian. Why is this morning different?"

"She's been gone too long," Austin told them. "No matter how long she's in there, she's never gone more than half an hour out here."

Dean checked his watch. It was almost nine-fifteen. Which

didn't tell him anything except the time. "Maybe she's taking longer because she found something."

"Sure, look on the bright side." He shoved a paw under the bottom of the wardrobe door and hooked it open an inch or two. "Listen."

"*Oui?* I hear nothing."

"That," growled the cat, "is because you're talking."

A moment later, the ghost shrugged. "I still hear nothing."

Then faintly, very faintly, just barely audible over the sound of Austin's tail hitting the floor, came the roar of a large and very angry animal.

The two men exchanged an identical glance.

"You are sure that is not Claire?" Jacques asked.

"Yes! Mostly," Austin amended after a moment's thought. "Either way, it can't be good. Dean has to go in and get her."

"Okay." Dean settled his glasses more firmly on his face and took a step forward.

"*Un moment.* You do not go alone, *Anglais.*"

"Yes, he does." Austin interrupted. "You have to weigh more than forty kilos to go on this ride; it's one of those stupid child safety features. Unfortunately, it also bars cats and ghosts, so I'm afraid Dean's it."

Jacques drew himself up to his full height, plus about four inches of air space. "If he carries the cushion, I go through with him."

"It doesn't work that way!" Austin directed a couple of angry licks in the direction of his shoulder. "And if it did, *I'd* be going through with him."

Dean reached past the cat and opened the wardrobe door. It was dark inside, much darker than it should have been. Another distant roar drifted out into the room. He squared his shoulders, flexing the muscles across his back, and bounced a time or two on the balls of his feet. Claire needed his help. Cool. "What do I do?"

"Step up inside and pull the door closed behind you, but don't latch it."

"Why not?"

"Only idiots lock themselves in wardrobes." His tone suggested any idiot ought to know that. "Once you're in there, think about Claire. Holding an image of her in your mind, walk toward the back wall. When you get to where you're going, keep thinking of her."

"Where am I going?"

"I have no idea. Once you arrive, look and listen for anything out of the ordinary. She'll be in the middle of it. Oh, and don't eat or drink while you're in there. Nothing. Zip. Zilch. Nada."

About ready to step inside, Dean paused. "Why not?" he asked again.

"Did you not read when you were a kid?"

"I, uh, played a lot of hockey."

Austin snorted. "I guessed. If you eat or drink inside the wardrobe, it holds you there."

The door half closed, he stuck his head out into the room. "How do I come back?"

"Think of this room and go through any opaque door."

"But do not return here without Claire," Jacques told him, "or I will make of your life a misery."

Dean accepted the warning in the spirit it had been given. "Don't worry. I'll save her."

As the wardrobe door swung shut, Austin leaped up onto the bed. "I hate waiting."

"You know," Jacques said thoughtfully, drifting over to join him. If you are wrong and she does not need saving, she is going to be not happy with you."

"Excuse me? If I am *wrong*?"

The inside of the wardrobe smelled faintly of mothballs. Dean found it a comforting smell as he turned away from the door and the argument gaining volume on the other side. It reminded him of the closet in the spare room at his grandfather's house. Unable to see, he took a tentative step forward, expecting, in spite of everything to whack his face on the back wall. Another step, and another. Still no wall.

A new odor began drifting in over the mothballs.

His grandfather's pipe tobacco?

He stopped and closed his eyes, suddenly remembering that he was supposed to be thinking of Claire, not of home.

"Holding an image of her in your mind . . ."

It was hard to hold a single image, so he cycled through the highlights of their short association as he took another step. Claire walking into the kitchen that first morning; Claire explaining how magic worked; Claire going up the spiral stairs to the attic. The smell of the pipe tobacco began to fade. She was his boss; she was a Keeper; she had a really irritating way of assuming she knew best or, more precisely, that he knew nothing at all.

When he opened his eyes, he could see a gray light in the distance.

Approximately thirty-seven steps later—he wasn't sure how many he'd taken before he'd started counting—he stood on Princess Street looking down the hill toward the water. Prepared for the strangest possible environment, he was a little disappointed to find himself in a bad copy of the city he'd just left. Everything was vaguely out of proportion, the street had been paved with cobblestones, and, although there were a few parked cars, there was no traffic. The half dozen or so people in sight paid no attention to him.

He could hear church bells in the distance and the cry of gulls circling high overhead.

There was no sign of Claire.

Hoping for a clue, he pulled out the card.

> Aunt Claire, Keeper
> Your Accident is my Opportunity
>
> (could be worse, could be raining)

The skies opened up, and it began to pour. Dean stuffed the card back into his wallet, noting that magic had a very basic sense of humor.

Fortunately, he seemed to have passed from October into August. The air was warm, and the rain was almost tepid. Pushing wet hair back off his face, he drew in a deep lungful of air and frowned at yet another familiar smell. Hoping he hadn't screwed everything up by thinking of home, he started running downhill toward the harbor. *Look and listen for anything out of the ordinary,* Austin had told him. Well, as far as he knew, there were no saltwater harbors on the Great Lakes.

It wasn't just a saltwater harbor. Signal Hill rose across the narrows where the Royal Military College should have been. Massive docks butted up against a broad thoroughfare and along the far side of it were the historic properties that should've been clustered around the Dartmouth ferry dock in Halifax.

"Okay. This is weird." But so far it didn't seem dangerous. Even the rain was letting up.

There were ships at nearly all the docks, most of them clippers and brigantines, but he saw at least two modern vessels as well. So which were out of the ordinary? While he stood there, undecided, someone bumped him from behind, muttered an apology, and kept moving.

Dean turned to see a heavily muscled man in an old-fashioned naval uniform, carrying a human leg over one massive shoulder, weave his way through the crowd on the thoroughfare and enter a windowless green building on the other side. The sign on the building read "Man-made Sausages."

No one else, from the little girl selling matches to the one-eyed, peg-legged street artist with a hook, seemed to think anything of it.

"Don't eat or drink while you're in there. . . ."

"Not much danger of that," he muttered. "I'll just find the boss. . . ."

From somewhere in town came the enraged roar of an Industrial Light and Magic special effect followed closely by a woman's scream.

"Claire!"

His work boots slipping on the wet cobblestones, Dean raced away from the harbor through a rabbit warren of narrow streets, all of them steeply angled regardless of the direction he was running.

The roar sounded again. Closer.

Just when he thought he was hopelessly lost, he pounded out from between two empty storefronts and into the intersection at Brock and King, across from the old city library.

In the center of the intersection, stomping jerkily about like one of the old stop-motion models, was a dinosaur. A T-Rex. Off to one side, were the squashed and nearly unidentifiable remains . . .

Dean clutched at his chest.

. . . of a 1957 Corvette.

"Oh, God, no!" Eyes wide behind his glasses, he staggered forward, hands outstretched. He was almost at the wreck when he felt the ground move, felt hot breath on the back of his neck, and had the sudden uncomfortable feeling he was a secondary character in a Saturday morning movie matinee.

He dove out of the way just in time. Rolled immediately thereafter to avoid being smacked by the massive tail. Leaped over a crumpled fender . . .

Sitting in the library, surrounded by reference material and a few of the more pungent if less literate clientele, Claire heard someone call her name. Loudly. One could almost say desperately.

The voice, even *in extremis,* sounded very familiar.

She'd been inside since the Historian's new pet had shown up, figuring sooner or later it would get bored and wander off and, if it didn't, she'd just go back out through the library door and home. Then, looking for a map, she'd gotten engrossed in the books. She had no idea how long she'd been in there.

"CLAIRE!"

"Dean?" Running her tongue over dry lips, she walked over to the window, wondering how the Historian had been able to copy Dean's voice so exactly. She felt her jaw actually drop when she realized she was hearing the original. "Dean!"

Had the T-Rex been animated better, Dean knew he'd have been dead and partially digested by now. Dodging a grotesque, chickenlike peck of the huge head, he found himself at the foot of the library steps.

The massive tail whipped around.

He jumped, cleared the tail, made a bad landing, stumbled back, and fell.

About a dozen stairs behind and above him, he heard the library door open and, at the same time, a small herd of pigs appeared on the other side of the intersection squealing loud enough to wake the dead.

Or attract the attention of the dinosaur.

As T-Rex lumbered toward the pork, something grabbed Dean by the shirt and tried to haul him backward up the stairs with no notable success. Before the pressure of the seams across his armpits cut off all circulation in his arms, he managed to get his feet under him and stand.

Claire released both handfuls of fabric as he turned to face her. Two steps apart, they were eye to eye. She went up one more step. "What are you *doing* here?"

Struggling to catch his breath, Dean gasped, "I came in to save you."

"To save me? Oh, for . . . Whose bright idea was that?"

Since she was obviously not thrilled by the thought of a rescue attempt, he squared his shoulders. "Mine."

"Don't be ridiculous," Claire snorted. "It was Austin, wasn't it? That cat is fussier than . . ."

A roar from the T-Rex jerked their attention back into the intersection. Ludicrously small arms raked the air, then it charged.

"Come on!" Grabbing another handful of Dean's shirt, Claire ran for the library door.

"It didn't take long with the pigs."

"That's because they weren't real. Only the Historian can do substance in here, all I can manage is illusion."

"Oh, great, so you've pissed it off?"

"Try to remember who's saving whose ass."

The solid stone steps shuddered as the dinosaur started up after them.

"Think about the bedroom!" Claire yelled as they reached the top step. Still clutching his shirt, she thumbed the latch and dragged him through the door after her.

The wardrobe shuddered to a mighty impact as they flung themselves out into the worried presence of Austin and Jacques.

Breathing heavily, Claire lay where she'd fallen, staring under the bed at a pair of fuzzy bunny slippers that weren't hers. Four paws, propelled by a ten-pound cat, landed on her kidneys and a moment later Austin's face peered into hers from over her right shoulder.

"Are you hurt?"

"I'm fine. I'm just a little thirsty." She rolled over, cradled him in her arms, and sat up. Dean had gotten to his feet and was busy trying to pull his T-shirt back into shape. "What," she asked the cat, "was the idea of sending *him* in after me? If I hadn't shown up in time, he'd have been killed."

"I heard roaring."

"You've heard worse."

"You'd been gone for over an hour."

"I lost track of time. I was reading."

"Reading?" Austin repeated, squirming free and jumping up onto the bed. "You were reading!"

About to mention the dinosaur, Dean's vision suddenly filled with an extreme close-up of a ghost. "Get my cushion," Jacques whispered, "quickly, and we will leave."

"But Claire . . ." Dean whispered back, trying to see around Jacques' translucent body.

"This you cannot rescue Claire from. And as much as I would like my cushion to remain, pick it up. We are leaving."

"I was worried sick and you were *reading?*" Austin repeated.

Something in the cat's tone suddenly got through. Eyes wide, Dean stared at Jacques who nodded frantically toward the cushion.

"It wasn't like that, Austin."

"It wasn't like what? It wasn't like you never even considered my feelings? Is that what it wasn't like?"

Careful not to break into the line of sight between cat and Keeper, Dean scooped up Jacques' anchor and the two of them raced into the sitting room.

"So what was it Claire save you from?" Jacques asked as they slowed.

Dean shrugged, the material stretched by Claire's hands riding on his shoulders like tiny wings. "A dinosaur."

"A what?"

"A very big carnivorous lizard."

"Ha! If I can go through the wardrobe, she would not have to rescue *me* from a big lizard. She would not have to rescue a real man."

"Real men admit it when they need help."

"Since when?"

"I think it started around the mid-eighties."

"Ah. Well, it did not start with me. I would have did what I went into the wardrobe to do."

"You would have *done* what you went into the wardrobe to do."

"That," said Jacques, staring down his nose at the living man, "is what I said."

"Okay." Dean half-turned toward the bedroom, gesturing with the hand holding the cushion. "If you're so brave, go back in there."

Austin's voice drifted out through the open bedroom door. ". . . consider more important than . . ."

Jacques looked thoughtful. "How big did you say was that lizard?"

Later, after tempers had cooled and apologies had been offered and accepted, Austin rested his head on Claire's shoulder and murmured thoughtfully, "Maybe it had nothing to do with either of us. Maybe it only had to do with Dean."

Claire stopped halfway across the sitting room and shifted her hold on the cat so she could see his face. "What are you saying?"

"Maybe he *needed* to go into the wardrobe; to begin tempering."

"Tempering?" Her eyes widened as the implication hit her. "Oh, no. Forget it. We don't need another Hero. They're nothing but trouble."

"Granted, but he fits the parameters. No parents, raised by a stern but ethical authority figure, big, strong, naturally athletic, not real bright, modest, good looking . . ."

"Myopic."

"What?"

"He's nearsighted," Claire said, feeling almost light-headed with relief. "Who ever heard of a hero in glasses?"

Austin thought about it for a moment. "Clark Kent?"

"Fake prescription."

"Woody Allen?"

"Get serious."

"Still . . ."

"No." She stepped out into the lobby, closing the door to her suite behind her. Patting the gleaming oak counter with her free hand, she headed for the kitchen. Since the unsuccessful search for the Historian had taken most of her energy, she had no memory of Dean actually finishing the work, but it sure looked good. Granted it would look better if they refinished the lobby floor, painted and recarpeted the stairs . . .

"No. I'm a Keeper, not an interior decorator, I have a job. If I can't find the Historian," she muttered, stepping into the kitchen, "there's more than one way to skin a cat."

Austin jumped out of her arms, landing by the sink and whirling around to face her. "I beg your pardon."

"Sorry."

He washed a shoulder. "I should hope so."

Hardly daring to breathe, Claire pulled the plastic container holding the site journal out of the fridge. Faint fumes could be detected seeping through the seal.

"Do you have to do that now?" Austin demanded. "It's twenty-five to ten. I thought we could have breakfast first."

"I have no intention of opening this when I have food in my stomach."

"That's probably wise, but factoring in wardrobe time, you haven't eaten for nearly twenty-four hours and, more importantly, *I* haven't eaten for two. After you deal with that, you're not going to want to eat for a while." He sneezed. "If ever. It's worse than the last time!"

"But the lid's still on."

"My point exactly." His first leap took him nearly to the dining room. Ears back, he headed for the hall. "If you want me, I'll be doing canine therapy next door. Out of my way, junior."

"Junior?" Dean repeated, flattening against the wall to avoid being run over by the cat. Still shaking his head, he turned the corner into the dining room and coughed. "What in . . ."

"If you want to do something useful," Claire told him a little breathlessly, setting the lid to one side, "you can find me a lifting thingie."

"A what?" he asked, noting with dismay that she was reaching for another fork.

"Something to lift the journal out of the liquid with."

Reminding himself that it was her hotel and she could therefore destroy as much of the cutlery as she wanted, Dean took his least favorite spatula from the spatula section of the second drawer and handed it over. "Did you and Austin work out, well, you know . . ."

"Yes. We did. Just so you don't worry in the future, we always do."

"You guys, you have a interesting relationship."

"Of course we do." She wiped one watering eye on the back of her hand. "He's a cat." Carefully, she slid the spatula under the journal.

Once again, the onions had turned indigo but, this time, there was still about an inch of brine sloshing around in the bottom of the container.

"Boss, I, uh, just wanted to say . . ."

"Not now, Dean."

"Okay." Left hand cupped over his mouth and nose, he walked over to the dining room side of the service counter. "How can you stand over it like that?"

"I do what I have to."

"And what do you have to do, *cherie*?" Jacques asked, appearing by her side.

"Watch." Holding the journal just up out of the brine so that none of the solution splashed out of the container as it drained, Claire carefully used the fork and flicked it open to the first of Augustus Smythe's entries. Although the paper remained a blue barely lighter than the letters, the writing was finally readable.

August 18th, 1942. I find myself summoned to a place called Brewster's Hotel. The most incredible thing has just taken place here. The Keeper who was, and who indeed continues to seal the site, attempted to gain control of the evil for her own uses.

Smiling broadly, Claire glanced up at Dean. "Isn't this wonderful!"

"Wonderful," he agreed, but he was referring to the little crinkle the smile folded into the end of her nose.

Jacques followed his line of sight, and snorted.

I cannot name the Keeper because she remains in the building, continuing to seal the site with her power—which is considerably more than considerable according to the arrogant s.o.b. of an Uncle John who helped defeat her. I hate how some of those guys get off on being "more lineage than thou," as if the universe shines out his ass.

"I guess that answers the Augustus Smythe personality question."

The other Keeper, Uncle Bob, isn't so bad. Is it because Bob's your Uncle?

"And that raises a few more."

Two of them wouldn't have been enough to defeat her if she hadn't . . .

Slipping the fork carefully under the damp paper, trying, in spite of her excitement, to keep breathing shallowly, Claire turned the page.

. . . had trouble wi th th e vir g i . . .

"Oh, no!" One by one, faster and faster, the letters slid off the paper and into the brine. For a moment, Claire stared aghast at a journal of blank pages, then the paper turned into a gelatinous mass and shimmied off the spatula. The resultant splash sprayed a couple of dozen letters up over Claire's hand and sweater.

She staggered back until she hit the edge of the sink, too stunned to speak.

Jumping forward, holding his breath, Dean slapped the lid onto the container. When the seal caught, he hurried around into the kitchen, plucked the spatula from Claire's hand and tipped it almost immediately into the garbage.

"You must wash your hand, *cherie*," Jacques told her. "There is em's upon it. And other letters there upon your sweater."

"I don't think it'll wash out," Dean offered.

Jacques sniffed. "It does not amaze me you also do laundry."

Slowly Claire lifted her hand to her mouth and touched her tongue to one of the letters.

The two men exchanged a horrified glance.

Her lips drew back off her teeth.

"I do not think she is smiling," Jacques murmured.

"Spider parts," Claire snarled. "That rotten, little piece of Hell!"

Both men flinched but nothing happened.

"Don't you see?" Claire's glare jerked from one to the other and back again. "The imp introduced spider parts into the solution. It couldn't have opened the fridge, so it had to have dusted the onions in the bin under the counter just before I started the second batch. It ruined everything!"

OH, VERY WELL DONE.
DO WE *GIVE* COMPLIMENTS?
WE GIVE CREDIT WHERE CREDIT IS DUE.
Hell was silent for a moment. NO, WE DON'T, it said at last.

"Mrs. Abrams is up to something; she's humming. It's an intensely scary sound. Why the long faces?" Austin asked, jumping up on the counter. He sneezed and turned a disgusted glare on the container. "Haven't you finished with that yet?"

"Oh, yes, I've finished with it." Claire pulled off her sweater and handed it to Dean who held it much the same way he'd have held a dead jellyfish. "It's all over. I'm not going to be able to undo what was done because I'll never find out what they did. I can't fix it. I might as well call the locksmith's cousin."

"What are you talking about?"

"Never mind." Moving mechanically, she turned, squirted a little dish detergent into her palm and washed her hands.

When Dean explained what had happened, the cat jumped down to rub against her legs.

"Spider parts can get onto onions a number of different ways; you don't *know* it was an imp. Or even that there is an imp."

"Don't start with me, Austin."

Wisely, he let it drop. "There's still the Historian," he reminded her.

"No, there isn't." She scrubbed her hands dry on a dish towel—which Dean retrieved to hold, two-fingered, with the sweater—and scooped Austin up into her arms. "I can't get out of that town she's built."

"The wardrobe Kingston?" Dean asked.

"Not quite Kingston," Claire told him bitterly. "There's a camp of killer girl guides to the north. When I take the bridge over the narrows and go east, I get hit with a snowstorm I can't get through. To the west there's a military academy. And south . . ."

"Un moment," Jacques interrupted. "Why can you not get by a military academy?"

"It's the men in uni . . ."

Claire put her hand over the cat's muzzle. "They think I'm one of their teachers and I'm AWOL. Attempting that route'll only get me stuffed into an ugly uniform and thrown in the brig until I agree to teach two classes in military history."

"The sea's to the south," Dean said. "What about one of the ships?"

"Get on a ship crewed by the Historian's people?" Claire shook her head. "I don't think so. It'd be faster just to drown myself and save them the trouble."

"Austin thinks you're trying too hard."

"Does he? Interesting he should know so much about a place he's never been." The cat in her arms became very intent on cleaning between the pads of a front paw. "No, it's obvious. I can't get to the Historian, and this . . ." She stared down at the jumble of letters and the sludge of the journal. Her shoulders slumped. ". . . this is less than useless."

"But what about studying the actual, you know, spell?"

"What about it?" She'd been spending an hour with Sara every morning and, so far, she'd developed an allergy to dust. Her ten minutes every other afternoon, the longest she could spend so close to Hell and a running monologue she couldn't shut off, had taught her a number of things she'd have rather not known about the Spanish Inquisition, World War II, and the people who program prime time TV but nothing about how to deal with the unique situation surrounding the site. "It's time I faced it; I'm going to be stuck here for the rest of my life."

After a moment, when the silence in the kitchen stopped ringing to the slam of a metaphorical door, Jacques sighed and said, "Would that be so bad, *cherie*?"

Claire paused on the verge of plunging into a good long wallow in self-pity, realizing he was actually asking, *Would it be so bad to spend the rest of your life here with me?* "You're missing the point, Jacques. If I were needed to seal the hole, doomed to become an eccentric recluse years before my time, it'd be different, at least I'd be doing something useful. Here . . ." A toss of her head managed to take in the entire hotel. ". . . I'm a passive observer, watching a system I can't affect, doing sweet dick all. It's like, like having last year's Cy Young winner sitting in the bullpen in case one of the starters blows a rotator cuff."

The ghost stared at her in bewilderment. "And that means . . . ?"

"It's baseball," Dean told him before Claire could explain. "It means she feels her abilities are wasted here."

"Wasted?" Jacques repeated. "Here where there is a hole to Hell in the basement and *une femme mauvaise* asleep upstairs? If there is something that goes wrong here . . .

DEATH! DESTRUCTION!
A FIVE HUNDRED CHANNEL UNIVERSE!

". . . your, what you call, abilities will not be wasted, *cherie*."

"But if nothing goes wrong . . ."

"We should all be so lucky," Austin interrupted, jumping out of her arms. He checked the dry food in his bowl and sat, tail wrapped around his toes. "You know this place needs to be monitored."

She waved a dismissive hand. "Well, yes, but . . ."

"And since you've been summoned here, this is where you need to be."

"That's the theory, but . . ."

"And since you can't access the information you need to deal with this unique situation, it seems apparent that you're the monitor needed for the site." The catechism complete, he flicked an ear back for punctuation. "If it helps, think of yourself as the world's last line of defense. A missile in a silo, hopefully never to be used. A sub . . ."

"That's enough," Claire told him shortly, breathing heavily through her nose. She'd always believed that the one thing she hated most was being lectured to by the cat, but she'd just discovered she hated being lectured to in front of an audience even more. "It's not helping. You want to know what will?" Whirling around, she yanked a large bag of chocolate chip cookies out of the cupboard. "This. This'll help." Tucking it under her arm, she pushed through Jacques, past Dean, and toward the dubious sanctuary of Augustus Smythe's . . . no, *her* sitting room.

"Perhaps I can see her point," Jacques mused as the distant door slammed. "Although, I am with her in this bull's pen, so at least she is not alone."

"And what am I?" Austin demanded. "Beef byproduct?"

"What is . . ."

"Never mind." Paws against the cupboards, he stood up on his hind legs to watch Dean check the seal on the plastic container.

"I'd better dump the rest of those onions."

"Why bother? You've been eating them for a week." He snickered at Dean's expression. "That which does not kill you makes you stronger."

"Spider parts?" Slightly green, Dean clenched his teeth and tried not to think about it.

"Never ask me what's in a hot dog." The cat dropped back onto four feet. "And if you're going to throw that out, double bag it so it doesn't leak. You'll contaminate the whole dump."

"Will the boss be all right?"

"Oh, sure. Just as soon as she comes to terms with spending the rest of her life standing guard in this hotel."

"Those are not easy terms," Jacques murmured reflectively. "To haunt this not very popular hotel is not how I myself thought to spend eternity. I will go to her."

"Hey, hold it." Dean grabbed his arm, and stubbed his fingers against the wall as his hand passed right through the other man. "She wants to be alone."

"And what do you know of it, *Anglais*? You can leave."

"Yeah, but I won't."

"So that makes you better than me? That you stay but do not have to." The ghost snorted. "I know why you stay, *Anglais*. It is not that it is so good a job, *n'est ce pas*?"

Dean's ears burned. "Austin says I'm a part of this. And Claire's mother says she needs me. And . . ."

"Oui?"

"And I don't run out on my friends."

The silence stretched and lengthened. Dean figured Jacques was taking his time to translate something particularly cutting but, to his surprise, the ghost smiled and nodded. *"D'accord.* If she must guard the world, we three will guard her."

We three.

It felt good being part of a team. It would've felt better standing back to back with Claire and taking on the world, just the two of them, but, deep down, Dean was a realist.

He hadn't ever really considered his future. He'd left Newfoundland looking for work, had fallen into this job, liked it well enough, and stayed. Because all his choices had been freely made, there seemed to be an infinite number still left to explore. He wasn't really very happy to discover that when a person reached a certain age, choices started making themselves. "The world's last line of defense—I wonder if the world knows how lucky it is," he mused.

The cat and the ghost exchanged expressions as identical as differing physiognomy could make them.

"Still, I can see her point," he continued in the same tone. "It's an awesome responsibility, but it must be some boring being on guard. Ow!" He reached down and rubbed his calf. "Why did you scratch me?"

"Never, ever say it's boring being a guard!"

"I didn't," Dean protested, checking for blood seeping through his jeans. "I said it must be some boring being *on* guard."

"Oh." Austin sheathed his claws. "Sorry."

Stuffing a fourth cookie into her mouth, Claire sank back into the sofa cushions and looked for something to put her feet up on. The coffee table practically bowed under the weight of the crap it already held and the hassock was on the other side of the room. Twisting slightly sideways, she chewed and swallowed and dropped her heels down on the plaster bust of Elvis.

"Thang you. Thang you vera much."

"You're kidding, right?" She lifted her feet and let them drop again.

"Thang you. Thang you vera much."

It seemed to have a limited vocabulary. "Why would Augustus Smythe waste power, even seepage, on something like you?" Unless. She chewed thoughtfully. "You don't sing, do . . ."

Her last word got lost under the opening bars of "Jailhouse Rock."

"Stop."

"Thang you. Thang you vera much."

"Sing."

A few bars of "Blue Suede Shoes."

"Stop."

"Thang you. Thang you vera much."

"Sing."

"Heartbreak Hotel." The opening bars of "Heartbreak Hotel."

"That's more like it." Claire had another cookie and prepared to wallow. From this point on, the future stretched out unchanging because to hope for change was to hope for disaster and to hope for disaster would strengthen Hell. She supposed she should call her mother, let her know how things had worked out—or rather how they hadn't worked out—but she didn't feel up to hearing even the most diplomatic version of "I told you so."

And if Diana was home . . .

The ten-year difference in their ages and a childhood spent being rescued by Claire from toddler enthusiasm meant that Diana had always lumped Claire in with the rest of the old people. She wouldn't be at all surprised to find Claire stuck running the hotel. It was what old Keepers did, after all.

Moving down to the second layer of cookies, Claire knew she couldn't trust herself to listen to that. Better not to call until Friday evening when she *always* called.

"You do know Elvis is running on seepage."

Claire sighed, exhaling a fine mist of cookie crumbs. "He's using a tiny fraction of what's readily available. He's not pulling from the pit."

"I wonder if that was the first excuse Augustus Smythe made." Austin jumped up onto the back of the sofa and gingerly stretched out along the top edge of the cushion.

"I doubt it." The song ended and Elvis thanked his audience before she could actually do anything.

"There is a bright side, you know. If Augustus Smythe hadn't been a sufficient monitor for all the years he was here, he would have been replaced. Since you're here now, obviously there's a better chance than there's ever been that something will go wrong."

Claire turned just enough to glare at the cat. "And I'm supposed to feel good about that?" But she reached out to see that the power loop remained secure.

YOU WERE DISAPPOINTED!

Get out of my head. She ate another three cookies so fast she almost took the end off a finger.

"You should cheer up," Austin told her.

"I don't want to cheer up."

"Then you should answer the door."

"There's nobody . . ." A tentative knocking cut her off. She glared at the cat as she called out, "What?"

"It's Dean. You haven't eaten yet today, so I made you some breakfast."

"It's almost noon."

"It's an omelet."

Names have power. Claire could smell it now: butter, eggs, mushrooms, cheese. All of a sudden she was ravenous. Half a bag of cookies hadn't even blunted the edge. When she opened the door, she found he'd brought a thermal carafe of coffee and a glass of orange juice as well. She held out her hands, but he didn't seem to want to relinquish the tray.

"You've, um, probably forgotten, but it's Thanksgiving today."

She hadn't so much forgotten as hadn't realized. A quick glance over at Miss October did indicate that it was, indeed the second Monday. And that she should replace Augustus Smythe's calendars. "Thank you. I'll call home."

"Yeah. Well, it's just that I was kind of invited to a friend's house for dinner."

"Kind of invited?"

"She's from back home, too, and we all made plans to get together and . . ." His voice trailed off.

"Go. Be happy. Eat turkey. Watch football." Claire reached over the omelet, grabbed the edge of the tray closest to his body and yanked it toward her, leaving him no choice but to let go or to go with it.

He let go.

"You've certainly earned a night off," she said, smiling tightly up at him. "Thank you for the food. Now go away, I haven't finished wallowing yet." Stepping back, she closed the door in his face.

"That was rude," Austin chided.

"Do you want some of this or not?"

It was enough, as she'd known it would be, for him to keep further opinions to himself.

Out in the office, Dean shook his head, brow creased with concern. "I don't know what I should do," he confessed to Jacques.

"Do what she says," the ghost told him. "Be with your friends. Eat the turkey, watch the football. There is nothing you can do here. She will come out when she is come to terms with this."

"*Has* come to terms with this. You could go in."

"I think not. What was it you said?" He started to fade and by the time he finished talking his words hung in the air by themselves. "I am pretty smart for a dead guy."

The interior of the refrigerator was as spotless as the rest of the kitchen. In Claire's experience, most crispers held two moldy tomatoes and a head of mushy lettuce but not Dean's. The vegetables were not only fresh, they'd been cleaned. She thought about making a salad and decided not to bother. Considered making a sandwich from the leftover pot roast and decided it was too much work. Reached for a plastic container of stroganoff to re-heat and let her hand fall back by her side.

In the end, she stepped away from the fridge empty-handed.

The familiar clomp of work boots turned her around.

"You're back early."

"It's almost nine. Not that early." Dean set a bulging bag down on the table and began removing foil wrapped packages. "We ate, did the dishes, had a cuffer—swapped stories," he explained as her brows went up. "And here I am, all chuffed out." Carefully lifting out a small margarine tub, he shot her a tentative smile. "Are you feeling better?"

"I spent the afternoon watching tabloid talk shows." She crossed the kitchen to stand by the table. "Now I feel slightly nauseated but better about *my* life."

"I think that's the idea."

Rubbing her temples with the heels of her hands, Claire snorted. "I certainly hope so. My mother send her regards, and my sister wants to know how you feel about European trawlers depleting the Grand Banks, but since she's only trying to start a political argument, you don't actually have to answer her." She picked up a package that smelled unmistakably of turkey. "What's this?"

"Thanksgiving dinner. I packed up some of the leftovers. The potatoes are cooked to a chuff, but you can't tell under the gravy."

When he got a plate and began arranging food on it, Claire folded her arms and shook her head. Only a young man could eat a full meal, then sit down and eat another. "I thought you were— How did it go—all chuffed out?"

"I am. This is for you." The feel of the answering silence drew his attention up off the food. "That is, if you haven't eaten. I mean, I don't even know if you like turkey. It's just that this was my first Thanksgiving away from home and I know how lonely I would've been without my friends and I thought that, well, that you should have some Thanksgiving dinner." Flustered, unable to read her expression, he spilled the gravy.

The accident and the subsequent wiping and rewiping and pol-ishing gave Claire a chance to swallow the lump in her throat. There were a number of things she wanted to say, but after the day's emotional ups and downs, she didn't think she could man-age any of them without bursting into tears—and Keepers never cried in front of bystanders. With the table restored to a pristine state, she reached out and touched Dean lightly on the arm. "Thang you," she said. "Thang you vera much."

THAT BOY IS SO NICE HE'S NAUSEATING. THERE MUST BE SOMETHING WE CAN TEMPT HIM WITH.

WE'VE TRIED. HE DOESN'T LISTEN.

ISN'T *THAT* JUST LIKE A MAN.

NOT WHERE WE'RE CONCERNED, Hell told itself tartly.

The next morning, Claire found a pair of Dean's underwear hanging off the doorknob as she left her suite. The imp must've spent the entire night dragging them up from the laundry room in the basement.

"I hope you gave yourself a hernia," Claire muttered, pulling them free.

Briefs, not boxers. Navy blue with white elastic.

"Boss?"

They wouldn't mash down into a small enough ball to hide. Keeping her right hand and its contents behind her, Claire turned. "What?"

"We've got lots of eggs, and I have to use them. I wondered if you wanted me to make you some for breakfast."

"Fine."

"How do you want them?"

"I don't care." He was wearing one of his brilliant white T-shirts and jeans, totally unaware of how good he looked. Briefs not boxers. Given how tightly his jeans fit, she should have been able to figure that out on her own.

"Scrambled?"

"Fine."

"With garlic and mushrooms?"

"Whatever."

Dean frowned. "You all right?"

"Fine."

He leaned left.

She shuffled just enough to cut down his line of sight. "Was there anything else?"

"Uh, no. I guess not."

"Good. You go ahead." Her right arm started forward to wave him away but she stopped it in time. "Go on. I'll be there in a minute."

Shaking his head, Dean disappeared down the hall.

Twenty years old, Claire reminded herself whacking the back of her skull against the door.

The hollow boom of the impact echoed throughout the first floor.

"Boss?"

"It's nothing," she called. Rubbing the rising bump, she contemplated doing it again. She'd had the perfect opportunity to prove the existence of the imp. There could be no other explanation for the underwear delivered to her door. So why, she wondered, had she acted like such an idiot?

"It's this place; it's messing with my head." Opening the door, she tossed the underwear into the sitting room. She'd figure out a way to get them back into Dean's laundry, later.

"Souvenir?" Austin asked as the briefs sailed by and landed on Elvis.

"Thang you, thang you vera much."

"You can both just shut up."

"They put over the top, how do you say . . . plaster board?" Jacques announced, pulling his head back out of the wall. "But the works for the elevator, they are all here."

"Should I start uncovering it?" Dean asked eagerly.

Claire shrugged. "Why not."

"Great, I'll go get my hammer."

"And what will you be doing, *cherie,*" Jacques asked as Dean ran off, "while he bangs out his frustrations on the wall?"

"I don't think Dean has frustrations." She ducked under the counter flap, heading for the phone. "But to answer your question, I'm going to finish packing Augustus Smythe's knick-knacks away."

"To make the place your own, yes?"

"Yes."

"So you are reconciled to staying here?"

An empty cardboard box dangling from one hand, she paused on the threshold, unwilling to take the final, symbolic step into the sitting room. "I might as well be, I haven't any other choice."

"You *are* needed here, Claire."

When she turned, he was standing right behind her. A step forward would take her right through him. His eyes had gone very dark and he was wearing the smile that made her stomach feel like she'd swallowed a bug.

"I could reconcile you." His hand caressed the air by her cheek. "It would take so little power."

At first Claire thought that the bells she heard were the ringing of desire in her ears, but then, over Jacques shoulder, she saw the front door open.

"Yoo hoo!"

She stepped forward, teeth gritted against the chill, Jacques dematerializing as she moved. There was no way Mrs. Abrams could've missed seeing him.

"Did you see that, Carlee, dear?"

"See what?" Claire asked.

"Nothing. Never mind. Of course you didn't."

Prepared for an argument, or possibly even hysterics, her satisfied chuckle confused Claire completely.

"I just came in to tell you that you've got guests. Two young men. I was on my way in from my Tuesday morning hair appointment—I like to get there early, you know, before poor dear Sandra gets tired—and I saw their car go up the driveway and I knew you'd want to know immediately. That's funny." Head cocked, she swiveled it about like an orange bouffant radar dish. "I don't hear Baby. He does so love to welcome your guests as they get out of their cars in the parking lot."

"Does he welcome them the way he welcomes the postman?" Claire wondered.

"Don't be silly, dear, there's a fence in his way. I'd best go check on the poor thing." Pausing on the threshold, she pointed back toward the gleaming oak counter. "You should put some paint on that, dear. All that bare wood looks somewhat indecent, don't you think?"

The two young men weren't much taller than Claire, although they had a wiry build and self-confident grace that suggested their height had never been an issue. Both had sharply pointed features, an eyebrow lying across each forehead with no discernible break, and short dark hair that picked up the light as they moved so that it seemed the very end of each individual hair had been dipped in silver.

Claire relaxed as a quick dip into identical gray eyes showed not only a lack of evil intent but that they carried significantly less darkness than the general population.

"You guys twins?" Dean asked, wandering over to the counter, hammer in hand.

"Actually," said one.

"We're triplets," said the other. "I'm Ron, never Ronald since that clown came on the scene, and this is my brother Reg. We're in town for the sportsman's show that's at the Portsmouth Center this week."

"Randy had a previous commitment," Reg explained with a toothy grin. "But *we'd* like a room. Our grandfather stopped here some years ago, and he spoke very highly of the place."

Must've been before Augustus Smythe took over, Claire thought. When Dean glanced her way, she had to hide a grin. It was obvious he was thinking the same thing. "All of our rooms are doubles," she told them making a mental note to have Jacques search the attic for a set of twin beds. "If you mind sharing, we could give you a deal on two rooms." It wasn't like the second room would be needed for other guests.

"Sharing's fine."

They were in constant motion and she'd lost track of which was which. "Breakfast is included in the price."

"Great but all we really need you to do is . . ."

". . . throw half a dozen raw eggs into a blender."

"We're in training."

For what? Salmonella? But they were guests, so all she said aloud was, "Well, if you'll give us a few minutes, we'll get room one ready for you."

"No hurry."

"We're going for a run down by the lake."

"We've been on the road since dawn and . . ."

". . . we don't do so well sitting still that long."

"We'll be back in about an hour."

Ron, or possibly Reg, grinned up, way up, at Dean. "See you later, big fella."

Reg, or as it were, Ron, nodded at Claire. "Ma'am."

They bounded out the door together. Claire had never seen anyone over the age of three actually bound before. Feeling a little out of breath, although she hadn't moved from behind the counter during the entire exchange, she wondered just when exactly she'd become a ma'am.

"Cool guys," Dean said. "Lots of energy. Should I go up and do the room?"

And was *Boss* really any better?

"Boss?"

Not really. "Why not? Has to be done."

She walked over to the desk as he went upstairs and dropped into the chair. *Keep your distance,* she reminded herself. *The way things have turned out, he'll be moving on long before you do.*

When Austin came into the office a few minutes later, she was sulkily updating the day's noninformation into the site journal. "What's with you?" she asked, noticing the cat's bottle brush tail, and half open mouth.

"Something stinks," he growled. "I smell dog."

"Two guests just registered." She hadn't noticed any particular odor, but if the twins were competing at the sportsman's show perhaps that meant they worked with dogs.

"It's coming from over here."

Rolling her eyes, Claire got up to peer over the counter at him.

"And it's not dog."

He was sniffing the spot where Reg, or possibly Ron, had stood to sign the register.

"Then what is it?"

"Werewolf."

WEREWOLVES?

THERE WOLVES. THERE CASTLE.

The silence that fell in the furnace room was the sort of antici-patory silence that fell just before a smack. In this particular case, it wasn't so much a smack as total, all encompassing destruction.

The silence continued a moment longer, then a very small voice said, OW.

NINE

"The seepage is building up again." Sitting on the edge of the bed, Claire pulled on a sock. "I can feel the buzz beginning."

Austin yawned. "What're you going to do about it."

"I don't know. I can stop the buzz by using it—which'll make Hell happy—or I can endure it and go slowly nuts—which'll also make Hell happy. There's got to be an alternative."

"I'll let you know if I think of one."

Claire rolled her eyes. "You do that."

"You going after the Historian this morning?"

Already halfway out the door, she threw an irritated, "What's the point?" back over her shoulder.

"Boss? You busy?"

Claire looked up from writing *Smythe;junk* on the outside of the sixth box of assorted odds and ends, mostly ends, she'd cleared from the sitting room. "Not exactly, no."

"Can I talk to you?"

"I think I can spare a moment." When he frowned, clearly considering the actual time he'd need, Claire sighed. "Figure of speech, Dean. What did you want to tell me?"

"Well, I was upstairs, wiping down the molding . . ."

She leaned slightly toward him, as though proximity would help the statement make more sense. "You were what?"

"Wiping down the molding. The trim around the doors," he expanded with an indulgent smile when she continued to look confused. "It collects dust. I didn't get to it last week because of the renovations. Anyway, you know the two guys in room one; the twins?"

"The triplets."

"Okay."

Claire managed to rearrange her face into her most neutral expression. "What about them?"

"I don't want to get them into trouble or anything, but they came in some late last night and I thought I heard it then, I just wasn't sure."

"Thought you heard what?"

"A dog."

"A dog?" Moving quickly to the counter, Claire swept Austin up into her arms before he could say anything.

"Yeah. And just now, I'm pretty sure I saw half a muddy paw print. I mean, if they're smuggling a dog into their room . . ."

Austin started to snicker.

". . . we ought to say something when they come back tonight because it's not necessary."

"What isn't necessary?" She shifted the cat's weight. He was laughing so hard he was becoming difficult to hold.

"Hiding the dog. You don't mind if they bring in a pet, do you?"

"No. I don't." Which was as much as she could manage with a straight face.

"A dog?" The twins exchanged identical smiles. "No," Ron continued, "we don't have a dog."

Dean frowned. "But I heard . . ." He faltered, caught and held by two pairs of frank gray eyes. They were telling the truth, he'd bet his life on it. "I guess maybe I didn't."

"You're welcome to come up and search the room," Reg offered.

"Any time," Ron added suggestively, brows rising and falling.

"No, that's okay." Feeling a little like he'd missed the punch line of a joke everyone else found incredibly funny, Dean shrugged. "I, well, we, that is the hotel, wanted you to know we don't mind animals in the rooms, that's all."

"Nice to hear. We'll remember that . . ."

". . . if we're by this way again."

"What's the lovely young man going to think of you when he finds out you've been lying to him?" Claire's reflection asked.

"I haven't been lying." She'd switched to a clear lip gloss on those days she wasn't able to use the mirror. It was faster than waiting to see what she was doing.

"You didn't tell him about the vampire, you're not telling him about the werewolves . . ." The reflection traced a dark red clown frown a quarter inch from her lips.

"But I'm not lying. If he asks . . ."

"And he's so likely to ask, isn't he? You promised, no more secrets."

"These aren't my secrets."

"We think it's sweet that you're trying to protect him."

Claire blinked, a little confused by the sudden change of topic. "What are you talking about?"

"You know. He's just a kid. Let's keep him safe. He'll thank you for it later."

No one did sarcasm quite like Hell.

When the twins left later that morning, they took three trophies with them. Although he only saw them from a distance, all three seemed to have a figure of a dog as part of the design. Dean decided not to ask.

"Boss, can I talk to you?"

Breathing heavily through her nose, Claire leaned out from behind her monitor. "What, again?"

"If this is a bad time . . ."

"A bad time? Would you like to see a bad time?" She waved him under the counter and around to her side of the desk. "Once, just once, I leave the wards off," she continued as he approached, ". . . and this is what happens."

"You spilled a cup of coffee on your keyboard?" Dean shook his head sympathetically. "That's rough."

"*I* didn't spill it."

"And don't look at me," Austin advised him from the top of the counter.

"It was the imp." Claire made a valiant attempt to unclench her teeth and nearly succeeded.

"Where'd it get the coffee?"

"I left my mug sitting here, half full, when I went in to lunch." It didn't need a Keeper to work out the cause of the two vertical lines over the bridge of Dean's glasses. He'd probably never left a half a cup of anything sitting around. He'd probably never even left a dirty cup sitting in the sink. "I forgot it was there, all right?"

"Sure." Head bent, hands dwarfing the keyboard as he gently twisted it from side to side, he remained unaware that the full force of her mood had turned in his direction. "Can't you drain it?"

"No." She felt as though she'd slammed into an affable brick wall—and had about as much effect as if she'd run full tilt into a real one. "It's already dry. Half a dozen of the keys aren't working." The wheels on the old chair shrieked a protest as she shoved it away from the desk. "I suppose I can write the stupid site journal out by hand, but it's a little difficult to build a database without a . . ."

Something small, something crimson and cream, raced along the wall under the window.

Claire snatched up the empty mug and flung it with all her might.

She missed.

The mug smashed into a hundred pieces.

Austin went three feet straight up.

"What're you trying to do to me?" he snarled as he landed, fur sticking out at right angles from his body. "I'm old!"

"It was the imp. You saw it, didn't you, Dean?"

"I saw . . ." He paused and replayed the scene as his heart rate returned to normal. "I saw something."

"A mouse," Austin told him tersely.

"I don't know, it was . . ."

"An imp." Claire's tone left no room for argument. "Somebody," she shot a scathing look at the cat, "has moved the trap."

"Probably the mice."

"Oh, give me a break."

Sitting down with his back toward her, Austin began washing his shoulder with long, deliberate strokes of his tongue.

Although Dean hoped it was his imagination, the air between cat and Keeper felt chilled. "I could take the keyboard apart," he offered, flipping it and frowning at the half-dozen, tiny, inset screw heads. "Maybe I can clean the coffee out of it."

"Take it apart? As in pieces?" On the other hand, she couldn't use it the way it was so how much worse could it get? "All right. But be careful."

"No problem." His enthusiastic smile faded as a bit of broken ceramic crushed under one work boot. "First off, I'll go get a broom and dustpan."

"Dean?"

He stopped on the other side of the counter.

"What was it you wanted to talk to me about?"

What was it? The sudden, deliberate destruction of the coffee mug had driven it right out of his head.

"Do you know what you are doing, *Anglais*?" Jacques leaned over Dean's shoulder and poked an ethereal finger at the keyboard. "Can you put the pieces back together when they all fall out?"

"That's not about to happen," Dean told him, inserting a Phillips head screwdriver into the last tiny screw. "These day's everything's solid state."

Leaning against the other side of the desk, Claire drummed bubblegum-colored fingernails on the CPU and bit her tongue. The buzz of the accumulated seepage had become a constant background noise as impossible to ignore as a dentist's drill, and the smallest things set her off. She'd yelled at Dean for returning the wallpaper sample books before she'd finished with them after telling him that she'd definitely made up her mind, at Jacques for going through the dining room table rather than around, at Dean again for waiting until after lunch before opening up her keyboard, and at Austin, just because. It was like continual PMS only without the bloating.

"That's got it." Setting the screw in the saucer with the others, Dean slid a pair of slot screwdrivers into the crack between the front and back of the keyboard and twisted in opposite directions. The plastic began to creak as the tiny levers moved off the horizontal. When the crack widened to half an inch, he pried the back of the keyboard carefully free.

The sudden flurry of tiny white pieces of plastic exploding into the air strongly resembled a small, artificial blizzard.

"Score one for the dead guy," Jacques observed when the last piece landed.

Dean scooped up one of the escapees. A tiny spring fell off one end, bounced on the desk, and rolled out of sight. "Sorry," he said, shoulders up around his ears as he peered up over the top of his glasses at Claire. "But I'm sure I can fix it."

It took an effort, but Claire managed to count all the way to ten before responding. "Just clean it up," she snarled, "and move on."

Dean's eyes widened and a muscle jumped in his jaw.

"Now what's your problem?"

"For a minute there you sounded . . ." He paused and shook his head. "It's okay. I'll just clean this up like you said."

"I sounded like what?" Claire growled. "Tell me. *Please.*"

He didn't want to tell her, but he couldn't seem to help himself. "Like Augustus Smythe."

She stared at him, saw that he was serious, and opened her mouth to call him several choice names. Snapping it closed on the first of them, she stomped into her sitting room and slammed the door.

Jacques snickered. "I must hand it over to you *Anglais,* you have the way with women."

"He said I sounded like Augustus Smythe!"

Austin rolled over and stared up at her. "No," he said after a moment. "Too high-pitched."

"It's the seepage." She rubbed at her temples where the buzz had lodged. "It's barely been two weeks since I cleared it out, and it's already making me cranky."

"Got news for you, Claire, you're way beyond cranky."

"Smythe couldn't have lived like this all the time."

"Feeling sorry for him?"

"No." Her lips pulled back off her teeth. "Wanting to wring his neck."

"Maybe you're more susceptible because you're a Keeper and under normal circumstances, which these aren't, you're able to adjust the seepage." The cat washed the black spot on his front leg thoughtfully. "Why not use it to close down the postcard?"

"Because the postcard is using seepage. If I close it down, in a few days I'll have a worse problem than before. And besides, I don't want to use it."

"The postcard?"

"The seepage!" She dropped down onto the couch and emerged from the depths a few moments later to add another forty-three cents and a plain gold ring that smelled of fish to the half-filled bowl of retrieved flotsam on the coffee table. "I can't go on like this."

The distant sound of a ten-pound sledge slamming through plaster board jerked her forward, almost tipping her into the precarious area between the coach cushions.

Austin yawned. "Maybe you should cut back on the caffeine."

"Maybe you shouldn't say anything if you can't say something helpful." Tapping her nails against her thigh, Claire gritted her teeth. "There has to be a logical solution."

"Why?"

"Shut up. Point: Power is seeping out around the edges of the seal two presumably dead Keepers created with another Keeper's power. A further point: It's not my power sealing the site, so I can't make adjustments. Yet another point: I can't just leave the seepage be because it's driving me nuts. And one final point: The only way to get rid of the seepage buildup is to use it, but using the power of Hell can't help but corrupt the individual using it no matter her intentions. So." She drew in a deep breath and exhaled noisily. "Where does that get us?"

"Absolutely nowhere," Austin told her, climbing onto her lap.

Claire slumped back into the sofa. "It was a rhetorical question anyway. What we need is a way to use the seepage without strengthening Hell."

"Can't be done. Hell works only in its own best interests."

Stroking the cat, Claire spent a moment wallowing in the innate unfairness of the universe, and then . . .

"Hey!" Austin fought his way out from between the two sofa cushions. "If you're going to stand suddenly, warn a guy!"

"Hell can be *made* to work against itself." Claire whirled around to face the cat. "I'll feed the seepage into the shield around the furnace room!"

The cat stepped over onto the coffee table and, with a solid surface below him, paused to smooth the ruffled fur along his side. "How?" he asked after a moment.

"Adhesion. The moment anything escapes from the pit. Slap!" She smacked her palms together. "Right into the shield but set up so that it's distributed evenly, like oyster spit building a pearl. Hell sends more out, the shield gets stronger. Hell sends nothing at all, nothing happens because the original shield is still in place."

After a moment, Austin nodded. "It's brilliant."

Claire picked him up and kissed the top of his head. "It's why I get the big bucks," she agreed.

Sledge over his shoulder, Dean bounded down the stairs into the lobby and rocked to a dead stop when he saw Claire's door open. "I uh, piled all the bits of your keyboard on the desk," he said as she emerged.

To his surprise, she smiled. "That's great. When I get a minute, I'll separate what's recyclable and throw the rest out."

He took a tentative step closer. When he realized he was holding the sledge across his body like a shield, he let it swing down until the head rested on the floor. "You're not angry, then?" he asked tentatively.

Claire shrugged. "Accidents happen."

"No, I meant about saying you sounded like . . ." Although she no longer seemed as crusty as she had, it didn't seem polite to say it again. "You know."

"I was angry because you were right."

Coming out from behind the counter, Austin performed an exaggerated double take. Dean tried not to smile.

"But," she continued, "I've come up with a way to solve the problem." She nodded toward the sledge. "How's the elevator coming?"

"We've got all four doors cleared. They didn't take anything out when they closed the system up, so it just needs the trim back around the holes. Jacques is in the attic right now having a look at the works."

"Jacques is?"

"It's old," Dean told her cheerfully, as though that explained everything. When it didn't appear to, he added, "It's the sort of machinery he's familiar with."

Walking over to the recessed doorway, Claire peered through the wrought iron scrollwork into the closet-sized space. She could just barely make out the cables. "Where's the car?"

"In the basement."

"Given what's in the furnace room, is that entirely safe?"

"Given gravity, the basement seemed safest."

Up on her toes, Claire sent a pale white light into the shaft. Everything she could see seemed in remarkably good shape, but she supposed there was no point in taking chances. "You're probably right."

Austin sat back on his haunches and stared up at her in astonishment. "That's twice."

She ignored him. "Do you think you can get it working?"

"Sure." Dean's grip slipped as he realized what he'd said. "I mean, yeah. No problem."

"Don't try it without me. I'd like to be in on the inaugural ride."

"It might not be safe. . . ."

"It'll be safer with me in it." Turning to go, she paused and took a deep breath. There was one more thing she'd resolved to do. "Oh, and, Dean? I'm sorry I snapped at you earlier."

"That's okay. It was nothing."

"It was something if I've apologized for it."

At that point, he decided it would be safer if he just kept quiet.

"Two admissions that someone else might be right *and* an apology. Circle this day on the calendar," Austin muttered as he followed Claire toward the basement.

"The boys seem to be getting along better," Claire noted as she opened the padlocks.

"They're not boys," Austin snorted from the top of the washing machine.

"It's a figure of speech."

"Dean likes you."

"Get real, he calls me Boss."

"He called you Claire when you fell down the stairs."

"He did?" Given the way her tailbone had impacted with the edge of the step, she wasn't surprised she hadn't noticed. "Means nothing."

"Then what about the way he looks at you?"

"He's twenty. The way he looks at women isn't under his conscious control."

"All right; what about the way you look at him?"

She twisted around enough to grin at the cat. "Like I said, he's twenty. It's an aesthetic appreciation."

Austin's tail beat out an audible rhythm against the enameled steel. "I know that babysitting a site at your age was the last thing you wanted, but it's given you a chance few Keepers get and you'll kick yourself if you blow it."

"Blow what?"

"The chance for a relationship."

"A relationship?" Claire sighed. "Have you been watching Oprah again?"

"No! Well, actually, yes," he amended. "But that has nothing to do with this."

"Forget it, Austin. Dean's attractive, yes, but he's too young."

"Jacques isn't."

"Jacques is too dead."

"Dean isn't."

She hung the chains on their hooks and turned to glare at her companion. "You're not the only one concerned about my having or not having a *relationship;* Hell suggested Jacques and I settle down for the duration."

"Just because something is an anthropomorphism of ultimate evil, that doesn't mean it hasn't your best interests at heart."

"Yes, it does."

"Fine. But your health is important to *me.*"

"My health?"

"It's been nearly six months."

"So?"

"If I remember correctly, the last incident wasn't terribly successful."

Her brows drew in. "What are you talking about?"

"I was under the bed."

"You were under the bed!"

"Hey, it's all just loud noises to me." He stretched out a back leg and stared down at the spread toes. "Mind you, some loud noises are more believable than others."

Claire counted to ten and let it go, reminding herself, once again, that no one ever won an argument with a cat.

Young Keepers started out believing that accessing the possibilities required inner calm and outer silence. After their first couple of sites they realized calm and quiet were luxuries they'd seldom have. Claire's first site had been in the sale bin at a discount department store. It hadn't been pretty, but it had prepared her for eventually working through the catcalls and attempted interference of Hell.

Breathing shallowly through her mouth, she adjusted the possibilities on the inside of the shield until the seepage began to adhere. It was a simple, elegant solution and she left the furnace room three hours later stinking of brimstone and feeling inordinately pleased with herself.

PRIDE IS ONE OF OURS, Hell called after her. When the only response was the slamming of the furnace room door, it examined the addition to its binding. IS SHE ALLOWED TO DO THAT? it asked sulkily.

NOTHING SEEMS TO BE STOPPING HER.

WE SHOULD BE STOPPING HER.

WELL, DUH.

As he heard Claire come into the lobby, Dean looked up from sorting the mail. "Good timing, Boss; you . . . you look like something they dragged off the bottom of the harbor."

"Thank you, Dean, I'm touched by your concern. You forgot to mention that I smell like something from the sewage treatment plant." She paused, took a deep breath, and ducked under the counter, swaying a little when she straightened on the other side.

Dean took a step toward her. "You okay?"

"I'm fine."

"You look exhausted."

"I'm a bit tired, yes. I've been working."

"On the pit?"

"By the pit."

"Is that safe?"

"It is now."

"I don't understand." He frowned. "Did you figure out how to seal it?"

"Wouldn't that be good news?" Austin asked before Claire could respond.

"Well, sure . . ."

"Then shouldn't you sound happier about it?"

"Stop being annoying just because you can," Claire suggested. Turning back to Dean, she shook her head. "No, I haven't figured out how to seal the pit, but I have solved a smaller problem. What did you mean when you said, good timing?"

It took him a moment to follow the path of the conversation. "The mail's finally here. You got a postcard."

Claire took the cardboard rectangle between thumb and forefinger, glanced at the photograph of a tropical paradise, then flipped the card over.

"Who's it from?" Dean asked, leaning forward.

"My sister, Diana. Apparently, she's in the Philippines."

Austin's ears went back. "Didn't they just have a huge volcanic eruption in the Philippines?"

"We don't *know* that was her fault." A tooth mark on the edge of the postcard had the distinct, punched hole appearance of Baby's games with the mailman. "Speaking of natural disasters, we haven't heard from Mrs. Abrams for a while."

"Maybe the blinds discouraged her?" Dean offered.

"Maybe we should put the wagon train in a circle," Austin muttered. "You should start to worry when the drums stop."

After a long hot shower, Claire spent the rest of the day sprawled in an armchair, watching a *National Geographic* video about killer whales. It was one of only eleven tapes she'd salvaged from Augustus Smythe's extensive collection. The pornography hadn't been the worst of it; his video library had also included every episode of "Gunsmoke" plus a nearly complete collection of "The Beverly Hillbillies."

Hell was not only murky, it filled out subscription forms.

"You coming, Austin?"

"You're kidding, right?" Tail lashing from side to side he backed up a step just in case Claire decided to force the issue. "You actually want me to get into that cross between a cage and a coffin, allow myself to be lifted three stories off the ground by an antique mechanism reinstalled by a cook under the direction of a dead sailor? I think not."

"It's perfectly safe."

"That's what you said about that cruise."

"Cruise?" Jacques asked by her ear.

"Bermuda Triangle. Long story," Claire told him.

"I wouldn't get into that thing," Austin continued, ears flat, "if I still had all nine lives. Not even if I'd rescued Princess Toadstool and picked up another life. If anything goes wrong, somebody has to be around to say I told you so."

"Suit yourself." Unfortunately for any second thoughts she might have been having, Claire couldn't back out now, not with the cat so vehemently opposed. He was quite smug enough without her giving him more ammunition. She closed the door, dropped the inner gate, and turned to the more corporeal of her two companions. "Are you sure you know what you're doing?"

"It's simple." Dean flashed her a confident grin. "All you do is turn this level from the off position to either the right or the left. Right takes us up, and left takes us down."

Claire sighed. "That's probably why they labeled it that way. I was asking on a more esoteric level, but never mind. Let's get this ride over with, shall we?"

"Anything you say, Boss." Feet braced, Dean wrapped both hands around the gleaming brass lever and swung it to the right.

Up in the attic, ancient machinery gave a startled jerk and wheezed into life, sending wave after wave of vibration through the stored furniture. The small, multicolored creature removing the last of the most recent marshmallows from the imp traps whirled around and fell to what served it for knees. In all of its short existence, it had never heard such a sound. Extrapolating from limited experience, it created a wild and metaphysical explanation that changed its life forever.

But that's another story.

Claire pressed one hand flat against the wall as the elevator lurched upward. "It works."

"I never doubted it." Looking like the captain at the wheel of a very small ship, Dean kept his eyes locked on the edge of the floor joists moving down on the other side of the iron gate. When the top edge of the first floor was almost even with the floor of the elevator, he lifted the switch back up into the off position. In the few seconds it took for the machinery to stop, the floors came level.

"Good eye, *Anglais*," Jacques muttered. "Such a pity you were born too late to make this a career."

"Yeah?" Stepping left, Dean hooked up the gate and reached for the latch on the outer door. "Well, it's a pity you died too early for me to . . ."

"To what, *Angla* . . ."

Careful not to step over the threshold, Claire leaned out of the elevator and peered up and down the beach, eyes squinted against the ruddy light of the setting sun. "This doesn't look like the lobby." The touch of the breeze on her cheek, the sound of the waves curling and slapping into pieces against the fine, white sand, the smell of the rotting fish they appeared to have cut in half worked together to convince her it wasn't illusion either. "I'm beginning to see why Augustus Smythe closed this thing up."

"Because he does not like to take the vacation? Perhaps because he did not have a beautiful woman to walk with by the sea." Wafting past her, Jacques turned and held out his hand.

Claire stared at him, horrified. "What are you doing out there? In fact, how can you be out there?" A quick glance showed that a doily taken from his old room remained crumpled in the back corner. "Your anchor's in here!"

"As to how, I do not know. As to what, I am inviting you to go for the walk."

"The walk? Jacques, I don't think you quite realize where you are." Had she been able to hold him, she'd have grabbed his hand and yanked him back into the relative safety of the elevator.

"And where am I, *cherie*? Where is this place that gives me such freedom?"

"I don't know. And that's my point!"

"Ah, you are frightened of the unexpected. I understand, *cherie,* you are a woman, after all." Lit from behind by the sun, his eyes gleamed.

She folded her arms. "If you're implying I'm not taking the same stupid chance you are because I'm only a woman, go ahead. I'm not going to fall for it."

"You wound me, *cherie.* I said I understood why *you* are frightened."

Dean moved out of the elevator too fast for Claire to grab him. "Are you saying I'm a coward?"

"Am I saying that?" Jacques drifted backward, toward the edge of the water. "*Non.* I would never think of such a thing."

"You better not be," Dean muttered. He drew in a deep lungful of air and smiled contentedly. "Man, this place smells just like home."

The ghost snorted. "If your home smells like this, *Anglais,* it is no wonder you clean so much."

The familiar salt air had put Dean in too good a mood to continue the argument. Shaking his head, he wandered down to meet the next wave coming in.

"Excuse me!"

Both men turned and, drawn by Claire's expression, found themselves returning to the elevator considerably more quickly than they'd left it.

"If you two are quite through exposing yourselves, maybe we could think about getting . . . now what?"

Dean had disappeared around the doorframe.

"This is some weird." His voice came from directly behind her. "There's just this door in the sand. From this side, you can't see the elevator at all."

"Don't step where it should be!" Claire shouted. She didn't want to think about what could happen should three realities—elevator, beach, and Dean—suddenly find themselves sharing the same space. When Dean reappeared, she backed away from the door, leaving him room to get in. "Come on."

Jacques stepped between them, his long face wearing the half rakish, half pleading expression she found so difficult to resist. "*Cherie,* how often is there the chance to enjoy such a sunset?"

"And how enjoyable will it be if I leave the elevator and it disappears?"

"So before you leave, we prop the door open with a rock. If only the door is real here, then the elevator will go nowhere."

"You don't know that," Claire muttered, but she could feel her resolve weakening. It was a beautiful beach; brilliant white sand stretching down to turquoise water, the setting sun brushing the entire scene with red-gold light.

"If I cannot convince you, *cherie* . . ." His eyes twinkled under lowered lids. ". . . then I dare you."

"You dare me?"

"*Oui.* I dare you to enjoy yourself, if only *pour un moment.*"

"You think I'm incapable of enjoying myself?"

"I did not say that."

"Well, I'm not. Dean . . ."

Dean had already found a rock. He rolled it up against the open door and, telling herself that Jacques' theory made a great deal of sense, Claire stepped over the threshold.

After a few moments of anticipatory silence, when neither the elevator nor the beach seemed affected, Jacques threw up his hands in triumph. "You see," he said, catching them again. "I am right."

Nearly body temperature, the water invited swimming, but both mortals contented themselves with tossing shoes and socks back into the elevator and wading through the shallow surf. Behind the open door, the beach rose up to become undulating dunes and finally a multihued green wall of jungle vegetation.

"Austin would love it here," Claire laughed, digging her toes into the sand. "It's the world's biggest litter bo . . . oh, my God! He'll be frantic!"

"I don't think it works that way."

Fighting to keep her balance in the loose footing, she whirled to glare at Dean. "What makes you such an expert?"

He held out his arm, watch crystal reflecting all the red and gold and orange in the sky. "The second hand hasn't moved since we got here."

"Oh, I see," she snarled, "time has stopped. Did it ever occur to you that it might be your watch?"

Crestfallen, he shook his head.

"*Excusez-moi.*" Jacques' tone laid urgency over the polite form of the interruption. "Something happens in the water."

About twenty feet from shore, the waves had taken on a lumpy appearance. Bits of them seemed to be moving in ways contrary to the nature of water, rolling from side to side as they headed for the shore. Then the center hump of a wave kept rising past the crest, the mottled surface lifting up, up, until it became obvious, even staring into the sunset, that what they were watching wasn't water.

"If I didn't know better," Dean murmured, one hand shading his eyes, "I'd swear that was an octopus."

"Octopi do not come so big," Jacques protested weakly.

"Well, it's not a squid."

A tentacle, as thick as Dean's arm, broke through the surf no more than four feet from where they were standing.

"Octopi, regardless of size, don't come up on the shore," Claire announced as though daring the waving appendage to contradict her.

The twenty feet had become fifteen. Fourteen. Twelve. Ten.

"On the other hand," she added as a suckered arm fell short and gouged a trench in the sand at her feet, "I don't think this is an octopus either. RUN!"

Stumbling and falling in the loose sand, they raced for the elevator.

A tentacle slammed into Claire's hip, throwing her sideways into Dean. He caught her and held on, dragging her forward with him, her feet barely touching down.

From the water's edge came the sound of a large, wet, leather sack being smacked against the shore.

Unaffected by the footing, Jacques reached safety first, turned, and went nearly transparent. *"Depeche toi!"*

Gesture made his meaning plain.

Dean shoved Claire forward, over the threshold and bent to roll away the rock. A tentacle wrapped around his right leg but before it could tighten, he pulled free and stomped down hard. It might've been a more effective blow had he not been in bare feet, but it bought him enough time. He leaped inside, dragging the door closed with him.

Claire slammed the gate shut.

The deep blue/gray tip of a tentacle poked through the grill-work in the small window.

Wrapping sweaty hands around the lever, Dean yanked it right.

The floor joists nipped off an inch of rubbery flesh. When it dropped to the floor, Claire kicked it into the back corner and turned on Dean. "Why up?" she demanded, loudly enough to make herself heard over the pounding of her heart. "We came into this through the basement and that's very likely the only way we'll get out. The basement is down!"

The floor of the elevator level with the second floor of the guest house, Dean locked the lever into its upright position. "I guess up just seemed more natural," he said. Grinning broadly, he sank down and reached for his shoes and socks. "Besides, we haven't seen what's on two or three."

Claire stared down at him in silence.

After a moment, one sock on, the other in his hand, he lifted his head. "What?"

"We haven't seen what's on two or three?"

The grin slipped. "Well, yeah."

She could see her reflection in his glasses. "Are you out of your mind?"

His brow furrowed. "We have to see what's on two and three. We can't quit now."

"Oh, yes, we can. We just got chased by a giant tentacled thing; that's quite enough excitement for one day."

After a moment, he shrugged. "You're the boss." Sighing, he pulled on his other sock.

"Do you believe him?" Claire asked Jacques, dusting the sand off her own feet. "He thought that was fun."

"Not fun," Dean protested. "Exciting."

"Dangerous," Claire corrected.

"But we all got away. We're all safe."

"We could have been eaten by something out of a bad Lovecraft pastiche!"

"But we weren't."

"Jacques." She turned to the ghost. "Help me out."

"He has a point, *cherie*. No one was hurt. And we are at the second floor. It would be a shame not to look."

Arms folded, she sagged back against the elevator wall. "There's just way too much testosterone in here."

"My watch seems to be working again, Boss."

"I'm thrilled."

Standing, Dean shot Jacques a "now what" glance, and received a "how the hell should I know" shrug in return.

"All right." Claire straightened. "A compromise. We'll look through the grille, but we won't actually open the door and we certainly won't join in the fun."

"Fun?"

"It's a figure of speech, Dean. Together on three so that we all see the same thing . . . one, two, three."

A familiar hallway stretched off in both directions, the doors to rooms one and two clearly visible.

"This is the second floor." Shoving up the gate, Claire pushed the door open and barely managed to stop herself from stepping out onto a familiar starship bridge.

"Make it so, Number One."

Slowly and quietly, she closed the door again. "And that wasn't."

"But what was it?" Jacques asked, peering out in some confusion at the second floor hall. "It was a military vessel?"

"It was an imaginary vessel, Jacques."

"What is an imaginary vessel? It is not real?" He shook his head. "But it was as real as the beach. And the not-a-squid."

"It was real here. And now. With the door open." The scene through the door remained the second floor. "But everywhere else, except on those occasions when it's a way of life, it's a television show."

Dean shook his head, as though trying to settle himself back into reality. "I could've walked out onto the real bridge of the starship. . . ."

"No." Claire reached out, intending to lock up, and found herself, instead, opening the door a crack. For one last look at the real bridge of the starship . . .

It looked like a balmy evening on top of Citadel Hill in downtown Halifax. Except for the two moons riding low in the sky and the woman in the distance with an agitated shrub on a leash.

Behind and above her right shoulder, Claire heard Dean murmur, "It changes every time you reopen the door."

"So the not-squid, it is gone? We could return to the beach?"

"Sure. Except the beach is gone."

Claire quietly eased the door shut, so as not to further agitate the shrub, and latched the gate. "All right," she sighed, her head falling forward until it rested against the fifty-year-old paint. "We're in this so far now we might as well see what's on the third floor. But . ." Straightening, she folded her arms, turned, and fixed each of her companions with her best *I'm a Keeper and you're not* stare. ". . . no one gets out. Understand?"

"But what if . . ."

"I don't care. No one leaves the elevator."

Through the grille, it *was* the third floor. It even smelled like the third floor.

"Do you think that *she* might have an effect?" Jacques asked nervously as Claire locked back the gate.

"Do I think that proximity to *her* could affect the elevator's destination? I don't know, but I don't think so. Those are strong shields." A puff of noxious air wafted in as she opened the door and stared out at the piles of blasted rock and steaming lava pools. "And then again, I suppose it's possible that . . ."

A terrified shriek cut her off.

Dean pushed forward, allowing himself to be stopped by the flimsy barricade of Claire's arm only because he wasn't certain of where the sound had originated.

A second scream helped.

Off to the right, close to one of the steaming red pools, two large lizardlike creatures held a struggling shape between them, snapping and snarling at each other over their captive's head. While accumulated filth and long dreadlocks made guessing age difficult, they did nothing at all to hide the gender of what seemed to be a completely naked twelve- or thirteen-year-old boy.

Captured. About to be devoured. Pushing Claire aside, Dean leaped forward, the porous surface of the rock crunching under his work boots. He heard her yell his name, felt her grab at his shirt, and kept running, throwing, "Stay where you're at!" back over his shoulder. With any luck she'd see that there was no sense them both going into danger. If he concentrated on speed rather than concealment, he'd could reach and rescue the kid before the two lizards finished quarreling over their catch.

The closer he got, the more the snarling began to seem like . . .

"Because it's my nesting site and I don't want the dirty little egg-sucker cooking right beside it. That's why!"

"So I have to carry it out of the nursery, all the way to cool ground? Is that it?"

"You caught it!"

"Crawling into your nest!"

"So now it's my nest, is it? And I suppose they'll be *my* hatchlings? *My* responsibility while you're off hunting with your friends."

. . . words.

And familiar words at that. Through a thick sibilant accent, it sounded remarkably like an argument his Aunt Denise and Uncle Steve'd had about dispatching a rat caught live in the kitchen. Which didn't actually change anything.

"Our nest, sweetie. I meant to say, *our* nest."

"You say that now. You don't mean it."

Through eyes beginning to water from the volcanic fumes, Dean noticed that the lizard with his aunt's lines was the larger by a significant margin. Sucking warm air through the filter of his teeth, he altered his path slightly so that he'd enter the smaller lizard's space.

The boy screamed again and lashed out with one filthy, callused heel. The smaller lizard howled and lost his grip. For a moment, the boy twisted and kicked, dangling only a foot or so off the ground then, just as it seemed he might get free, the larger lizard grabbed his ankle with her other hand.

"Honestly. You can catch them, why can't you hold onto them?"

"It kicked me!"

"Stop acting like such a hatchling and remember you're about to be . . ." The lizard's amber eyes widened. "Behind you, Jurz! It's another one!"

Belatedly, Dean realized that the "other one" she was referring to was him. He realized it when Jurz, moving much faster on his bulky back legs than he'd expected, whirled around, pushed off with a thick tapering tail, and landed behind him, grabbing both his upper arms in a painful grip. He froze as talons pierced his shirt and punctured the skin. Even if he'd been able to turn, the lizard's body would have blocked his view of the elevator.

"Good gorg, Coriz, this one's huge!"

Coriz leaned forward and peered nearsightedly down at him, holding the boy tighter against her chest. "And it's a funny color."

Dean felt his hair being lifted by the force of Jurz' inhalation.

"And it's clean! Maybe," he added thoughtfully, "we could eat it."

"Eat it! Are you out of your mind?" Coriz sat back on her tail, shifting her hold on the boy. "It's still a filthy egg-sucker no matter how clean it is. People get sick from eating those vermin!"

"Hey!" The insult broke through the terror. "Who're you callin' vermin?"

Both lizards stiffened. The boy continued struggling.

"Look, this whole thing is a major misunderstanding." It took an effort to speak calmly with five small, painful holes in each arm, but Dean managed. Coriz stared at him—with no nose, nor eyebrows, nor lips to speak of, he couldn't read her expression, but he could feel the weight of Jurz' gaze on the top of his head. He obviously had their attention. All he had to do was stall until Claire arrived to save him. "Why don't we just talk this over. . . ."

"Talk?" Coriz squeaked and dropped the boy.

Who took off at a dead run, occasionally using his hands against the rock for better speed as he escaped.

"Talk?" she repeated, rearing back on her tail. "It TALKS?"

"Of course it doesn't talk," Jurz muttered nervously. "It's just making sounds, imitating speech."

Although he couldn't be positive, Dean thought the female lizard looked relieved. "No! You're wrong!" Struggling drove the talons in deeper. "I'm talking!"

They ignored him.

"Imitating speech, of course." Coriz sighed, the tension leaving her narrow shoulders.

"I'm not imitating . . ."

"Still, it does seem somehow more evolved than the others we've caught."

Jurz' grip shifted, poking new holes into his left arm. Without the talons filling the punctures, the originals began to dribble blood. "Do I kill it?"

"Of course you kill it."

"Hey!"

"Hopefully, it hasn't bred. Just imagine if the egg-suckers started to think." She shuddered. "They do enough damage to the nests now."

On cue came the horrible sound of smashing shells.

"MY BABIES!"

Jurz dropped Dean, smacked him toward the lava pit with his tail, and raced after his howling mate. Fortunately, he misjudged either the distance or the weight of the object he was attempting to sink.

Legs out over the pit, bottoms of his jeans beginning to scorch and his feet inside the steel toes of his workboots uncomfortably hot, hands abraded by the hardened lava, Dean stopped himself at the last possible instant. Rolling forward, he collapsed as flat as the terrain allowed, trying to catch his breath.

"Come on!" Claire knew she didn't have a hope of lifting Dean if he was actually injured, but that didn't stop her from grabbing at his arm and hauling upward. "Jacques isn't going to hold them for long." The fabric compacted warm and damp under her hands.

Sucking in an unwelcome lungful of air, Dean shook her off and, coughing, heaved himself up onto his feet. "Jacques?"

"He's dead. They can't hurt him." Claire gaped at the smear of red across her palms. "How bad is it?"

"Not bad."

"Can you run?"

He shoved his glasses back into place. "Sure. No problem."

Side by side they pounded back toward the elevator propelled by enraged howls and French Canadian invective.

Twenty feet from safety, Jacques caught up. "I have no smell," he explained, effortlessly keeping pace. "*Les lezards,* they count the eggs but that should not take them . . ."

The howls changed timbre.

" . . . long."

When Dean stopped to roll a hunk of obsidian away from the door, Claire hip-checked him over the threshold, grabbed the rock, and flung it toward their pursuers.

The howls changed again.

"OW! Coriz, they hit me with a rock!"

"Egg-suckers don't use weapons."

"But I've got a bump!"

The door cut off further diagnosis.

"What part," Claire gasped, dropping the gate into place and turning to glare at Dean, "of no one leaves the elevator did you not understand?"

"They were about to kill the kid."

"So? He was robbing their nest. Stealing their eggs. Making omelets."

"I couldn't just watch him die!"

"Then we should have closed the door."

"You don't mean that."

She did. Or she thought she did until she met his eyes and discovered that he believed she'd have gone to the rescue herself had he not been there. "Forget it. Go straight to the basement. No arguments."

Dean pushed the lever all the way to the left. "No arguments," he agreed. Passing the second floor, he glanced over at Jacques. "Did you really break one of their eggs?"

"And how do I do that?" the ghost asked, pushing his hand through the wall of the elevator. "I touch nothing."

"I stomped on a bunch of shells that had already hatched," Claire explained. "Jacques stayed behind to distract them."

"Why didn't you . . ."

"Use magic? Because the possibilities were different there and, since you decided to play hero, I didn't have time to work out a way through. Look at me, I'm filthy. I had to lie down on that black stuff with my feet still in the elevator to reach a rock for the door, and if you ever pull such a stupid, boneheaded stunt again, I'm leaving you to cook in the lava pit! Do I make myself clear?"

Ears burning, Dean ducked his head. "Yes, Boss."

"When we reach bottom, I want a look at those arms."

"It's nothing." A drop of blood traced a trail over the back of his hand, down his index finger, and dripped onto the floor.

She glared at him through slitted eyes. "I'll be the judge of that."

"A glass of rum in the belly and one on the wounds. He will be fine, Claire."

"I have antibiotic cream in my bathroom," Dean offered hurriedly. "I can take care of it."

"Bring the cream to the dining room." As the bottom of the elevator settled into its concrete basin, Claire tossed up the gate, picked up the doily, and stomped out into the basement.

"You stink like an active volcano," Austin complained, jumping down off a shelf. "Have a nice time?"

All three brushed by him without answering. Dean went into his apartment. Jacques followed Claire up the basement stairs.

"Guess not." He stuck his head over the threshold and sniffed at the bit of tentacle lying on the floor. His ears went back. "Who let the sushi out of the fridge?"

"So stoic," Jacques murmured sarcastically as Dean, sitting on the dining room table, tried not to jerk his arm out from under Claire's ministrations. "So much a man."

"Stuff a sock in it," Dean grunted.

"So articulate."

"Stop it. Both of you." Shirtless, Dean had pretty much lived up to Claire's expectations. Eyes locked on the wounds instead of the rippling expanse of bare chest, she dabbed antibiotic cream on the punctures and fought to keep her mind on the job. "None of these are deep. You were lucky. He could've ripped your whole arm off. Both arms." She was babbling. She knew it, but she couldn't seem to stop. "Ripped both your stupid arms off and thrown them on the ground." He not only looked great, he smelled terrific. Which had nothing to do with the matter at hand. Nothing at all. "You'd have bled to death before I could get to you. You could have been killed."

Jacques snickered. "Such a *magnifique* manner beside the bed, *cherie.*"

"I'm just saying," she began, and stopped. "I'm just saying," she repeated, "that I need him to run this hotel and . . ." If she hadn't looked up and seen Dean watching her, his expression teetering halfway between hope and disappointment, she could've left it at that. ". . . I've gotten used to having him around and I don't . . ." The end of one finger covered in cream, she poked at the last three punctures. ". . . want him dead."

"Ow."

"Sorry."

"About what?" Austin asked, jumping up onto the table beside Dean. "And what happened to your arms? And, just out of curiosity, why don't you have any chest hair?"

While a blushing Dean shrugged into his shirt, Claire answered the first two questions.

"And the chest hair?" the cat prodded when she finished.

She picked him up and dropped him on the floor.

"You're just mad because I was right," he muttered as he jumped back up again. "I can see the sign now. This elevator holds a maximum of . . . How many dimensions?"

"That's not important."

"It will be to the elevator certification guys."

"I'll get some drywall and reseal the doors tomorrow," Dean offered.

"No." When three pairs of eyes locked on her, she shrugged. "I'd like to study it for a while, maybe I can fix it. It's perfectly safe if you all stay off it."

"And if *you* stay off it, *cherie.*"

"I know enough to stay in it."

"Penny for your thoughts?" Austin asked from the other pillow.

Claire rolled onto her side and stroked his head. "That only works if you hand me the penny," she reminded him.

"If I had hands . . ."

She smiled. "I was thinking about . . ." *How Jacques and I make a good team. How I felt when I saw Dean lying on the rocks. How one of them's too young and the other's too dead. How a Keeper should be able to keep her mind on the job even if it has been six months which is a bit of personal information relevant to absolutely nothing.* ". . . the elevator."

"Really?"

Why doesn't Dean have any chest hair? "Uh-huh."

"Liar."

ISN'T THAT OUR LINE?

TEN

By the last Saturday in October, it was obvious that the seepage had been successfully contained. Hell had tried directing it, spreading it, and cutting it off completely; nothing worked. When a sudden cold snap drove Claire into the furnace room to adjust the heat, she found Hell hunkered down and sulking.

It continued to make personal appearances, however. As long as evil existed, Hell explained wearing Dean's face in Claire's mirror, personal temptation would be its stock in trade.

Cautious experimentation with the elevator determined that if the door was opened by someone outside in the hall, passengers could actually exit onto the desired floor. Seepage, or lack of it, affected neither the mechanical functioning nor the variety of destinations. As far as Claire could determine, the elevator had no actual connection to Hell and only a tenuous connection to reality.

But there *was* one unfortunate casualty of the seepage slowdown.

"I guess this'll be the next thing you'll get rid of," Austin sighed, perched on the silent bust of the king of rock and roll.

The sitting room, emptied to essentials, had a lobotomized look, as though all personality had been surgically removed. Stripped of their accessories, Augustus Smythe's florid, over-sized furniture seemed self-consciously large.

Although she'd had every intention of removing the plaster head, Claire surrendered to the pale green stare making unsubtle demands from the top of the high-gloss pompadour. "If it means that much to you, it can stay."

"Will you start it up again?"

"No."

"You could adapt it to run off the middle of the possibilities."

"No."

"But . . ."

"I said, no. It'd be easier to go out and buy a complete set of

CDs and a stereo." Either Augustus Smythe had taken his stereo with him when he'd abandoned the site, or, unlike most men, who tended to buy stereo equipment before unimportant things like groceries or clothing, he'd never owned one.

"If you're afraid of a bit of hard work . . . ."

"Don't start with me, Austin. Elvis has left the building." Before the cat could claw his way through her resolve, Claire turned on a heel and headed for the bedroom. The bust hadn't been the only amusement in Augustus Smythe's rooms to run on seepage. Grabbing the fringed curtain hanging over the postcard, she flung it open and barely managed to bite back a startled scream.

"What?" Diana twisted far enough to see that nothing particularly startling had slipped into the space behind her. When she saw that nothing had, she shrugged and directed her attention back out of the postcard. "You don't look so good, Claire. Maybe you ought to sit down."

Not really hearing her sister's suggestion, Claire staggered backward until she hit the edge of the bed and sat. "What are you *doing* in there?"

"Practicing postcards. Mom said you had one running so I thought I'd see if I could tap into it . . ."

Claire began breathing again. Diana's room had not been part of Augustus Smythe's dirty little picture gallery.

". . . that way you could see me, too, and I couldn't be accused of spying on you."

Theoretically, that wouldn't be possible; as a Keeper, Claire would know if she were under observation even by another Keeper. However, since Diana had just tapped into a powerless postcard with no apparent difficulty, something that Claire doubted she could have managed even with nearly ten extra years of experience, she wasn't about to declare it couldn't be done. So she did the next best thing: "You postcard me, and I'll rip your liver out and feed it to you."

Diana grinned. "As if. You think I'm stupid enough to get that close?"

"Speaking of close, when did you get back from the Philippines?"

"Last week. I landed in San Francisco, stuck my two cents into a site Michelle was dealing with by Berkeley, took Amtrak to Chicago, helped One Bruce seal two small sites—both of them in the middle of major intersections, can you believe it—and flew home from there. I can't wait until I get to do this stuff on my own."

Claire couldn't remember hearing about any earthquakes or train derailments, and since Chicago seemed to be functioning at least as well as it ever did, she breathed a sigh of relief. "What about school?"

"I'll catch up." Dropping into an ancient beanbag chair that she'd long outgrown but refused to get rid of, Diana leaned left until she had to brace herself against the floor, then repeated the movement to the right.

"What are you doing?"

The younger woman straightened. "I was trying to get a better angle on your room. Mom says Dean's a major babe, so I was looking for him."

"Mom said Dean was a major babe?"

"Not exactly; she said he was 'quite an attractive young man' and I translated."

"This is my *bedroom*."

Diana snorted. "So that's why you have a bed in it."

"I don't even want to know why you think Dean might be in here."

"Well, jeez, Claire, I hope I don't have to explain it to you. At your age." After a self-appreciative snicker, she crossed her legs and settled back until it looked as though she'd perched on the crushed remains of a red vinyl flower. "Go and get him, *please*."

Even through the postcard, Claire felt the pull of power her younger sister laid on the magic word. "No," she said, folding her arms. "I am not putting Dean on display to fulfill your prurient interests."

"Ooo, prurient. Big word. So are you guys getting it on?"

"Diana!" Righteous indignation propelled her onto her feet. "Dean's a nice guy who does most . . ." Diana's left eyebrow rose. There was as little point in lying to her as there would have been in her lying. ". . . almost all . . . okay, all of the work around here. A nice guy. Do you even know what that means?"

"Sure, I know. It means he's not getting any."

"Diana!"

"Relax, I'm just yanking your chain." Lips pursed, she made a disgusted face. "Man I hope I'm not as big a prude when I'm almost thirty. I told One Bruce and Michelle about you getting stuck on an unsealable site and they both said that Keepers are sent where they're needed. Not very helpful, I thought. Anyway, since you're settled, I gave them both the phone number. They seemed to think that with you in one place and me still in training and us in contact because we're family, we have a chance to actually lay some lines of communication between Keepers. Which reminds me, the Apothecary is thinking of setting up as an on-line server so we can start using e-mail to stay in touch. Here we are, joining the twentieth century in time for the twenty-first."

Carrying on a conversation with Diana was often like shopping in a discount store: piles of topics crowded the aisles, stacked ceiling high in barely discernible order. The trick was pulling one single thing out to respond to. "The Apothecary doesn't even have electricity."

"I know. He says he can work around it. So what about you and this Jacques guy Mom mentioned?"

Claire sighed. "Jacques is dead."

"I know. But if the Apothecary can run e-mail without electricity . . ." She let her voice trail off but her eyebrows waggled suggestively up and down. "It sounds like what you really need is Jacques possessing Dean's body."

HELLO.

"That is never going to happen." Although Claire directed her response as much at Hell as at her sister, only her sister acknowledged it.

"I know."

"You know, you know, you know; you're beginning to sound like Austin."

Diana fixed Claire with an exasperated stare. "Keeping the peace, fulfilling destiny, that doesn't mean we can't be happy."

"I am as happy as I can be under the circumstances."

"Now who's sounding like Austin. What makes you think I'm talking about you?"

Claire winced. That had been incredibly insensitive of her. "I'm sorry, Diana. Did you have a problem you want me to help with?"

She grinned and shook her head. "No. But if you want, I'll come by and figure out how to deal with Sara, seal the pit, and get your butt on the road again."

"Diana!"

"Oh, chill, Claire." Dark brows dipped into a disdainful frown. "I'm five hundred and forty-one kilometers away, *she's* not going to hear me."

"Your butt is in a sling if she has!" Claire could feel nothing through the shield. Unfortunately, that only meant *she* hadn't yet gone through the shield. "If you'll excuse me, and even if you won't, I'm going to go check and see if you've started Armageddon." Ignoring protests, she closed the curtain with one hand and pulled at the neck of her cotton turtleneck with the other, telling herself that the room hadn't suddenly gotten warmer. She wasn't quite running as she crossed the sitting room.

"Can I assume you're not hurrying out to feed me?" Austin asked. "Who were you talking to?"

"Diana."

"Subverting a powerless postcard? Typical. What did she have to say for herself?"

"Nothing much. *Her* name. Out loud. Through a power link. If she's woken *her* up . . ."

Austin caught up to Claire at the door. "What are you going to do."

"Beats me. You know any good lullabies?"

Out in the lobby, Dean looked up from prying open a new gallon of paint as Keeper and cat raced for the stairs. "Problem, Boss?"

"I don't know."

"Need my help?"

Five weeks ago, even three weeks ago, she'd have snapped off an impatient "No." What good would a bystander be against a Keeper who'd attempted to control Hell? Today she paused and actually considered the possibilities before answering. "There's nothing you can do."

"Is it *her?*" Jacques asked, materializing as they started up the second flight of stairs.

"It could be," Claire panted, silently cursing the circumstances that made the elevator inoperative. It seemed to take forever to open the padlock, and the lack of noise from inside room six was surprisingly uncomforting.

The shield was intact. Aunt Sara lay, as she had, on the bed. The only footprints in the dust were Claire's, laid over her mother's, laid over her own and Dean's. She stepped forward, following the path, and studied the sleeping woman's face with narrowed eyes.

No change.

Sighing deeply, she took what felt like her first unconstricted breath since Diana had called Aunt Sara's name.

And sneezed.

Nose running, eyeballs beginning to itch, she backed out of the room and relocked the door.

"We are safe?" Jacques demanded from the top of the stairs. "*She* sleeps?"

"*She* sleeps," Claire reassured him, wiping her nose on a bit of old wadded-up tissue she'd found in the front pocket of her jeans.

"Admit it," Austin prodded as they started back downstairs, the ghost having gone on ahead to fill Dean in on the details, "you're a little disappointed."

Claire stopped dead and stared at the cat. After a moment, she closed her mouth and hurried to catch up. "All right, that settles it. We're taking a break in the renovations. You've been sucking up too many paint fumes."

"You're not willing to wake her yourself," Austin continued. "But you'd love to know who'd win if you went head-to-head. Keeper to Keeper."

"You're out of your furry little mind."

"One final battle to settle this whole thing. Winner takes all."

"Get real."

"I can't help but notice that you're not making an actual statement of denial."

PRIDE IS ONE OF . . .

"Yours. So you've said."

HAS ANYONE EVER POINTED OUT THAT IT'S VERY RUDE TO INTERRUPT LIKE THAT?

"Sorry."

USELESS APOLOGY. SINCERITY COUNTS.

"Get out of my head."

"Jacques told me what happened; is everything okay?" Dean asked as they descended into the lobby.

"Austin's senile," Claire told him tightly. "But other than that, things seem to be fine."

He watched her walk down the hall toward the kitchen and shook his head. "Once again," he sighed, "I'm left muddled." Stepping back, he put his right foot squarely down in the paint tray.

Two things occurred to him as he watched the dark green pigment soak into his work boot.

He hadn't left the paint tray there.

And he couldn't possibly have seen a five-inch-tall, lavender something diving behind the counter.

For the first Saturday since Claire'd begun handing out the money for groceries, there was considerably more than seventy dollars in the envelope. Dean whistled softly as she pulled out the wad and began counting the bills.

"One hundred and forty, one hundred and sixty, one hundred

and eight-five dollars." Tossed back into the safe, the envelope landed with non-paperlike clunk. "One hundred and eighty-six dollars," Claire corrected as she pulled a loonie out of the bottom corner.

"Premium cat food all around," Austin suggested from the top of the computer monitor.

"You're getting a premium cat food."

"I'm not, it's geriatric. I don't care how much it costs, it's not the same thing as that individual serving stuff they show on TV."

"And would you like it served in a crystal parfait dish, too?"

He sat up and looked interested. "It wouldn't hurt."

"Dream on."

"You're just mean, that's what you are." Lying down again, he pillowed his chin on his front paws. "Tempt me, taunt me, then feed me the same old beef byproducts."

"If it isn't for Austin, what's it for?" Dean wondered. "We've got lots of food."

"Frozen and canned," Claire reminded him, handing over the money. "Maybe you're supposed to stock upon fresh."

He fanned the stack with his thumb. "This is gonna buy a lot of lettuce."

In the end, unable to shake the feeling that she needed to be involved, Claire decided to go with him. It would be strange to leave the hotel so soon after going out to buy the new keyboard—something most site-bound Keepers would not be able to do—but with Hell itself reinforcing the shield, what could go wrong?

Austin, when applied to for his opinion, yawned and said, "The future is unclear to me. I'm probably faint from a lack of decent food."

"What if I promise to bring you some shrimp snacks?"

He snorted. "Too little, too late."

"He'd tell me if he saw a problem," Claire assured Dean a few minutes later as she climbed into the passenger side of the truck. "He's too fond of being proven right not to."

Baby heralded their return two-and-a-half hours later with a deafening volley of barks and a potent bit of flatulence.

"Couldn't have a wind from the north," Claire muttered, staggering slightly under the weight of the grocery bags she carried. "Oh, no. Has to come up off the lake and right over the canine trumpet section. What *has* that dog been eating?"

"Well, we haven't seen Mrs. Abrams for a while," Dean pointed out, unlocking the back door.

"Yoo hoo! Colleen dear. Have you got a moment?"

Silently accusing Dean of invoking demons, Claire took a step back and smiled over the fence. "Not right now, Mrs. Abrams. I'd like to get all these groceries inside."

"Oh, my, you have bought out the stores, haven't you. Are you having a party?"

Since she asked in the tone of someone who expected to be invited should said party materialize, Claire was quite happy to answer in the negative.

One hand clutching closed her heavy sweater—a disturbing shade of orange a tone or two lighter than her hair—Mrs. Abrams eyed the bags with disapproval. "Well you surely can't be planning on eating all of that yourself. It's extremely important for a young woman to watch her weight, you know. I don't like to brag, but when I was young I had a twenty-two inch waist."

"I've really got to go put these things away, Mrs. Abra . . ."

"I only need a moment, dear. The groceries will keep. After all, this is business. A very close, personal friend of mine, Professor Robert Joseph Jackson— Maybe you've heard of him? No? I can't understand why not, he's very big in his field. Anyway, Professor Jackson is coming to Kingston on November third. He's so busy over Halloween, you know. I'd love to have him stay here, of course, but Baby has taken such a strange dislike to him." She beamed down at the big dog. "I told him that I knew the nicest little hotel and that it was right next door to me, and he said he'd be thrilled to stay with you."

Claire could feel the bag holding the glass bottle of extra virgin olive oil beginning to slip. "I'll be expecting him, Mrs. Abrams. Thank you for recommending us." Rude or not, she began moving toward the door.

"Oh, it was no trouble at all, Colleen dear. I'm just so happy to see that you've taken my advice and have begun fixing the old place up. It has such potential you know. I see that young man is still with you. So nice to see a young man willing to work."

"Isn't it," Claire agreed as Dean rescued two of her four bags. "Good day, Mrs. Abrams."

"Professor Jackson will need a quiet room, remember." The last word rose to near stratospheric volume as her audience stepped over the threshold and into the hotel. Dogs blocks away began to bark.

"I wonder if we're asking for trouble, renting a room to a friend of Mrs. Abrams."

Dean turned from putting the vacuum pack of feta cheese in the fridge as Claire set her bags down on the counter beside the others. "More trouble than a hole to Hell in the basement?"

"You may have a point."

"He may," Austin agreed, leaping from chair to countertop. "But fortunately his hair hides it. While you were out, a guy named Hermes Gruidae called. He's bringing a seniors' tour group through tonight, retired Olympians, and needs four double rooms and a single. I said there'd be no problem."

"Retired Olympians?" Dean fished a black olive out of a deli container and popped it in his mouth. "What sports?"

"He didn't say. He did mention that they're not very fond of restaurants and wondered if you could provide supper as well as tomorrow's breakfast. You being Dean in this case since I doubt they'd want beans and weiners on toast. I told him that would be fine. They'll be here about seven. Dinner at eight." He blinked. "What?"

Arms folded, Claire stared down at him suspiciously. "*You* took the message?"

"Please, I've been knocking receivers off hooks since I was a kitten."

"And you took Mr. Gruidae's reservation?"

"Well, I didn't write anything down if that's what you're asking although I did claw his name into the front counter."

"You what!"

"I'm kidding." Whiskers twitching, he climbed into one of the grocery bags. "Hey, where's my shrimp snacks?"

By six-forty-five the rooms had been prepared, the paint trays and drop cloths had been packed away, and Dean was in the kitchen taking the salmon steaks out of the marinade. Assuming that ex-Olympic athletes would be watching their weight, he'd also made a large Greek salad, and a kiwi flan for desert.

Wondering why she was so nervous, Claire checked the newly hunter green walls above the wainscoting in the stairwell and was relieved to discover that although they still smelled like fresh paint, they were dry. "Lucky for us that when Dean says he'll get to it first thing in the morning, he means predawn." Crossing over to the counter, she watched Austin race through a fast circuit of the office. "What's with you? Storm coming?"

"I don't know." He flung himself from the top of the desk to the top of the counter and skidded to a stop in front of Claire. "Something's coming." After three vigorous swipes of his tail, he added, "It feels sort of like a storm. Almost."

At six-fifty-two, a wide-bodied van of the type often used to shuttle travelers from airports to car rental lots parked in front of the hotel.

"Looks like they're here," Claire announced, moving toward the door.

Austin bounded to the floor and raced halfway up the first flight of stairs. "So's the storm."

"What are you talking about?"

His ears flattened against his skull. "Old . . ."

"Of course they're old, it's a seniors' tour." Adjusting her body temperature to counteract the evening chill, Claire went out to meet the driver as he emerged. He was a youngish man, late thirties maybe, wearing a brown corduroy jacket over a pair of khakis, one of those round white canvas hats that were so popular among the sort of people willing to pay forty five dollars for a canvas hat, and a pair of brown leather loafers. With wings.

"I have them taken off the sandals every fall," he told her, noticing the direction of her gaze. "I don't know what I hate more, cold feet or sandals and socks." He held out a tanned hand. "Hermes Gruidae; the second bit was assumed for the sake of a driver's license. You must be Claire Hansen. I believe I spoke to your cat about our reservations."

"He's not *my* cat," was the only thing Claire could manage to say.

"No. Of course not." Hermes looked appalled. "I wasn't implying ownership, merely that it was a cat I spoke to."

"Uh, right. I just came out to tell you that there aren't any stairs around back if you want to let your people off in the parking lot instead of out here."

"Not a bad idea, but I don't think you could get them to use a back door." He winced as an imperious voice demanded to know the reason for the delay. "They're a rather difficult bunch actually."

The voice had been speaking flawless Classical Greek—although Claire spoke only English and bad grade school French, Keepers were language receptive, it being more important in their job to understand than to be understood. "Retired Olympians," she muttered, examining the words from a new angle. "Oh, God."

"Gods, actually," Hermes corrected, sounding resigned. He

hustled back out of the way as an elderly man in a plaid blazer stomped down onto the sidewalk.

"You listen to me, Hermes, I'm not spending another moment sitting in that . . . Hel-lo." Smiling broadly, he stepped toward Claire, arms held out. "And who is this fair maiden?" he asked in equally flawless English, capturing her hand. "Surely not Helen back again to destroy us with her beauty."

"Not fair and not a maiden!" snapped a woman's voice from inside the van. "Keep your hands to yourself, you old goat. Get back here and help me out of this thing."

Belatedly Claire realized that her fingers were being thoroughly kissed and an arm had slipped around her waist, one liver-spotted hand damply clutching her hip.

"Zeus! I'm warning you . . . !"

Silently mouthing, "Later," Zeus gave her one final squeeze and returned to the van.

Objectively, the Lord of Olympus was shorter than Claire would have expected him to be, had she actually spent any time thinking about it, and someone should have mentioned that the white belt and shoe ensemble wasn't worn north of the Carolinas after Labor Day. He'd been handsome once, but over two millennia of rich food and carnal exercise had left the square jaw jowly under the short curly beard, the dark eyes deep-set and rimmed with pink over purple pouches, and his Grecian Formula hair artfully combed to hide as much scalp as possible. An expensive camera bounced just above the broad curve of his belly, the strap hidden in the folds of his neck.

And if that was Zeus . . .

Hera, clawlike hand clutching her husband's arm, reminded Claire of an ex-First Lady from the American side of the border. Her skin stretched tight over the bones of her face, her makeup applied with more artifice than art, she looked as though a solid blow would shatter her into a million irritated pieces. "The Elysian Fields Guest House? Honestly, Hermes, is this the best you could do?"

"It's the best for our needs," Hermes told her soothingly.

Claire found herself being examined by bright, birdlike eyes behind a raised lorgnette.

"Oh, a Keeper," Hera sniffed. "I see."

The second man out of the van paused to stretch, both hands in the small of his back. Incredibly thin and still tall in spite of stooped shoulders, he was dressed all in black—jacket, shirt, pants, shoes—with a crimson ascot at his throat. A hawklike hook of a nose made even more prominent by the cadaverous cheeks completely overwhelmed his face although a neatly trimmed silver goatee and full head of silver hair did what they could to balance things out.

A tiny white-haired woman in a lavender pantsuit draped in a multitude of pastel scarves followed him out. "Oh, look, Hades!" Wide-eyed, she pointed gracefully toward the eaves of the hotel. "A white pigeon! It's an omen."

Hades obligingly looked.

The pigeon plummeted earthward, hitting the ground with a distinct splat.

"Did I do that?" Hades asked. "I didn't mean to."

"Senile old fool," Hera muttered, pushing past him.

"Never mind, dear." On her toes, Persephone rubbed her cheek against his shoulder. "Next time, just don't look so hard." Capturing a scarf as it slid out from under a heavy gold brooch, she fluttered ring-covered fingers around her body. "Oh, dear. I've forgotten my knitting."

"Never mind, Sephe. I've brought it out for you."

Claire had no idea who the woman handing Persephone her knitting bag might be. Running over the remaining goddesses in her head offered no clues. Pleasant looking, in the sensible clothes favored by elderly English birdwatchers, she reminded Claire of a retired teacher pulled back into duty and near the end of her rope.

As though aware of Claire's dilemma, she walked over and held out her hand. "Hello. You must be our host. I'm Amphitrite."

Her palm was damp and felt slightly scaly. "Pleased to meet you."

"She's Poseidon's wife," Persephone caroled. "Unless you're into those boring old classics, you've probably never heard of her."

"Shape-shifter's daughter," Hera sniffed in classical Greek.

"Hera." Persephone danced toward her, diamond earrings catching the light from the street lamp. "The eerperkay nunderstandsay reekgay."

Hera stared at the Queen of the Dead. "You are pathetic," she said after a moment.

"Who's pathetic?" Poseidon's gray hair and beard flowed in soft ripples over his greenish-gray tweed suit. He blinked owlishly around at the gathered company through green-tinted glasses, waiting for an answer. "Well?" he said after a moment.

Amphitrite took his hand and led him away from the van, murmuring into his ear.

"Well, of course she is," Poseidon snorted. "Inbreeding, don't
you know."

"Excuse me?" Knees up around his ears, Hades squatted by
the pigeon's body. "This bird is dead."

Claire saw acute embarrassment in Hermes' eyes as he sagged
back against the van's side and she hastily hid a smile, remembering that these relics weren't only his responsibility—they
were also his relatives.

Next in the open door was a man with a short buzz of steel-
gray hair over his ears, a broad, tanned face with an old scar
puckering one cheek, and the stocky rectangular build of someone who'd spent a lifetime doing hard physical labor. He swung
forward on a pair of canes—Claire assumed they were aluminum
until she heard the sound they made as they hit the concrete sidewalk. Steel. Uncapped—and swung himself out after them.
"Dytie," he bellowed over a broad shoulder, "are you coming?"

"No darlin', just breathing hard," laughed a voice from the
dark interior of the van.

The assembled company sighed, unified in resignation.

Aphrodite? Claire mouthed at Hermes. He nodded. Which
made the man with the canes Hephaestus.

The goddess of love had filled out a bit since the old days. The
hair was still a mass of ebony curls, piled high, and the eyes were
still violet under lashes so long they cast shadows on the curve of
pale cheeks although the cheeks had more curves than they once
did and the tiny point of the goddess' chin nestled in a soft bed of
rounded flesh. Although tightly bound into an approximation of
her old shape, it was obvious that within the reinforced Lycra
Aphrodite's body had returned to its fertility goddess roots.

Men could get lost in that cleavage, Claire thought. *Come to
think of it, men have.*

"Hermes, darling, it's a lovely little hotel. I can't wait to see
the inside."

"You can't wait to see the inside of a hotel?" Hera rolled her
eyes. "What a surprise."

"Bitch."

"Slut."

Sighing deeply, Hermes indicated that Claire should lead the
way. Feeling a little like the pied piper, she started up the stairs.

The retired Olympians followed.

"Hades dear, do leave the pigeon where it is."

Claire had no idea how Hermes did it, but he managed to get them all into their rooms by seven-twenty with the promise that their luggage would follow immediately. Since Dean was still cooking, Claire went back outside to help.

"Small pocket in the space-time continuum," Hermes explained as her jaw dropped at the growing pile of suitcases, trunks, and garment bags covering the sidewalk. "Aphrodite travels with more clothing than Ginger took on that three-hour cruise, Hera uses her own bed linens, Persephone has more jewelry than the British royal family, and Poseidon always packs a couple dozen extra towels."

"It'll take forever to get all this stuff upstairs."

"Not hardly." He grinned. "After all, quick delivery is my middle name. If you'd be so kind as to keep an eye open for the neighbors . . ."

Since the only neighbor likely to be watching seemed to have deserted her post, Claire gave the all clear. Hair lifted off her forearms as Hermes twisted the possibilities and the luggage disappeared.

"Still a few perks left," he said with quiet satisfaction. "Thanks for your help. I'll just run the van around to the parking lot."

Wondering how much help she could've been, Claire went back inside.

"So," Austin asked from the countertop. "What are you going to tell Dean?"

"About what?"

"The ex-athletes he's expecting."

"Do you think he can handle the truth?"

The cat paused to wash a back leg. "Better that you tell him than he finds out the hard way. And if that lot's staying here so they can be themselves, he will find out." Peering at the floor, one paw braced against the side of the counter, he glanced up at Claire. "You know, a really nice person would lift me off here and keep me from straining old bones."

Claire scooped him into her arms and headed for the kitchen. "Hades killed a pigeon just by looking at it. I suppose Dean should be warned."

"You suppose? He should?" Austin snorted. "If you're tired of having him around, wouldn't it be easier just to fire him?"

"I am *not* tired of having him around. I'm just not looking forward to explaining something he has no frame of reference for. You have to admit that not many kids get a classical education these days."

"You want him to get a classical education? Wait'll Aphrodite gets a look at him."

When they got to the dining room, they found Hermes leaning over the counter inhaling appreciatively. "I hope you don't mind," he said as they approached, "but I've introduced myself to Dean and explained a bit of the situation."

"Really?" The counter was covered in food, so Claire set the cat down on the floor. He shot her an indignant look and stalked away. "Which bits?"

Recognizing her tone, Dean hurriedly turned from the stove. "Mr. Gruidae . . ."

"Please; Hermes."

". . . explained that the guests aren't actually ex-athletes but from a place called Mount Olympus. In Greece."

"And this means to you?" Claire asked.

Dean sighed, clearly disappointed. "That none of them knew Fred Hayward. He was an old buddy of my granddad's who was on the Canadian hockey team at the Olympics in 1952. Great guy. He died in 1988 and I just, well, you know, wondered."

Claire exchanged a speaking glance with the messenger of the gods, picked up a stack of plates and began setting the table. "Dean, do the names Zeus and Hera mean anything to you?"

"Sure. I watch TV. I mean, they're kids' shows, but they're fun."

Hermes looked so distraught, Claire pushed him into a chair and attempted to convince Dean that there were distinct differences between television gods and real ones—even after retirement—and that if he didn't keep those differences in mind, it was going to be an interesting meal.

"So retired Olympians meant a bunch of old Greek Gods? The real ones?"

"Some of them, yes." She grabbed a handful of cutlery.

"Like in myths and stuff?"

"Post-myth but essentially, yes."

"Forks go on the left."

"I know that."

Holding a baking sheet of potato wedges roasted with lemon and dill, Dean turned and looked thoughtfully down at Hermes. "You're the guy on the flower delivery vans and stuff? The real guy?"

Hermes smiled and spread his hands. "Guilty."

"How come you're taking these retired gods on this road trip, then? Aren't you retired, too?"

"To answer your second question first: not as long as I remain on those flower delivery vans. As for the first bit, they were bored and I'm also responsible for treaties, commerce, and travelers. In the interest of keeping peace in the family, I try to get some of them out every year. This year, we've just finished a color tour of Northern Ontario. Zeus took a million pictures, most of them overexposed, and any leaves that weren't dead when we arrived were as soon as Hades finished admiring them. Now, if you'll excuse me . . ." He stood and twitched at the creases in the front of his khakis. ". . . I'd best wash the road dirt off before supper."

"Hermes."

One step from the door, his name stopped him cold.

Claire stepped in front of him and held out her hand. "Before you go, maybe you'd like to return the butter knife you slipped up your sleeve."

"That I slipped up my sleeve?" He drew himself up to his full height, the picture of affronted dignity. "Do you know who you're talking to, Keeper?"

"Yes." The missing knife flew out of his cuff and landed on her palm. "The God of Thieves."

Hades and Persephone were first down for dinner. Trailing half a dozen multicolored gossamer scarves, white hair swept up and held by golden combs, Persephone appeared in the dining room as though she were entering, stage right, and announced, "It feels so nice and homey to have an attendant spirit, doesn't it, dear?"

Murmuring a vaguely affirmative reply, Hades came in behind her, brushing the ends of scarves out of his way.

Behind the Lord of the Dead, looking perturbed, came Jacques. As god and goddess took their seats, he wafted over to the kitchen. "I am not a servant," he muttered as Claire folded napkins down over the baskets of fresh garlic buns. "Pick this up, put that there. . . . Who does she think she is?"

"The Queen of the Dead," Claire told him. "Not that it matters, you're noncorporeal, you can't touch anything."

"The things they have, I can touch. And also, I cannot leave them. I come when she calls. Like a dog."

"Jacques, get that scarf for me."

"What do I say? I am to fetch, like a dog."

"Jacques, do hurry, it's on the floor."

He paused, halfway through the counter and turned a petulant expression on Claire. "For this, I deserve a night of flesh."

Claire shook her head in sympathy as the goddess called for him a third time. "Perhaps you're right."

"I am?"

"Jacques, my scarf!"

"Is he?" Dean asked, glancing up from the salmon steaks and watching Jacques fly across the room with narrowed eyes.

Claire shrugged. "I said perhaps. He's stuck working for them, I just wanted to make him feel better about it."

He waved the spatula. "*I'm* working for them."

"Yes, but you get paid."

With his face toward the stove, she almost missed him saying, "I could be made to feel better about it."

All at once she understood. "This is the night you go out drinking with your friends from home, isn't it? And I never even thought to ask you if you'd mind staying here, I just assumed." This dinner had nothing to do with lineage business, and she had no right to commandeer a bystander's support. "I'm sorry. There'll be a little extra in your pay this week."

He looked up, turned toward her, flushed slightly, and after a moment said, "That wasn't what I meant."

Afraid she'd missed something, Claire never got the chance to ask.

"Sexual tensions," Aphrodite caroled from the doorway. "How I do love sexual tensions."

"*Not* at the dinner table," Hera snarled, pushing past.

"Fish." Dripping slightly, Poseidon wandered into the kitchen and peered nearsightedly down at the platter of salmon. "Finally, an edible meal." He straightened and blinked rheumy eyes in Claire's general direction. Fingers of both hands making pincer movements he moved closer. "Wanna do the lobster dance? Pinchy, pinchy."

"No. She doesn't." Still holding the spatula, Dean moved to intercept. He didn't care who the old geezer was, a couple of his granddad's friends had been dirty old men and the only defense was a strong offense. The God of the Oceans bumped up against his chest.

"Ow."

"Serves you right." Aphrodite pulled her husband from the kitchen and steered him toward his chair. "You promised you'd behave."

"My nose hurts."

"Good."

When all the gods but Zeus had assembled, Hermes cleared his throat and gestured toward the entry into the dining room, announcing, "The Lord of Olympus!"

"Where'd the trumpet fanfare come from?" Dean murmured into Claire's ear.

Claire shrugged, an answer to both the question and the gentle lapping of warm breath against her neck.

Striding into the room like a small-town politician, Zeus clapped shoulders and paid effusive compliments as he circled the table. The recipients looked sulky, senile, or indifferent, depending on temperament and number of functioning brain cells. Finally settling into his seat at the head of the table, he lifted his sherry glass of prune nectar and tossed it back.

With the meal officially begun, everyone began buttering buns and helping themselves to salad.

"Stupid, irritating ritual," Hephaestus muttered as Claire set his plate in front of him.

"If it makes him happy," Hermes cautioned.

"What's he going to do to me if he's unhappy, run over me with that domestic hunk of junk you're driving?" The God of the Forge smiled tightly and answered himself. "Not unless he wants to trust to secular mechanics the next time it breaks down."

"It's so pleasant to be ourselves," Amphitrite said quickly as Zeus frowned down the table. "But shouldn't you be eating with us, Keeper?"

Claire had already been over this with Dean. "As guests of the hotel, you're my responsibility. Besides, Dean did all the cooking."

"And it looks like a lovely meal. I find men who cook so . . ." Aphrodite's pause dripped with innuendo. ". . . intriguing."

"You find men who breathe intriguing," Hera muttered

"Harpy."

"Flotsam."

"More nectar?" Claire asked.

"I thought dinner went well," Austin observed, climbing onto Claire's lap. "Everyone survived."

"You have salmon on your breath."

He licked his whiskers. "And your point is?"

"Pick it up. Put it down. She drops a stitch in that infernal knitting and I must pick it up for her. If I were not already dead, that woman would drive me to chop off my own head." Jacques collapsed weightlessly down on the sofa beside Claire. "I thought that you should know, His Majesty, the Lord of the Dead, is downstairs talking to Hell and Her majesty wants him to come to bed. She is getting—How do you say?—impatient?"

". . . them to sit down and they did, but what they didn't know was that I'd shown them to the Chair of Forgetfulness and they couldn't get up again because uh, they, uh . . . Who was I talking about?"

THESEUS AND PIRITHOUS.

"I was?"

YES.

"Oh. They weren't the ones with the pomegranate seeds?"

NO.

"Are you sure? There was something about pomegranate seeds."

THE LADY PERSEPHONE ATE SEVEN POMEGRANATE SEEDS AND HAD TO REMAIN WITH YOU IN TARTARUS FOR PART OF THE YEAR.

"No, that wasn't it."

YES, IT WAS.

Hades' voice brightened. "Do you know my wife?"

Listening at the top of the stairs, Claire was tempted to leave Hades right where he was. Another hour or two of conversation and Hell would seal itself. Unfortunately, there was an impatient goddess in room two. Fortunately, it took very little to convince Hades, who'd forgotten where he was, to return to her.

KEEPER?

Almost to the door, herding the Lord of the Dead up the stairs in front of her, Claire paused. "What?"

IF WE WERE CAPABLE OF GRATITUDE . . .

"I didn't do it for you."

NEVERTHELESS.

Backed up against the dishwasher, the goddess of love so close he could see her image in the reflection of his glasses in her eyes, Dean had no easy out. The room started to spin, beads of sweat formed along his spine, and he knew that in a moment he'd do something he'd be embarrassed about for the rest of his life. He wasn't entirely sure what that was likely to be, but it certainly appeared that Aphrodite had a very good idea. Taking a deep breath, he dropped his shoulder, faked right, and moved left.

Fortunately, Aphrodite's corseting insured that her reach impeded her grasp.

Distance helped. With the length of the kitchen between them, he began to regain his equilibrium although his jeans were still uncomfortably tight. "The decaf's in the pot on the counter there, ma'am. Help yourself."

Tipping her cleavage forward, the goddess smiled. "You going to sweeten it for me, sugar?"

He pushed the sugar bowl toward her.

Her fingers lingered on his as she picked it up, and her expression segued from seductive to delighted. "Why, you're just a big old . . ."

"Dytie!" Even from the second floor landing, Hephaestus' voice carried. "Are you bothering that boy?"

"Why, yes, I do believe I am."

"Well, stop it and come to bed!"

To Dean's relief, she picked up her cup and turned to go, tossing a provocative, "Pleasant dreams, honeycake," in his general direction. He had an uncomfortable feeling it wasn't merely a suggestion.

Coming back downstairs from returning Hades to his wife, Claire stepped aside to let Aphrodite pass.

"You know, Keeper," the goddess said, leaning close, "that boy of yours is a treasure."

"Dean's not mine."

"Sure he is. Or he could be if you gave him a little bitsy bit of encouragement."

"Encouragement?"

"You're right." She patted Claire on the shoulder with one plump hand. "He won't understand subtle. Kick his feet out from under him and beat him to the floor."

"Dytie! You coming?"

"Not yet, darlin', and don't you start without me." Adding a quiet, "You remember what I said," she sashayed on past, and Claire descended the rest of the way to the lobby.

Hearing noises in the kitchen, she hurried down the hall. It could be a god getting a late night snack, but on the other hand, it could also be a god attempting a senile manifestation of ancient, eldritch powers with catastrophic results. The odds were about equal.

"Oh. It's you."

Dean closed the dishwasher and straightened. "I couldn't sleep without putting the dishes away."

"Kick his feet out from under him and beat him to the floor."

"Boss? You okay?"

She blinked and started breathing again. "Sorry. Just thinking of something Aphrodite said."

His ears turned scarlet.

"That boy of yours is a treasure."

"Are *you* okay? She didn't . . . well, you know."

To her surprise, his blush faded. "Would you care?" he asked, meeting her gaze.

"Of course I'd care. While you're under this roof, you're my responsibility and she's . . . well, she's a little overpowering. You wouldn't have much choice. Any choice."

"I'm not a kid," he said quietly, squaring his shoulders.

"I know that."

"Okay." Eyes on his shoes, Dean moved toward the basement stairs. "I'm done here."

"Lock your door."

He paused and stared back at her, his expression unreadable. "Sure."

Confused, Claire went to her own rooms, hoping that Jacques had been released from his attendance on Persephone. The way she was feeling, if he pushed her tonight . . .

Unfortunately, or perhaps fortunately since she knew she'd regret it in the morning, Jacques' nightly petition had been preempted by a goddess.

Dean had a suspicion that a locked door would stop no one in the hotel except him. He locked his anyway.

Right about now, down at the Portsmouth, Bobby would be attempting to wrest control of the jukebox away from the inevitable crowd of country-western types. He'd be unsuccessful, and Karen would have to go over. They'd have finished talking about the news from home and begun making plans to go back. Mike would be suggesting Colin'd had enough to drink and Colin'd be telling Mike to mind his own business.

The same thing happened every Saturday night.

Lying on his bed and staring up at the ceiling, Dean realized Claire hadn't actually asked him to stay and cook dinner. They'd both simply assumed he would because it needed to be done.

That seemed to make him more than a mere employee.

What would Aphrodite have done if he hadn't moved?

As more than a mere employee, did that give him . . .

Would she have done it right there in the kitchen?

. . . a chance to talk with Claire as an equal or would that whole Keeper thing . . .

So she was a bit older, but she was a goddess. She was probably a lot more flexible than she looked.

Claire was a bit older, too. . . .

"Okay. That's it." That was as far as those trains of thought were merging. Closing his eyes, he resolutely counted sheep until sleep claimed him.

Next door, in the furnace room, Hell sighed.

"Claire. Claire, wake up."

Pushing Austin's paw away from her face, Claire grunted, "What is it?" without actually opening her eyes.

"I just thought you ought to know there's a swan in your bathroom."

"A swan?"

"A really old swan."

"I am not going to sleep with you for a multitude of reasons, but for now, let's just deal with the first two." She flicked a finger into the air. "One, I am not even slightly attracted to poultry." A second finger rose. "And two, you're married."

"Hera's sound asleep." Shaking off his feathers, Zeus stepped out of the bathtub; chest out, stomach sucked in over skinny legs. "We're perfectly safe if no one wakes her up, and no one's going to wake her up."

Eyes closed, Claire missed seeing an orange something with yellow highlights speed out from under the sink and disappear through the open bathroom door. She groped for a towel and held a terry cloth bath sheet out in Zeus' general direction. "Here. Cover up."

When she felt him take it, she opened her eyes. Wrapped around his waist, the towel was a small improvement.

Leaning toward her, Zeus leered. "Would you prefer a shower of gold?"

"No."

"An eagle?"

"No."

"A satyr?"

"No."

"A white bull?"

"I said no."

"An ant?"

"You're kidding."

"Eurymedusa, daughter of Cleitus, bore me a son named Myrmidon when I seduced her in the form of an ant."

"Must've been some ant."

"Ant it is, then." Before Claire could stop him, his features twisted, his eyes briefly faceted, and a hair from each eyebrow grew about three feet. Panting, he collapsed against the vanity. "On second thought . . ." His right clutching his chest, he flung out his left arm, the flesh between elbow and armpit swaying gently. ". . . take me as I am."

Claire sighed. "Out of respect for your age and your mythology, I don't want to hurt you, but if you don't get out of my bathroom and go back to your own bed, you're going to be very sorry."

"I could call down the lightning for you," Zeus offered, continuing to support his weight on the sink. "And with any luck it'll strike more than once. Wink, wink, nudge . . ." The second nudge remained unvoiced as a violent banging on the door to Claire's suite cut him off.

"Open this door right now, you tramp! I know you've got my husband in there!"

Zeus paled. "It's Hera."

"What was your first clue?" Claire snapped, furious that the Lord of Olympus had involved her in such a humiliating situation. "I'll stall her, you get back to your own room."

"How? She's right outside the door."

"How did you get into my tub?"

His face brightened. "The tub. Right." Staggering back to it, he stepped inside and pulled the shower curtain closed. "I'll hide in here. You get rid of her."

Claire yanked the shower curtain open. "I meant that you should disappear the same way you appeared."

"I can't."

"You can't?"

"I'm old. Do you have any idea how much effort that took?" His lower lip went out in a classic pout. "Not that you appreciated it."

"Keeper, I'm warning you!" Mere wood and plaster did little to hinder Hera's volume. "Open this door, or I'll blow it off its hinges!"

"Can she?" Claire demanded.

Zeus shrugged. "Probably not."

"All right. I've had enough. Get out of there."

"But . . ."

"Now."

Muttering under his breath, the god obeyed.

Once he stood squarely on the bath mat, Claire grabbed his wrist and dragged him, mat and all, toward her sitting room.

"Where are we going?"

"We're going to explain this whole mess to your wife." Working one-handed, she released the wards around the sitting-room door. "This is your problem, not mine."

Zeus winced. "Actually, Keeper, if you've studied the classics, you'll know that's not how it usually . . ."

The door crashed open.

Framed in the doorway, her eyes blazing, Hera shook her hands free of the feathers trimming the sleeves of her peignoir and pointed a trembling finger at Claire. "I knew it, another one who can't keep her hands off him!"

"That's not . . ."

"Well, I know how to deal with you, you hussy, don't for a moment think that I don't!"

"Hera, I was asleep. I found him in my bathroom."

The goddess' lips thinned to invisibility. "That's what they all say."

"It's the truth."

"Ha!"

Claire could feel the possibilities expanding in unfamiliar ways. Yanking Zeus another couple of feet forward, she thrust him toward his wife. "Tell her!"

"I'm so sorry, my little myrtle leaf." Clutching the towel, he scuttled to Hera's side. "I was lured!"

"Shut up, you old goat. I'll deal with you later. But for now . . ." The finger still pointing at Claire began to tremble. ". . . we'll see how many husbands you seduce as a linden tree!"

The world twisted sideways.

When Claire could see again, everything seemed strangely two-dimensional. And green. By concentrating on where her neck should be, she lowered her head and took a look at her body. She wasn't a linden tree. She rather thought she was a dieffenbachia. And pot-bound at that.

"Isn't that a house plant, my love?"

"Shut up," Hera snarled. "I know what it is."

How dare she! Claire thought, leaves rustling. *How dare she assume that I would ever have anything to do with that dirty old man!*

A number of white flies with glowing red eyes, settled down on her stem. ANGER IS ONE OF OURS.

I know *that*. Carefully reaching toward the middle of the possibilities, Claire began to pull power. When she regained her own body, she was going to . . .

REVENGE IS ALSO ONE OF OURS.

Who asked you? Vaguely aware of a vibration in her fake terra-cotta pot, Claire swiveled her stem toward the doorway as Austin and Hermes pounded into the sitting room. *Oh, great. An audience. How much more embarrassing can this get?*

Hermes took one look at Claire and whirled to face Zeus. "Dad! What have you done?"

"It wasn't me."

"It's always you!"

More vibration. Heavier, mortal footprints. *Well, I guess that answers my previous question.* She needed watering and that made it difficult to concentrate but she tried to pull power faster before anyone else showed up to see her like this.

"Boss? I heard shouting. Are you all right?" Wearing his jeans, his glasses, and not much else, Dean looked around at the assembled company, eyes widening when he took in Zeus' equivalent state of undress. "Where's Claire?"

"Down here." Austin rubbed against her pot.

"She's shrunk, then?"

"She's a plant."

What are you looking at me for? Claire wondered. When he tried to touch a leaf, she snatched it away from his fingers.

He straightened. "Why?"

"Because my father," Hermes answered, "can't keep his withered old pecker in his pants."

"Here now, a little respect," Zeus began, but when he saw the expression on Dean's face, his voice trailed off and he sidled over behind Hera.

Weight forward on the balls of his feet, Dean brought his hands up, fingers not quite fists. "Change her back."

Hermes sighed. "As attractive as all that flexing is, it's not going to get you anywhere. At least not right now," he amended, glancing over at his father and Hera. "Let me deal with this." Adjusting the belt of his bathrobe, he fixed the Goddess of Marriage with a steely glare. "Try to remember this isn't some mortal or nymph you're unjustly accusing here. Even in a vegetative state, this is a Keeper. Eventually, she'll change herself back."

Hera sniffed. "I don't believe you."

"Then believe the cat. Would he be so calm if Claire's form were dependent on your whim?"

Austin yawned.

"Dean." Hermes turned around, came face to muscle with Dean's chest and took a moment to reengage cognitive faculties. "You know Claire better than I do. How do you think she feels about all this?"

"About being a plant?"

"Yes. Do you think she'll be angry when she's herself again."

"Oh, yeah."

Hermes shifted his attention to the goddess. "Change her back, Hera. Or you're going to have to deal with an angry Keeper."

"What can she do?"

"She can confine everyone to Olympus. For all the years of her life, it'll be nothing but shuffleboard, listening to Ares screw up the plots of old war movies, and actually looking forward to the night the Valkyrie come by for choral singing."

The goddess folded her arms. "So what."

Austin stretched and stood. "She can also cancel your cable."

Round circles of rouge stood out against suddenly pale skin.

"She didn't know what she was doing, lambie-kins." Zeus reached out a tentative hand and patted his wife's arm. "Change her back. For me."

"For you?" Penciled brows drew in, wrinkles falling into their accustomed place. "All right. Since you got her into this, I'll change her back for *you*."

He started for the door.

Hera grabbed the two, three-foot eyebrow hairs and yanked him back to her side, her other hand gesturing toward Claire.

The world didn't so much twist as flicker.

Fortunately, Claire had already pulled nearly enough power to effect the change on her own. Using the path Hera had opened, she stretched, straightened, and felt her lips draw back off her teeth. She couldn't remember ever being so angry.

Hell's silence stopped her after a single step. She could feel how much it was enjoying itself at her expense. Breathing heavily, she smoothed her pajamas and forced a smile. "Thank you for your intervention, Hermes. Now go to bed. All of you."

YOU STILL WANT TO SMASH THEM.

"Extra points for overcoming temptation," Claire told it. When the ex-Olympians hesitated, she added, "I'm going to try to forget this ever happened."

"Not very convincing," Hera muttered.

"Best you're going to get," Claire told her through clenched teeth.

The goddess nodded and, still holding Zeus' eyebrow hairs, headed for the stairs.

"Ow! Honeybunch, that hurts. . . ."

Hermes bowed slightly and followed.

Only Dean remained.

She had her hand raised to remove the humiliating memory from his mind when he asked, "Are you okay, Boss?" and she realized that was all that mattered to him. He didn't care that she'd been a plant as long as she was all right now.

But there were one or two things they still had to be clear on.

"I *didn't* invite Zeus in."

"Okay."

"He just appeared in my bathtub. As a swan."

Dean looked appalled. "I'll scour the tub tomorrow."

"I could have gotten rid of him on my own if Hera hadn't shown up."

"I don't doubt it for a moment."

And he didn't. "Good night, Dean."

"Good night, Boss."

"You know," Austin said as the door closed behind him, "that *Boss* is beginning to sound rather like an endearment."

This was not the time, nor the mood, to deal with that. "At least the others didn't show up."

"I suspect they keep a low profile when Hera's on the rampage."

Claire slapped the wards back up and staggered to the bathroom. "I need a drink."

"May I suggest a little compost tea?"

"No."

"So you'd as leaf not?"

"Oh, shut up."

Back in his own apartment, Dean pulled Claire's business card from his pocket expecting that it would give him some indication if she really wasn't all right.

> Aunt Claire, Keeper
> your Accident is my Opportunity
>
> (100% organically grown)

Reassured, he went back to bed.

The Olympians left directly after breakfast. Claire watched them climb into the van, fighting over who was sitting by what window, and raised a neutral hand in response to Hermes' wave. The moment the van pulled away, she raced upstairs.

"Where are you going?" Austin demanded.

"Something woke Hera last night. I'm going to find out what it was."

"With grape flavor crystals?"

"You'll see."

Standing by the bed in room one, she flung the crystals into the air. When they settled, there were tiny purple three-toed footprints on the bedside table.

"Go get Dean and Jacques," Claire said.

Unusually quiet, Austin left the room.

"When Hermes said Poseidon leaves a room damp, he wasn't kidding."

"You think you have problems? I work like a dog for that Persephone and she does not even tip."

"You're dead. What would you do with money?"

"So I am dead." Jacques sniffed disdainfully. "It is, how do you say, the principle of the thing."

As they rounded the bed and saw Claire's expression, they fell silent. She pointed toward the bedside table. "I want that imp caught," she said.

It wasn't as easy as all that. Both men, the living and dead, were unsuccessful. The traps remained empty. Claire's mood grew worse.

"If anything's going to get done," Austin sighed, leaping down off the bed as the bathroom door slammed the next morning, "I've clearly got to do it myself."

"Uh, Boss? I can finish the wallpapering myself if you'd rather be somewhere else."

Fighting the urge to photosynthesize, Claire stepped out of the shaft of sunlight. "No. I said I'd help."

Wondering how much trouble he'd be in if he mentioned she was being more of a hindrance, Dean rolled the next sheet through the tray and laid it against the wall. "Could you please hand me the smoother."

"The what?"

Hands still holding the paper to the wall, he turned to point and froze.

Claire frowned and followed his line of sight.

Picking his way over the folds in the drop cloth, Austin crossed the dining-room table with something small and squirming in his mouth. Its legs were froglike and ended in three toes. Its arms, nearly as long as its legs, ended in two fingers and a thumb. Its eyes were small and black and it appeared to have no teeth. Covered in something between fur and scale, it changed color constantly.

As Austin drew even with Claire, he spit the imp out. "Yuck, those things taste awful."

The imp leaped off the table, scrambled up the wall, and dove under the wet wallpaper.

As the bulge headed for the ceiling, Claire snatched up the last full roll and, swinging it like a club bat, smacked it down again and again. And again.

When her arm dropped to her side, Dean pulled the roll from limp fingers.

Breathing heavily, she looked up at the barely noticeable lump. "I'm feeling much better now."

In the furnace room the silence filled all available space and pushed against the shield. After a moment, it found a voice.

SHE DESTROYED MY IMP!

YOUR IMP?

MY IMP. NOW, IT'S PERSONAL.

ELEVEN

Claire woke from uneasy dreams where images of Hell unfolded like overdone special effects, realized the date, and gave serious consideration to remaining in bed. Although the origins of Halloween were far older than the beliefs that had defined the pit in the furnace room, greeting card companies had seen to it that pointy-hatted hags and men in red long johns with pitchforks had risen to dominance over history.

If Hell intended to try anything big, it would make the attempt on October 31.

WELL?

NO. TOO OBVIOUS. SHE'LL BE EXPECTING SOMETHING TO HAPPEN TONIGHT.

BUT IF NOTHING HAPPENS, WON'T THAT MAKE HER SUSPICIOUS?

Hell considered it a moment. YOU'RE RIGHT. It sounded surprised. I WILL BIDE MY TIME. YOU MAY DO AS YOU PLEASE.

BUT WITHOUT YOU . . .

TRY HARDER.

"Diana's more likely to be a catalyst than a help, Mom."

"I don't like the thought of you there alone, tonight of all nights."

Which was the truth as far as it went. On the other hand, Claire couldn't really blame her mother for trying to get Diana out of the house on Halloween, not after the incident with the gob stoppers. "Don't worry, I'll be fine. Thanks to the seepage, the shield's never been as strong."

Claire felt as much as heard her mother's sigh. "Just be careful."

"I will."

"Doublecheck *her* shielding."

"I will."

"Your father says that you should try to convince Jacques to pass over. He says it isn't healthy for a spirit to be hanging about on the physical plane and that the links between worlds are weak over the next twenty-four hours. He says . . ." She paused and turned her mouth from the receiver. "Do you want to talk to her, Norman?" This second sigh held a different timbre. "Your father, who seems to think I have nothing better to do than pass on his commentary, says Jacques' presence could call other spirits and that you'd best ward against it unless you want to house a whole company of ghosts."

"Tell Dad that Jacques has been haunting this place for over seventy years and that hasn't happened yet. Tell him it's probably because of the nature of the site—ghosts don't want to be near it."

"Do you want to talk to him?"

"No, you can tell him. I'd better go now, Mom." Leaning out over the counter, she peered down the hall toward the dining room but couldn't see anything. "Dean and Austin are alone together in the kitchen."

"Is that a problem?"

"It could be. The geriatric kibble has been disappearing, but I don't think Austin's been eating it. I want to catch them in the act."

"Do you think they're destroying it?"

"No. Dean would never waste food."

"Surely you don't think *he's* eating it."

"No, but he does do all the cooking . . ." After final good-byes, Claire ducked under the counter and headed for the back of the building. Rounding the corner into the kitchen, she stopped short. "What are you doing?"

Dropping a handful of pumpkin innards into a colander, Dean looked up and smiled. "We forgot to get one on Saturday so I went to the market this morning."

"You're carving a jack-o'-lantern? Have you forgotten what's in the basement?"

"No, but . . ."

"Do you really think that, under the circumstances, it's a good idea to attract children to the door?"

His face fell. His shoulders slumped. "I guess not. But what'll we do with all the candy?"

"What candy?"

"All those bags of little chocolate bars and stuff we bought on Saturday."

"There's two bags less than there were," Austin pointed out from his sunny spot on the dining room table.

"Two bags?" Dean stared aghast at Claire who glared at the cat.

"Tattletale." Assuming there'd be no little visitors to the door, she'd also assumed the candy was for home consumption and acted accordingly. All right; perhaps a bit more than accordingly.

Sighing deeply, Dean stroked his hands down the sides of the pumpkin, fingers lingering over the dark orange curves. "I suppose I could do some baking. If I want to see the kids' costumes, I guess I can go to Karen's place tonight."

It was honest disappointment in his voice. He wasn't trying to manipulate her—regardless of how she might be responding. Claire couldn't decide if that was part of his charm or really, really irritating. "All right. I guess one jack-o'-lantern and a few candies can't hurt."

"Depends on how they're inserted," Austin observed.

"So you're what they call a Keeper these days." Her mother's image in the mirror folded her arms over her chest. "Put the boy in danger just because you can't bear to say no to him." Red eyes narrowed. "I certainly hope you're not feeling guilty for continually saying no to him on other fronts."

Claire finished brushing her teeth and spit. "What other fronts?"

"Don't tell me you haven't noticed his raging desires? His burning passion that only you can quench."

"Did you just acquire another romance writer?"

"Go ahead, scoff. It's no skin off my nose . . ." Skin disappeared off the entire face. ". . . if you break his heart."

"Oh, give it up, I am *not* breaking his heart." Dropping her toothbrush on the counter, Claire stomped from the bathroom.

The image lingered. "A mother knows," it said with a lipless smile.

"Is it that you want me to be gone?" Jacques demanded, his edges flickering in and out of focus. "I thought you were happy to have me here, with you."

Claire hadn't intended to hurt the ghost's feelings, but since feelings were pretty much all he was, she supposed it was inevitable. "All I said was that if you want to cross over, tonight would be a good night to go. The barriers between the physical world and the spiritual will be thin and . . . Austin!"

He looked up and drew his front leg back out of the rubber plant's green plastic pot. "What?"

"You know what."

"You'd think," he muttered, stalking from the sitting room, his tail a defiant flag flicking back and forth, "that after seventeen years she'd trust me. Use a flowerpot just once and you're branded for all nine lives."

When the cat's monologue of ill-usage faded, Claire turned her attention back to Jacques. "You're stalled here," she reminded him, "halfway between two worlds and, someday, you'll have to move on."

"Someday," he repeated, his fingers tracing the curve of her cheek. "If I, as you say, move on, will you miss me, *cherie*?"

"You know I will."

"Pour quoi?"

"Because I enjoy your company."

"Not as you could."

"What you seem to need is Jacques possessing Dean's body."

She shook the memory out of her head before Hell could comment, but Jacques seemed to see something in her face that made him smile.

"Perhaps you desire me to leave because you are afraid of the feeling I make in you. Of the feeling I have for you."

"Jacques, you're dead. Only a Keeper can give you flesh, and I'm the only Keeper in your . . ." About to say, life, she paused and reconsidered. ". . . in your existence."

"Then it is fate."

"What is?"

"You and I."

"Look, I just wanted to ask you if you wanted to move on; since you don't, I have things to do." Pulling enough power to brush him out of the way if he didn't move, she headed for the door.

He drifted aside to let her pass.

Fingers wrapped around the doorknob, she paused, expecting Jacques to put in one final plea for flesh. When he didn't, she left the room feeling vaguely cheated.

"What're you doing, Boss?"

Claire set the silver marking pen on the desk and worked the cramp out of her right hand. "I'm justifying tonight's potential danger. Trying to be a Keeper in spite of the situation." She nodded toward the huge wooden salad bowl half full of miniature chocolate bars, eyeball gum, and spider suckers. "Every piece of that candy has a rune written on the wrapper that'll nullify anything bad the kids might pick up."

"Like fruit and nuts instead of candy? Kidding," he added hastily as Claire's brows drew in. "I mean, I know there's sickos out there and I think it's great you're doing something about it."

"Thank you. Every time one of those sickos slips a doctored treat past street-proofing and parents, there's another hole ripped in the fabric of the universe and, given the metaphysical baggage carried by this time of the year, anything could slip through. Early November is a busy season for the lineage."

The chocolate bar he picked up looked ludicrously tiny as he tossed it from hand to hand. "Can I ask you something? Why don't you stop them before the kids get hurt?"

"You mean why don't we make everybody behave themselves instead of just cleaning up the mess once it's over? My sister used to ask that all the time." She'd stopped, but Claire suspected Diana still believed the world would be a better place if she were in charge. So did most teenagers; trouble was, Diana had power enough to take a shot at it. "It's that whole free-will thing; we're no more allowed to make choices for people than you are. We're just here to deal with the metaphysical consequences."

"Is there anything I can do?"

"You can stand in the doorway and hand this stuff out."

"I meant . . ."

"I know." There were times, Claire reflected, when a facetious comment just wasn't enough. "You're good people, Dean. That helps strengthen the universe all by itself."

"Kind of like moral Scotchgarding," Austin told him, unfolding on one of the upper bookshelves. "Now could one of you, preferably the taller one, help me down."

After the cat had settled on the monitor and Dean had returned to the kitchen to fetch the pumpkin, Claire tossed another chocolate bar into the bowl and said, "Thanks."

"No problem. You were having an honest, in-depth conversation, so I figured you'd soon run out of things to say."

"You know . . ." She poked him with a sucker stick. ". . . you can be really irritating."

"Only because I'm right."

The candy hit the bowl with more force than necessary.

"I'm right again, aren't I?"

"Shut up."

* * *

Dusk settled over the city, the streetlights came on, and clumps of children, many with bored adults in tow, began moving from door to door.

In the furnace room, the bits of Hell left off the newly formed personality, sent out invitations.

As the first group of kids climbed the stairs, the wards incised into the threshold with a salad fork . . .

"Why a salad fork?"

Claire shrugged. "It was the first thing I grabbed."

. . . remained dark.

Only two of the four wore anything recognizable as a costume. One of the others had rubbed a bit of dirt on his face although it might not have been intentional. They stood silently holding out pillowcases as Dean offered the bowl.

"Do you want to take a handful or should I do it?" he asked enthusiastically.

After a silent consultation, the largest of the four jerked her head toward the bowl. "You do it. You got bigger hands."

"Aren't you guys supposed to say 'trick or treat'?" Claire wondered as Dean dropped the runed candy into the bags.

A little boy, dressed vaguely like Luke Skywalker, giggled.

"What's so funny?"

Their spokesman rolled her eyes. "Trick or treat is way uncool." Clutching their pillowcases, they turned as one, pounded back to the sidewalk, and raced away.

"When I was a kid, I'm sure we worked harder at this," Claire muttered as she closed the door.

Cross-legged on the countertop, Jacques rematerialized. "When me, I was a kid, we knock over Monsieur Bouchard's . . . How do you say, outside house?"

"Outhouse. Privy."

"*Oui*. We knock it over, but we do not know Monsieur Bouchard is inside."

They turned to look at Dean.

He shrugged. "I don't really notice any difference."

One princess, one pirate, and four sets of street clothes later, the wards on the threshold blazed red.

Claire opened the door.

The Bogart grinned, showing broken stubs of yellow teeth. "Trick or treat."

She dropped a handful of unruned candy on its outstretched hand. "Treat."

"You sure?" It looked disappointed at her choice. "I gots some good tricks me."

"I'm sure."

Without bothering to rip off the wrappers, it popped a pair of chocolate bars into its mouth. "Good treat," it announced after a moment of vigorous masticating and an audible swallow. "Same times next year?"

"No promises."

The Bogart nodded. "Smart Keeper." A backward leap took it to the sidewalk where it paused, almost invisible in the increasing dark. "Biggers coming," it called and vanished.

"That wasn't a kid in a really good costume, was it?" Dean asked as Claire stepped back and closed the door.

She checked the wards. "No. And on any other night you probably wouldn't have seen it."

"What was it, then?"

"Do you remember those sparks off the energy that I told you about the first day I was here?"

He frowned thoughtfully and scratched at the back of his neck. "The ones you see that keep you from driving?"

"Essentially. There are places where the fabric of the universe is practically cheesecloth tonight so a lot of sparks are going to get through. Once through, it seems some of them are being called here. That was a Bogart."

"Humphrey?"

"I doubt it."

"Was it dangerous?"

"No." Dropping down onto the stairs, she stretched her legs out into the lobby. "But it could've gotten destructive if I hadn't bought it off."

He glanced down at the salad bowl. "With chocolate bars?"

"Why not?"

"Okay. What did it mean by biggers?"

"Bigger than it. More powerful, more dangerous."

"Will they be coming all night?"

"I don't know. They might stop coming if we blow out the jack-o'-lantern and turn off the front lights, but they might not."

"So we should blow out the candle and turn off the lights and see what happens."

Her eyes narrowed. "No."

"No?"

"I'm not cowering in the dark."

"But you didn't even want to do this." He was wearing what Claire had begun to recognize as his responsible face. "It was my idea and . . ."

"So?" She cut him off and stood as Austin announced more children approaching. "Since we've started it, we're going to finish it. And you might as well enjoy it."

The gypsy and the ghostbuster—although they might've been a pirate and a sewer worker, Claire wasn't entirely sure—looked startled when she opened the door before they knocked.

"How did you know we was coming?" the gypsy/pirate demanded.

Claire nodded toward the window where Austin could be seen silhouetted beside the pumpkin. "The cat told me."

The ghostbuster/sewer worker snorted. "Did not."

"My dad says this place is haunted," the gypsy/pirate announced.

"Your dad's right."

"Cool. Can we see the ghost?"

"No."

They accepted her refusal with the resigned grace of children used to being denied access to the adult world.

"The cat told me?" Austin asked as she closed the door.

"Hey, it's Halloween."

"Then you should have shown them the ghost," Jacques pointed out with a toss of his head.

"Jacques!"

Catching it one-handed, he set it back on his shoulders at a rakish angle. "If you give me flesh, I could not do that."

Suppressing a shudder, Claire glared at him. "If I gave you flesh right now, I'd smack it."

His grin broadened. "*D'accord.*"

"No."

"Tease."

The wards blazed red.

"Well . . ." Claire glanced around at the man, the cat, and the ghost as she reached for the door. ". . . let's check out the next contestant."

A young woman stood on the step. She had short brown hair, brown eyes, and matching Satin Claret lipstick and nail polish.

Claire tapped her own Satin Claret nails impatiently against the doorjamb. "You've got to be kidding."

The young woman shrugged. "Trick or treat?"

Behind her, Claire heard Dean gasp. "Boss. It's you."

"Not quite. It's a Waff, a kind of Co-walker. Technically, it's a death token."

"A what?"

"Don't worry about it." Folding her arms, Claire looked the Waff in the eye and said in her best primary schoolteacher voice, "You've no business being here. Go on, then. Off with you! Scram!"

Looking embarrassed about the entire incident, the Waff slunk down the steps and out of sight.

"Honestly," Claire sighed as she closed the door. "They used to get chased off by mortals, you'd think they'd know better than to even try against a Keeper."

"I doubt it had a choice," Austin pointed out, scratching vigorously behind one ear. "Once it was called, it had to come. Things are going to get a lot worse before they get better."

"Do you know that, or are you pontificating?"

He licked his nose and refused to answer.

Three sets of street clothes, a couple of Disney characters and a Gwyllion later, Dean headed for the kitchen under the pretext of getting coffee. He *was* going to get coffee, but that wasn't his only reason for going to the kitchen.

The Gwyllion had looked rather like one of the city's more colorful bag ladies and had been mumbling what sounded like directions to the bus station when Claire'd banished it with an iron cross she'd pulled out of her backpack. Without a backpack of his own, Dean opened the bread box for the next best thing.

A fairy bun.

Technically, it was a leftover brown'n'serve from supper, but in a pinch it'd have to do. As an Anglican minister, his granddad had fought a continual battle against the superstitions that rose up in isolated communities and had told him how even in the sixties many of the more traditional men would carry fairy buns into the woods to protect them from being led astray by the small spirits. Dean had never thought to ask what exactly his granddad had meant by small spirits but reasoned that anything that could make it up the steps to the door had to count.

He wrapped the bun in a paper towel and carefully squashed it down into the front right-hand pocket of his jeans. Turning to go, a movement in the parking lot caught his eye.

His truck was the only vehicle out there. If some of the older kids were about to do any damage, it would have to be to *his* truck.

Over his dead body. That truck had brought him from New-foundland to Kingston in February and, in one of the worst win-ters on record, had gone through everything he'd asked it to. And one thing he hadn't asked it to, but the gas pumps hadn't actually exploded and the police had determined that the large patch of black ice had been at fault rather than his driving, so technically it had been an uneventful trip. Anyway, he loved that truck.

Moving quietly to the window, he pushed aside enough of the vertical blinds to allow him to scout the enemy; no point in rush-ing out like an idiot if his truck was safe.

The most beautiful woman he'd ever seen looked in at him, smiled, and gracefully beckoned him closer.

Dean swallowed, hard. He could feel his Adam's apple bob-bing up and down like a buoy on high seas.

Her smile sharpened.

Moving from space to space between the vertical slats so that he wouldn't have to take his eyes off her, Dean shuffled toward the door.

"Dean?" Austin brushed up against his shins. "What are you looking at?"

His tongue felt thick. He had to force it to make words. "Irre-sistibly beautiful woman."

"Out there? In the parking lot?"

"Needs me. Needs me to go to her."

"Uh-huh. Look again."

A sudden sharp pain in Dean's calf jerked the world back into focus. Out in the parking lot, the beauty was no longer quite so irresistible. Her eyes held dark shadows, her teeth were far too white and there didn't seem to be much in the way of boundary between where she ended and the night began. Feeling as though he were standing on the edge of a fog-shrouded cliff, Dean stuffed trembling fingers into his pocket and grabbed one end of the fairy bun.

Belief is everything when dealing with baked goods.

A misty figure, vaguely woman-shaped directed her burning gaze down toward the cat and hissed angrily.

"Yeah, yeah, whatever. Nice try, now get lost. Come on," he added as the spirit disappeared, "let's get me a piece of that pork left from dinner, then get you back to the lobby before something else shows up."

Conscious of the blood slowly soaking into his jeans, Dean fed and followed without an argument.

"Well?" Claire asked impatiently as they came out into the light.

"I was right. He was in trouble. Judging from his reaction and the noise it made before it disappeared, I'm guessing it was a Lhiannan-Shee."

"A fairy sweetheart?"

"Not a sweetheart," Dean protested remembering its final appearance.

"We all have our bad days." Claire grabbed him by the elbow and spun him around. "Are you all right?"

"Sure." He felt a little light-headed and his skin prickled where the hair had risen all over his body, but he still had his soul, so the rest seemed too minor to mention.

"What happened to your leg?"

"Austin."

"Hey, I had to get his attention, didn't I?" Austin demanded as Claire turned a raised eyebrow in his direction.

"By attempting an amputation?"

Industriously washing a front paw, he ignored her.

"I know a man who die from a cat scratch," Jacques announced rematerializing halfway up the stairs. "The scratch, it went . . . How do you say, *septique*?"

"Septic."

"*Oui.* Had to cut it off and he dies."

"Died."

"*Oui.*" He smiled at Dean. "Should we cut off your leg now or later?"

"I'm fine."

"I'm insulted," Austin snorted. "My claws are clean."

"Maybe you'd better go wash your leg," Claire suggested, nodding toward her suite. "Use my bathroom. There's some antibiotic cream in the medicine chest."

At the sight of the roughly circular stain, Dean sucked in air through his teeth. About three inches in diameter, it was an ugly red-brown, darker in the center of the top curve. "Oh, man. I'll be right back."

"Where are you going?"

"To change. I don't get these jeans into cold water soon, I'll never get the blood out."

"Don't look out any windows!" Claire yelled as he ran for the basement. "I don't believe him," she muttered over the sound of his work boots clumping down the stairs. "One minute he's terrified, the next, a laundry problem drives the whole experience from his mind."

"He is right about the bloodstain and cold water," Jacques pointed out. "You see these?" He slapped his thighs. "Cover with blood when I fall in the lake and now, for eternity, clean."

Claire helped herself to a chocolate bar. "Don't you start."

A few moments later, Dean reentered the lobby in jeans so clean the creases were a lighter shade of blue.

"Well?"

He smiled. "I've been hurt worse while still on the bench."

"Next time I'll dig a little deeper," Austin muttered as another group of kids arrived.

For about half an hour, a steady procession of the neighborhood children climbed up the steps to claim their loot. Claire kept a wary eye on the wards while Dean stood in the open doorway, happily handing out the candy. By the time the crowd thinned and the stairs emptied, it was full dark.

"Uh, Boss? There's a real evil-looking cow down on the street."

"A cow?"

"Yeah. It's got barbed horns and glowing red eyes."

"Considering how the rest of the stuff's been manifesting, it's probably a Guytrash."

"What should I do?"

"Shut the door; it'll go away."

Brow creased, he did as he was told. "These things can't hurt the kids, can they?"

"Have you ever heard of a kid being hurt by a cow on Halloween?"

"Well, no, but . . ."

"This kind of manifestation can't hurt you if you don't believe it can hurt you, and frankly, not many people believe in the traditional ghoulies anymore." The wards blazed red and Claire reached for the door. "There's probably enough race memory left to give them a bit of a scare, but isn't that what tonight's abo . . . oh, my." She stared up at the very large man wearing what looked to be black plastic armor and shivered a little at the menace in the black plastic eyes.

"Truth or dare?" His voice was darker; deeper even, if that was possible.

It was essentially the same question. The trick was, never for an instant to show uncertainty. "Truth."

"You think you can do it alone, but you can't."

"What are you talking about?"

"You've had your truth." She could hear amusement in the dark tone. "Now, it's *my* turn."

"Hey, Nicho! Look who it is!"

A pair of six- or seven-year-olds charged up the stairs and grabbed onto the trailing black cloak.

"You are so cool, man."

"You're our favorite."

"It's *really* you, isn't it?"

He turned enough to look ominously down at them. "Yes. *Really.*"

"Cool."

"Way cool."

"Can we have your autograph?"

"Will you come home with me and meet our mom?"

"No, no! Better! Come to school with us tomorrow."

"Yeah, you could slice and dice those guys who won't let us on the swings."

"Slice and dice!"

The features of the mask were, of course, immobile, but Claire thought she could detect a faint hint of building panic as the question and comments continued at machine-gun speed.

"You looked a lot taller in the movie."

"Where'd you get those cool boots?"

"We loved the way you iced that guy without even touching him."

"You gonna be in the prequel?"

"I got the micro machine play set that looks just like you."

"I drew a picture of you on the inside cover of my reader. It was pretty good, but I got in trouble."

"Can I hold your light sa . . ."

"No." He yanked his cape from their hands.

"Oh, come on, just once."

"Me, too."

"I said, no."

"We wouldn't break it."

"Yeah, don't be such a jerk."

Breathing labored, he rushed down the steps, strode out onto the sidewalk, and disappeared.

"Cool."

"Yeah. Way cool."

The taller of the two looked speculatively up at Claire. "You got any gummy bears?"

* * *

"I'm melting, I'm melting . . ."

Swinging the empty bucket, Claire closed the door on the dissolving manifestation. "At least she stuck to the script."

"I always thought the CBC was overreacting about the effects of the American media," Dean said thoughtfully, "but now I'm not so sure."

"Aren't you a little young to be out so late."

The tiny girl watched the candy drop safely into her bag before answering. "My daddy just got home."

The shadowy figure at the bottom of the stairs raised an arm in a sheepish wave.

"I see. Well, what are you supposed to be?"

She tossed her head, setting a pair of realistic looking paper horse ears waggling, and spun around so Claire could see the tail pinned to the back of her jacket. "I'm a *pony*."

"Oh. Sorry."

"You've got a cat in the window," she continued. "I want a cat, but my stepmom's allergic. Can I come in and pet your cat? Just for a minute." Head to one side, she smiled engagingly. "Please."

"What about your father?"

She spun around again. "Daddy! Can I go pet the cat?"

The arm lifted in what could have been a wave of assent.

Like most cats, Austin was not fond of small children. Claire grinned and was about to step out of the way when she noticed the threshold seemed to be a darker color than the surrounding wood. Reaching into her pocket, she pulled out a paper packet of salt and, as the child's eyes widened, ripped it in half and threw it in her face.

The glamour faded.

The runes blazed red.

The little girl stretched six, seven feet tall, costume vanishing although the horse ears remained, curved fangs protruding from her lower jaw, oversized hands scraping at the bricks on either side of the door.

Daddy breathed fire.

Claire and Dean together slammed the door.

"That was close," Claire said with feeling as the latch finally caught.

Shoulders against the wood, Dean let out a breath he couldn't remember taking. "Do you always keep salt in your pocket?"

"Strange question from a man carrying a brown'n'serve."

* * *

"Aren't you guys a little old to be out tonight?"

One of the three identical junior skinheads scowled, differentiating himself momentarily from the other two. "Aren't you a little ugly to be passin' judgment?"

"Yeah. Just give over the fuckin' candy."

The teenager in the middle elbowed them both hard in the ribs. "What we meant to say, *ma'am,* was trick or treat."

Claire thought about it a moment as the boys postured. "Trick," she said at last and closed the door.

The boy with his boot thrust in on the threshold got a nasty surprise. They could hear his shriek even through the heavy wood.

"I think the bitch broke my fuckin' foot, man."

"They were going to egg us anyway," Claire explained. "I figured, why waste the candy."

"Egg us?" Dean repeated.

She grabbed his arm, stopping his charge. "Don't worry about it."

"These guys won't stop with eggs!"

"I think they will." A few minutes later, watching out the window as the last of the thrown eggs paused inches from the hotel and swept back, like all the rest, to smash on the now dripping and furious thrower, she sighed. "I guess I was wrong."

The hunk of broken concrete followed the same path as the eggs.

"Tricky downdrafts. That had to hurt."

Claire put herself bodily between Dean and the door as he tried to follow the will-o'-the-wisp dancing up and down the stairs. She allowed herself one small thought about the firm resilience of his stomach, then dug her shoulder in and shoved him far enough into the lobby to be able to close the door.

"That's it," she said when he was safely behind the counter. "It's ten o'clock. There won't be any more kids. I think we can blow out the candle and turn off the outside lights, honor intact."

The pumpkin lid refused to lift and all the air blown in through the carved face wouldn't put out the candle.

"Oh, nuts."

Two of the remaining four chocolate bars acquired almonds. Two didn't.

"Granddad?"

"No tricks, Dean, I promise. Come on out, we have a lot to say to each other."

"But you're dead."

"Never said I wasn't, but this is the night the dead walk."

"The restless dead."

"You think I'm not restless after what you did? Think again!"

"But Aunt Carol loves the house."

"I left it to you, you ungrateful whelp."

"Granddad, let me explain." One foot lifted to clear the threshold, Dean felt something crunch in his pocket and shoved a hand in to feel what it was.

The fairy bun.

The steps were empty.

"I thought I told you not to open that while I was gone." Claire stepped out of her sitting room as he jerked back and closed the door. "What was out there?"

"The ghost of my granddad."

"He's dead? Sorry, stupid question." She went out into the lobby and searched his face. "It wasn't actually him, you know."

"Yeah. I know."

"You don't look so good. Maybe you should go to bed."

"Will they keep coming?"

"Yes. Probably until dawn."

He lifted his chin and squared his shoulders. "Then I'll stay."

"What was *that*?"

"Fachan. They've gone back to the classics."

"That roast was for tomorrow's supper."

"Trust me, he wouldn't have been happy with candy."

Dawn seemed a long time coming.

"Any candy left?"

Claire tipped the bowl up on its side and tried to focus on the contents. Half a dozen empty wrappers fell out. "Looks like I've finished it."

"What were those last two things again."

"An ogre and a Duergar. Why?" She blew a weary bubble.

Dean pulled off his glasses and rubbed his eyes. "Did you really spin straw into gold?"

"It was going around in a circle, so technically it was spinning." The Duergar hadn't been entirely happy, but since it had the treat, it couldn't trick. The ogre, on the other hand, had ripped the railing out around the area and tossed it and the hotel sign out into the street. Treating an ogre meant feeding it dinner.

Ogres were man-eaters. The trick was knowing that.

Austin lifted his head off his paws and yawned. "Sun's up. And the candle just went out." He leaped off the windowsill as the pumpkin collapsed in on itself, smoking slightly.

Shoving his glasses back on approximately where they belonged, Dean stood and headed for the door. "I think I'll get that stuff off the road before there's an accident."

Dragging herself up onto her feet, Claire waited a moment until the world stopped spinning. "I think I'll go throw up."

THAT'S IT? YOU SCARED THEM A TIME OR TWO AND YOU DID A LITTLE DAMAGE AND YOU TIRED THEM OUT, BIG DEAL. THE KEEPER FIELDED EVERYTHING YOU THREW AT HER AND NEVER ONCE DREW POWER FROM LOWER THAN THE MIDDLE OF THE POSSIBILITIES.

SO LET'S SEE YOU DO BETTER. The rest of Hell sounded miffed.

BETTER?

OKAY. FINE. *WORSE.*

WAIT FOR IT. . . .

Down on one knee, the police constable poked at the hole torn in the concrete setting and shook his head. "When exactly did this happen?"

"About four A.M."

"Four-*twelve*," Mrs. Abrams corrected. "I know because when I heard the noise, and it was a terrible noise, I looked at my alarm clock and even though I bought it before Mr. Abrams died, God bless the man, it still keeps perfect time."

"Four-twelve," the constable repeated. "Did you happen to see who did it?"

"Oh, no! I wasn't going to expose myself to that kind of destructive hooliganism. That's what the police are paid for and that's why I called them."

"I was actually asking Ms. Hansen."

Since there'd been a chance of flying glass, Claire had stayed away from the window and so could truthfully answer, "Sorry, I didn't see anything."

"It was probably a gang of students from the university. They get a few too many drinks in them and go crazy."

"That sounds reasonable," Claire agreed as he stood. It wasn't what had happened, but it sounded reasonable. Most of the vandalism in Kingston conveniently got blamed on wandering gangs of students from the university who'd had a few too many drinks. Occasionally they were spotted in the distance, but no one ever managed to identify individuals since, like other legendary creatures, they vanished when too closely approached.

"When you arrest them," Mrs. Abrams said, so determined to do her civic duty that she clutched at the constable's sleeve, "you let me know. I'm the one who called. Mrs. Abrams. One *be* and an *ess*."

"You're the lady with the dog, aren't you?"

"You've heard of my Baby?" she beamed up at him.

The constable sighed. "Oh, yeah."

Another call dragged the grateful police officer back into his car and away. Mrs. Abrams transferred her attention to Claire.

"You haven't forgotten that Professor Jackson is coming to stay the day after tomorrow, have you, Kimberly, dear?"

"We're looking forward to it, Mrs. Abrams."

"I'm sure you'll take wonderful care of him. I'll likely be over to visit him while he's there. Only because Baby dislikes him so, you know. We wouldn't ever do anything compromising. Although," she simpered, "I used to be quite progressive in my younger days."

The worst of it was, she was telling the truth. Shuddering slightly, Claire went inside and spent the rest of the day trying to catch up on her sleep without dreaming of Mrs. Abrams and the professor in progressive positions. Had she not checked to insure all shields were holding, she'd have assumed the dreams, in graphic detail with full sound and color, had risen up out of the pit.

"You Claire Hansen?"

Claire checked, but the courier had not been called by Hell. Which made sense after she thought about it a moment; if something absolutely had to be delivered the next business day, Hell'd prefer it to be late. "Yes, I'm Claire Hansen."

"Sign here."

"Why?"

Although the young woman's expression made a rude comment, she kept her tone professional. "I got a package for you."

"You want me to sign for it, then, Boss?"

"*You* Claire Hansen?" the courier demanded.

"No, but . . ."

"Then *she's* got to sign it."

In return for her signature, Claire was handed a large, bulging manila envelope and an illegible receipt.

"Who's it from?" Dean asked as the courier carried her bike back down the front steps and rode away.

"More important," Jacques murmured appreciatively, rematerializing by the window, "what does she wear? Her legs, they look like they are painted black."

"They're tights."

"*Oui,* they are tight. Me, I do not complain, but they are allowed?"

"Sure."

He heaved a heavy if ethereal sigh. "I died too soon."

"The package is from Hermes," Claire interrupted with heavy emphasis.

Austin snickered. "Someone doesn't like not being the center of attention."

Ignoring him, she pulled a folded towel from the envelope and frowned. "Why would Hermes send us a towel?"

"It's one of ours," Dean declared, fingering the fabric. "It must've gotten accidentally mixed in with his stuff."

"He's the God of Thieves, Dean. I doubt it was an accident, and since I also doubt his conscience got the better of him, I wonder why he sent it back." A piece of paper, both sides filled with line after line of script, fell from a fold. "Maybe this explains it. *Dear Keeper,*" she read. *"Three days ago, I left your establishment with one of the items traditionally liberated from hotel rooms. Since that time, two ferries have attempted to sink out from under us and would have sunk had Poseidon not been on board to command the waves to carry us to shore. Our vehicle has broken down seven times. Hephaestus is happy, no one else is. For the first time since we began traveling, the border guards asked to see identification and then, when I informed them we were heading to Rochester, searched the van. The pocket in the space-time continuum didn't bother them as much as the cameras Zeus bought in Toronto but lost the receipts for. When we were finally allowed into the United States but warned by the most officious person it has ever been my displeasure to meet that we wouldn't be able to return to Canada—and, I might add, your admirable system of socialized medicine—Aphrodite had a flare up of an old complaint, and the clinic visit maxed out her credit card. While we were waiting for her, someone stole our travelers' checks. They were not American Express.*

The list continued for the rest of the front and onto the back of the paper and ended with:

So I return to you the item divination has determined is the cause of our recent difficulties. Please excuse the small scorch mark. Your security system is admirable if excessive.

—Yours in mythology,

Hermes.

"What security system?" Dean asked.

"I suspect that after all these years with an active accident site, the hotel's capable of providing its own security." Claire patted the terry cloth fondly. "Offhand, I'd say it's a *really* bad idea to steal our towels."

STOPPING THE SEEPAGE WON'T WEAKEN THE SHIELD, Hell told itself sulkily.

I'M NOT STOPPING THE SEEPAGE. I'M GATHERING IT.

TWELVE

Professor Jackson was a man of medium height trying to be tall. Under a hat last fashionable in the forties, he carried his chin high and his weight forward on the balls of his feet. Something about him suggested carpetbags to Claire although a quick glance over the counter showed only a perfectly normal, gray nylon suitcase.

"Am I your only guest?" he asked, signing the register with a precise flourish.

"At the moment." Claire dropped the key to room one into his outstretched hand. "Next floor up, turn left at the top of the stairs."

An expectant gaze drifted down to his luggage and then around the lobby, slid over Austin but rested for a moment on Claire. When she made no response, he sighed dramatically, picked up the suitcase, and started up the stairs.

At the sound of the professor's door closing, Austin opened his eyes. "Why don't you like him?"

"I don't know. Maybe because Baby's taken a strange dislike to him."

"That would only be strange if Baby actually *liked* anyone."

"Good point." Staring down at Professor Jackson's signature, Claire traced the loop of the "J" with one finger. Unless he was one of those rare nonpoliticians who believed their own lies, it was his real name and occupation. "I can't help thinking he's dangerous."

"How?"

"You're the cat, you tell me."

Austin thoughtfully washed his shoulder. "He looks like he's in his late fifties."

"So?"

"Ten years younger than Mrs. Abrams."

"Your point?"

"Do I have to spell it out? He's ten years younger than she is. He's younger. She's older. They're . . ."

Claire's eyes narrowed. "I don't care."

"Do you *want* to be a lonely old recluse?" Austin demanded, tail tip flipping back and forth.

"All right. Let's just get this settled once and for all." She drummed her fingernails against the counter. "I like Dean. He's a nice man and he's very attractive. Under normal circumstances, where I'd be moving in then moving out when the job was done, I might consider, were he willing, a short physical dalliance."

"Dalliance?"

Ignoring feline amusement, Claire went on. "However, I'm not going anywhere, and he's barely twenty. He's not going to be content staying here as chief cook and bottle washer forever."

"So you're going to give up now because you can't have forever?"

"I didn't say that."

"So you'd be willing to sleep with him and then move on, but you're not willing to extend the same courtesy to him?"

"I *really* didn't say that."

"So the problem is, you really want the one you can't have."

Claire stared at the cat for a long moment. Twice, she opened her mouth to say something, anything, but the words wouldn't come. Finally, she turned and walked away.

As the door to her sitting room closed behind her, Austin stretched out on the counter. "What would she do without me?"

"We lock the front door at ten-thirty."

"Why?"

"Pardon?"

Professor Jackson fixed Claire with an interrogative stare. "Why do you lock the front door at ten-thirty? Why not at ten? Or at eleven? Or at ten-forty-five? You don't know, do you? You've just always done it that way. Most people go through life without noticing what's going on around them. If I could show you the world beyond your pitiful little daily routines, well, you'd be amazed."

"Would I?"

"Amazed," he repeated. "I'll be back before ten-thirty."

"I can't help wondering," Claire said as the front door closed behind him, "just what exactly he's a professor of."

"Some kind of philosophy," Dean answered, coming into the lobby as she finished speaking. "He holds an appointment from an eminent Swiss university."

"That explains the accent."

Dean looked confused. "What accent?"

"Exactly. He's probably never been closer to Switzerland than a box of instant hot chocolate. I'm curious; how did you find this out?"

No closer to understanding than he had been, Dean shrugged and moved on. "Mrs. Abrams stopped me on my way up the driveway to make sure the professor got in okay."

"On your way up the driveway?"

He nodded. "She leaned out her window. I had to stop or the cab of the truck would've taken her head off. She was, um . . ." He paused, uncertain of how to describe the bouffant vision, her hair oranger and higher than he'd ever seen it.

"She was what?" Claire demanded. "Irritating?"

"No. Well, yes. But also, dressed up."

"Is *that* all."

Dean nodded. It was a weak description, but it would have to do. If she'd been dressed any more up, she could've rested her chin on them. Shuddering slightly, he tried his best to forget.

Conscious of Austin apparently asleep on the other end of the counter and Jacques watching bull riding in her sitting room, she tried not to sound stilted as she asked, "Did you have a good afternoon?"

"Sure." When she seemed to be waiting for further information, he added. "I went over to my friend Ted's. We gapped the plugs and points and changed to a winter-grade oil."

Since she had no idea what that meant, it seemed safest to make a noncommittal kind of sound.

"Did you want me for anything, then?"

"No." When he turned to go, she jumped into the pause. "That is, unless, if you like, we could maybe order a pizza and all three of us could watch a movie together this evening?"

"All three of us?"

"Four if you count Austin, but he'll lose interest if no one feeds him."

"Pizza and a movie?"

"Well, Jacques won't be eating. It's just I saw this ad, in the paper, and there's a pizza place on Johnson that rents videos, too, so you can have them both delivered. Together." She knew she was overexplaining, but she couldn't seem to stop. "I just thought that instead of cooking you might want to, uh, join us."

Chaperone us, decoded the little voice in her head. It wasn't coming from Hell, but then, it didn't have to.

"Sure."

Except this time *sure* meant, *if I have to*. Claire had begun to learn the dialect. "What's wrong?"

'Nothing. It's just, there's a game on . . .'

"No problem." Briefly, she wondered what sport, then dismissed the question as one of little importance. "We can watch the game."

His smiled blazed. "Great. Double cheese, pepperoni, mushrooms, and tomatoes?"

"That would be fine."

"I'll just go hang my jacket up and then I'll call."

On the way down the stairs, he checked the business card.

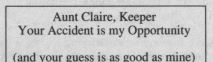

Aunt Claire, Keeper
Your Accident is my Opportunity

(and your guess is as good as mine)

Stretched out on his back, all four paws in the air, Austin opened one eye as Claire drummed her nails against the countertop. "You're not fooling anyone, you know."

"Get stuffed."

As the first period careened toward the end of its allotted twenty minutes, Claire gnawed on a length of pizza crust and wondered just exactly what she thought she was doing. While Jacques had originally resented Dean's intrusion into their evening, an involved discussion of how hockey had changed since his death had considerably mollified him. After an unsuccessful attempt to understand the fundamentals of icing, Claire gave up and tuned out.

If she didn't want to be alone with Jacques, all she had to do was remove his anchor from her sitting room; a simple solution that hadn't even occurred to her. Why not?

"Why not, what, *cherie*?"

"Did I say that out loud?"

"Oui."

She glanced over at Dean, who nodded. This was not good. In a working Keeper, the line between the conscious and subconscious had to be kept clearly defined. Fortunately, Montreal chose that moment to score, and by the end of the period the conversation had been forgotten by everyone but Claire. And Austin.

"Looks like things are coming to a head," he muttered under

the cover of yet another beer commercial. "Going to have to be resolved sooner or later."

"They've been resolved. Too young and too nice, and too dead."

"Dead's relative."

"It is *not*."

"Then can I have some pizza?"

"No."

"No, what, Boss?"

Before she could answer, they heard the front door open. Austin reached out and pressed the mute on the TV remote. "What?" he demanded, tucking the paw back under his ruff. "You trying to tell me that you guys don't want to know if he's alone?"

He wasn't.

"Mind the legs now, Professor. They're good quality, I only have good quality things, but they're not as young as they once were, you know, and I don't want to try and use them someday and find them warped."

At the unmistakable sound of Mrs. Abrams' voice, Jacques faded slightly, muttering, "Someone for everyone. *C'est legitime,* it's true what they say." He'd been strongly enough affected not to add an *entendre.*

Austin poked a paw through the ghost. "Get out in the lobby and see what they're talking about."

"Claire said I am not to spy on the guests."

"So spy on the neighbor!"

He started to dematerialize, then thought better of it and glanced at Claire.

"Go ahead."

"Jacques, don't." Dean's hand went through an ethereal arm. "They have a right to their privacy."

"Jacques, go. Or they'll be upstairs and we'll never know."

Turning toward Dean, Jacques spread his hands in a gesture that clearly indicated whose side of the argument he came down on and vanished.

"Don't tell me," Claire cautioned Dean before he could speak, "that you're not curious because I won't believe you. I mean, good quality legs?"

"Well, for a woman her age . . ." His voice trailed off as Jacques reappeared.

"They carry a small folding table."

"A card table?"

I see no cards but she is wood and square, like so." He held his hands out just beyond shoulder width.

"The table is?"

"Oui."

"They're going to play cards." Claire knew she had no right to feel relieved, but a card game was a lot less disturbing than what she'd been imagining. *Get a grip, Claire. Irritating old women have as much right to a sex life as you do. . . .*

"I'm glad Mrs. Abrams has a friend to share her interests," Dean said happily, reaching for the remote as the second period started.

Grinning broadly, Jacques rolled his eyes. One fell off the edge of the coffee table.

. . . maybe more.

With eight minutes still on the clock until the second intermission, Claire felt the hair lift off the back of her neck. "Something's happening."

"It's a power play for Montreal," Dean explained. "New Jersey got a penalty for high sticking, so they have one less man on the ice. They're only one goal ahead so Montreal wants to lengthen their lead."

"That's not what I meant." Claire heaved herself up out of the sofa and onto her feet. "Austin . . ."

"Yeah. I feel it, too." Tail twice its normal size, he jumped down onto the floor, breathing through his half-open mouth.

"It's coming from inside the hotel."

"The furnace room, then?" Dean asked, eyes locked on the television. Montreal had the puck. Hell could wait another twenty-three seconds.

"No, it's not the furnace room, and it's not *her* either."

"That's good."

"No, that's bad. An unidentified power surge in this building can't be good."

"Claire." Jacques stared at her through the translucent outline of his hand. "I am fading."

She was about to tell him to *stop* fading when the near panic in his declaration broke through. "You're not doing it on purpose?"

"Non."

"Medium."

How Austin had hissed a word containing no sibilants, Claire had no idea and no time to investigate. "Professor Jackson! They're not playing cards, they're having a seance and something's gone wrong; come on!" She ran for the door, the cat close on her heels.

The buzzer sounded the end of the power play, releasing Dean's attention. "Hey! Where are you going?"

"To save Jacques!"

He caught up in the office. "From what?" he asked as the four of them, Jacques nearly transparent, crossed the lobby.

"Professor Jackson is a medium," Claire told him starting up the stairs at full speed. "A real medium. Not a fake. They're rare—thank God. They have power over spirits."

"Comme moi?" His voice had faded with him.

"Yeah, like you." She missed a step, would've fallen except Dean grabbed her arm. "Thanks." Charging out into the second floor hall, she banged on the door to room one with her fist. "Mrs. Abrams! Professor Jackson! Stop what you're doing and open the door! Now!"

"Cherie . . ." One hand stretched toward her, Jacques disappeared.

"No!" Whirling around she reached through the possibilities for power, but before she could blow the door off its hinges, Dean stepped back and slammed the sole of his work boot into the lock. The effect was much the same.

Professor Jackson stood in the midst of a blazing vortex of tiny lights dancing on a manic wind—although stood wasn't entirely accurate as his feet dangled a good six inches off the floor. Sitting on the corner of the bed, the card table pulled up over her knees, Mrs. Abrams stared wide-eyed, one hand pressed up against her mouth, the other making shooing motions toward the lights.

"What's happening?" Although the hall had been silent, one step over the threshold, Dean had to shout to make himself heard.

"It looks like Jacques is more than he can handle."

Dean's eyes widened. "Jacques is attacking him?"

"Jacques is not doing anything. The professor started something he couldn't control."

"Then where is he?"

"Who?"

"Jacques!"

Claire waved a hand toward Professor Jackson. "He's in those lights. Bits of him may even be in the professor!"

"Connie!" Mrs. Abrams' shriek cut through the ambient noise like a vegetarian through tofu. "You've got to do something!"

Which was true.

"Dean! Try and keep Mrs. Abrams calm."

"While you do what?"

"While I rescue Jacques!"

"Be careful!" Body leaning almost forty-five degrees off verti-cal, he fought his way through the wind to the bed.

"It's the residual power from when *she* made him flesh!" Ears flat against his head, Austin had tucked himself into the angle be-tween floor and wall, claws hooked deeply into the carpet. He stared up at Claire through narrowed eyes. "Can you bring him back?"

"I think so!" Reaching for calm, Claire shuffled quickly for-ward, never breaking contact with the floor; at about half Dean's weight, she couldn't risk being blown away. A little better than an arm's length from the professor, she marked her spot and started to spin. She moved slowly at first, barely managing to keep her balance; then the power lifted her and she began to pick up speed as she rose into the air. The room whirled by, faster, faster, until the walls began to blur and the tiny points of light were pulled from their orbits around Professor Jackson. *Oh, dear; I really wish I hadn't had that third slice of pizza. . . .*

"Catherine! What do you think you're doing? You've got to save the professor!"

"She's trying to, Mrs. Abrams!" Dean wasn't entirely certain Mrs. Abrams had heard him. With Claire picking up speed, the winds had doubled in intensity. He ducked as the lamp from the bedside table flew by, cord dangling. The table followed close be-hind. On one knee beside the bed, he was horrified to feel it begin to shift. Throwing possible consequences, as it were, to the wind, he flung himself down beside the old woman, grabbed her around the waist with one arm, and blocked the professor's flying suitcase with the other. Under him, the bed bucked and twisted, fighting to throw off the extra weight that kept it on the floor.

The card table never moved. The flame of the single candle never flickered.

Even behind the protection of his glasses, the wind whipped the moisture from his eyes. Lids barely cracked, Dean watched the little lights leave the professor and move to circle Claire. Sometimes singly, sometimes in clumps, they did one figure eight around both spinning figures, then settled down in their new orbit. When all the lights had shifted, including a few pulled painfully from under the professor's skin, he breathed a sigh of relief and almost got beaned by a worn leather shaving kit sucked out of the bathroom and into the maelstrom.

It wasn't over yet.

Now the lights began to orbit a new position equally distant from both spinners. The third point on the triangle. Once again they traced a single figure eight and then began to spin in place.

The bed lifted, four inches, five, six, then banged back down onto the floor.

A familiar form began to take shape in the center of the lights. And then the lights began to spiral inward.

Muscles straining, Dean somehow managed to keep a protesting Mrs. Abrams on the bed. At least he thought she was protesting—he couldn't hear a thing she was shouting over the roaring of the wind, the pounding of his heart, and the cracking of her heels against his shins.

One by one, the drawers were sucked out of the bureau.

With every light that disappeared Jacques grew more defined.

Dean frowned. Too defined. "Claire! His clothes!"

She didn't seem to hear him but maybe the clothes came last.

More and more lights were absorbed until only a few remained. Jacques seemed more solid than he ever had.

Dean's gaze dropped. He almost let go of Mrs. Abrams in shock until he remembered the force of Jacques' spin had to be distorting reality.

The last light slid in under Jacques' left arm.

Nothing happened. All three bodies continued to spin. The wind continued to howl.

Although it was difficult to tell for certain with her face flicking in and out of sight, Dean thought that Claire frowned. The index finger of her right hand curved up to beckon imperiously.

One final light, almost too small to see, sucked free from the professor, circled Claire and smacked Jacques right between the eyes. Which opened.

The wind quit.

The candle flame went out.

". . . member of the Daughters of the Parliamentary Committee and if you don't stop this, this moment, I'll be speaking to my MP!" Mrs. Abrams' ultimatum echoed in the sudden silence. "Well." She tossed her head, the lacquered surface of her hair crackling against Dean's chin. "That's better."

In the confusion of three bodies and various pieces of furniture hitting the floor, Dean managed to get across the room to Claire's side before Mrs. Abrams could react to his presence. One of the bureau drawers bounced off his left shoulder, but he considered bruising of minor importance compared to being caught with his arm, uninvited, around her waist. She *might* thank him for keeping her out of the whirlwind, but the odds weren't good.

"Claire! Are you okay?"

"I'll be fine when the room stops whirling," she muttered.

"The room isn't moving."

"Says you." But she opened her eyes and lifted an arm. "Help me sit up."

"Candice! I demand an immediate explanation!"

With his left arm supporting her back, Claire shifted her weight against Dean's chest. "Mrs. Abrams," she sighed. "Go to sleep." They winced in unison at the sound of another body hitting the floor. "Put her back on the bed, would you, Dean."

The warmth of the sigh had spread through fabric to skin.

"Dean?"

He released her reluctantly. "But you . . ."

"I'm okay. Nothing wrong that a little vomiting couldn't cure." Dragging a dented wastebasket out from under the lamp and cradling it in her arms, she smiled wanly up at him. "No problem."

"If I could help, *cherie*?"

This was not something Dean could face on his knees. He stood, then turned, to find Jacques shrugging into a red-and-gray-checked flannel bathrobe. Reality, he noticed as the robe closed, appeared to have returned to normal proportions.

"Help Dean," Claire instructed from the floor. "I'll crawl over and check the professor."

"But, *cherie* . . ."

"I know. But not until we've got this mess cleared up."

About to add his protest to Jacques', Dean suddenly realized that if the ghost—or whatever he was now—was with him, he wouldn't be with Claire. "Come on." He jerked his head toward the bed. "You take her feet."

"*Cherie* . . ."

"Not now."

As Claire started crawling toward the professor, Jacques shrugged and, stroking both hands down the nap of the robe, followed Dean.

Austin had reached and done a preliminary diagnosis on the sprawled body of Professor Jackson by the time Claire arrived. "He's having trouble breathing."

"He's got a ten-pound cat sitting on his chest."

"I'm big-boned," Austin amended, primly stepping off onto the floor. "I think he's blown a fuse or two."

"Serves him right." Setting the wastebasket to one side, Claire bent over the professor and lifted his left eyelid between her thumb and forefinger.

"So giving Jacques flesh was the only solution?"

"If you had a better one . . . ?"

"Me? Oh, no."

Letting the eye close with an audible snap, Claire glared at the cat. Traces of the matrix Aunt Sara had created to give Jacques flesh had been causing the problem; it made logical sense, therefore, to use those traces to solve the problem. She couldn't have come up with a faster or more efficient solution. That was her story and even in the relative privacy of her own mind, she was sticking to it. "What are you implying?"

"Me? Nothing." As the professor's head gently lolled toward him, Austin reached out a paw and pushed it back. "Hadn't you better pay attention to what you're doing?"

Teeth clenched, Claire carefully pulled power. After a moment, Professor Jackson moaned and opened his eyes. "Where am I?" he asked breathily.

In ten years as an active Keeper only one person had asked a different question upon regaining consciousness and since, "Do it again," was actually a statement, Claire had always assumed it didn't count. "Never mind," she said, brushing his eyes closed. "Go to sleep."

When he, too, had been laid out on the bed, at a respectable distance from Mrs. Abrams in spite of Dean's protest and Jacques' alternative suggestion, Claire told the two men to leave the room.

"*Cherie,* we have not so much time."

"I know. But I gave you flesh to save you—and to save him," she added nodding toward the bed. "Not to . . . um . . ." Very conscious of Dean's presence, she couldn't finish, but when Jacques took her arm and turned her slowly to face him, she didn't resist. His fingers, lightly stroking her cheek, were cool. His mouth had twisted up in the smile she found so hard to resist. When his lips parted, she mirrored the motion.

"Ow! Austin!"

"May I remind you," he said as she stumbled backward and would have fallen had not Jacques and Dean both grabbed an arm, "that the bodies *already* on the bed need tending; memories need changing."

"I was going to . . ."

"Please, no details. Just take care of these two first."

Lips pressed into a thin line, she jerked free and nodded toward the door. "Fine. Everyone out."

Not even Jacques argued.

"You take this calmly," he said thoughtfully to Dean, as the door closed behind them.

Dean shrugged. He didn't feel calm. He didn't know how he felt. "You don't seem very affected either," he pointed out as they followed Austin down the stairs. "Except that you're walking kind of carefully . . ."

"I am not use to feeling the floor."

". . . and you keep touching yourself."

Jacques drew himself up to his full height, which, with both feet on the ground was considerable shorter than it had been. "Do I make these personal comment about you, *Anglais?*"

"Sorry." Ears red, Dean shoved his hands in the front pockets of his jeans. "So, uh, what do we do now?"

"I do not know."

"I do." Leaping down the last three stairs into the lobby, Austin turned and stared up at them. "Forgetting for the moment that one of you is dead and one isn't, and refusing to borrow trouble since none of us has any idea of how this is going to turn out, I think you should feed the cat."

"Wasn't there a half a slice of pizza left?" Claire asked, dropping onto the sofa almost two hours later. "I'm starved."

On the other end of the sofa, Austin opened one eye. "I let the mice take it," he said. "I didn't think anyone wanted it."

Pinching the bridge of her nose with one hand, Claire waved away the information with the other. Mice. Fine. Whatever. "Where are the guys?"

"Here I am." Jacques emerged from the bedroom, fiddling with the belt of the professor's robe. "I forget how many sensation in the world; old, new . . ."

Then the bathroom door opened and Dean came out, glasses in his hand, the edges of his hair damp. Claire opened and closed her mouth a time or two, but no sound emerged.

Dean's ears turned scarlet as he hastily shoved his glasses on. "I'm sorry, Claire. I used your towel. It's just it was getting late and the game just ended and I was after waiting up for you . . ."

"Game?"

"Oui. Hockey with ducks," Jacques explained, lip curled.

"Hockey," Claire repeated.

Austin snickered. "I know what new sensations you were thinking about."

"Shut up."

"Someone's got a dir . . ."

Dragging him onto her lap, she cupped her hand over his mouth. "Someone also has opposable thumbs," she reminded him.

The sound of voices in the lobby diverted attention.

"Mrs. Abrams leaving," Claire explained, covering a yawn. "She remembers a lovely seance where Professor Jackson contacted the ghost of the young man she'd seen standing in the window of room two as a girl and then more recently in the dining room, and the lobby, and the office, and back in the window of room two."

Jacques winced as her voice picked up an edge toward the end of the list. "I am sorry, *cherie.* I thought she see me only once."

"You thought she saw you and you didn't tell me?"

"I did not think it important."

"If I'd known, I could've prevented this whole incident from happening."

"*Oui,* but then I would not have flesh."

Claire decided to avoid that issue for a few moments longer and slid right on by without even pausing. "Well, now she believes that you've gone happily to your final rest, passed over into the light, so . . ." She managed energy enough to jab a finger at the ghost. ". . . stay away from windows!"

"I will."

"And if she happens to accidentally see you . . ."

"I tell you, *immediatement.*"

"Good." Yawning, Claire sagged back into the sofa. "The funny thing is, I'm not the first Keeper to mess with her head. There's a whole section of early memories that've been dramatically changed."

"Mr. Smythe told me that she lived in the house next door her whole life," Dean offered. "He said it used to be Groseter's Rooming House and Mr. Abrams was a roomer who didn't move fast enough and got broadsided." When Claire lifted her head to stare at him, he shrugged apologetically. "That's what *Mr. Smythe* said. Anyway, she's always saying things aren't like they were when she was a girl. Maybe she was poking around and saw something she shouldn't."

"You mean *besides* Jacques?"

Without an actual exhalation, Jacques' sigh lost emphasis, but he made up for it with the peripherals. Bending over the back of the sofa, he tucked a curl behind Claire's ear. "I am sorry the old woman cause you problems, *cherie,* but I am a long time dead and I am not surprise someone sees me."

"Not surprised." She started to move into his touch and when she realized, jerked her head away.

He smiled. *"Oui."*

"I think . . ." Reaching up, she flicked the curl back where it had been. "I think she probably wandered into the furnace room, maybe followed the Keeper down."

"Her?" Dean asked, jerking a thumb toward room six.

"Probably Uncle whoever. During the months *she* was Keeper here, Mrs. Abrams was a teenager; too old to go poking around the neighbor's . . ." Another yawn cut off the last word. ". . . basement."

"Time for bed, *cherie.*"

Dean jerked up onto his feet. "Yeah, I, uh, should get down, um, downstairs." Unable to say what he wanted to say—and not entirely sure what that was—he couldn't seem to put a coherent sentence together. "It's, uh, been a long, you know, day." Feeling the blood rise in his cheeks and wishing that the floor would just open up and swallow him whole, he headed for the door.

"Dean, wait."

With one foot in the office and one foot still in Claire's sitting room, he waited. Because she asked him to. He wondered if she knew how much he'd do for her if she asked him to.

To his surprise, he felt her hand in the small of his back, moving him out into the office. She followed and closed the door.

"After everything we've been through this last month, I thought you should know that Jacques and I aren't . . . that is, I'm not . . . I mean, we won't . . ."

"Why not, then?"

Claire stared up at him in astonishment. "Why not?"

Overcoming the urge to grab her and shake her, Dean nodded. "Yeah, why not? You gave him the flesh he's been bugging you for."

"Only to save him and the professor and only until dawn."

"Okay. But since you both want to . . ." He raised a hand to cut off her protest. "I'm not blind. I can see the way you two are together. Why shouldn't you take advantage of it?"

"He's dead?"

"Are you asking me if that's a reason?"

"No," she said slowly. "I guess not. Even though Jacques' body died, his passion, his personality, even his physical appearance, they stayed. And now they have substance." Standing so close she could smell the faint scent of fabric softener that clung around him, Claire looked up and tried to see past her reflection in his glasses. "And you're okay with this?"

Dean blinked. The way he'd played out this scene, he asked her, "Why not?" and she said, "Because it's you I really want," and things moved to a satisfactory if somewhat undefined conclusion from there. He hadn't intended to talk her into it. Since that's what he seemed to have done, although he wasn't entirely certain where things had gone wrong, there seemed to be only one way out. "Sure. Go ahead."

Claire expected *sure* to mean, *Would it matter to you if I wasn't?* It didn't and she couldn't seem to find an actual translation. "I'm not saying that I'll rearrange my life to spare your feelings, but I don't want you to be . . ." She'd intended to say hurt but the assumption that her actions would cause him pain just sounded too egotistical. Even for a Keeper. ". . . upset."

"Not a problem."

It was, actually, but every Keeper learned early in her career that sometimes a lie had to serve. People were entitled to emotional privacy. "Good night, Dean."

"Good night, Boss."

She watched him go down the hall, listened to him go down the stairs, until a furry weight against her shins distracted her. "What?"

"*Sure* meant I'm not so stupid that I can't see you've made your choice, so if I get all bent out of shape about it I'll look like some kind of a wuss moaning on and on about what I can't have, so I'm just walking away and pretending it doesn't matter."

Claire blinked. "How do you know that?"

"It's a guy thing."

"Yeah. Right." Stepping over Austin and purposefully closing the door in his face—not that a closed door ever stopped him—Claire went back into the sitting room to find Jacques sprawled in the armchair poking himself on the bridge of the nose with an old wooden ruler. "Why are you doing that?"

"I have never done it before." He tossed the ruler aside and stood. You have said what you have to say to our young friend?" When she nodded, he reached for her hands. "*Bien*. Now I will say something to you."

"Jacques . . ."

"*Non.* My turn." His grip tightened around her fingers, cool and still weirdly insubstantial. "I desire you. You know how I wish to use this flesh you have given me, but I will not make pressure on you."

"Put pressure on you."

"That also. If you decide we will not be together tonight, I have a bed still of my own in the attic. But know that you are to me more than a way to break a very long time without a woman."

"Jacques."

He winced. "Too much? I should not have said the last about the woman, I know. It is funny, I am, how do you say . . . nervous."

"That's how we say it." This was the moment she had to decide. On the one hand, Jacques was sexy and funny and there'd been a frisson between them from the moment she'd forced him to materialize. On the other hand, he was dead. That would definitely be a problem for most people. "I don't want to be like *her.*"

"You are not anything like *her.*" Releasing her hands, he cupped her face.

"I don't want to just use you."

"Use me, *cherie.* I can stand in."

"Stand it."

"We are both needing each other, Claire. Stop worrying about regrets you might have tomorrow. This is now."

He was going to kiss her; it hadn't been so long that she couldn't recognize the preliminaries. She just didn't know how she was going to respond. Fifty-three seconds later, she found out.

"Oh, my . . ."

PERFECT. SHE'S DISTRACTED.

WE SHOULD BE UP THERE, the rest of Hell protested. WE'RE MISSING A TERRIFIC OPPORTUNITY TO SCREW WITH HER HEAD.

I'VE GOT BETTER OPPORTUNITIES DOWN HERE.

The power seepage had been gathered in one place, prevented from escaping into the shield.

ARE YOU GOING TO CREATE ANOTHER IMP?

YOU KNOW WHAT YOUR PROBLEM IS? YOU DON'T THINK BIG ENOUGH. THAT'S WHY YOU'RE GOING TO SPEND AN INFINITE AMOUNT OF TIME DOWN IN THAT PIT.

YOU CAN'T GET THE SEEPAGE THROUGH THE SHIELD.

OH, YES, I CAN.

NO, YOU CAN'T.

YES, I CAN.

N . . .

ARE YOU ARGUING WITH *ME?* The silence seemed to indicate that, no, it wasn't. "GOOD. I CAN GET THE SEEPAGE THROUGH THE SHIELD USING THE CONDUIT THE KEEPERS HAVE PROVIDED.

The hoarded seepage began moving.

Low wattage lights went on in the rest of Hell as realization dawned. BUT THAT POWER GOES RIGHT UP TO *HER!*

YES.

SHE TRIED TO USE US.

AND FAILED.

WE'D RATHER NOT RISK THAT AGAIN.

NO ONE ASKED YOU. *SHE* WILL TAKE CARE OF THIS YOUNG KEEPER FOR ME.

Up in room six, under dust-covered lids, Aunt Sara's eyes began to move in her first dream in over fifty years.

"Jacques, wait. I felt something . . ."

"This?"

"No. . . . Oh. Yes."

"Hey, Diana." Phone cradled against her chin, Claire did up her cuff buttons and listened to the sounds of Dean moving about in the kitchen making breakfast. "Is Mom home?"

"Hey, yourself," her sister responded suspiciously. "What are you doing up so early in the mor . . . Oh my God! You did it, you slept with the dead guy!"

Recognizing that the move was completely illogical but needing to do it anyway, Claire held the receiver out in front of her and stared at it.

"Don't bother denying it." Diana's voice came tinnily out through the tiny speaker. "I can hear it in your voice."

"Hear what in my voice?" Claire demanded, the receiver back to her mouth.

"You know, that post-necrophilia guilt. How was he? I'd make a crack about him being a stiff, but you'd blow."

"Diana!"

"Don't get me wrong, I understand your choice. I mean, even ignoring the whole forbidden fruit thing, Keepers have responsibilities—busy, busy, busy—and after a night in the sack, a dead guy's not going to expect you to settle down and play house. So did you give him back his actual flesh, or did you make some minor additions?"

Breathing heavily through her nose, Claire attempted to keep her voice level. "*Is* Mom home?"

"No. Lucky for you. What kind of an example are you setting here for your younger sister?"

"Tell her I called."

"Should I . . ."

"No. Just tell her I called."

". . . of course I landed on my feet, but the other guy . . ." Austin let his voice trail off as Claire came into the kitchen. Wrapping his tail around his toes, he sat and stared unblinkingly up at her.

Claire glanced over at Dean, who shrugged, then back at the cat. "What?" she sighed.

"Nothing. I just figured the first meeting between you and Dean the morning after would be awkward, and I wanted to start things off right. I think you two can take it from here." Looking smug, he leaped down to the floor and padded away.

The silence stretched.

Having made his decision to cut a net he had no hope of hauling, to save the boat so he could fish another day, to suddenly get caught up in regional metaphors he'd never previously considered using, Dean should have slept the sleep of the just, the sleep of the man who has recognized that he'd lost the battle but by no means lost the war. As it happened, he slept hardly at all, Claire's bedroom being right over his. His imagination, deciding to make up for twenty years of benign neglect, had kicked into overdrive the moment his head hit the pillow. He'd finally gotten a few hours' sleep on the couch in the next room.

"So," he said at last, "you're up early. Where's Jacques?"

Before Claire could answer, he blushed and held up both hands. "I'm sorry. I didn't mean that to come out the way it sounded."

"What way?"

"Like I had a right to know." He took a deep breath, adjusted his glasses, and said, "Did you want some coffee, then?"

"Sure." When Dean shot her a surprised glance before reaching for a mug, she hoped she'd got the nuance right. She'd intended *sure* to mean, *nothing's changed between you and me.* Dean could continue feeling how he felt about her—a little unrequited whatever it was he felt wouldn't hurt him—and she'd continue thinking of him as an incredibly nice, gorgeous kid who just happened to do windows. She'd come to that conclusion while dressing, wondering why she was making such a big deal out of Dean's reaction. "Jacques went back to the attic. He said he needed some time to think."

"Ah."

The silence fell again.

"Professor Jackson's not down yet."

Dean gratefully looked at his watch. "No, but then it's just turned eight."

"Ah."

Before the silence extended far enough to elicit a conversation about the warmer than seasonal weather, the front door opened. And closed.

Dean frowned. "Stay where you're at," he muttered, untying his apron, "I'll get it."

Sighing, Claire started walking toward the lobby. "What have I told you about this kind of thing?"

"Specifically?"

"Generally."

"You're a Keeper and you can take care of yourself?"

"Bingo."

Bent nearly double, stroking Austin as he wound around black leggings and chunky ankle boots, the young woman in the lobby seemed to be neither a threat nor a guest. When she straightened, one hand rising to try and brush disheveled blonde curls down over the purple-and-green swelling on her forehead, Claire got the impression of a person just barely hanging on to the end of her rope.

A quick glance at Dean showed him ready to pound whoever, or whatever, had brought such a fragile beauty to such a state.

The delicate jaw moved slowly up and down on a piece of gum. The weary motion seemed so involuntary it came as a bit of a shock when she stopped chewing to speak. "I've been walking all night," she offered tentatively, "and I need, um . . ."

"A room?" Claire asked.

She glanced back over her shoulder before answering. "I haven't any money."

"That's all right." Keepers went where they were needed;

sometimes, need came to them. Without turning, Claire lightly touched Dean's arm. "Go make up room three."

"Sure, Boss."

No one spoke again until he'd disappeared up the stairs.

"This is a beautiful cat." A trembling hand ran down the black fur from head to tail. "Is he yours."

"Not exactly."

"I had a cat once." She closed shadowed eyes. When she opened them again, she stared around the lobby as if wondering where she was.

Austin nudged her.

"I saw your sign. I thought, if I could lie down for a few hours, I could figure out what to do. But I can't pay you. . . ."

"The room's there and it's empty," Claire told her, stepping forward. "You might as well use it."

Clearly too tired to think straight, she shook her head. "That's not how it works."

"That's how it works here."

"Oh." She looked up the stairs and thin shoulders sagged. "I don't think I can."

"I'll help." By the third step, Claire had wrapped the girl's weight in power. Reaching the first floor hall, hoping the professor wouldn't chose this moment to head downstairs for breakfast, she led the way to room three, pausing outside the door to allow Dean to leave.

When he opened his mouth to speak, she shook her head and pushed past him. He couldn't help until they knew what was going on.

Settling the girl on the edge of the bed, Claire stepped back and watched Austin make himself comfortable beside her. "Do you mind if he stays?"

"Oh, no." Her hand reached out to stroke him again. "You and that big man, are you happy?"

Claire blinked, completely taken aback. "There's nothing between me and Dean."

The ugly bruise on the girl's forehead darkened, surrounded by an embarrassed flush. "I'm so sorry. It's just that you looked . . ."

"Postcoital," Austin murmured when she paused.

"Ignore that, *please*," Claire suggested, spitting the magic word through clenched teeth, "I'll leave you now, get some sleep. We'll talk later."

*   *   *

HELLO. . . .

NOT NOW. I DON'T WANT THE PISSANT LITTLE EN-
ERGY WE CAN PUSH OUT OF HERE WASTED ON TRI-
FLES.

YOU DON'T WANT? WHAT ABOUT WHAT WE WANT?

Time passing suddenly became the loudest sound in the furnace room. After a moment, the rest of Hell answered their own
question.

NEVER MIND.

By the time Claire got back to the kitchen, Professor Jackson
had descended for breakfast. He seemed extraordinarily pleased
with himself as he ate his bacon and eggs. He hummed slightly
as he spread jam on his toast, and he stirred his coffee with the
air of a man who'd lived up to his own extraordinary expectations. Fortunately, he'd lifted himself to such exalted heights, he
was far beyond making casual conversation with mere hotel
staff.

Wiping his mouth, he rose from the table and graciously informed both Dean and Claire that he'd be leaving as soon as he
packed.

"Well?" Dean demanded the moment the professor was out of
earshot. "Who is she? What happened? Does she want us to call
the police?"

"I have no idea, but Austin stayed with her so we'll soon find
out."

"Austin?"

"Why not. She's tired and vulnerable. . . ."

Dean nodded, understanding. "He'll be a nonjudgmental comfort to her."

"No, he'll take advantage of it. He's a cat, not Mother Theresa."
Claire poured herself a bowl of cereal and sat down. "It shouldn't
be much longer."

On cue, Austin jumped up onto the counter. "All right; bacon."
Glancing over at Claire, he added, "Which I, of course, can't eat
even though I've been gathering vital information about the
young woman in room three."

Claire sighed. "One small piece."

"Two."

"One and the dregs of milk from my cereal."

"Not if it's bran; last time I was in the litter box all morning."

"It's not."

"Deal."

They waited more-or-less patiently while he ate and not at all patiently while he washed his whiskers.

"First of all," he said, at last, "it's not what you think. Her name is Faith Dunlop. . . ."

"She told a cat her name?"

"Don't be ridiculous; I hooked her ID out of her pocket when she fell asleep." He snorted. "Who tells a cat their name?"

"Just get on with it."

"Who hit her?" Dean demanded.

"No one. She walked into a door. Our little Faith was leaving in a hurry because she'd just helped her boyfriend rip off a convenience store out on North Montreal Street. When they split up to throw off pursuit, she had the bag of loot. Unfortunately, she left it on a bus and now she's afraid to go home because this is the second time something like this has happened and the boyfriend is going to be very unhappy."

Claire stared at Austin in astonishment. "This is the second time she's left the loot on a bus?"

"If I understood her correctly—and between the sobbing and the gum she wasn't very coherent—the last time she left it in the women's washroom at a fast food restaurant but essentially the same scenario, yes."

"She's afraid of her boyfriend?" Dean growled. Behind his glasses, his eyes narrowed to a line of blazing blue. "Oh, I get it; first off, he forces her into a life of crime and then, when she can't perform to his satisfaction, he beats her."

"She walked into a door," Austin protested.

"Sure. This time. But what'll happen when she gets home? She's terrified of him, or she wouldn't have been out all night, forced to throw herself on the kindness of strangers."

Claire sighed. She'd just discovered two things about Dean. The first, which was hardly unexpected considering the rest of his personality, involved taking the side of the weak against the strong. The second, that at some point in his scholastic career he'd been forced to read *A Streetcar Named Desire*. "You don't know any of that for certain."

He folded his arms across his chest. "I know what I see in front of my face."

"I don't know how you can see anything with your eyes slitted closed like that."

"It's obvious what happened!" His jaw thrust slightly forward.

"It's never that obvious." Pouring herself a cup of coffee, she asked Austin if he'd got a look at Faith's home address when he snagged her ID. When he admitted that he had, she headed for the phone.

Hurriedly picking up the empty cereal bowl and putting it in the sink, Dean followed. "What are you doing?"

"Calling Faith's apartment and telling the boyfriend where she is. Once he's here, I can protect her, but until I hear the whole story, I can't help her."

"You're after helping her right into the hospital!" Rushing forward, Dean put himself between Claire and the phone. "Look, you can put yourself into whatever weird relationships you want, but you can't make those kind of choices for Faith."

"Weird relationships?"

"Uh, oh." Ears close to his head, Austin ducked under the desk.

Claire's nostrils flared. "I thought you said you were okay with it?"

"Well, what else was I supposed to say? You're the Keeper; you always know what you're doing, and you never listen to me. I can't even get you to put your dirty dishes in the sink!"

He was right about the dishes. Claire took a deep breath and forced it out through clenched teeth. "Move away from the phone, Dean. I know what I'm doing."

"And I don't?"

"I didn't say that."

"But you're always implying it. After all, I'm just the bystander and all this lineage stuff is way over my head. Okay. Maybe it is. But this," he stabbed a finger toward room three, "this is people stuff, and I know people stuff better than you."

"The moment Faith entered this hotel, she *became* lineage stuff."

They locked eyes for a long moment. Finally, Dean jerked away from the phone. "Okay. Fine. If you're not after listening to me, I'll go and do the dishes. That seems to be all I'm good for around here."

"Dean . . ."

"You know where to find me if you want something unimportant taken care of." Heels denting the floor, he stomped back to the kitchen.

"I told you so," Austin muttered, still safely hidden under the desk.

"Told me what?" Claire asked, fingers white around the receiver.

"That Dean's all bent out of shape about you pounding the mattress with Jacques."

"Jacques wasn't even mentioned!"

He stuck his head out and stared up at her in disbelief. "You really aren't any good at this people stuff, are you?"

Just after ten, Professor Jackson checked out. He paid in cash and, although a number of smaller things had been broken the night before, he made no mention of them. Since, technically, Claire had broken them, she let it slide.

"I'll just go up and clean the room, then, shall I, Boss?"

Claire'd been trying to think of a way to apologize—although in spite of a nagging feeling that she was in the wrong, she wasn't sure for what—but Dean's emphasis on that *Boss* changed her mind. She'd wait until he decided to stop being so childish.

At eleven, she tried Faith's home number again. She'd left two previous messages on the answering machine, and when the same annoying little song came on telling her to *not make a peep till the sound of the beep,* she decided not to leave a third.

When Dean came downstairs at eleven-forty carrying a wastebasket full of broken lamp, the office was empty, but a thin man in a Thousand Islands baseball cap and jean jacket that looked two sizes too large was limping across the lobby. "Can I help you?"

He jerked around to face the stairs. Pale lips, under a sparsely settled mustache, lifted in what could have been a smile but was probably a twitch. "Hi. Yeah. I'm here for Faith."

"Faith?"

"Yeah. I'm Fred." The tip of his nose was an abraded pink that vibrated slightly with every word. "She's not gone?"

"No." Dean descended the last three steps and was disappointed to see that he still towered over Faith's boyfriend. He'd been hoping for a big man, one he could flatten without guilt. "What happened to your foot?"

"My foot?" Eyes wide, Fred stared down as though amazed to see a foot on the end of his leg. "Oh. That foot. I had an accident, eh." He laughed nervously. "Dropped a cash register on it. Hurts like hell."

NOT QUITE. BUT IT COULD.

Dean set down the wastebasket and jiggled his baby finger in his right ear, anger momentarily swamped by confusion. "Did you hear that?"

"Hear what?"

"Nothing."

DON'T YOU JUST WISH YOU COULD WIPE THIS KIND OF SCUM RIGHT OFF THE FACE OF THE EARTH?

"Well, yeah, but that wouldn't solve anything."

"What?" Fred backed up a step, looking like a small rodent suddenly face to face with a very large cat.

"Did I say that out loud?"

"What?"

If Fred was a monster, Dean decided, he hid it well. On the other hand, a man facing a much larger man was often a different person than a man facing a woman. "Look, you wait here. I'll check if Faith wants to see you."

"Is she all right? Is she hurt? The message said she was just tired." What seemed like near panic jerked the words out in a staccato rush.

"She's fine."

"Then why wouldn't she want to see me?"

Dean sighed. "Just wait here, okay?"

Fred's gaze skittered around the office as though checking for traps. When it finally got back to Dean, he nodded. "Okay."

Shaking his head, Dean started up the stairs.

THOSE KIND OF WEASELS ARE THE FIRST TO PICK ON SOMEONE WEAKER THAN THEMSELVES. YOU SHOULD SHOW HIM HOW IT FEELS.

Dean's fingers curled up into fists.

VIOLENCE IS ONE OF OURS.

Down in the lobby, Fred shifted his weight off his bad foot and stared mournfully at the stairs. He didn't want to wait, he wanted to see Faith.

Which was when he noticed the elevator. A fascination for all things mechanical drew him across to it, limp almost forgotten. He opened the door, peered past the gate, down into the shaft, and could just make out the top of the car. It seemed to be in the basement.

Brow furrowed under the brim of his cap, he opened the door immediately to his left.

The basement stairs.

It was easier going down the stairs than up. He could take the elevator to the top of the hotel and go down to Faith's room, missing the big guy with the glasses entirely.

No one would mind. Elevators were there to be used.

Leaning outside the door to room three while Faith put on her face, Dean polished his glasses with the hem of his shirt and tried not to think about how much he'd enjoy flattening Fred's quivering pink nose.

ONE, TWO, SPLAT. THAT'S THE TICKET.

Lost in memories of a childhood spent riding the old elevator at the S&R Department Store, Fred touched two fingers to his cap brim, murmured, "First floor, ladies lingerie," and twisted the brass lever to *UP*.

Sitting in the bathroom, reading the Apothecary's new catalog, Claire heard the unmistakable sound of an ancient elevator starting up.

By the time she reached the lobby, it was just passing the first floor. She didn't know the man inside.

Dean frowned as he heard the elevator rise to meet the second floor, then he shrugged. Claire'd said she was through testing, but obviously she'd thought of something else to try.

Then he heard:

"Second floor, housewares and cosmetics."

By the time he got across the hall, all he could see was the bottom third of a pair of grimy jeans and Fred's worn and grubby running shoes.

He had to beat the elevator to the third floor. If Fred opened the door . . .

HE'LL GET WHAT HE DESERVES. FAITH'S TERRIFIED OF HIM. YOU SAW THAT YOURSELF. THERE'LL BE ONE LESS ABUSIVE WEASEL IN THE WORLD.

Dean hesitated.

Then Faith's door opened. When she stepped out into the hall and saw only Dean, her smile dimmed. "Where's my Pookie?"

Claire reached the second floor and saw Dean charging toward her. Then past her. The elevator had passed and was still moving up. Gasping for breath, she took the next flight of stairs two at a time, but had only reached the landing when Dean, who'd barely looked as though he were touching down at all, reached the top.

The growl of the motor stopped.

Unless he was a total klutz, it would only take seconds for the man inside to open the gate. The taste of old pennies in the back of her throat, Claire staggered into the third floor hall as the elevator door started to open. Before the latch cleared, Dean threw himself in front of it and slammed it shut.

"Hey!"

Chest heaving, Claire staggered up on rubbery legs as Dean stepped back and, after making sure that it had indeed closed completely, pulled the door open.

"It's just I've got this sore foot," Fred began hurriedly. "And you know, the stairs are steep, and . . ."

Dean cut off the rest of the excuse by reaching in, grabbing the smaller man by the front of his jacket, and pulling him out into the hall.

"Pookie?" Faith's anxious voice drifted up from the second floor. "Is that you?"

"Yeah, Baby, it's me." Fred smiled, or twitched, nervously, eyes flicking from Dean to Claire and back to Dean. "She calls me Pookie."

"You must be the boyfriend," Claire hazarded.

"Yeah. I'm Fred."

She jerked her head toward the stairs. "Go on."

Fred sidled out of Dean's reach and limped quickly away.

Dean hadn't moved since he pulled Fred from the elevator. Worried, Claire took a step toward him. "Are you okay?"

He lifted horrified eyes to her face. "I hesitated."

"When?"

"When I heard the elevator go by. I heard a little voice say, he'll get what he deserves, and I . . ." He shook his head in disbelief. ". . . I hesitated."

About to reassure him that it was no big deal, Claire suddenly realized that for Dean, it was. For the first time in his life, he hadn't automatically done the right thing. If she couldn't convince him to let it go, irrational guilt would eat at him for the rest of his life. *That's it, Claire, no pressure.*

Wrapping her fingers around his forearm, she gave him a little shake. "You saved him, Dean. I couldn't have gotten here in time."

"You don't understand. I actually thought about letting Fred . . ." Unable to continue, he shook free of her grip and stumbled back away from her.

Claire sighed. How unfortunate that smacking some sense into him would probably scar his psyche forever. "Dean, listen to me. I know you think I'm lousy at people stuff but I'm older, I'm a Keeper, I know; people think unworthy thoughts all the time."

LIKE THE ONE WHERE HE'S ON HIS KNEES AND . . .

Shut up. "It doesn't count if you don't act on it."

"But I hesitated."

"And then you made up for lost time. Trust me, they cancel each other out."

Dean forced a smile. "I appreciate you trying to make me feel better, Boss, but nothing can cancel out what I've done." The smile slipped. "I should go see if Faith needs my help." Trailing misery behind him like streamers of smoke, he started for the stairs.

Which was when Claire realized . . . "Dean, did you say you actually heard a little voice?"

"Yeah."

"How did it sound?"

Two steps down, he stopped and leaned back out into the hall. "Sound?"

"Can you describe it?"

"I guess." He frowned, brows dipping down below the upper edge of his glasses. "It sort of sounded like it was talking in block caps."

Should she tell him? Would it help? No. If Dean knew he was hearing the voice of Radio Free Hell, he'd be more convinced than ever that his hesitation had damned him. "Dean, do me a favor. If you hear the voice again, *please* ignore it."

After a moment, he nodded. "Okay."

A sudden shriek of laughter from below had them both clamping their hands over abused ears. Side by side, they hurried downstairs.

The second floor hall was empty so they kept going.

Inhaling his clean, fabric softener scent, Claire wasn't thinking of either Fred or Faith. After nine months, she wondered, what had finally given Hell a way in?

In room six, directly across from the open elevator door, Aunt Sara licked her lips.

Baseball cap skewed, Fred pulled out of the clinch as Claire and Dean emerged from the stairwell. "You were so good to Faith, you oughta know; we're giving up our life of crime."

"Although it wasn't really a life of crime," Faith protested. "It was only two stores and we paid for them taco chips."

"I think you've made a wise decision," Claire told them, smiling. "What do you think, Dean."

He shrugged and looked miserable. "I'm not one to say."

Claire rolled her eyes. This *I'm a horrible person stuff* was going to get old, really fast. "But you're glad they've decided to go straight, aren't you?"

"Sure."

That was good enough for Fred. "Thanks. Truth be told, we weren't any good at it."

Faith's lower lip went out, making her look like a pouty angel. "We coulda practiced more, Pookie. Or got a gun."

"No guns. People get hurt when you got a gun." He patted her shoulder. "I'm takin' that job with my cousin Rick." Turning back to Claire and Dean, he added, "Rick's got a truck, eh, and he hauls stuff."

"You're not gonna call the cops, are you?" Faith asked, leaning past him and twisting a curl around her finger.

"No."

"See, Pookie, I told you they were good people."

Dean winced.

Claire resisted the urge to stamp on his foot and give him something to wince about. Instead, she herded their modern Bonnie and Clyde to the front door and waved them out toward the waiting world. "Go home. Go straight. Be happy."

At the bottom of the steps, Faith turned and smiled beatifically back in at Claire. "Thank you for letting me use the room and everything."

"You're welcome."

"You figure their parents were cousins?" Austin asked when she closed the door.

"I have no idea."

He yawned, stretched, and glanced over at Dean. "What's with him? He looks like he just tried to kill somebody."

Dean stared wide-eyed at the cat. "You can tell?"

Austin sighed and flicked an ear toward Claire. "What's he talking about?"

"When he heard Fred going upstairs in the elevator, he hesitated before racing off to save him."

"Not much point in removing only one of them," Austin agreed.

"You're not helping," Claire snapped before Dean could react. Crossing the lobby, she poked him in the chest. "Stop tearing yourself up over this. You aren't a horrible person. You've got to be the nicest guy I've ever met."

NICE GUYS FINISH LAST.

"Get out of my head."

WE WEREN'T TALKING TO YOU.

Oh, Hell . . .

"Dean?"

"If you don t need me for anything, I'd like to go downstairs and do some serious thinking about my life." He spun on one heel and hurried off before she could answer, which was probably a good thing since she couldn't think of anything constructive to say.

Walking over to the counter, she scooped Austin up into her arms and stroked the top of his head with her cheek. "This is not good."

"What? That after living unaffected next to Hell for almost a year, Dean spends a month and a half in your company and all of a sudden he's willing to kill?"

"He hesitated! Then he saved the guy!"

"Face the facts, Claire, you've got him tied in knots. He's not thinking, he's reacting and that's exactly the sort of situation Hell loves to exploit."

THE CAT'S RIGHT.

"Of course I am; but who asked you?"

She set him back on the counter. "I'm not Dean's problem."

JEALOUSY IS ONE OF OURS.

"He said he was fine with me and Jacques."

YOU'RE REALLY NOT A PEOPLE PERSON, ARE YOU?

"Take your own advice and stop listening to Hell." Austin paused to lick at a bit of mussed fur. "Let Dean do his serious thinking, and maybe he'll solve the problem on his own."

"Cherie?"

"And speaking of problems."

Shooting Austin a warning look, she turned to face Jacques. Translucent in the light from the office window, he looked exactly the way he had the first day she'd set eyes on him. She realized that she'd been expecting their night together to have changed him, but, unfortunately, it seemed to have changed only her perception of him—men were just so much more attractive when they were opaque.

"You are more beautiful this morning than I have ever seen you." His eyes twinkled. It was a disconcerting effect since Claire could see the door through them. "I have been thinking. One night cannot balance so many years alone; perhaps this afternoon . . ."

"No."

His grin faded. "But *cherie,* was I not all I promise I would be?"

"Yes, but. . ."

The grin returned. "Give me flesh again, and we will drive away the but."

"Look, Jacques, you're dead, so you have nothing to do, but I'm alive and I have . . ."

STRANGE TASTE IN MEN.

Shut up. ". . . responsibilities."

Jacques looked interested. "Like what?"

"Like feeding the cat," Austin declared in a tone that suggested he shouldn't have had to mention it.

"And?" Jacques wondered.

"And that's not important right now. What's important is that you're dead and I'm alive . . ."

"Cherie, non."

". . . and no matter how many times I give you flesh, you'll still be *dead!*" The words echoed in the empty lobby. From the look of pained betrayal on Jacques' face as he dematerialized, he wouldn't be back any time soon. "I didn't mean to hurt him," she sighed. "I just wanted him to . . ."

"Go away. And he did, congratulations." Critically inspecting a front paw, Austin snorted. "I'm not sure this is as clean as it could be."

Claire grabbed the edge of the counter, bent over, and rhythmically banged her head against the wood.

THAT WAS FUN.

THIRTEEN

For the first time in weeks, as the pipes banged out the news that Claire was in the shower, Dean wasn't lost in daydreams of soap and water. Kneeling by the bed, he pulled out his old hockey bag, the only luggage he'd brought from back home. It was pretty obvious that Claire thought they could just go on as though he hadn't been willing to murder Faith Dunlop's boyfriend for no greater crime than being a total moron. Maybe she could, but that sort of thing changed a guy.

Changed the way he looked at himself.

Maybe it was time he moved on.

"I see Dean's truck is gone."

Claire picked up her breakfast dishes, stared at them for a moment, and then carried them over to the sink. "He left about ten minutes ago."

Austin sat by his empty dish and curled his tail around his front feet. "He left without feeding the cat."

"You have such a rough life." She picked up a can and a knife and froze, eyes locked on the empty parking lot.

After a moment, Austin sighed. "Get a grip! He went for groceries, like he does every Saturday morning."

"I know." Under blouse and sweater, she could feel goose bumps lifting. "I just had this incredible sense of foreboding."

"Which is nothing compared to what you're going to have if you don't feed the cat."

"Can't you feel it?" she asked, scooping food into his dish. "When I think of Dean, I get the feeling that events are poised on the edge of a precipice."

"A simple solution, *cherie;* do not think of Dean."

Straightening, Claire drew in a deep breath. She hadn't been looking forward to this, not after the way she'd smacked Jacques away from her yesterday.

When she turned, the ghost was sitting cross-legged on the

dining room table—a position he favored because of how it irritated Dean. He grinned at her. "Why the long face, *cherie?* The day, she is sunny, Dean is gone, and me, I am here for company."

Claire searched his face unsuccessfully for any lingering sign of hurt and betrayal.

"Ah." The grin broadened. "You cannot see enough of me."

"Yesterday . . ."

"I am dead since 1922," he reminded her, with a matter-of-fact shrug. "I cannot carry all my yesterdays with me. Although," he winked, "some I remember very well and am anxious to repeat."

"Not now . . ."

"*Oui*, not now, not here. Although," he glanced around and smiled broadly, "you and me on this table; it would give the old lady something to see, yes?"

"No."

"Fraidy-cat." He blew her a kiss and dematerialized.

"Some of us," Austin muttered, jumping onto a chair and then up onto the counter, "don't appreciate the word cat being used in a derogatory manner. If you've left the television on PBS, he's going to be right back."

"It's probably still on TSN. I didn't check."

He rubbed his head against her elbow. "You okay?"

"I don't know. Nothing's changed with Jacques and everything seems changed with Dean. I can't figure it out."

"It's simple. Jacques is dead, he can't change. Dean's alive, he can't not change. Now me, I'm a cat. I don't need to change."

She reached down and scratched him gently between the ears. "What about me?"

"You need to move your fingers a little to the left. More. Ahhhhh. That's got it."

An hour later, perched precariously on top of the stepladder, eyes squinted nearly shut against the thin November sun, Claire razored masking tape off the windows. As expected, there'd been no change in the shields around Aunt Sara and Hell. She'd written as much in the site journal and now had the rest of the day to fill. Jacques was watching television, Dean was still out, and if the masking tape didn't come off soon, it'd be there until Hell froze over.

SHE'S THINKING OF US.
SO? KEEP WORKING.

WE'LL NEVER WAKE *HER* USING SEEPAGE. The rest of Hell sounded sulky.

I DON'T NEED TO WAKE *HER*. I MERELY NEED TO UNBALANCE THE BALANCE OF POWER. *SHE'LL* DO THE REST.

WHO?

HER.

HER?

NO! *HER,* YOU IDIOT!

Picking bits of tape off the edge of the blade, Claire could just barely make out the unmistakable shapes of Mrs. Abrams and Baby by the driveway. Baby seemed to be sniffing the fresh concrete around the base of the railings.

"I don't suppose you want to go chase that dog off our property?"

"You suppose correctly." Sprawled in a patch of sunlight, Austin didn't bother opening his eyes. "But I'll pencil in a visit for later in the afternoon."

"I can't see the fun in bothering a dog that neurotic."

"You can't see the fun in shredding the furniture either. Don't worry about it."

When Baby's head rose suddenly, ears flattened against his skull, Claire leaned forward to see what had caught his attention. The approaching pedestrian seemed to have no idea of the danger.

"Oh, no." Although details had been washed out by the light, she knew that shape. Knew the way it moved. Watched it make a fuss over the big dog who, after a moment of visible confusion, actually wagged his stump of a tail.

Climbing down off the ladder, reluctantly deciding it might be safer if she wasn't holding the razor blade, Claire walked to the door and opened it.

Mrs. Abrams turned as she came out onto the step. "Yoo hoo! Courtney! Look who's here! It's your sister, Diana. She's come for a visit; isn't that nice?"

"Swell."

Diana looked up from murmuring endearments in under the points of Baby's ears. "Isn't this the sweetest doggie you've ever seen?"

"Oh, yeah, he's a real cream puff."

Giving the Doberman a final pat and telling Mrs. Abrams she hoped to see her again, Diana picked up her backpack, ran up the front steps, and paused to examine Claire critically. "You ought to let your hair grow out, I can't believe you're wearing mascara in the house, and didn't I tell you that nail polish was bad for the environment?"

Claire stepped back and motioned her sister inside. "I don't want to. I don't care. And what are you talking about?"

"Nail polish remover is like, so toxic." She turned on the threshold to wave at Mrs. Abrams and Baby, then bounded inside. "Nice paint job. Forest green. Very trendy. Hey, Austin."

He lifted his head, sighed deeply, and let it fall back to the countertop. "Shoot me now."

ANOTHER KEEPER!
IT'S A CHILD. KEEP YOUR MIND ON YOUR WORK.
BUT THERE'S TWO OF THEM!
AND THERE'S VERY NEARLY AN INFINITE AMOUNT OF ME.

The rest of Hell considered the implied threat. GOOD POINT.

"Diana, why are you here?"

"I'm needed."

"For what?"

"I'm a Keeper." She ducked under the flap into the office. "We go where we're summoned, and I was summoned here."

"Here?"

"Uh-huh. Right here. Are you still using this old computer? You must've bought it, what, two, three years ago?"

"Three and a half, and don't touch it."

"Chill, I'm not going to hurt it." She tapped lightly on the monitor. "Oops." At Claire's low growl, she grinned. "Kidding. It's not even turned on."

"Diana."

"What?"

Claire took a deep breath and tried to remember where the conversation had diverged from the important questions. "Do Mom and Dad know you're here?"

"No. I snuck out in the middle of the night." Diana rolled her eyes. "Of course they know I'm here. They're Cousins. I'm a Keeper. And, at the irritating risk of repeating myself, I was summoned."

"All right. You were summoned. So?"

"So I guess I'm here to help you."

"You want to help?" Austin muttered. "Take a man off her hands."

"As if. Didn't Mom tell you? I'm a lesbian."

Claire sighed. "Isn't everyone?"

"You know, Claire . . ." Arms folded over her black jean jacket, Diana's eyes narrowed. ". . . I get the feeling you're not happy to see me."

"It's just . . ."

". . . that the thought of you and Hell in the same building is enough to give anyone with half a brain serious palpitations," Austin finished.

"No problem." Diana raised both hands to shoulder height, backpack sliding down her arm to swing in the crook of her elbow. "I solemnly swear to stay away from the furnace room. Now are you happy to see me?"

Claire's better judgment suggested she send Diana home immediately, summons or no summons. She had no idea what part of her kept repeating, *but she's your kid sister,* as though that had any relevance at all. Whatever part it turned out to be, it was doing a good job of drowning out her common sense. "All right. I'm happy to see you. Now what?"

"Now, you give me the guided tour."

There was a soccer game on in her sitting room; a dozen guys in green and white appeared to be running circles around a dozen guys in red and black. Claire wasn't even certain that they'd played soccer in Canada when Jacques died, but he was interested enough in this particular match that he'd faded out until only a faint distortion remained in the air above the sofa.

"Imbecile!"

Claire'd been half hoping he wouldn't be there at all, but since he was, and since she couldn't come up with any kind of a believable reason for him not to meet her sister, she called his name.

"Do you see that? The ball goes right by him, but he does not move to kicks it!"

"Kick it."

"Tabernac! Qui t'a dit que tu puisse jouer a balle?

"Jacques, there's someone here who wants to meet you."

He snorted. "Why not? These people, they are asleep!"

Reaching past him, Claire picked up the remote and muted the TV. "Could you focus?"

"Focus?" He looked down through himself. "Ah, *d'accord.*"

By the time Diana came into the room, his edges had firmed up. His eyes widened and he walked through the sofa toward her. "Another Keeper? And so young and beautiful."

Recognizing the reaction, Claire sighed. "Jacques, this is my sister Diana."

"Diana, fair huntress of the bow. Although," he added thoughtfully, "given how the rest have fallen, no doubt she is now fat and old."

"What are you talking about?"

"It's a long story," Claire answered before Jacques had a chance. "There, you've met him. Let's leave, so he can get back to his game."

Jacques glanced speculatively at her through his lashes. "Are you ashamed of me, *cherie?*"

"It's not you," Diana told him. "It's me."

"I'm going to the kitchen for a coffee, you kids have a blast working it out. Wait a minute!" Claire jabbed a finger in her sister's direction. "You just forget I said the word blast."

The coffee helped. Claire sank into her regular chair at the dining room table and took another long swallow. Showing Diana the hotel had been exhausting. When they ended up in front of room six for the second time, Claire had accused her sister of clouding her mind. The resultant denials had lasted down all three flights of stairs and had been no more believable in the lobby than they had originally.

She'd emptied the mug and begun worrying about what Jacques and Diana were discussing when Dean's truck drove up. The feeling of impending doom returned. All the hair on her body standing uncomfortably on end, she hurried outside, ostensibly to help him carry in the groceries.

Reaching past him for a pair of canvas bags, she tried to sound nonchalant as she asked if he was all right.

"Sure."

He sounded all right; depressed maybe, but not doomed. She checked for the taint of dark or eldritch powers and found only that frozen peas were on sale for a dollar thirty-nine. "No trouble at the grocery store?"

"No."

"No trouble with the truck?"

"No." Dean held open the back door and stood aside so Claire could enter the building first. "What's the matter?"

"I don't know."

"Okay. I understand now why you don't trust me."

Teeth gritted, she put the bags down and turned to face him. "No, really, I don't know."

"She doesn't know why I'm here? Or she doesn't know when I'm leaving? Which?"

Claire's nostrils flared. She'd intended to tell Dean about her premonition but *not* in front of her sister. Diana in the same room with impending doom practically guaranteed Armageddon. "She'll be leaving on Sunday night because she's got school on Monday morning and she's already missed too much of it this year. Dean, this is my sister Diana."

"Hey." She waggled a hand in an exaggerated wave.

It was the first time Dean had felt like smiling all morning. Although the sisters looked superficially alike—dark hair and eyes, short and thin—energy popped and fizzed around Diana as though she'd been carbonated. "Hi."

"So you're from Newfoundland?"

"That's right." Picking up the bag with the produce, he began putting things away.

"I've never been there."

"You'd have noticed," Claire added, passing over a package of luncheon meat.

"So." Diana picked up a loaf of bread and examined it critically. "Did you always want to work in a hotel?"

"No. I just needed a job."

"I hear Augustus Smythe was a real tyrant."

"He wasn't so bad."

"Worse than Claire?"

He stared down into a net bag of cooking onions. "Different."

"Still, I guess you get to meet a lot of interesting people working here. Vampires and werewolves and . . . Ow! Claire!"

They were standing about ten feet apart but, obviously, that hadn't been far enough. Dean had no idea of what was going on and no intention of getting between them. "Yeah," he said, folding the bags and putting them away, "lots of interesting people."

"How long are you planning on staying around?"

"Actually . . ." He took a deep breath, let it out slowly, and turned to face Claire. "Actually, I've been thinking of leaving."

"Leaving?"

"Yeah. You know, getting on with my life."

Silently congratulating herself for maintaining a neutral expression, Claire wondered why her reflection in his glasses looked as though she'd just been punched in the stomach. "When?"

"Soon. If you want, this can be my two week notice." When Claire gave no indication of what she wanted, he shrugged. "Nice meeting you, Diana. I've got to go make some phone calls."

"Well, thud," Diana said, as he disappeared down the basement stairs.

Claire felt as though she were waking up from a bad dream, the kind where she was trying to cross the road but her feet kept sticking in the asphalt and there were two trucks and a red compact car bearing down on her. "What do you mean, thud?"

"Thud. The sound of the other shoe dropping." Diana straight-armed herself up to sit on the edge of the counter. "A little more than a month ago, Mom said Dean was the most grounded guy she'd ever seen and now look at him. You've just cut the ground right out from under him, haven't you?"

"I have not."

"He must really dig your looks 'cause it can't be your personality."

"Diana!"

"I mean, Jacques is cuter than I expected and, okay, he makes me laugh with those corny pickup lines, but he's dead. In spite of the glasses, Dean's big-time beefcake. If *I* can see that, you should be able to. You had the perfect opportunity here, and you blew it."

"The perfect opportunity for what?" Claire demanded.

"For making the best of the situation and building a partnership with a really nice guy. Not my personal cup of tea, but a lot of people would jump at the chance."

"Why can't a man and a woman run a hotel together and just be friends?"

"Well, gee, I don't know, Claire. You're the one doing the horizontal mambo with the dead guy, you tell me?"

"We're not talking about Jacques!"

"Sure we are. Enlighten me; if you needed to bed one of them, and obviously you felt a need, why Jacques and not Dean? Don't answer, I'll tell you. They're both bystanders so that's not it. Is it because Dean's alive? No, from what I hear that's never been a problem in the past. Oh wait, could it be because you're an agist?"

"A what?"

"You heard me, an age-ist! You think I'm incompetent because I'm younger than you, and you ignore the evidence and think Dean's a kid for the same reason."

"I don't have to stand here and listen to this."

"True."

"I have work to do."

"Okay. Go do it."

"Fine. I will." About to leave the kitchen, Claire whirled back around to glare at her sister. "Don't blow the place up while I'm not watching."

"I came to help, remember."

"Oh, you've been a *big* help."

Leaning back and kicking her heels against the lower cabinets, Diana waited until she heard the door to Claire's sitting room slam shut before she smiled triumphantly. "Made her think."

"And I'm all for that," Austin agreed, jumping up beside her. "As long as you *don't* blow the place up while she's not watching."

"I promised I'd stay out of the furnace room."

"Good for you."

"How come Claire screwed things up so badly?"

The cat shrugged. "She's a Keeper. She's trained to come in post-disaster and deal with the mess, so she has to make a mess of any potential relationships before she feels competent to deal with them."

"I'm a Keeper and I don't do that."

"Yet," Austin said, looking superior.

Golf had replaced the soccer game and Jacques was gone. Still steaming, Claire turned off the television and stomped through to the bedroom. In order to get far enough from her sister to keep from wringing her neck, she'd have to leave the hotel. Yanking open the wardrobe door, she stepped inside.

Right at the moment, she'd enjoy dealing with a troop of killer Girl Guides.

Still sitting on the counter, Diana searched the cupboards for cookies, found three-quarters of a bag of fudge creams, and sat happily eating them while she worked out a way to fix Claire's life.

Obviously, Claire needed to leave the hotel.

Since no other Keeper had arrived to take over the site, the site had to be closed.

In order for the site to be closed, the exact parameters of the current seal had to be determined.

"And since there's only one remaining witness . . ." Scattering cookie crumbs, Diana jumped down off the counter. ". . . the logical solution would be to ask her." She snapped her fingers toward the kitchen and headed for the stairs.

Behind her, the crumbs cleaned themselves up and dropped into the garbage.

Paying only enough attention to keep from tripping over unexpected phenomena, Claire strode deeper into the wardrobe.

There were, Diana realized, a couple of ways to get into room six. The first involved pulling enough power to melt the locks, but that kind of heat would probably also burn down the building.

She went looking for a set of keys.

I should have told her flat out that it was none of her damn . . . darned business. Her mind on other things, Claire moved toward a soft gray light. *I am not an agist.*

"Hey, Dean, sorry to bother you, but I wanted to go poke around in the attic 'cept the door's locked and Claire's gone off with her keys."

"Claire's gone? Where's she at?"

"Oh, she stomped off into the wardrobe." Rocking backward and forward, heel to toe, Diana grinned up at him. "We had a fight, and she took off to think about what I said. I don't know if you've noticed, but Keepers have this tendency to think they're always right."

Dean's brows rose. "Aren't you a Keeper, then?"

"Well, sure, but that doesn't make Claire any less of a pedagogue."

"A what?"

"A know-it-all." Her eyes gleamed. "Although I'm leaving off a few choice adjectives. The attic?"

"Okay, sure." He pulled his key ring from his pocket dropped it in Diana's outstretched palm. "It's the big black one. You, uh, know about Jacques, then? The ghost? He might be in the attic."

"Yeah, Claire told me all about him." Closing her hand around the keys, she reached out and punched Dean lightly on the arm. "Don't worry, you're better off without her. She snores."

Don't worry? If Claire told her sister all about Jacques, Dean thought, watching Diana bound back up the basement stairs, *what did she tell her about you, boy?*

"Don't stand around with your thumb up your butt. What do you want?"

Claire's wandering attention snapped home. She was standing in a long room, lined with floor-to-ceiling bookshelves. Directly in front of her, sitting at a library table stacked with shoe boxes, was an older woman with soft white curls, wearing an ink-stained flowered smock. "Historian!"

"I know who I am," the Historian snapped. "Who the hell are you?"

"Claire, Claire Hansen. I'm a Keeper."

"You wouldn't be here if you weren't. Wait a minute." The Historian's eyes narrowed, collapsing the pale skin around them into a network of grandmotherly wrinkles. "I remember now, you were here three years, twelve days, eleven hours and forty-two minutes ago looking up some political thing. Did you finish with it?"

"The site?"

"No, democracy."

"Uh, not yet."

"Crap. You wouldn't believe the amount of paperwork it generates." She sighed and pushed away from the desk, giving Claire her first good look at the computer system nearly buried in shoe boxes.

"Is that one of the new 200MHz processors?"

"New? It was obsolete months ago. History. That's why it's here. So, since I tend to discourage social visits, what can I do for you?"

It took Claire a moment to get past her anger at Diana and remember. "Kingston, Ontario, 1945; two Keepers stopped another Keeper from gaining control of Hell."

"How nice for us all."

"I need to know how they did it."

"Damned if I know." When Claire frowned, the Historian sighed. "Keepers, no sense of humor." She pointed an ink-stained finger along the bookshelves. "The forties are about a hundred yards that way. The year you're looking for was bound in green." Then, muttering, "Hansen," over and over to herself, she opened up a shoe box that had once held a size nine-and-a-half cross trainer, and pulled out a digital tape. The plastic case appeared to be slightly charred. "When you get home, tell your sister I'd like to have a word."

The padlock slid into her hand with a satisfactory plop. Diana slipped it into her pocket and returned her attention to the key ring. Dean had the master neatly labeled with a piece of adhesive tape.

All she had to do now was push.

Heart pounding, she gripped the doorknob.

I'll just bring Aunt Sara up to partial consciousness, ask her a few questions, and take her back down again. Piece of cake.

What good was power if she never got to use it? Claire was going to be so pissed when she got home and found her younger sister had all the answers.

Sara, herself, turned out to be a bit of a disappointment.

While the old adage, *the more human evil looks the more dangerous it is,* was undeniably true, Diana had been expecting at least some outward indication of the heinous crime Sara had attempted—small horns, visible scars, overdue library books—but from the look of things, she hadn't even been having a bad hair day. The only incongruous point about her whole body was that her very red lips glistened, dust free.

. . . but had there not been problems with the sacrificial virgin, the Keepers would never have arrived in time. Not until Aunt Sara had Margaret Anne Groseter suspended over the pit and had made the first cut did she realize that the girl, although only fifteen, was not suitable.

Feeling as though the big green binder of 1945, Kin to Kip, had just smacked her on the back of the head, Claire read that paragraph again.

Margaret Anne Groseter.

"Mr. Smythe told me that she lived in the house next door her whole life. He said it used to be Groseter's Rooming House and Mr. Abrams was a roomer who didn't move fast enough and got broadsided."

"It's not possible."

For Mrs. Abrams to have been fifteen in 1945, she had to have been born in 1930. Which would put her in her late sixties. With a virtual thumb blocking the bouffant orange hair of a mind's eye view, Claire supposed it was possible.

"I used to be quite progressive in my younger days."

It was, Claire reflected, occasionally terrifying knowing the exact measure of the fulcrum that Fate used to lever the world.

Stepping through the shield, Diana had a momentary qualm. The emanations rising from the sleeper were stronger than she'd expected. It wouldn't be easy accessing power surrounded by such potent malevolence.

"On the other hand," she cracked her fingers and moved up to the head of the bed, "if it were easy, everybody'd be doing it."

. . . however, it took the combined strength of both Keepers to achieve the necessary balance of power between Sara and the pit, and even then she nearly broke free of their restraints.

Given the urgency of the situation, the Keepers on the scene felt it best to use a slam, bam, thank you, ma'am approach.

The Historian clearly believed in making history accessible to the masses.

Reaching carefully through the middle possibilities for power, Diana trickled a tiny amount into the matrix that held Sara asleep.

As the patterns in the dark emanations changed, a howling Austin raced into the room, trailing a cloud of shed fur. "Diana, stop! You don't know what you're doing!"

I TOLD YOU NOT TO WORRY ABOUT THE SECOND KEEPER. SHE'S HELPING US!
DO WHAT?
SHUT UP AND BE READY.

The cat gathered himself to leap just as Sara's lips parted and drew a long breath in past the edges of yellowed teeth.

NOW!
At the top of an infinite number of voices, Hell shouted Sara's name up the conduit.

With the seepage added to Diana's power, the balance tipped.
Sara opened her eyes.
Her own eyes wide, Diana tried to block the power surge. One second. Two. A force too complicated for her shields to stop slammed into her, dropping her to her knees.
Yowling, Austin landed on the end of the bed.

Sara smiled and raised a finger.

The energy flare caught him full in the face, lifted him into the air, and smashed him against the wall between the two windows. The first bounce dropped him into the remains of the fern. The second dropped him unresisting to the floor.

"NO!" Unable to stand, Diana crawled toward the body. A warm hand clamped down on one shoulder stopped her cold.

"I don't think so."

As Sara's grip dragged her around to face the bed, Diana put up no resistance. When Sara's eyes met hers, she grabbed for all the power she could handle and smashed it down on the other Keeper like a club.

Sara didn't even bother swatting it aside. She absorbed it, twisted it, and wrapped it around Diana like a shroud. "My mouth tastes like the inside of a sewer," she muttered, running her tongue over her teeth. "Christ on churches, but I could use a cigarette."

. . . unfortunately, as both Keepers were drawn from troops about to leave for the European theater, this temporary solution . . .

"Claire Hansen?"

"In a minute. I've almost got it."

"Suit yourself, Keeper, but I just got an e-mail telling me to re-activate that bit of history you're reading."

Claire looked up from the binder. "What do you mean reactivate?"

"Probably got a couple of loose ends tying themselves up."

"Probably?" Claire scrambled to her feet. Any loose ends had come untied since she'd left. "What's happening?"

"How should I know? I don't mess with the present, I do history. Put the book back on the shelf before you . . ." The Historian sighed and moved a black three onto a red four as Claire raced away through the ages. "And they wonder why I don't like company."

"Would it have hurt them to have dusted me on occasion? I don't think so." Lifting a thrashing Diana about three feet off the floor, Sara tied the laces of the young Keeper's black high-tops together and used them as a handle to drag her through the air toward the door.

Chewing on the power gag that held her silent, Diana dug her fingers into the doorjamb.

"Let go or lose them, your choice." It was clearly a literal offer. "I, personally, don't care. I know what you're thinking," she continued as Diana reluctantly released the wood. "You're thinking that all you have to do is delay me and sooner or later more Keepers will arrive. Well, they won't. And do you know why? Of course not, you're a child. . . ."

Tiny wisps of steam rose up from Diana's ears.

Sara smiled and ignored them. ". . . you couldn't possibly comprehend how I work. Over fifty years ago, two interfering busybodies put a shield around me. Specifically, around me. It's still there. No one will know I'm awake until it's much too late."

As the sound of Sara's gloating receded down the hall, several small, multicolored figures came out from behind various pieces of furniture and moved purposefully toward the limp body of the cat.

Running full out, Claire still hadn't reached the end of the bookshelves.

"Stop thinking about the past!"

Distorted by echoes, it could have been anyone's voice. Claire didn't waste time turning to check. She needed a door. She couldn't get home without going through a door.

"Hello, handsome. Are there any more at home like you?"

Pressed up against the wall in the lobby, Dean had a sudden memory of a fish flopping about the gaff that pinned it to the bottom of the boat. It didn't stop him from struggling, but it did give him a pretty good idea of how successful that struggle would be.

When he finally sagged, exhausted, he felt the sharp points of fingernails lift his chin off his chest.

"Very nice," Sara cooed. "I've always been a big fan of flexing and sweating." Slipping her fingers into the front pocket of his jeans, she pulled the denim away from his body and dropped the keys into the pouch. "Thanks so very much for your help. I don't suppose you have a cigarette on you?"

Dean shook his head and dragged himself out of the pale depths of her eyes. They were same gray/blue as the heart of an iceberg only less compassionate. He nodded toward Diana's thrashing body. "She said she was going into the attic. I thought Keepers couldn't lie."

"Bystanders can't lie to a Keeper, but we're actually very good at lying to . . ." Sara ducked and the old leather-bound registration book whipped over her head and slammed corner first into the wall. As the ancient binding gave way and yellowed pages fluttered to the ground, she measured the dent between thumb and forefinger. "Nice try, Jacques. I'm amazed you managed that much ectoplasmic energy." Leaning toward Dean, she whispered, "He must've gotten lucky in the last couple of days."

Eyes watering, Dean turned his head away. Her breath would've peeled the paint off the gut cans at the processing plant.

"Hey!" A fingernail opened a small cut in his cheek. "You sleep for that long and see what kind of a morning mouth *you* wake up with."

The brass bell rose off the counter and smacked into her shoulder.

"This is getting tiresome, Jacques." She turned to face the office. "Technically, I should have dust and ash for this, but we'll just make do with an abundance of dust." A gentle push sent Diana down the hall toward the basement stairs. With both hands free, Sara scraped a bit of fuzz off the front of her skirt and drew two symbols in the air.

Dean braced for bad poetry, but he needn't have bothered.

Both symbols glowed red.

Jacques snapped into focus between the symbols. Eyes wide with terror, he twisted and fought, and when Sara smacked her palms together, he exploded into a thousand tiny lights that scattered in all directions.

Praying silently, Dean worked his left hand free and snagged two of the lights as they went by. They burned as they touched his skin, but he closed his fingers around them and faced Sara with both hands curled into fists.

"Well," she said, "that takes care of him. You, however, I can use."

SHE'S GOING TO TRY IT AGAIN!

WOULD YOU STOP WORRYING! A FEW DECADES AT HER BECK AND CALL AND THEN WE'RE FREE.

AND YOU THINK SHE'LL WANT HELL WAITING FOR HER WHEN SHE DIES?

After a long silence, Hell muttered, YOU MIGHT HAVE BROUGHT THAT UP BEFORE.

SHE'S SEALING THE PIT! WE CAN'T STOP HER!

NO. NOT FROM IN HERE. . . .

First there were no doors, and then there was nothing but doors. Claire'd charged into three saunas, two walk-in freezers, something animated she couldn't identify, and more hotel rooms than she wanted to count.

"Yoo hoo! Cornelia! Diana! I was taking Baby out for his walkies and I just popped by to see if you . . ." Mrs. Abrams froze on the threshold, her mouth opening and closing but no sound emerging. Finally she managed a strangled, "I remember you!"

"That was an oversight on somebody's part," Sara observed as she tied the laces of Dean's work boots together. "*Please,* come in and close the door."

One hand pressed against the polyester swell of her bosom, Mrs. Abrams shuffled forward.

"And the door," Sara prodded. "Don't forget to close it."

Although her movements were pretty much limited to impotent thrashing, Diana managed to bring herself closer to the wall. Twisting left, she slammed her heels into the plaster.

Mrs. Abrams jerked at the sound and took a step backward, toward escape.

Sara raised a hand, and Diana found herself wrapped even more tightly in power. All her strength, all her attention, focused on drawing air through constricted passageways.

"Margaret Anne. Close the door."

Margaret Anne Abrams, née Groseter, had been fifteen the last time Sara had commanded her. A lot of water had passed under the bridge since then, and little old ladies were not without power of their own. Taking a breath so deep it stood each orange hair on end, she rallied. "Don't you talk to me in that tone of voice, young woman! I'll have you know that I'm the head of the Women's Auxiliary at our church and I've five times been volunteer of the year at the hospital. Look at you, you're all covered in dust. If I were you I'd be ashamed to go out in that . . ." Her voice trailed off as Sara's pale eyes narrowed and she expelled the last of the breath in a squeaky cry for help. "Baby!"

Secured by a leather leash to his own front porch, Baby lifted his wedge-shaped head off his paws.

He heard his master calling.

Lips pulled back off his teeth, the big Doberman surged up onto his feet and out to the end of his leash. The leather held.

The porch, on the other hand, surrendered to the inevitable.

Claire knew she was close. She could feel the hotel, but a dozen doors remained between her and the end of the hall, and she couldn't shake the fear that time, usually so fluid outside reality, had decided to march to a linear drummer. In other words, it was passing. Quickly.

Behind the first door to her right, sat a tiger. Fortunately, judging from the debris around its cell, it had just eaten.

"You're only delaying the inevitable," Sara muttered, as with a crooked finger she drew Mrs. Abrams farther into the lobby. "There's nothing you can summon, old woman, that can hurt . . ." Her eyes widened.

Baby had lived his whole life for this moment. Years of frustration propelled him over the threshold in one mighty leap.

The remains of the porch swept Mrs. Abrams off her feet, tangling her in the twisted wreckage.

Baby's front paws slammed into Sara's chest.

She hit the floor, bounced once in a cloud of dust, and lost the collar of her jacket as the extra weight on the end of Baby's leash stopped him a mere fraction of an inch short.

Breathing heavily, the Keeper scrambled to her feet, careful to stay clear of the snapping mouthful of too-long, too-pointed, and too-many teeth.

Fixated on her throat, Baby missed his chance at a number of other body parts as they passed.

A wave of Sara's hand closed the door. The sound it made, the sort of sound that put a final period on both rescue and escape, was almost a cliché.

"Margaret Anne, as much as I'd love to finish what we started so long ago, I've got all the sacrificial bodies I need." She raised her voice to be heard over Baby's frantic snarling. "This time, there's no mistake about the qualifications."

Dean hung limp in the air, but Diana took a moment out from breathing to glare.

Sara ignored them both. "*Please,* go to sleep, Margaret Anne." As Mrs. Abrams slumped forward, Sara glanced down at the Doberman, still desperately trying to rip her to pieces. "You," she said, "have got a single-minded way of going after a goal I rather like."

Nearly throttling himself, Baby made an unsuccessful lunge for her ankle.

"In fact, you remind me of me. Good dog."

The words meant nothing. The tone sent Baby into a frenzy of barking.

Dragging Dean and Diana behind her, Sara started down the basement stairs.

With seven doors to go, Claire paused in the center of the hall.

She could hear barking.

The distinctive, just barely sane barking of a big dog forced to live a lapdog's life. Who, with the fraction of brain that hadn't been bred out of it, intended to get even.

Laying her ear against each door only long enough to check for a rise in volume, Claire moved quickly down the hall.

Three doors. Four.

She opened the fifth door and flung herself out of the wardrobe. The volume of the barking didn't so much rise as expand to fill every available space with sound.

Baby was in the hotel.

Under normal circumstances, that would have been a problem, but being torn apart by a psychotic Doberman would be significantly preferable to life with Sara controlling Hell. Claire leaped over a pile of laundry, raced through the sitting room, and slid to a halt in the office.

Baby ignored her. Toenails scrabbling against the lobby floor, he dragged the ruin of the porch and the snoring Mrs. Abrams another inch closer to the basement.

Unwilling to scan the hotel lest she give her presence away, Claire decided to follow Baby's lead. Adding up the dog, the porch, and Mrs. Abrams, the odds were good Austin hadn't been responsible; not one hundred percent, but good.

Her back against the wall, she slid past, losing nothing more significant than a percentage of her hearing, and sped down the basement stairs, grateful that Baby's barking would cover any possible noise she might make.

The door to the furnace room was open.

Her heart beating so loudly she could hardly hear herself think, Claire paused by the washing machine and reached for calm.

A Keeper without self-control could control neither the power accessed nor where in the possibilities that power was accessed from.

Evil favored the chaotic mind.

Whites and colors should be sorted before washing.

Claire blinked, breaking contact with the box of laundry detergent. This was as calm as she was going to get.

Wiping damp palms against her thighs, she slipped behind the masking angle of the furnace room door and peered inside.

Still wearing the dusty clothes she'd been put to sleep in so many years before, Sara stood on air over the pit, back to the door, both hands raised, head bowed. Her fingertips were red where the blood had dripped down from her nails.

Suspended horizontally over the pit in front of her, shirtless, blood dripping from a number of shallow cuts on his chest, Dean appeared to be unconscious but still alive. It took a moment to spot Diana wrapped in overlapping bands of power and propped, mummylike, against the wall.

Wait a minute . . . Dean was over the pit and Diana was up against the wall?

Claire took a closer look at the power holding her sister. Most of it held her in place and kept her quiet but threaded throughout it, head to toe, was a conduit set up to pour Diana's considerable power into Sara—already in place because there'd be no opportunity to stop the invocation and set it up later.

Which meant that Dean was over the pit because . . .

No wonder he was always blushing.

But at twenty? Looking like a young, albeit myopic, god?

Hey! she told herself sternly, *now is not the time.* The problem was, it was easier, much, much easier to think about Dean than to come up with a plan to save the world.

It had taken two Keepers to stop Sara the first time she'd tried this. How could she possibly do it alone?

Not alone—if I can reach Diana without attracting Sara's attention, I can use the conduit myself. With Diana's power joined to mine, Sara's extra twenty years of experience shouldn't count for much.

As the evil Keeper began a new chant, Claire realized that were two small problems with her plan. The first was that Sara sealed Hell. With Sara removed, Hell would surge free. Claire would have to sign herself onto the site so that her power would become the seal when Sara's power was removed. Which meant, if there wasn't power enough left to close the hole, she'd be stuck here. In the hotel. For the rest of her life.

And Dean was leaving.

She didn't even know where he kept the toaster.

The second problem was that Sara also held Dean. Literally. Attacked from behind, Sara would let go and Dean would fall into the pit.

When she hooked up with Diana, Sara would know. She'd have to strike immediately. If she saved Dean first, Sara would have time to marshal a defense.

If she let Dean fall . . .

What point in saving the world if she let Dean fall?

She'd just have to find a way to save him, and that was that. Timing her footsteps to Baby's frenzied barking, she crept down the stairs toward Diana.

Down in the pit, Hell gloried in the strength it gained from each drop of sacrificial blood.

THERE ON THE STAIRS, the rest of Hell pointed out to itself, IT'S THE OTHER KEEPER.

SO?

SO SHOULD WE TELL *HER?*

Another drop of blood evaporated in the heat. Hell breathed it metaphorically in and laughed. YOU MEAN, SHOULD WE HELP *HER?* WE DON'T HELP. ANYONE.

Baby had managed to drag the whole mess another three inches toward the basement stairs. Tongue hanging out, collar cutting into the thick muscles of his neck, he kept barking and pulling in the certain belief that he had his enemy on the run.

And then, in the fraction of a second between one bark and the next, a familiar voice told him to be quiet.

The barking stopped. Claire froze.

Sara drew her fingernails along Dean's side. As blood welled up from four parallel lines, she began a new chant.

Claire recognized the guttural Latin. There wasn't much time left. Lower lip caught between her teeth, she started moving again.

A sterile dressing wrapped around his head and over his left eye, Austin had the rakish look of a wounded pirate. Breathing heavily, slightly scorched, he lay on his side on a litter made of an old silk scarf carried by twelve mice wearing multicolored frock coats, breeches, and tricorn hats.

This was so far outside Baby's experience, he sat panting and stared.

Still a safe distance away, the mice stopped and Austin opened his one good eye. "Somebody," he said without lifting his head, "is going to have to undo that collar."

Dean didn't so much regain consciousness as hijack it; consciousness wanted nothing to do with the whole situation.

HOW YA DOIN' GORGEOUS?

He'd have jerked back at the sound of the voice, but he couldn't figure out how to operate his body. Which scared him a lot more than Hell. He had a friend, Paul Malan, who'd gone into the boards at the wrong angle and now Paul played ball hockey from a wheelchair.

HE'S IGNORING US!

CAN HE DO THAT?

HEY, BUDDY! IN CASE YOU HAVEN'T NOTICED, THIS IS A LOT WORSE THAN BALL HOCKEY!

Thankful that somewhere along the way he'd lost his glasses, Dean ignored the voices because Claire had asked him to. She'd even said, "please."

He blinked, hit by a sudden realization. The voice he'd heard yesterday in the hall had been the voice of the pit.

BINGO.

And he'd listened. He'd hesitated.

OH, FOR . . . SIX SECONDS OUT OF TWENTY SQUEAKY CLEAN YEARS!

He deserved to go to Hell.

YOU'RE KIDDING, RIGHT?

Except he didn't want to die.

Over, or maybe under, the voices in his head, he could hear the drone of words chanted in a language he didn't understand. Slowly, working within the invisible bands that held him, he turned until he could see along his left arm. Gazing past his clenched fist, out over the edge of the pentagram, he could see Diana Hansen. She was just a kid, he realized, she'd never have believed that she'd set this whole mess in motion. If by some miracle he got out of this, he was after kicking her right in the butt.

Her back against the wall, barely daring to breathe, Claire crept the last few feet to her sister's side. Once she took Diana's hand, she'd control both their power.

Dean's eyes widened as Claire slid into his field of vision.

Rescue!

Claire saw the word in Dean's eyes and flinched.

Dean saw her flinch.

* * *

Sara chanted louder, spitting out consonants. The pentagram began to glow.

Maybe because he was suspended over a hole to Hell. Maybe because he'd been breathing the fumes of his own evaporating blood. Maybe because he'd spent almost a year next to a metaphysical accident site.

Maybe just because he could read it on Claire's face.

Dean knew.

She couldn't save him and the world.

He'd hesitated.

He was being given a chance to make up for that.

Hell could have him, but it couldn't have the world.

Do it, he told Claire silently.

Claire shook her head. There had to be another way.

The pentagram began to dissolve.

It was almost worth it to know she was willing to risk the world for him.

Do it.

Because she had no other choice, she did.

Claire grabbed Diana's hand and opened the conduit. Quickly retracing the pentagram, she etched her own name into the pattern.

Sara turned.

Dean fell.

Claire hit the other Keeper with everything both she and Diana had.

Suddenly finding herself in a sphere of blinding white light, Sara flung up a bloodstained hand to cover her eyes. Lips too red parted . . .

. . . and she laughed.

Designed to prevent any sort of metaphysical power from waking a Keeper bent on cataclysmic evil, the shield Sara had worn for more than fifty years held.

Stepping down to the floor, Sara straightened her jacket and nodded toward Diana. "I thought our friend here too young for this site. Not," she added after a critical inspection of Claire, "that you're so much older." Her smile was frankly patronizing. "You killed him for nothing, you know. Power can't pass into this shield."

Claire dragged Diana aside as a bolt of red light blew chunks of rock out of the wall.

Sara's smile broadened. "How nice for me that it passes out of it just fine."

Teeth clenched against rising nausea, Claire stepped forward, but before she could speak, Sara raised her hand again.

"Oh, yes, you can enter the shield physically, pummel me if you like, but don't expect me to stand here and allow . . ."

Which was when Baby launched himself from the top of the stairs.

Sara had time to scream as she fell back but only just.

Clinging to each other for support, Claire and Diana walked to the edge of the pentagram and cautiously leaned forward.

GOT HER!

OW! BE CAREFUL, SHE KICKS!

Claire felt her power fill the pentagram, holding Hell off from the world. That was it, then. A lifetime in the Elysian Fields Guest House.

Diana swallowed and found her voice. "Poor Ba . . ."

THAT'S OUR PUPPY! IS HE GLAD HE'S HOME?

WHO'S A GOOD DOGGIE-WOGGIE, THEN? WHO'S A GOOD BOY!

"Doggie-woggie?" Claire repeated.

Before Hell could answer, Diana dug her nails into Claire's arm. "Look! *She's* still part of the pattern. If you tie the pentagram to her before it fades, she'll pull the hole in after her!"

Still buzzing from the power she'd passed, it took Claire a heartbeat to understand. "I can close the site?"

"Yes!"

"Forever?"

"Yes!"

Sara's name had begun to fray. "No."

"Are you out of your mind? This may be your only chance!"

"No!" Claire yanked her arm free. "Dean's in there and I'm not closing that hole until he finds his way out." When Diana began another protest, she cut her off. "Hell can't hold a willing sacrifice. They have to let him go."

"They do?"

"If you paid more attention to what was going on and less to what you just happen to be powerful enough to do . . ." She bit it off. Now was not the time. "Yes. They do."

"Okay, fine, but they're not going to help him find his way or give him a boost out, and Sara's name is already fading! You haven't got time to wait. Don't let his sacrifice be in vain."

Claire reached for more power and poured it into the pentagram. From where she was standing, it was a long reach to the middle of the possibilities. Her vision was starting to blur, and she wasn't entirely certain she could feel her toes. "I can hold it," she snarled through clenched teeth. "I can hold it for as long as it takes."

"All right." Diana shrugged out of her jean jacket. "Then I'm going in after him."

"Oh, no, you're not!" Claire had a strong suspicion she sounded like their mother. At the moment, she didn't much care. "This isn't like going across the border for cheap electronics! You want to help, reactivate the conduit and start feeding me . . ." The "S" tried to straighten out. She forced it back into a curve. ". . . power."

"That'd make me part of the seal and we could be stuck here together indefinitely. You want him out, someone has to go and get him."

"Not you!" A subliminal growl snapped the second "a" back into line. "You'd never survive."

"But Dean . . ."

"Dean has the strength of ten because his heart is pure." Which was when Claire drew a second conclusion from Sara's choice of sacrifice. Fortunately for Diana, she had other things to deal with at the moment. "The rules protect him."

"What rules?"

"I know this is hard to believe at seventeen, but there are always rules." She definitely couldn't feel her toes and was starting to have doubts about her entire left foot. "It takes extraordinary conditions for the living to pass over and then come . . . The living!" Eyes locked on the pentagram, Claire grabbed her sister's arm. "Find Jacques!"

"Jacques' gone. *She* blew him into ectoplasmic particles."

"Then gather him!"

"Me?"

"You're always complaining how no one ever lets you do anything. Just be careful where you're pulling power from this close to the pit."

"You had to ruin it with advice," Diana complained as she started to spin. "Couldn't just assume I'd do it right."

All things considered, Claire felt she had precedent for that assumption, but she let it go as the wind began to swirl around the furnace room. A moment later, a stream of tiny lights poured down from the basement.

"There's two missing," Diana panted as the lights refused to coalesce. "I don't know where they are."

Vaguely Jacques-shaped, the lights dove into the pit.

"NO!" Claire reached out but caught only a single light.

Teetering as the room continued to spin, Diana stared at her sister in astonishment. "I thought that's what you wanted him to do?"

"He doesn't know that! He doesn't know Dean's down there. Jacques has still got connections to *her, she* could've dragged him down.'

"So what do we do now?"

Claire gritted her teeth, clenched her fist around the single piece of Jacques she'd managed to save, and dug in. "We wait."

"Wait?" Diana's voice rose nearly an octave. "For how long?"

"Until we can't wait any . . ." All of a sudden, Claire could feel a familiar twisted touch groping up toward the pentagram. *"She's* using her name to pull herself free. Link with me!"

"No! I'll be stuck with you, holding that thing, and there'll be two Keepers lost because you can't let Dean go. Because you feel guilty about how he felt about you when you didn't feel the same for him and turned to Jacques, who you can't possibly have a future with instead."

"Diana! This is no time for relationship therapy!"

"You've lost them both. Let them go before *she* starts this whole thing all over again."

Her connection to her name had strengthened. The sound of triumphant laughter boiled up over the edges of the pit.

"I'm not leaving them there!"

Diana laid her hand on her sister's arm and to Claire's surprise her voice was gentle as she said, "You're a Keeper. Seal the s . . . son of a bitch."

Down in the pit, something that had once been Mrs. Abrams' Baby barked as Dean rose up into the furnace room surrounded by a cloud of tiny lights. When both his feet were on the ground, and before either Claire or Diana could get their mouths shut to say anything, he opened his left hand.

Two lights few out.

Claire peeled her fingers back off her palm. The final light spun up into the air.

Jacques rematerialized.

Dean coughed once and stumbled forward. Together, Claire and Diana eased him down onto the bottom step, then Claire turned back toward the pit.

She could feel Sara clawing her way up her name, closer and closer to the edge of the possibilities. Holding tightly to the seal, Claire broke all the remaining links but Sara's.

The building shook as the pentagram, etched into solid rock, slid toward the center of itself. The inner edges disappeared. Flickering through the visible spectrum and one or two colors beyond, hundred-year-old words of summoning poured into the hole.

"Claire!" Stretched out like smoke in a wind, Jacques streamed toward Hell, caught in the binding.

Even if there was time, unraveling the binding would free Sara's name.

"I don't think so . . ." Wielding power like a sword, Diana slashed through the pattern where Jacques was caught.

Not subtle, but effective.

As the points flipped up and over, Claire broke her name free.

CURSES, FOILED AGAI . . .

The unmarked bedrock of the furnace room floor steamed gently.

Diana let out a breath she couldn't remember holding. "Wow."

Dean jerked to his feet as Claire swayed. "You okay?"

Actually, she had no idea how she was, but okay would do for the moment. "Sure. What about you?"

He frowned. Until Jacques had appeared out of the darkness, he'd stood on the slope leading upward toward the glow of what were probably the fires of the damned and had known he'd been forgotten. Sure, Hell was busy with Sara, but still . . . "I hesitated," he said.

Claire felt her lip curl. "Get over it. You were willing to die to save the world. You're a terrific person!"

"You mean that?"

She cupped his face between her palms and moved close enough that he could see her clearly without his glasses. "Yes. I have never meant anything more in my life."

Keepers lied quite easily to bystanders; but he believed her. The load of guilt lifted off his shoulders. "Thanks." Pulling free, he took a step back. "There's something I nccd to do."

"Ow!" Diana rubbed the spot where Dean had applied the side of his work boot. "What did you kick me for?"

His silence said it all.

"Oh. Never mind."

* * *

"You've done a wonderful job, Claire, but are you certain you don't want me to come to Kingston and check things out?"

"Quite certain, Mom. The site is closed." Claire had put the furnace room through every test she could think of, and she'd even allowed Diana to come up with a few. To all intents and purposes, there'd never been a hole to Hell. Or an Aunt Sara. "Dean drove Diana to the train station. She'll stay with friends in Toronto tonight and head home first thing tomorrow morning."

"Well, I'm sure that's the plan." Martha Hansen sounded doubtful.

"Don't worry, she gave me her word she'd go straight home."

"Claire Beth Hansen! Did you put a geas on your sister?"

Claire grinned. "Yes."

"Good. But how on earth did you manage it?"

"I agreed with her when she opened her defense with 'all's well that ends well,' and while she was still reeling in disbelief I slipped it by."

"You *agreed* with her?"

Her grin broadening, Claire explained. "I had every intention of tearing a strip off her for being so adolescently arrogant, thinking she could wake Sara without consequences, but then I realized that she was right. Keepers go where they're needed. The two of us in combination were needed to close down the site, so it's entirely possible that everything that happened was intended to happen. Diana, me, Dean, Jacques; even Hell had a hand in its own demise by squeezing a Hell Hound through the tiny window of opportunity between Sara's original capture and her power being used to temporarily seal the site."

The phone remained silent.

"Mom?"

"If Diana's reckless disregard for consequence was necessary to help save the world, she's going to be impossible to live with." Claire very nearly felt her mother's sigh. "Still, I expect your father and I can come up with a few things to say to her when she gets home." Sara's choice of sacrifice had not been elaborated on, but parents were perfectly capable of drawing their own conclusions. "You said that Dean was driving her to the station; how is he? Is it safe for him to drive?"

"He's fine, Mom. Really. He was a willing sacrifice, completely ignorant of what that meant, and he believed that in falling he'd burn in Hell forever. With that kind of karma, he could've just walked through the possibilities to the light. If

Jacques hadn't found him so quickly and brought him back to the basement, I expect he'd have started tidying the place up."

"What do you mean, he had no doubt he'd burn in Hell forever? He's been living next to the site for almost a year completely unaffected."

She'd been hoping she'd slipped that by. "There was an incident." Leaving out the bits that Diana would be sure to embellish on later, Claire explained about the elevator and Faith's boyfriend. "He hesitated."

On the other end of the phone, Martha snorted. "Oh, for . . ."

"That's what I said. But this whole sacrifice thing grounded him again. He's as good as new."

"I see." The pause spoke volumes. "What happens now?"

Claire chose to misunderstand. "Now, I expect I'll be summoned somewhere else. Austin says I'll be able to leave by tomorrow, that help is on the way."

"Claire . . ."

"He's down to his last life, you know. But he says he's not worried."

"Very well. If that's the way you want it. Give Austin our love."

An uncomfortable moment later, Claire hung up and sighed.

What happens now?

Jacques was waiting in her sitting room. He had to know she'd be leaving—that she couldn't stay and he couldn't come with her.

This wasn't going to be a pleasant interview.

"Jacques?"

He stopped pacing and turned to face her. "*Vôtre mère,* your mama, is she good?"

"She's fine."

"*Bon.*" Drifting out through the coffee table, he waved a hand at the sofa. "Please, *cherie,* I have things to say."

Since she wasn't looking forward to saying the things she had to, Claire sat. If listening was all that she could do for him, she would at least do that.

"You are ready? *D'accord.*" He rubbed his hands against his thighs, a living gesture Claire'd never seen him make before. "I am decided, it is time I move on."

You're *leaving* me? Somehow, Claire managed not to voice her initial reaction.

His expression grew serious. "I have seen Hell and I do not belong there, or they would not have allow me to leave. There is not enough evil in me for them to hold." The corners of his mouth twitched up. "It helped that you held my heart."

When he smiled, Claire had to smile with him. "That wasn't your heart."

"*Non?* Ah, well, close enough." He took a step back and held out his hand. "Will you help me?"

So much for her speech about change being constant. Claire ripped up her mental notes, stood, and laid her palm against Jacques', his fingers wrapping around hers like cool smoke. "Of course. When?"

"Now. I have found the courage to face *her.* I have found the courage to descend into Hell for *l'âme,* the soul, of Dean, who I do not even entirely like. I think while I have found my courage, I should use him, it, to face what is on the other side."

"Did you want to wait and say good-bye to Dean?"

"No. You tell him I say *au revoir, adieu, bonne chance,* and that if he does not use it, it will fall off."

"Maybe you'd better stay a few more minutes and tell him yourself."

Jacques shook his head, a strand of translucent hair falling into his eyes. "No, *cherie.* Now. There has always been—will always be—an excuse to stay. Dean, he will understand. It is a guy thing."

"A guy thing?"

He shrugged. "I hear it on Morningside." One hand still wrapped about hers, he laid the other against her cheek. "Thank you for the night we shared. I think I saw heaven a little bit in your arms."

"You think?"

"I am fairly certain." He grinned. "When you talk of me, could you perhaps exaggerate a little?" When she nodded, her cheek moving up and down through his hand, he squared his shoulders under the heavy sweater. "*D'accord.* Then I am ready."

Claire reached through the possibilities and opened the way. Squinting a little, she stepped back to give him room. "Just follow the light."

His features almost dissolving in the brilliance, he took a step away from the world, and then he paused.

"Au revoir, cherie."

"Good-bye, Jacques."

"Si j'etais en vie, je t'aurais aime."

And then he was gone.

"If I were alive, I would have loved you?"

Blinking away the spots in front of her eyes, Claire tried to focus on the cat.

Austin carefully climbed onto the hassock and sat down. "Not a bad exit line."

"You're supposed to be resting?"

"I am resting, I'm sitting."

"You should go to the vet."

"No, thank you." He twitched his tail around his toes and his lip curled under the lower edge of the bandage. "It's been taken care of."

"By the mice?"

"Are you calling me a liar?"

Locked in the gaze from his remaining eye, Claire shook her head. "No. Not as such. But if I may point out, *I* haven't seen any mice."

"You haven't seen Elvis either."

Claire glanced over at the silent bust. "So?"

"So that doesn't mean he's not working in a 7-11 somewhere. Did you take care of Mrs. Abrams?"

"She thinks Baby died a natural death about six months ago, and now that she's done mourning, she's going to get a poodle. But while we're on the subject; how long did you know Baby was a Hell Hound?"

"I knew it from the beginning."

"Well, why didn't you tell me?"

Austin snorted. "I'm a cat." Before Claire could demand a further explanation, he cocked his head. "There's Dean's truck. Maybe you'd better go take care of that last loose end."

"The hotel is yours if you want it."

Dean paused, one hand on the basement door, and turned to face Claire. "No, thank you. I don't want it. You'll be leaving?"

She nodded. "Soon. Tomorrow, probably. Austin says that someone'll be along."

"So you pretty much knew my answer before you asked?"

"Pretty much. But I still had to ask. How long . . ."

"I guess I'll wait until that someone shows up and play it by ear."

"Okay. Good. Um, Jacques is gone. He said to tell you good-bye and that you'd understand why he didn't wait."

"Sure."

When the silence stretched beyond the allotted time for a response, Dean nodded, once, and went downstairs.

As the sound of his work boots faded into the distance, Claire pounded her forehead against the wall. That hadn't gone well. There were a hundred things she wanted to say to Dean, starting with, *Thanks for driving Diana to the train station.* and moving on up to: *Thanks for sacrificing yourself to save the world.* Somewhere in the middle she'd try to fit in *Maybe you and I . . .*

"Maybe he and I what?" she asked herself walking back to the office and jerking her backpack down off the hook. "Could be friends? Could be more than friends?" Yanking the cables from her printer, she shoved them into the pack. "He's an extraordinary guy. Not brilliant maybe, but good, kind, gorgeous, accepting . . ." The printer followed the cables. ". . . not to mention alive."

Maybe she'd had that rare chance that few Keepers ever got and for whatever reason, pride or blatant stupidity, she'd blown it.

What happens now?

The site was sealed.

She was leaving.

He was leaving.

It was over.

Folding a pair of jeans neatly along the crease, Dean set them into his hockey bag. He wanted to be ready to go as soon as possible after that someone arrived.

"Austin says that someone'll be along."

He'd never be able to look at a cat without wondering. As for the rest of it, well, he knew who he was again, so the rest of it didn't matter.

A stack of white briefs, also neatly folded, tucked in beside the jeans.

There'd been a lot left unsaid upstairs in the hall. Claire'd been looking sort of aloof and unapproachable, but also twisting a lock of hair around one finger. Dean had to smile at the combination as he added all but one pair of socks to the bag.

Diana had given him continual advice on the way to the station. About half of it, he hadn't understood.

It didn't much matter.

Claire was leaving.

He was leaving.

At least she hadn't offered to rearrange his memories. He'd have fought to remember the last eight weeks.

"What in tarnation have you done to my hotel?"

Claire, who'd been waiting in the office, stared down at Augustus Smythe, opened and closed her mouth, and finally managed a stunned, "You?"

"Who else would be willing to run this rattrap?"

"But . . ."

"Used to be a hole to Hell in the basement. That sort of thing has to be monitored." He shrugged out of his overcoat and tossed it up on the counter. "They say I'm retired, with full pension for years of service rendered, but I know better." Bushy brows drawn in, he glared around at the renovations. "So you opened up the elevator; lose anyone?"

"No."

"Tried it since the hole closed?"

"No, but . . ."

"Never mind. I'll convince that harpy next door to go for a ride." To Claire's astonishment, he smoothed back his hair and grinned. After a moment, the grin rearranged itself into the customary scowl. "Well? Haven't you got somewhere else to go?"

Now that he mentioned it, she had.

The summons grew stronger as she shrugged into her backpack and held open the cat carrier for Austin to climb in. Reaching for her suitcase, she stopped, straightened, and decided Jacques was right. There'd always be a reason to delay.

She reached for the suitcase again, shifted it to her left hand, and picked up the cat carrier with her right. "Tell Dean I said good-bye."

And then she left, ignoring the muttered, "Idiot," that could have come from either the Cousin or the cat.

The summons drew her west. She passed the park, and the hospital, and the turnoff to a house Sir John A. MacDonald, Canada's first Prime Minister had lived in briefly before he entered politics.

The definitive November wind, cold and damp, blew in off the lake, stiffening her fingers around the handles of her luggage. By the time she reached the lights at Sir John A. MacDonald Boulevard, she decided that the summons was taking her farther than she wanted to walk. Even in a bad mood and feeling vaguely guilty about pretty much everything.

"You need a lift?"

He wasn't entirely unexpected.

Frowning, Claire turned to face the truck. "You don't know where I'm going."

Leaning across the front seat, braced against the edge of the open window, Dean shrugged. "So?"

"Just get in!" The cat carrier rocked in Claire's grip as Austin shifted his weight. "I'm freezing my tail off out here."

"You told him which way we'd be heading."

"What part of *get in* don't you understand?" he snarled, poking a paw out through the wider weave in the front of the carrier.

There were people crossing the street toward her. Another few feet and they'd be close enough to hear.

Claire got in the truck.

Fastened her seat belt.

As Dean shifted into drive and started across the intersection, she held the top of the cat carrier open just far enough for Austin to climb out.

"What happens next?" Dean asked.

Claire shrugged and squirmed around to set the carrier behind the seat with her suitcase. "I don't know."

There was still a lot that had to be said.

"You did know the speed limit on this street is 40k?"

And a lot that didn't.

Dean nodded. "Okay. We'll play it by ear."

"You've been to Hell," Austin snorted, stretching out on Claire's lap, "you should be up to it."

HEY! WHO TIDIED THE BRIMSTONE?

TANYA HUFF
VALOR'S CHOICE

"Readers who enjoy military SF will love Tanya Huff's
VALOR'S CHOICE. Howlingly funny and very
suspenseful. I enjoyed every word."
—*scifi.com*

Staff Sergeant Torin Kerr was a battle-hardened professional.
So when she and those in her platoon who'd survived the last
deadly encounter with the Others were yanked from a well-
deserved leave for what was supposed to be "easy" duty as
the honor guard for a diplomatic mission to the non-Confedera-
tion world of the Silsviss, she was ready for anything. Sure,
there'd been rumors of the Others being spotted in this sector
of space. But there were always rumors. Everything seemed
to be going perfectly. Maybe too perfectly. . . .

0-88677-896-4 $6.99

Tanya Huff

FIONA PATTON

"Rousing adventure, full of color and spectacular magic"—*Locus*

In the kingdom of Branion, the hereditary royal line is blessed—or cursed—with the power of the Flame, a magic against which no one can stand. But when used by one not strong enough to control it, the power of the Flame can just as easily consume its human vessel, as destroy whatever foe it had been unleased against. . . .

☐ **THE STONE PRINCE**   UE2735—$6.99

☐ **THE PAINTER KNIGHT**   UE2780—$6.99

☐ **THE GRANITE SHIELD**   UE2842—$6.99